MYTH OF ORIGIN

A SCIENCE FICTION ADVENTURE

MATILDA SCOTNEY

Myth of Origin: A Science Fiction Adventure
ISBN: 978-0-6487545-4-1

The best prophet of the future is the past
- Lord Byron

PROLOGUE _

IN THE YEAR 4331, the Triumvirate, governing body of the three inhabited planets of Venus, Earth and Mars, received a submission from an Earth faction called The Nexist Mutuality. The manuscript, entitled Myth of Origin, emphasised Earthers' purity and claimed ancestral tainting of the Venusians by a race called "Indigo"—a species long held by the Triumvirate to be mythical.

The manuscript further challenged the accepted Venusian Charter of the Colonisation of Earth. The Nexist Mutuality disputed the Charter's validity, contending it may have been subject to alteration to favour the Triumvirate's account that Earth was uninhabited until the Venusian's arrival. With no supporting evidence, The Nexist Mutuality added to their submission, claiming an unknown superior race of humans settled Earth, most likely as an experiment in colonisation, centuries before the Venusians arrived.

The Triumvirate privately considered the document's contents preposterous and without merit, but in the interests of diplomacy, agreed to an investigation. Publicly, and on all points, they dismissed the Nexists' claims before quietly relegating the submission to the archives on Venus, where the Triumvirate assured themselves it would merely gather dust.

But the Nexist Mutuality has a long memory…

CHAPTER ONE _

Source: Retrieved Seeker-20 space module.
Seeker Exploratory Project.
Recovery Date: 3/4/4598: Location of salvaged ship:
Rille Lunar Base

Data recovery file: Pilot's log.

There would be no welcome mat. I watched the grey curve of the moon as the ship sank silently to rest, that same forsaken greyness that arched away from me on countless other moons, countless other worlds, so there seemed little point in hurrying to release my flight harness—any survey of this moon, of the blue planet beyond would reveal only what I can see with my own eyes. I will search the emptiness of this place and strain my ears to hear a sound, even though I know the only echoes will be my own sighs. Space. Out here, I found only bleakness. Emptiness. No life. No reason to hope.

I have long since ceased to see the angled elegance of a rocky landscape, the spiritual beauty of twin moons in the heavens. My heart no longer leaps in anticipation of meeting new life. Each new moon, each new planet is as the one before—a rock orbiting aimlessly in these eternal skies, billions of toys created by an unthinking god to dangle enticingly before his children, for their amusement during their sojourn on his one inhabited world.

I am self-banished. To stay would have meant death, but leaving separated me from everything I knew, even those who cannot and will not accept me, nor my kind. For years I traversed the galaxy, and in all that time, the only human voice I heard was my own, until there was no longer need for words, until I found no further need to listen to my thoughts. I fancy there are other voices from time to time, but I know it's my solitude that speaks. Not even the little green men of a child's fertile imaginations have found a place out here. In space, each planet, lush and fertile, or barren and bleak, is cold and desolate, where there is none to give a cheery smile nor wave.

So why was I so sure, as I felt the familiar rumble of the outer doors, that my experience here would not advance my search for those like me? I believed they came from the stars, and now I know that I am one of them.

I stepped from the ship, my home for all those wasted years, and recognised the familiar loneliness of the place. The distant blue planet beyond rose bright and shining in the heavens in stark contrast to this landscape, grey, brittle, cold…

It was then I became aware of the door fashioned into the rock. I felt the splash of tears on my face as I pushed against the hard surface, calling as I did, even though I knew no human ears could hear my cry. The door was closed, my way barred, and it was then, I knew, really knew, the desolation of being truly alone.

CHAPTER TWO _

Charlie Maitland stood at the drinks port as her coffee, or at least what passed for coffee here, dripped with painstaking slowness through a filter attached to an ancient dispenser, just one of the antiquated food and beverage ports here on Rille station. Prepacked and stored in mostly out-of-date vials, the coffee was ready for fusing with a concoction of sterilised condensation and a barely alluded-to infusion of recycled water that passed through the same processing plant as the personnel's bodily waste. If you thought too hard about it, there was no way you'd drink anything. But Charlie wasn't here for the coffee; she just wanted an excuse to spend a few extra minutes with the tall, good-looking man next to her.

"Sam, I swear this stuff will be the death of us," she declared, looking up at him and wrinkling her nose in disgust at the pungent, mass-produced and over-processed coffee smell. Sam leant his elbow against the wall and rested his temple against his hand, waiting for the sluggish stream of murky brown liquid to deliver itself into the cup. He hated the coffee too, but like Charlie, he appreciated the ritual that granted him a few more minutes in her company before starting his shift.

"If we stay on this base much longer, my dear Charlie," he came back with a grin, "life itself will be the death of us. Even this last roster is almost too much to bear. If it wasn't for you…" his voice trailed away. He knew she felt the same.

Charlie didn't answer, just whacked the top of the dispenser, hoping it would hasten the coffee's delivery. It didn't. The vibration of her hammering generated a few splashes of hot water, although it did change the machine's tone from an even buzz to a musical clang. Sam would soon be gone, and with him, any modicum of happiness. The knowledge Charlie was unlikely to follow him to Earth any time soon had a profound effect on them both. Sam's presence these last three months made Charlie's life tolerable—better than tolerable, especially when they were both on night shift together. It meant they could spend their days in her quarters, making love, laughing, talking, sharing food. It was all a relief from the unremitting stream of nothing to do save closing a wound on a careless engineer or the occasional broken bone that took her only a few minutes to fix. When Sam left, Charlie would be back to her lonely, uneventful existence as Medical Officer in the salvage yard on Rille Lunar Base, where patching up the engineers who worked on the ageing transport fleet was the order of the day. Most of the shipbuilding had transferred to Mars, but the Triumvirate, in its questionable rationale, elected to maintain a repair depot on the moon. All Triumvirate employees and graduates completed a stint here, whether they were top of their class or right at the bottom. It was as inescapable as death and taxes. Charlie hadn't expected it so soon; it commonly happened in the last year of a graduate's indenture, but the previous doctor let himself out an airlock, and the position fell to her.

The dark, endlessly processed liquid eventually got delivered. Still, they didn't pick up the cups in triumph, even after waiting so long, because the resulting beverage was simply never worth celebrating.

Charlie took a sip and peered at Sam over the rim of the cup, "If nothing else, it'll shock us into staying awake."

Sam made a suggestive flick of his eyebrows, "We didn't get much sleep, did we?" then puckered up his face in a gag as the potent brew hit the back of his throat.

Charlie knew how he felt. The coffee was unpleasant, but like clockwork, each morning they drew a cup, and each morning gagged at its awfulness, but here, anyone who passed by would see nothing suspicious, only two officers ready for duty, available and on time. The Triumvirate discouraged close relationships on Rille, so Sam and Charlie never made public just how close they had become.

"The engineers are commencing work on the Seeker ship they brought in," Charlie said. "I hear it's sealed from the inside. Do you think they'll find anyone? Any remains?"

Sam had heard those same rumours. "If they do,

they'll be calling for your services."

There wouldn't be much Charlie could do to help someone who'd been deceased for over twenty years, a post-mortem possibly, but who knows what happens to a body that returns from so far out in space? There was no precedence. Still, it would be an interesting exercise. "Well, if they don't," she replied, "they'll be calling for yours."

Sam Mead was a Senior Metallurgist and Data Analyst, just concluding his roster on Rille Base. Unless he came back voluntarily, which was unlikely because no-one ever put up their hand for Rille assignments, this was likely to be his last. He had one previous, brief spell here during training, hopefully never to be repeated. Still, he somehow ended up reassigned because no-one else was available, much the same way as Charlie. This time though, he encountered the sweet and funny Dr Charlotte Maitland, so he would say that the Triumvirate made a good move for once. It would be hard if they asked him to extend, almost as hard as leaving Charlie. Sam was the Triumvirate's brightest and best, destined in time to be the Leading Officer, the loftiest rank available to any Triumvirate member enrolled in either transport or engineering. Sam's wealthy parents paid for his education, and even though he couldn't dodge these postings, it was easier for him to get the plum jobs in between. For indentured officers like Charlie, the Triumvirate owned your ass and sent you wherever they chose for three years after graduation. So, as no-one ever volunteered, every officer ended up on the moon at some point.

The problem was Charlie had been here two months longer than her allotted roster. The base governor, Miller, advised they had not yet found a suitable replacement, but Charlie quickly learned the governor had other, nefarious reasons for keeping her on the base.

Checking no-one was in the vicinity, Sam bent down and brushed his lips against hers. "I need to get going. Your cabin later?" Supremely confident of his place in her life, he didn't wait for an answer. She had become more to him than just a distraction from the tedium of the menial work offered on the base. "I'll see you then," he smiled.

Charlie nodded and watched him walk away. She liked Sam very, very much. She had a thing for tall men with dark, wavy hair. Sam also had soft grey eyes and a fancy Northern Continent accent, educated and proper. As a bonus, Sam had muscles. Charlie liked muscles, too. Idly, she sipped at the coffee, hating the bitterness of the long-awaited brew. She took one more awful mouthful, then released the cup and its contents into the disposal unit. When Sam left, she wouldn't look at this coffee dispenser ever again.

Sick Bay beckoned, a haven of monotony with a healthy dose of nothing to do chucked in for good measure. Her feet never seemed as willing to head there as they did to leave at the end of a shift, when they magically became energised as she scampered back to her quarters, either for a romantic rendezvous with Sam, facetime with mum and dad, or to get ready for an extended exercise session. Sick Bay was a prison within a prison, forced confinement until the Triumvirate let her out, although it looked as if the Dean of Schedules had forgotten her very existence.

Finding her way barred even before she took one step, Charlie focused on the shiny button at her eye level on the man's tunic.

"So," Governor Miller sneered. "It's still you and Mead, Mead and you?" Governor Miller always sneered. What could one expect from a sneering, condescending type of man? Charlie heard the breath whistling through the fat, hairy nose that sat stuck in a permanent sneer above his sneering lips. He was a great big sneer. In her mind, she hissed out the 's' of *sneer*. She wished she could squeeze that nose so hard, he would gasp for breath and beg for mercy.

Charlie stepped to the side without looking up, but Miller anticipated and moved with her. She clenched her teeth and muttered, "Governor, let me pass. I have work to do."

Miller snorted a laugh. "No, you don't, Charlie. Most of the staff are cutting up that ship before your boyfriend goes in for the evaluation." Charlie recoiled as he stepped closer, his breath hitting her in the face as he bent towards her. He brushed a sweaty finger against her cheek and dropped his voice to a sickeningly husky drawl. "You've got time for me."

These encounters, engineered by Miller for when no-one else was around, invariably followed the same pattern, with him waiting until Charlie was alone somewhere on the base. The second-class engineers and technical crew accommodations were located elsewhere, so finding a deserted corridor with her in it wasn't hard. However, this corridor was a distance from his office, so coming here would have required effort on the governor's part. He'd learned Charlie was with Sam here most mornings and that they would go in separate directions to their destinations, so it was an opportunity too good to miss. Miller once considered installing a camera in Charlie's quarters, but he didn't have the technical know-how to set such a thing up himself. Asking an engineer would raise suspicions; besides, a previous clumsy attempt at seducing a crew member who, unbeknownst to him was a Triumvirate senator's daughter, earned him a reprimand. Right now, he needed to be out from under the Triumvirate's eye, but that minor episode in history wouldn't stop him from having a little fun.

Governor Miller cupped Charlie's cheek in his hand and pressed his thumb to her mouth. Squeezing her eyes tight shut, she curled her lips inwards so he couldn't touch them, making her disgust evident. Undeterred, he moved his thumb to under her jaw, pushing hard to force her face upwards. Backing up against the wall, she opened her eyes.

There it was. Miller loved that look. Defiance. Challenge. It was all the same to him. He'd singled out the slightly built, athletic, flat-chested, almost boyish Charlie the moment she arrived at the facility. Attracted by her fine blonde hair and wide, innocent blue eyes, he assumed an indentured officer would be so desperate not to jeopardise her career, he could do as he pleased. He made the mistake of not checking the person behind Charlotte Maitland's kid-like exterior. She hated bullies. And Governor Miller was the worst she'd ever encountered.

"I hear you put in another request to transfer back to Earth?" he whispered in her ear, his disgusting mouth shifting from sneer to smirk. "I can make that happen."

Charlie got a full blast of his pungent breath as she jerked her chin from his grip.

"I didn't put the application in to you, Governor," she spat, unaware her fiery rebuttal of his advances was part of the appeal. She knew he'd let her go eventually. She just had to suffer these next few minutes. At only a little over five feet, Charlie hated looking up at him because it meant gazing up those huge, hairy nostrils, but she did it anyway. "This time, Governor, my request went to your superiors." She took another step to the side. "It's not for you to grant or deny."

Miller straightened himself and put his arm out as a barrier. "I have friends, Charlie," he sniggered. "Why do you think you've been here longer than three months? Do you honestly think I don't have a say in who stays and who goes? Imagine what it will be like with lover boy out of the picture?"

Charlie refused to let him intimidate her. Standing in silence for a moment longer, she made a third attempt at sidestepping him, but he grabbed her arm. Senior officers could not handle subordinates unless in an emergency. Miller knew what would come next, and he rather liked this part. Charlie delivered a stinging slap to his hand as she wrenched free. Miller would have to justify why Charlie felt the need to slap him if he reported her, so he just took it as part of the sport. He knew this slip of a girl sent complaints about him to the Triumvirate; he'd taken steps to ensure those comments didn't even make it off the moon, intercepting each transmission, along with her petition for reassignment. With his contacts, he'd got everything about Dr Charlotte Maitland "lost" in the system. Had she been a little more amenable, he might have made matters simpler, but up to now, she made excellent sport where the other women on the base were too fearful to refuse him.

Charlie followed up her slap with a hard shove. Too large for her to knock to the floor, this time Miller let her pass. For such a slight girl, Charlie had significant strength, but Miller only ever laughed as he took the impact. Reporting her for slapping or shoving him would, at the very least, draw attention to the fact she was long overdue for reassignment. He grinned nastily to himself as he watched her stalk down the empty corridor to Sick Bay. He was tired of her games, but the challenge of breaking that spirit, showing her who was in charge, was still his motivation. The day had barely begun, but by the end, he told himself with no small measure of smugness, she'd be on her knees, begging him. He tilted his head. On her knees sounded perfect.

Charlie plopped herself down at her desk and asked the

nurse droid to sanitise her face and hands. Someone in the consulate had seemingly swept her four complaints about Governor Miller under the rug. Ignoring him, kicking him, elbowing him, yelling; it all seemed to make him worse. Only getting off the moon would get her out of his way. He disgusted her. Considerably older than she, a married father of seven, malicious, overbearing, with breath that would sour cream and to boot, no-one on Rille Base liked him. There were other women here, and Charlie guessed a few had submitted not so willingly, but now it seemed he'd fixed his sights on Charlie, and that knowledge brought fresh humiliation. If her transfer didn't happen soon, she decided, she would take a life suit and float back to Earth.

Life will be unbearable here without Sam, she thought, as tears pricked behind her eyelids. There was no way he'd be able to visit while she was stuck here with Miller; he'd never get clearance.

The nausea that predictably followed an encounter with Miller subsided, and Charlie leaned back in her chair. Running her hands through her hair, she waved away the nurse droid. There was no point in being maudlin. Sam planned to take up her cause the minute he got back to Earth. He would remind the Dean of Schedules in person that they'd forgotten someone on Rille Base. She feared telling Sam about Miller; it might spoil their last few days together. Either way, she doubted she'd get a quick resolution.

Sick Bay had all the charm of a cemetery with lights. Nothing of significance ever happened, and most days,

Charlie didn't even get to see a patient. She hadn't performed so much as a minor operation, despite her distinctions in surgical procedures, and she hadn't picked up a dermal beam or isolator in months.

She yawned. With the prospect of nothing to do stretching before her, she speculated on studying the psychiatric effects of boredom. She felt too jaded to bother, so instead, with a lazy roll of her head, she gazed through the glass partition between her office and the therapy area. Two medical technicians sat on an examination couch, chatting while they recalibrated and tested—probably for the tenth time, several old medical recorders and devices destined for the cargo and transport vessels that travelled the major Triumvirate planets of Earth, Mars, and Venus.

Charlie peered at the nurse droid. Unless she used it to clean her face and hands, there was no current demand for its services. Each day, it just perched on its hook, collecting dust and growing cobwebs, its circuits fogging up with endless days of doing nothing, just like Charlie's medical and surgical skills. Sam Mead was the only beacon of light, but once he left…

Charlie lifted her feet onto her desk. The displays above her head afforded views of the station to make her instantly aware of a medical emergency. They showed "green" status, which meant her presence wasn't currently required anywhere else on the station. There was some action happening in engineering, so she scanned that; anything to lessen the monotony. Colourful sparks from cutting tools showered the compact, one-person Seeker ship. There didn't appear to be human remains on board, and Charlie wondered where they went; there should have been at least a few bones, but the engineers had pushed on from the cockpit and were now engaged in cutting out the rear section of the hull.

Keeping one eye on the engineering view, Charlie flicked on a historical narrative of Seeker ships. History lessons in high school talked about them, but Charlie didn't bother retaining the information. The Seeker Program held no particular interest for her—human biology had been her favourite subject—but boredom can make even the most bizarre things appealing. As a Seeker ship was now in the hangar, she supposed it was at least topical and might be worth reacquainting herself.

Charlie made "blah blah blah" noises as she advanced the preamble and attributions to this scientist and that, puckering up her face at an image of Governor Miller's father, a vocal opponent of the Seeker program. She didn't like him for any other reason than that he fathered the son she despised. Miller senior was dead these ten years, and she knew little else about him, but his history of begetting a ghastly son was sufficient.

The colourful and imaginative narrative, aimed at first-year high school students, gave a lively account of the many fantastic myths of beings from other worlds, unidentified flying objects in the night sky, and unverified glimpses of strange creatures in forests and remote mountain ranges. Then came the dull, colourless section that described the events leading to the Seeker Program's foundation.

Charlie's attention drifted. The UFO and monster stories were never proven, but Charlie rather liked those tales, even if she considered them fanciful. She always dreamed of becoming a physician but travelling to the other Triumvirate planets or anywhere else in space held little appeal. So far, her only assignments had been on her native Earth and a brief trip to the Martian Penal Colony. This appointment on the moon hardly counted as space travel. Sam had been to all inhabited worlds in the system, Venus, Saturn, Mars, the space station near Jupiter and the exclusive settlement on Europa. If she went with him, Charlie thought, she might change her mind about space travel.

The female narrator droned out the stock question aimed at the youthful audience. "Who colonised Earth?"

"Venus colonised Earth," Charlie intoned in reply; she at least knew that part by heart, just as she knew the Venusians bypassed the inhospitable, lower gravity and dusty atmosphere of Mars as not worth their time.

Charlie asked the next question before the narrator, "And who colonised Mars?" Then she answered herself, "Earth."

After a few generations, Earth thought Mars the ideal place to stash all their rubbish, so Mars became a waste processing depot. As labourers were in high demand, the Triumvirate agreed to install a Martian penitentiary, thereby killing two birds with one stone. Somehow, the justice system felt getting the criminals off Earth and providing them with something productive to do, like sorting rubbish for recycling, would be an excellent way to improve mental health and rehabilitate the recidivist element of the Southwestern provinces of Earth. The shipyard installation also brought colonists to Mars. Several factories sprang up, dividing available employment between the free settlers, who migrated to find work, and day-release criminals who had a somewhat more straightforward existence, with food and accommodation provided. The seedy, shanty towns of Mars were also attractive to the unemployed, the bohemian, the shady, and just misfits fleeing the law.

Without giving it much thought, Charlie believed the root of all life in the solar system stemmed from Venusian colonisation, with the Venusians being the original occupants of Venus and most likely evolving from a primordial source. Some maintained fanciful notions that aliens colonised Earth prehistory as a cosmic experiment or that humans were an inferior subspecies of an alien race who would someday come back to claim all the planets in the system. That is if they even left. This theory, the Myth of Origin, was created when its proponents outrightly rejected Venusian colonisation. The scientific community examined the document's claims before rejecting them, with the findings shoved somewhere at the back of a government data rondure. The population of all three worlds, for the most part, continued to accept the traditional beliefs that the Venusians colonised Earth.

From time to time, the document got resurrected to promote boredom amongst schoolchildren during compulsory history lessons.

The narrator ran through a series of questions even the youngest primary school child could answer. Still, Charlie had to think about some of them. The narrator spoke of the mining operation that eventually emerged on Saturn with makeshift accommodation on a space station. The planet's surface was too hostile for a permanent settlement, but for the fly-in/fly-out workers, the pay was excellent and worth the inconvenience. Venus and Earth housed the largest densities of population; both beautiful, fertile worlds, although Earth had its fair share of crime and social issues. The more affluent families lived on Jupiter-Europa in exclusive communities.

Then the question, *"What happened next?"* came.

This was the only part Charlie found of any interest. The worlds functioned in accord until a hundred and fifty years ago when a solitary man gained notoriety by stirring up the Myth of Origin research, resurrecting the notion Earth's colonisation took place courtesy of a superior human race, and Venus was never part of the equation. For that reason, the argument ran, the Triumvirate, the supreme authority, should be conducted from Earth. When most citizens rejected his claims, he adjusted them with a sub-theory that humans were a diluted result of a species called Indigo that inhabited Venus in ancient times, embellishing the theory that Earthers drove them from the solar system. The man even produced some convincing data and imaging of flying objects in the sky. He got the desired effect even though no-one asked how the humans drove the Indigo away, seeing that Earthers didn't have space travel until the Venusians provided it.

The man gained enough of a following to attract the Triumvirate's attention, notably because in response, a formerly obscure movement resurfaced, which tried to convince Earth's more gullible residents they needed protection from the possibility of an extraterrestrial threat. The Venusians found themselves extensions of the movement's policies, which cited them as aliens and heirs of the Indigo. This movement, the Nexist Mutuality, or simply "Nexists", were the original authors of The Myth of Origin. They rejected the notion Earthers descended from colonisation by Venus and ensconced themselves solidly in their superiority and purity of race. The Triumvirate, made up mainly of Venusian senators, condemned the Nexist claims, but that made the Nexists create even more noise. Urging the government to erect a mined and patrolled border throughout the solar system—an almost unimaginable feat of engineering—the Nexists pushed their agenda to keep out any undesirable, passing alien who might spy on and ultimately contaminate the Earth. The perimeter minefield would have the bonus, the Nexists argued, of keeping away the original aliens who created Earthers and therefore stopping them from retaking the planet.

Each time Charlie heard the politicking on the history channel, she thought about the absurdity of the historical Nexists. There was no real meat to their claims, and the man who reignited the proposals didn't get more than fifteen minutes of fame; even that notoriety got buried in the kerfuffle he created. But the sudden interest fostered an unforeseen response. A new faction grew within the Triumvirate ranks, a separate political party calling themselves Unionists. The Unionists preached that contact and friendship with other species, if there were any, would deflect the risk of an alien invasion.

The Unionists, heavily represented within the Triumvirate, influenced the development of a program to send probes beyond the limit of the solar system, with recordings of salutations and entertaining facts—at least to the people who sent them—about the populated planets. Not a single probe elicited a response, not from outside the solar system anyway, only one that blew up when it bumped into Saturn. The message scattered itself on all shipping channels, corrupting comms traffic, causing cargo delays, disruption, and chaos through all communication satellites.

The Nexists and the Unionists bickered for decades; the Nexists on the dangers of such ventures and the Unionists, undismayed by the probes' failure, on the wisdom. The Triumvirate ignored the Nexist minority and drafted a manned space exploration program. They called it:

The Seeker Program.

The Nexists, with no foothold in the Triumvirate, urged that the Seeker's scripted message also include the term "defended" as it related to the system, so if the Seeker's encountered any other species, those species would be considered "warned". The Nexists coupled this with unreasonable demands for revisions to the program, hoping the delays would cause the Triumvirate to abandon its plans. In turn, and with significantly more political clout, the Unionists openly accused the Nexists of plotting to sabotage the Seekers.

In the end, it didn't matter; the question of the cost of the program caused a political divide within the Triumvirate itself. Earth, a minor player in decisions with only a consular presence, garnered the most followers in vetoing the program, probably boosted by wealthy, covert Nexists. Venusians, closer to the direct administration of the Triumvirate, remained solidly behind the Unionists, as did one or two of the leading families on Europa. There, however, most remained politically on the fence.

Then one silly, decidedly senior Union sympathiser and Triumvirate Senator made the loose-lipped comment in passing during interviews for the Seeker program that "perhaps aliens already walk amongst us, perhaps even the Indigo are still here." The ill-thought-out remark generated widespread panic, principally among Nexists, whose leaders were swift to react, reassuring their followers that the Unionist hierarchy must know something they were not disclosing. The Nexists vowed to defend Earth against any aliens biding their time to take over the Triumvirate.

There even followed a bloody and pointless civil war as Nexist sympathisers rounded up anyone they thought might be Indigo or alien, with no objective evidence to back up their claim, then occupied several regions of Earth and Venus as strongholds against the supposed alien invasion. The Nexists resorted to terrorism and murder, but against the hastily gathered Venusian forces, their occupation of several provinces on Venus was swiftly quashed, and their brief and bloody reign on Earth came to an ignominious end. For their trouble, Nexists found themselves at the end of their own smoking gun; anyone discovered to be a Nexist from then on, promoting the cause, or merely a sympathiser, got rounded up and sent to Mars. It didn't matter because the Nexists still won when the cost of the civil war put the Seeker program on hold. It happened more than a hundred and fifty years before Charlie was born, but she knew some Nexists still kicked about on Earth, although they took care not to fall foul of the law. Decades went by before the Triumvirate resurrected the Seeker Program.

A technician poked his head around the door.

"Doc, we've brought up one of the obsolete nurse droids from the stockpile. We've got nothing else to do; d'you mind if we see if we can get it to work?"

He would have been better asking engineering if he could fiddle with the droid's innards, but Charlie supposed he was on her time. She waved him away with a grin, thinking she might even join him, but instead, she glanced back at the display of the Seeker ship.

Much of it lay in chunks on the hangar bay floor, and Charlie reflected on what a waste of time the Seeker program turned out to be, a money pit that attracted criticism from disillusioned Unionist supporters and people-pretending-not-be-Nexists alike. Governor Miller's father, a minor senator in the Triumvirate, was one of the program's most outspoken opponents. His speech was required reading at school. In that speech, Miller's father argued for the cohesion of the Triumvirate worlds, that exploration of the universe might attract unwanted, possibly hostile attention. He further demanded that resources be directed to defence rather than exploration, so convinced was he there were enemies to be had "out there". He cleverly phrased his speech to reflect objectivity, publicly distancing himself from what he called "outdated and unenlightened policies" while his words played right into the hands of the Nexists. The Triumvirate criticised him for his equivocal use of language, even though no-one could prove any link between Senator Miller and Nexism.

It turned out his views generated a lot of sympathy. By then, only twenty of the single pilot Seeker ships had launched. A fickle public forgot the civil war and rallied in support of Governor Miller. Facing opposition and wishing to appease Earth, the Triumvirate agreed to pause the Seeker Program's second launch until they received word from the pilots who had already left. Two years later, with no such word received, the government quietly terminated the program with the lone pilot in each ship declared lost. Still, the damage was done. The Unionists lost support, and the remaining redundant ships duly dismantled, their components finding homes as spare parts in the Mars shipyards.

Today, according to the narrative—which was quite a few years out of date, the radical Nexists and the Union are just a distant memory. History to study at school. Dull history, Charlie thought, as dull as the last couple of minutes she spent reviewing it.

Sam's appearance in the hangar drew Charlie's attention to the engineering view. She leaned forward; they must have discovered something, although she was more interested in admiring Sam than in anything they might find on the ship, which to her, was just a piece of historical space junk. A sudden yell and flurry of activity on the viewer startled her to attention as the status changed to amber, which meant injury incoming to Sick Bay. Charlie jumped to her feet.

"Incoming from engineering," she hollered as Sick Bay suddenly shifted into a hive of industry. Three injured crewmembers arrived within minutes, the nurse droid activated itself, and the three casualties settled on lounges, awaiting triage. Charlie felt a pang of disappointment when she discovered they required only wound repair, a minor burn and resetting of a broken finger, injuries easily handled by technicians and the nurse droid. Charlie would have liked to clean a wound, reposition a bone or treat a burn, but the Triumvirate considered its medical officers above such menial tasks. She exhaled hard and went back to her office. Fancy wishing someone had been maimed just to alleviate boredom. It seemed life on Rille Base was turning her into a psychopath.

CHAPTER THREE _

In the early afternoon, the sight that greeted Sam on his arrival in Sick Bay was the facility's medical officer's boots up on the desk, her eyes closed, and her mouth open as she dozed. Her backside was perched perilously close to the edge of her seat, but Sam couldn't resist tickling her nose. He chuckled as he startled her awake.

"Commander Wells wants you and me to attend a conference about the Seeker ship," he said, pointing to the viewer. "I'm not sure why she asked for you, Charlie, there are no human remains on board, but I said I'd collect you. I analysed some of the data by applying one of my new techniques; what I discovered was a bit curious, so I reported it to Wells." Sam shrugged. "She glanced at my conclusions, then shut me down."

Charlie twisted her body and stretched out her limbs; snoozing in that chair hadn't been a good idea, now she had a paralysed backside, a throbbing pain in her tail-end and on top of that, pins and needles in her feet. She stood, wincing and hopping from one foot to the other to get her circulation moving.

"That is odd for Wells to include me," she agreed, "but nothing's happening here, so even a debriefing is a bit of a change." Charlie sighed. "I spent six years at medical school so I could watch a technician regenerate a dermis and autosplint a broken finger."

Sam commiserated with her. "You're wasted here."

Charlie nodded slowly and headed for the door, throwing cold water on her face as she passed the sink. "We all are, Sam."

The briefing room on the Governor's level doubled as a dining area and entertainment theatre as each need arose, remodelled according to the rank of dignitary attending. Only lowly base personnel were in attendance today, so hard seats, side tables and spectator paraphernalia were provided as basic. A visual display console dominated the front of the room. Charlie glanced around, recognising one or two of the individuals assembled, although the presence of Captain Suliman, a former freighter captain and long-term patient from the Mars penal colony who'd been here since before she arrived on the moon, surprised her. Suliman was rough, seldom spoke and only got to be called "captain" because he once owned a ship. The Triumvirate would never let a character like him into their military chain of command. Sam sat opposite Charlie, and Governor Miller positioned himself behind a solid lectern at the head of the assembly. Close to Miller stood Commander Wells, the thin, grey-haired, sour-faced, dedicated second officer. Charlie didn't know the other three attendees; an older man with drawn features and a wisp of grey hair who wore a Triumvirate military uniform; a thin, pimply skinned face man in his early thirties who stared straight ahead and acknowledged no one, and a nervous round-bodied fellow of indeterminate age, with a shock of red hair and a chubby face full of freckles. Miller offered no introductions.

In her other position as Senior Science Officer, Commander Wells took the floor and displayed an image of the Seeker ship as it appeared before dismantling.

"As you know," she began, her tone clipped and unmelodic, "twenty-two years ago, the Triumvirate launched twenty Seeker ships to determine the existence, or non-existence, of extraterrestrial life. They equipped each ship with advanced life support systems, antigravity and engine magnitude of greater than one-quarter past light speed." Commander Wells eyeballed her audience. Her delivery always sounded scripted, crisp, as though reeling off her words line by considered line. Any interruption drew a steely *"I haven't finished"* glare.

Commander Wells changed the image to the Seeker ship following its dismantling, gutted and in pieces all over the hangar floor. Its frame, the bones picked bare, suspended above.

"This ship was the last to launch and piloted by Pilot Amira Santer." Wells switched the image to a room-wide holographic impression that settled around her audience, giving them the opportunity for closer examination of the ship. Following the engineers' ministrations, it was nothing more now than an empty shell and only increased Charlie's bewilderment at her presence in these proceedings.

"Like many Seekers," the commander continued, "Pilot Santer was Venusian, in possession of all the physical, spiritual and cultural attributes the Triumvirate encourages us to expect from her race. We would, therefore, in this case, expect precise data recorded at all times, along with detailed charting of systems and any species the pilot encountered."

A murmur of agreement followed. Venusians were nothing if not thorough, and that ship looked to contain nothing of value.

"However," Commander Wells snapped; she hadn't invited comments. "In this instance, our expectations of Venusian thoroughness have disappointed. We received data containing a brief report, an incomplete star chart and little else. Santer didn't return with the ship, which suggests to us she abandoned her mission when she came upon what she presumed was the remnant of a civilisation. Either that, or she met with foul play, hostile action or perhaps died from a mishap or sickness, but there are no signs of the ship coming under attack." Wells replaced the impression with another, more familiar image.

"Thoughts on this, if you will."

An image of Earth peeped above the moon's arc, easily recognisable, gloriously blue and with wispy clouds at the pole. Beautiful, but nothing unexpected. Wells's audience looked from one to the other, speculating as to what she expected them to think.

Charlie spoke up. "Earth?"

"Look again, Doctor Maitland. You are from the Northwest Islands, are you not? They are just coming into view now. Does this area look like your home?" Wells highlighted the island group where Charlie grew up. She had to admit, it looked different; similar, but the archipelago where she was born had ninety islands. This had only a handful. She looked at Sam, but he only shrugged.

"No? That is because this is not Earth," Wells said with a note of triumph. Charlie could have sworn it was the first time a smile ever cracked the officer's mouth. "We believe this planet, this system, is inhabited. Santer's report is from a moon orbiting the Earth-like world. We have no way of knowing if she ever reached the blue planet, and we do not know how she programmed her ship to return to the exact coordinates of its origins. Pilot Santer did not have an engineering background, and we built these ships to be piloted. If she encountered superior technology, we cannot know what harm the Seeker program might still yet wreak on us."

Governor Miller took the floor with a nod to Commander Wells.

"I sent you all the report from the ship. Did any of you read it?"

Sam was the only one with a response. He'd seen it on the ship; Miller must have sent it to the others. Why hadn't they acknowledged it?

"And?" Miller leant forward and placed his elbows on the lectern, his head tilted to one side as he waited for Sam's answer.

"It's not a report," Sam said slowly, unsure how to describe the text he extracted from the data storage. "It's more a fragment of prose, an outpouring of emotion from someone who spent more years than she planned, alone, in space." Sam shook his head, "As a report, it tells us nothing. As a piece of poetry, it is rather thought-provoking as to the mental state of Pilot Santer."

Miller was glad to hear his assessment. Having the document's contents reduced to the ramblings of a crazy woman worked well. He hadn't sent the report to anyone else; he could easily explain why they had not received it as a comms error. Sam Mead removed the ship's data, so there was no way around that, but Miller was not interested in the opinions of the others present in the room.

"We have yet to analyse the rest of the data," Miller continued, "but there is little else, only some incomplete imaging of the system. It looks identical to our own, but we have no way of substantiating her findings. Of paramount concern is that Pilot Santer discovered an entrance, a doorway into a cliff on this moon that we assume, given she is not here, she somehow persuaded to open."

Unfortunately, Pilot Santer hadn't provided an image of the doorway. Charlie would have liked to have seen it. A structure built by an alien civilisation. That would be really something. She raised her hand.

"Why do you assume that? Does it say so in the report?"

"No, it doesn't," Sam cut in sharply. "It only mentions the doorway." He looked at Miller. "How *did* you come by that assumption?"

Miller was unfazed. "Santer discovered a means to return the ship to us and record her most recent coordinates. Why would she not return? Santer's abilities only ran to piloting and minor maintenance to the navigational systems. Did she want to alert us to her discovery? Could it be what she found was hostile, and now, years later, she has discovered a way to send a warning? Or perhaps, as the Unionists believed, the species she discovered were so friendly, she stayed, and the ship is a postcard to say she is having a good time and wishes we were there?"

Suliman, prepared only to be an observer at these proceedings and indifferent as to why he was summoned, saw only one possible solution. He ignored Miller's sour humour and flagrant political undertone and spoke up.

"The only way to know for sure is to go look."

Miller smiled then, something he only did when he was getting his way.

"That is precisely what we intend to do."

None of this made sense to Charlie, Pilot Santer would have known the risks. From memory, Charlie understood each Seeker underwent rigorous psychological assessment. Their mission was to catalogue new civilisations if they found any, but not to make contact. She raised her hand again.

"If Pilot Santer was afraid, why would she take the time to compose an essay? And why would an unfriendly species allow her to send a warning?"

The drawn-featured man spoke then. "The danger may be that what she found is friendly, at least on the face of it, friendly enough to test the waters of our system, see if we respond to their overtures. Despite the requirement a Seeker needed to prove political neutrality, Pilot Santer may be a Unionist."

A debate followed, but Charlie barely listened. Instead, she, the pimply-faced man, and the round man sat in silence as the provocative undertones of Unionist and Nexist politics filled the room. Charlie felt out of place. They should not be having this conversation. Nexist discussions were frowned upon, but both Wells and Miller seemed willing to reveal their political leanings.

Crossing her arms and legs protectively, she felt herself shrinking into her chair. Her presence at this briefing made no sense until that point, even if the story of the door in the cliff had briefly piqued her interest. Now, a sense of foreboding took hold. Sam, at the point of argument with the thin, sickly-looking man and obviously trying to piece all this information together, caught her watching him, but even his smile couldn't warm the chill making its way up her spine.

Miller eventually brought the deliberation to an end when Sam pointed out the governor sounded decidedly

Nexist, a comment Miller didn't qualify with a denial.

"An expedition to locate Pilot Santer or her remains and establish the truth of her findings is due to leave in two days," Miller declared, deflecting Sam's accusation. "Those assigned are here. Commander of the mission…"

Sam's sudden outburst of disbelief ended when Wells thrust her palm close to his face in an unmistakable "stop". Sam sat back. He didn't like where this briefing was going.

Miller waited while Wells put Mead back in his place. "This is not open for debate, Mr Mead."

Sam found Miller's dismissiveness unacceptable. As far as he was concerned, if the Governor was sending them all on an expedition, it was most positively a matter of debate. He stood and fixed Miller with a determined gaze, ignoring the thin-lipped Wells who still stood beside him. She thrust up her chin and inhaled noisily, but this time, at a slight gesture from Miller, did nothing.

"*Governor,*" Sam emphasised his superior officer's title. "We have received no official orders from the Triumvirate; therefore, I disagree. It *is* open for debate, and I challenge you to justify commanding any of us present to embark on a mission based on a possibly specious and whimsical piece of poetry. Pilot Santer imaged areas of that solar system, but she didn't image the door she allegedly saw on that moon. I must ask, why not? Your premise for sending this expedition is not based on fact. The entire purpose of the Seeker mission was to catalogue other inhabited worlds if they existed, nothing more. You propose risking this crew's lives to find a nebulous doorway in a system that has similarities to our own. I believe, with respect, your proposal is reckless."

"Noted, Mr Mead." Miller held Sam's gaze, "Nevertheless, I am sending an expedition."

"What makes you think a venture like this will succeed?" Suliman asked. He excluded himself from the political controversy, and throughout the briefing, remained slumped messily in his chair, legs stretched out, clad in hospital-grade slacks and looking in need of a bath and a shave. But then he always looked like that. He lifted his hand as an afterthought as he spoke, allowing it to flop back on the side table. Suliman couldn't stand protocol, particularly in a setting such as this, but he did know something about engines. He eyeballed Miller before speaking.

"Queter technology only works in light craft. There's no way to create the necessary fields for speed-of-light or above in a larger ship." He thumbed at the image of the Seeker module, now tidily back inside the screen. "And you just dismantled the only one left. It wouldn't be much of a crusade."

"You have been out of circulation too long, *Captain* Suliman," Miller responded with sickening smugness. "We have a ship, capable of Mag 4. If our calculations are correct, again estimating the time the Seeker ship should have taken to make a return journey if it had superior speed, the expedition will take around three years. Naturally, one would have to factor in the possibility of making contact, possibly hostile contact."

All eyes were on Suliman, busily tapping the tip of his finger on the side table. "What ship?" he asked.

"You know the ship well, Suliman," Miller replied. "Your old ship, the Millstone."

At that, Suliman wrenched himself upright and roared with laughter, slapping his hand on the table.

"Hell's Bells, Miller!" he cried. "You're joking! The Millstone is junk, held together with resin and string. That hull couldn't take Mag 4. Hell, it could barely take .5 light. How would you get around the light speed issues close to planets?" Suliman slumped back, shaking his head and snorting. He glowered at the others under hooded eyes, his moment of disbelieving mirth evaporating. "I nursed that ship for thirty years," he muttered. "I know its limitations." He finished up with a sarcastic grin at Miller. "You're in cuckooland, Governor."

Miller had no military authority over Suliman, but Suliman still had three years of a criminal conviction to run and was in his custody, so in theory, Miller could do what he liked. He walked over to stand behind Suliman's chair.

"Where have you been for the past nine months, Captain Suliman?"

"Here, getting my liver fixed," Suliman mumbled without turning to look.

Miller then strolled to each seat, inviting the incumbent to look up at him as all the while, he addressed Suliman, sounding both disinterested and condescending simultaneously.

"Yes, a liver that's processed many, many crates of

whisky, I understand. Let us be honest, Captain, most of the time, you were too drunk to notice your surroundings, too drunk to see what was going on under your nose on the Mars shipyard."

Suliman sneered again. All authority tried his patience, Governor Miller's in particular, but what he said was true, no denying.

"Technology didn't stand still while you caused trouble on Mars," Miller continued, injecting as much contempt as possible into his voice. "You made yourself unwelcome in almost every medical facility on Earth. The worlds didn't stand still after authorities brought you here for you to detoxify for—remind me, how many times is it?—the *eighth time*? The Millstone got an upgrade, Captain. I expected more gratitude."

"I bet you did," Suliman said under his breath, but Miller ignored him.

"It's not the most luxurious ship I grant you," Miller announced to the rest of his shocked audience, "but she will suit our purpose."

Suliman tossed a scornful glance at Miller and repeated his prediction.

"She'll fall apart at light speed."

The governor clasped his hands behind his back and resumed his parade of victory around the room. He expected that old cargo pirate to buck against this.

"Not according to our evaluations, she won't," he declared. "She holds up well, and I will say again, this is not a matter for debate."

Suliman couldn't care less what Miller thought. He learned a few things in the judicial system, and something smelt fishy to him.

"So why upgrade the Millstone?" he demanded. "That Seeker ship only came back a few days ago; you couldn't have been anticipating this mission."

Miller inclined his head. "The Triumvirate used the Millstone to test a Queter engine prototype."

"Bullshit!" Suliman spat. "You could have built an entirely new ship in the time it took to install Mag engines. You can't graft healthy tissue onto a dead body and expect it to get up and start walking around."

Miller thought for a moment. "Well, that's quite an image, Suliman, but we didn't choose to build a new ship at enormous expense to the Triumvirate."

Suliman shrugged. The governor was lying; this smacked of private enterprise.

"So, who's flying it?"

Miller embraced his sense of power, allowing it to send shudders of triumph the length of his body. He curled his mouth into a vicious grin of victory.

"You are, Suliman," he announced. "You have three years of your sentence to run; space will contain you as well as we can here."

Again, Suliman lifted his hand and let it drop with a heavy clatter back on the desk in a gesture of resignation. He was still a prisoner. The Triumvirate owned him.

Miller nodded to the moribund-looking man. "Commander Thale will be the commanding officer. The crew will comprise Professor Rice—" Miller pointed to the nervous, rotund fellow positioned between Suliman and Sam, "— who is an eminent historian, and Matthew Livesey," to whom Miller gave a slight, dismissive flick of the hand. "The only Triumvirate member on board apart from Commander Thale will be Doctor Maitland."

Charlie felt the colour drain from her face. For a second, she felt suspended, paralysed. How could Miller select her for this mission? She didn't have the skills for any assignment outside the neighbouring planets. Sam caught her dismay and spoke up on her behalf, not understanding why Miller would choose Charlie—any of them, over him.

"Am I not to be included on this fool's errand, Governor?" Sam inquired.

"No, Mead, you're needed elsewhere."

"Then why Doctor Maitland? Surely she's needed elsewhere too?"

"Ships doctor, Mr Mead. We have no idea what the crew may encounter."

Sam slapped his hand on the desk. "Then send a junior physician! It's a waste of Doctor Maitland's abilities."

Miller raised his voice to drown out Sam's protests.

"This mission has a top classification. Discuss it with no-one. Between now and departure, remain in your quarters. You may connect to your families but text only. I will deliver orders within the hour. Dismissed."

CHAPTER FOUR _

Miller's statement stirred up Charlie. Shaken, she found her feet but had to concentrate on putting one foot in front of the other as she made her way to the exit. Why her? Without training for deep space travel, she would be unprepared. Even the Seeker pilots underwent basic training in possible scenarios because there wasn't enough knowledge about space outside their solar system, and look what happened to the Seekers. What was Miller thinking?

A sudden, fiery wave of realisation sent Charlie's blood boiling, driving away her shock and indignation. Vengeance! This was Miller's revenge, a way of ensuring her silence for the next few years. Her body twisted slowly to stare across at him, deep in a victory conversation with Commander Wells. Taking a single, deep, ferocious breath, she clenched and unclenched her fists. With her outrage growing, she took a step towards the governor. Charlie had no coherent plan on what she would do when she reached him, although it would likely end in a court-martial. At least the others in the room would witness it. Then, she could reveal to the magistrates just how nasty their governor truly is. In the passion of her fury, it sounded like a better option than getting launched into space to god knows where.

Sam stole her moment. Charlie's body language was just too dramatic, and he placed himself between her and Miller. Unaware of Miller's lechery towards her, Sam thought her rage stemmed from Miller selecting her for the mission. Grabbing Charlie's arm, he shepherded her out the door, ignoring her whispered cursing as she unwillingly stomped along beside him. Miller saw Sam steering the angry woman away. He'd allow them a few minutes; there was still time for Charlie to change his mind. Although he doubted she would.

Sam and Charlie only just made it to her quarters when Miller sent Sam a request to return to the debriefing room. Sam dropped an apologetic kiss on the top of her head, but it did little to appease Charlie, who huffed and snarled about unfairness at his departing back. She spent the next hour crying and hurling objects around her quarters. With three years of her indenture still to run and Sam stopping her from wringing Miller's neck, there was no alternative but to do as ordered. The Triumvirate paid for Charlie's six years of medical training and added in a bonus surgical residency on Europa as a carrot at the end of her indenture, so she was hugely in their debt. The only drawback was it meant her time was at their disposal for four years after graduation rather than the usual three. It wasn't so bad; her lifestyle was comfortable until her assignment to Rille, a place from where she couldn't seem to get unassigned. Throwing herself down on her bed, she lamented the monitoring of medical postings in the Triumvirate, and the plankton-brained officials in administration.

After reflecting, weeping, and cursing about the situation, Charlie dried her eyes and supposed she should send a message to her parents. She had no option but to lie and tell them her posting was imperative and high classification, which meant she would be out of communication, possibly for a few years. Listening to their pride and words of encouragement, she embellished the lie, telling them it might mean advancement but that they must not speak of it to anyone. As expected, they stacked on effusive praise, following her lead at the gravity of being singled out for such an exclusive mission, even if Charlie could not offer them any details other than they could not contact her. Her mother shed a few tears, which threatened to set Charlie off again, but she pressed her tongue hard against the roof of her mouth and refused to give. An image of the family's pet hairy toothclaw lizard came up at the end of the audio, making Charlie feel doubly lonely. She continued to stare at the display until her eyes demanded she blink.

Turning aside from the picture of her beloved toothclaw, Charlie glanced around her cabin. She'd always considered it cramped, but at least it was her sanctuary, and she didn't want to leave it other than to go to Earth and back to her mum and dad. Her bed was still a mess from when Sam had been here yesterday and where she'd thrown the pillows on the floor in anger just now. *"I'm gonna miss you, Sam,"* she whispered aloud as she spied Sam's shirt draped over a chair. Reaching out, she picked it up, holding it to her face and breathing in Sam's warm, spicy scent. Stuffing the shirt into her bag, it became a souvenir, a lucky charm that for years—she didn't know how many—would be her only connection to the man who had captured her heart.

Hours later, her door slid open, and Sam stepped through, checking along the walkway that no-one saw him. He gathered Charlie into his arms, and she sobbed against his chest.

"What the bloody hell's going on?" he breathed, stroking her hair, trying to soothe not only Charlie but himself as well. The thought of her leaving was just as overwhelming for him, and he couldn't accept Miller's reasoning for sending her. He held her away from him and looked into her eyes, red-rimmed and swollen from several hours of weeping. He planned on smiling a reassuring smile, but Charlie cottoned on that Sam had something to tell her, and it wasn't just commiserating on her being shipped off on a fool's errand.

"What is it, Sam?" Charlie sniffed as she drew his hands from the side of her face, holding them in front of her. Sam sighed and shook his head.

"I'm not supposed to be here." He kept his voice low, even though only Charlie could hear him. "Miller told me I wasn't to contact you before the mission, but I have to tell you something just in case he confines me to quarters."

That Sam was twitchy about this "something" worried Charlie. Not much made him lose his cool, so she waited while he prevaricated, his expression changing as different thoughts went through his head. She gave him a little encouragement.

"Come on, Sam. Spit it out."

Sam took a deep breath. "You remember the gadget I was tinkering with—or was in the process of developing, the one that peeled back layers of old data that's eclipsed by new?"

Charlie nodded; besides her, it was his pet project.

"Well, this time," he said, his voice barely above a whisper, just in case by some weird quirk, Miller had bugged Charlie's quarters, "when I pulled the data from the Seeker ship, I put it under the display and found a data shadow, an eclipse. I disregarded it at first because when people make an error, with a date or a time, for example, they can delete it and reinsert the amended information. The most recent shadow is retrievable if anyone is interested enough, but this shadow… Charlie, it was never meant to be found. I've fudged data myself; it requires skill. That's why I developed that tool. This data had layers of encryption sequences; my god, whoever didn't want it found embedded it *so deep*. I checked the signature of the shadow data…"

There would be a punch line. Charlie didn't even need to ask whose signature.

Sam's eyes widened. "Commander Wells's signed it. I looked closer. Both the date and log had evidence of tampering—Charlie, that ship returned more than a year ago. I have never seen such a, such a—" he gripped her shoulders, struggling for a moment before coming up with an unoriginal conclusion, "—tampering of data."

Charlie frowned. "It can't be. I saw it tractored in myself only days ago."

"That's what they want us to believe," Sam nodded. "After I located the eclipse, I looked around the rest of the ship and found a piece of plant material, all dried out and powdery. I think it was once someone's lunch, left behind, a sandwich or something; the point is, it was pretty old. I ran the cellular analyser over it, and its rate of deterioration matched with the date on the eclipse…" Sam's voice trailed away as his thoughts went over the events in the hangar. "You got three emergencies this morning?"

"Yes," Charlie confirmed, "nothing serious."

"I engineered those. I feel terrible about it, but I wanted to run a non-routine investigation on the ship's exterior without arousing suspicion. The only place concealed from visuals is underneath, so I took a scraping off the hull for analysis. Nothing special showed until I retrieved some matter out of the seam of the hull. I found a microscopic sample of soil, Martian soil. Charlie, that ship has been on Mars. That lunch was probably a Martian sandwich."

Charlie pulled a face. "Mars? Why?"

Sam blew out his breath with a whistle. "You tell me."

"Maybe then they found a body," Charlie said, "and it's on Mars."

Sam hadn't found evidence of that. "There's no residue of anything organic except that lunch and the signatures of our engineers here. At first, I thought the Triumvirate must have stored the ship on Mars, but there are no signs of any dismantling." Sam set his mouth in a firm line before continuing, "My gut says someone hid it."

"Do you think Miller is behind this?"

Sam threw up his hands. "Who else? After that debate in the briefing room, I believe now the Triumvirate know nothing about the Seeker ship, and I'll put money on it they don't know about the expedition. That's why all the secrecy. Miller revoked my comm access, so I can't alert anyone. When I get back to Earth, I'm going straight to the consulate and make them listen. I may raise enough suspicions to get the mission cancelled before you're out of comms range."

"What suspicions are you going to raise, Sam?" Charlie asked. "That Miller is acting without Triumvirate sanction? That he hid a Seeker ship on Mars? They'll want proof, and there's not much to support a conspiracy. Have you spoken to the engineers who dismantled the ship? They might back you up."

"That's just it, Charlie. They won't talk." Sam rubbed his face and gave a weary sigh. "I don't know. It's like…" he couldn't explain it, "like they've been told to keep quiet or something."

To Charlie, it felt that more was at stake than Amira Santer's whereabouts, the Seeker ship's return or even a ruse for Miller to get his own back for her rejections. Sam might be right to consider a conspiracy, but…

"No-one's going to believe ill of Miller, Sam. Like he says, he's got friends."

Sam stiffened his shoulders. "I know, but it just… feels wrong. Don't you think it's convenient he suddenly has a ship ready to haul you all off into the great unknown? I don't buy that 'we were testing out a prototype' bullshit. If they were, with the types of metal used in Mag engines, who would be the ideal choice to be on that project?"

Charlie didn't need to say Sam would have been the ideal choice.

"I don't want to go on this mission, Sam," she said as she made sad, tiny plucking movements at the front of his shirt. "I'm not trained for deep space. I've only ever been to Mars. I always thought when I travelled, it would be in a people carrier."

"Apart from Thale, none of you are qualified, although I don't know much about Suliman. I can't fathom Miller's reasoning and…"

Charlie put her arms around Sam and leaned her head against his chest. Perhaps, under the circumstances, now would be the right time to tell him the truth. He stopped talking and held her close as she whispered, "I think I know why he picked me."

Sam had to tell her about the sandwich and the soil, but he didn't plan on it spoiling what time they had left. He ran his fingers through her hair, appreciating its silkiness; baby's hair, he always thought. She was such a little squirt of a person, a delightful concoction of daintiness and fierceness, strength and softness. He didn't want her to go, but she couldn't defy orders either. For an indentured employee, disobedience was occupational suicide. And it was only three years. She heard his voice rumbling in his chest.

"Okay, why did he pick you?"

Charlie felt sad. Sam had no idea what was coming.

She tilted her head up to look at him—confession time.

"I rejected him."

Sam made a noise between a laugh and a snort as he peered down at her, but one look at her face stopped him. She was deadly serious.

"Rejected him?" he asked. "How?"

"He took a fancy to me when I first arrived," Charlie admitted. "I've been fighting him off ever since."

Sam studied her face, her wide eyes so close to tears. "Why didn't you tell me?"

"I tried to tell the consulate more than once," she sighed. "And I've pushed and shoved him and generally made myself thoroughly distasteful, but nothing seems to work. Sending me on this mission is a punishment. I thought I could handle Miller, and I knew if I got you involved…"

The revelation shocked Sam, "Why couldn't he just send you back to Earth?"

"He's sending me because he can and because he doesn't need me calling him out to the authorities." Charlie laid her head back against Sam's chest, drawing comfort from him. "Miller's a vindictive bastard who thinks someone might believe me when I reveal him for what he is. When, if, we get back, I don't doubt I'll be conveniently assigned to one of the far corridor mining installations, never to be heard of again."

"Surely he'd know you'd tell me?"

"Evidently not. Miller seems to have no worries with you returning to Earth."

"Charlie," Sam said, "I'll find out everything I can about this—this mission, whatever it is. I know it's three years, but I promise, I'll still be here when you get back, and I guarantee you won't be going to any corridor outposts."

But Sam's words brought no comfort. "I'm afraid Miller might try again, perhaps use the mission as leverage, that if I give in, he won't make me go."

Sam tucked Charlie's wispy hair behind her ears and attempted a smile, although he understood now why Charlie looked about to murder Miller in the debriefing room. He now felt like that himself towards the man. He didn't even know how he would keep his hands off Miller for the next week until his assignment ended. He leaned his chin against the top of her head.

"I would rather be without you for three years," he said, "ten years even, than you give in to that jerk."

Charlie looked up and managed the smile Sam waited for, then he kissed her, let her go and headed for the door. He stopped there, "Did you talk to your oldies?"

Charlie nodded. "Briefly."

"I'll go see them when I get to Earth," Sam promised. "Now, I daren't get caught here." He grinned. "If I can, I'll sneak back later. Don't start without me!"

The last night found Charlie packed and ready to leave a clear eight hours before needed. Making her way to the hangar, she lamented Miller had not allowed her to check medical facilities onboard the Millstone. As Miller restricted all contact with the other crew members, she couldn't ask Suliman. This secret mission, it seemed, had to be a secret even from each other until launch.

The unlikely crew gathered at the hangar bay. Suliman, looking as if he still hadn't bothered to shower or shave, seemed to have no gear. As the only one allowed to board the ship, Charlie hoped he'd already taken on at least a shaving kit and a few changes of clothes; otherwise, three years with a smelly crewmate would seem like three hundred.

CHAPTER FIVE _

The Millstone lived down, and then some, to all Charlie's expectations. Of indeterminate proportions, the original aged hull was cobbled together with parts of other salvaged craft, and covered in paint scratches from multiple unintentional contacts with other vessels over the course of its history. The result was a multicoloured concoction that didn't look like it would ever get off the launch pad. The upgraded engines and necessary modifications to the outer hull were evident, making the ship look cumbersome and too heavy at the rear. The lowered ramp had a rusty sheen with welded panels for reinforcement. Suliman was right; space junk—a decommissioned, clunky, grubby ex-light cargo vessel that looked like its erstwhile owner, shabby and unkempt.

Rice, the historian, stood next to Charlie, his voice trembling as he fought tears.

"A millstone is a weight, Doctor Maitland," he whimpered, "used historically for grinding flour. They also used them to drown people as punishment." He pulled a handkerchief from his pocket and blew his nose noisily. "That's what this is, a gargantuan punishment. I've only ever been on an interplanetary shuttle, and I always have to sit in the front seat because I get space sick. I don't know how to pilot or crew."

Charlie felt for him. She'd cried herself out last night and again, after a long goodbye, when Sam left her cabin in the early hours. Rice glanced up as Charlie placed her hand on his shoulder.

"You'll be fine, Professor Rice. It's strange to me too."

Rice nodded and gulped. He dried his tears and stuffed his hanky back in his pocket.

"Thank you, Doctor Maitland, you're very kind."

Commander Thale appeared, emaciated and sickly looking in the hangar lights, a caricature with narrow crimson lips slashed into his white face. His disdainful glance at Rice's red-rimmed eyes and flushed face gave Charlie immediate cause to dislike the man.

"We need to get underway," he stated, with no formalities or greeting. "There is no reason to delay. Doctor Maitland? We have stocked the medical bay; it will meet your requirements, and you can peruse it at your leisure once we have cleared the perimeter. Professor Rice?" Thale stood back and waved the little Professor onto the ramp. Rice scuttled past him without looking up, just before Livesey arrived to board the ship. He passed Charlie and Thale without a word.

The narrow cockpit was initially constructed for only the pilot and first mate, but three other seats were now needed to accommodate the extra bodies. While the seats were secure, the arrangement left a lot to be desired from a safety standpoint. Charlie immediately evaluated the seating risk and made a mental note the configuration needed to be addressed. Still, there was little she could do about it right now. She and Rice were short, but Rice's frame was substantially broader. He would find his seat snug, with the possibility of some of his midriff spilling into the narrow space between seats. Suliman, a towering man of large stature, was already in the pilot seat, which appeared to accommodate his bulk comfortably. Thale, occupying the cargo mate's chair, was, in contradiction, such a shadow of a man, he took up little room, and as he couldn't fly the ship, Charlie wondered why he took the larger seat which would have accommodated Rice's bulk more adequately. Power, Charlie supposed. Just showing them who's in charge. Livesey deposited himself in a bulkhead side seat. Of average height with long, skinny legs, he'd made a good choice. None of this was ideal, though. A section of the bulkhead which protruded from the floor for no apparent reason would prove an impediment if she and Rice needed to get out in an emergency. If the forward two seats were still occupied, they would be trapped unless they clambered over the back of the seat. With the low cockpit ceiling, she doubted Rice would manage any gymnastics. The seating logistics needed further study, but Charlie envisaged little else to do on the voyage other than rearrange the furniture.

"Stow your kit in the locker in the corridor, Doctor Maitland," Suliman instructed, thumbing towards the door and reading Charlie's mind as to the tight squeeze. "You too, Rice. There's only one bunk room on board, and they've used any storage to squeeze in extra bunks, so it's going to be tight."

Charlie stowed her bag in the locker and packed herself into her seat between Rice's midriff roll and the armrest. Livesey still hadn't uttered a word and continued to stare straight ahead as the ancient ship rattled their bones, thundering and farting its way into space. As a bonus, neither Miller nor Wells came to wave them goodbye.

CHAPTER SIX _

After leaving orbit, Suliman invited them on a grand tour of the ship, which took a princely ten minutes. It housed all utilities in separate and not particularly private closets. The galley, which turned out to be the most significant room on board, boasted a meal preparation section, a drinks port, a cold larder, deep enough—according to Suliman—to hold several bodies, and a bench with five low stools. Despite being of a more practical size than its neighbouring closets, the galley still was a tight fit. If the five crew members happened to be seated at the same time, at least one occupant's bottom would jut out into the corridor when placed upon one of the seats. Worse still and to Charlie's dismay, the bunk room contained five bunks. Suliman found her discomfiture mildly entertaining.

"Sorry, Doc," he grinned, "they only catered for two crew when they built this ship. The designers didn't gear it for splitting the sexes either. Have your pick of the bunks, just pick a top one, or all you'll see are our hairy arses if we come to bed after you."

"Thanks, Suliman," Charlie saw no way around these sleeping arrangements. "I expect I'll get used to it."

Suliman grunted. "I never did. I don't play nice with other people. I prefer solitude."

Charlie knew that, but still, she gave him a tight-lipped grin. "Thanks for the heads up."

The Sick Bay, renamed Medbay on this ship, considering the modest size of the Millstone, turned out to be well equipped if Charlie looked at it in the context of a first-aid post. She guessed she'd have to wing it if any genuine emergency arose. According to the medical records Miller supplied, only Thale suffered any significant health issues. Specific instructions to control his condition were on file, along with dedicated equipment for Charlie to keep track of the disease and provide pain relief. Charlie toiled through the diagnostic and scanning equipment, marvelling at how Thale was still alive if he needed this much support. She found ordinary supplies such as bandages, which she had only ever seen once at med school, as a primitive back-up for failed wound care tech. Charlie turned the wadded cloth this way and that; she recalled how to use it, but it seemed so "quaint", as did a medicine chest equipped with various potions for an afflicted crew member to take orally, again if the tech failed. All these outmoded items she organised into a container labelled "field medicine". She just hoped no-one ever needed major surgery, because little was automated and even less linked to the ship's power supply.

Charlie's boots made "tacky" noises on the dirty floor as she moved around. She also discovered suspicious, grubby marks that looked like dried body fluids all over the work surfaces, including the examination bed. A cradle holding a simple nurse droid—little better than a hollow cylinder with arms—sat against the wall. Upon activation, it advanced to greet Charlie, requesting instructions, all the while comically puffing dust and cobwebs out its ports.

Although its dustiness raised a smile, Charlie sighed as she inspected the droid before sending it back to its cradle. It wasn't sterile, and with power off for so long, the little droid, whose primary function was to close wounds, instil painkillers and generally assist, needed a program overhaul and reset. The list of things needing attention in the tiny medical bay grew, and she supposed cleaning up would occupy some of her time. Although not now, she decided. Getting to know her crew and potential patients needed to be the priority.

She found the rest of the team in the galley. Without a word, Livesey pushed a cup of coffee across the bench towards her. Smiling her thanks, Charlie sat down. She expected solemn faces, but instead, she encountered a general air of moderate resignation, which was good, because having just left the filthy medbay, she didn't much feel like cheering up anyone.

"Who's flying the ship?" Rice asked, frowning at Suliman.

Suliman had no time for historians. He didn't care about the past; the present was bad enough without carping on about what went before, and historians were a waste of space. But then he thought that about most people.

"A trained monkey, Rice," he replied sarcastically, "didn't you see me bring it on board?"

Rice didn't get sarcasm. To him, it was masked ridicule, and he expected all insults to be directed his way, so his round face contorted as he failed to work out the nuances of Suliman's reply. "I mean, is it on autopilot or whatever it is that lets you be in here?"

Thale dismissed the exchange with a wave of his hand.

"This ship has full autopilot, Professor Rice, and Captain Suliman is under the impression he has a sense of humour."

"Not me, Commander," Suliman snorted. "I don't think any of this is funny."

"Well, as we're all here," Thale said, "we can discuss the mission parameters."

"I don't know much about missions, Commander," Charlie responded, "but what is there to discuss? The ship is on a heading, and we're following it to find a door in a rock and see what happened to Pilot Santer. That's all Governor Miller required."

"Yes, Doctor," Thale inclined his head, his weary eyelids sliding down over his eyes. Charlie supposed he meant the slow blink as implying patience with a junior officer, but instead, the expression came over as patronising. Two strikes at not liking him so far. Thale continued, "We are also to confirm the source of the message and establish who sent the Seeker ship back, or did you miss that part of the briefing?"

"Take it easy with the patronising, Thale," Suliman cut in, reading Thale's expression just as Charlie had. "What the doc means is we've got the coordinates for the source. As I understand it, Miller just wants to be sure there aren't any little green men waiting to hop across and steal Earth." He waggled a finger at Thale, "You don't look as if you'll see this mission through."

"Until then, Suliman, I'm in command," Thale retorted without acknowledging Suliman's personal observation of his appearance. "As I said, we need to discuss mission parameters such as what we do if we run into problems, how to proceed when we arrive at the coordinates and establish a code for eventualities as we travel. As we are all here, it makes sense…"

"I'm here, alright," Rice jumped in, "but I don't know why. I'm a civilian, I got back from Venus, and the next thing, I'm diverted to Rille Base, no explanation, nothing."

"You must have done something to piss off Miller," Suliman said. "Or the government."

"I wonder if we all did," Charlie added. The four men looked at her and waited for her to proceed. "I think the reason we *are* here is as important to Miller as to why there's a mission at all. I think it's personal." She made eye contact with Thale, who dropped his gaze. If Miller was behind this, almost certainly the Commander he selected would be the one with all the knowledge, but was he going to share? She doubted it. "We're on a three-year mission into the unknown; we're like Seekers," she said. "Even if the coordinates Pilot Santer set are correct, what are the chances we'll make it home?"

And with Charlie's last comment, Livesey spoke for the first time. A simple statement of fact that displayed no emotion.

"That's Miller's aim."

"What do you mean?" Rice's eyes bulged and flitted from side to side.

Livesey leaned forward and joined his hands in front of him. For someone who spoke so little, his accent and his words were both articulate and considered.

"We're chosen because we're expendable in some way, all of us. The Triumvirate didn't set up this expedition. Governor Miller organised it, working alone. Commander Thale? You're terminally ill, and that's why you agreed to this mission?"

Thale made a few grunting noises, the question unexpected, but he gave, in part, an honest answer.

"I won't deny it, I've given my life to the Triumvirate, and Governor Miller granted me this last command. If I die at some stage, that command will fall to Captain Suliman."

"Me!?" Suliman exploded. "I don't want bloody command!" He pointed to Charlie. "Doctor Maitland's Triumvirate, she can have it." He flipped a glance at Livesey, ignoring Charlie's look of horror. "How do you know all this, anyway?"

"I overheard my parents talking to Miller," Livesey admitted. "I have acute hearing, and I—well, I eavesdrop. They're part of the few who know about this mission. I didn't finish advanced education, I have never held any positions, and one of the reasons I'm here is because I'm a colossal disappointment to my high-achieving family."

Suliman asked him the other reasons, and although Livesey hesitated, he didn't answer.

"Who is your family, Mr Livesey?" Charlie enquired when no answer was forthcoming. "I don't know any prominent families by the name of Livesey."

"My mother's name is Miller. Her first husband's name was Livesey."

"As in Governor Miller?" Suliman laughed and slapped his knee.

"As in Governor Miller," Livesey replied.

Thale stood then. "As none of you seems inclined for a sensible conversation," he said, "I will retire to the cockpit, but when the time comes, I expect you to take orders."

Suliman, perched on the stool at the exit, blocked the doorway with his massive frame. He didn't move as Thale squeezed past. If there were protocols for observing when a commanding officer left their presence, such as standing or saluting, no-one bothered. Charlie recognised this would be the tone for the whole mission. Thale might be in charge, but it was no guarantee anyone would respect or even listen to his orders.

With Thale in the cockpit, the four crewmembers took the chance to talk. Rice went first.

"I can understand Miller wanting you out of the way, Suliman. You look like you might be a pain in the neck, but if us not coming back was their plan, things just got a lot clearer."

Charlie asked why.

"I suppose you may as well know,' Rice said, "I just got back from Venus. I might be fat, but I'm not stupid, and I gained access; highly illegal access…" he ignored Suliman's grin and raised eyebrow; Suliman hadn't expected espionage of the short professor, "…to some artefacts. I look harmless, so no-one suspected me, but I snuck into the Venusian underground vaults. I couldn't resist, but it was purely research and curiosity. I ended up locked in there for four days before being detected." Rice indulged himself with a grin. "I found an antechamber with reams of ancient documents, all buried in a box vault. I had to lever the lid off. I don't think the Triumvirate has ever set eyes on them. One chronicle was made of a kind of silk with the bulk of the text in a dialect not unlike Venusian; it certainly read like Venusian, what I could understand of it. Interspersed, in different writing, was patois—simple language as if someone with lesser education co-authored the text. I think it was French, which is the deadest language in existence. I didn't understand it all, but the parts of the document I could read cited, rather convincingly, the arrival of humans in our solar system." His face wrinkled in puzzlement. "If a species capable of intergalactic space travel brought humans to our solar system, why would they inscribe the history of their arrival on cloth? Why not use technology?"

"Technology degrades," Livesey said. "Some textiles last forever if properly preserved."

Rice acknowledged that point. "I know that. It may have been a ceremonial scripture. I've heard of them, but historians have never found any that old. I wish I'd left well enough alone," he added miserably.

"So what did the cloth say? Did it confirm the existence of the Indigo?" Livesey asked.

"The Indigo? No, not directly," Rice replied, "but I thought it might tie in because it spoke of a purple flame. Purple is indigo. The text speaks, in formalised language, about being driven from their homeworld. The manuscript uses terms like 'we' and 'us' without ever mentioning the species. It also tells of 'invasionary forces' and 'ferocious battles' and fleeing to the stars. There's heaps I couldn't understand, and as I said, at one point, the dialect, even the tone of the writing changed. It was French, I'm sure of it, but how that got into the document, I have no idea."

"Perhaps several people authored that text," Charlie suggested.

Rice nodded. "Most likely. I gleaned bits and pieces after that, enough to know the race settled Venus, then Earth, and that they had the technology to travel through space, which ties in with our regular belief system. They also referenced the 'humans' travelling with them, so they obviously picked some up on their travels. I found a second document, a schematic that detailed the coordinates of their ships on Venus. The texts aren't fake; I'm certain, that's why I don't think the Triumvirate has seen them; otherwise, they would have produced the manuscripts, unearthed those ships and put the matter of the Myth of Origin to rest once and for all."

"So, you're saying the Nexists were right?" Suliman said. "Earth was colonised by aliens?"

"Maybe," Rice shrugged. "Although they colonised Venus first."

"Are the Venusians deliberately keeping those texts from the Triumvirate?" Charlie asked.

Rice pulled a face. That was anyone's guess.

"Dunno, my hunch is no-one knows they're there. You should have seen the place; it's got dust dunes—undisturbed dust dunes. They set off my allergies. That's how I got found, someone heard me sneezing, but I shut the antechamber and hid it first."

Suliman gave a scornful snort. "The Indigo are a superstition, like ghosts and vampires, and the Myth of Origin is just something to talk about in history in schools. What makes you think these documents confirm their existence?"

Rice shook his head. "I didn't say they did, Suliman, but it's as good an explanation as any. At least the Indigo exist in our mythology; other aliens don't."

"He has a point, Suliman," Charlie said. "Does it matter what name we give them?"

"I don't think it does," Rice agreed. "I went to the

Venusian Peninsula after the janitor let me out, but the place was a wilderness, and I had no way of knowing how the topography might have changed since the time of the entry in the chronicle. Anyway—" his face flushed red in embarrassment, "I stupidly told the janitor what I found and where I was going, although I didn't mention the antechamber. He reported me, and I got arrested when I tried to board a transport back to Earth. They searched me for copies, but I persuaded them there was no facility to copy in the vaults. That seemed to satisfy them, then they told me to expect some comeback for entering a secure facility. But I didn't foresee this, getting sent out into space."

Charlie knew how he felt. "You must have hit a nerve with someone, Professor Rice. Perhaps you saw something the 'someone' hoped didn't exist."

"But if, for argument's sake, the Venusians kept that document secret," Suliman added, "Why would they report you to the Triumvirate?"

"Not Venusians," Rice shook his head vigorously. "They had Earth accents. The people who arrested me at the Venusian spaceport were security in civilian clothes."

Suliman frowned. "That's suspicious in itself. They might have been Nexists. If so, you would have thought they'd be happy to have their theory proved."

"Except they reject the idea of the Indigo," Rice pointed out. "They say their aliens created Earthers first; the document I found refutes that." He turned his attention to Charlie. "What sin are you guilty of that got you banished, Doctor Maitland? Was it as trivial as Suliman being an ass, Thale dying, me exposing government secrets, or Livesey being the village idiot?"

Charlie grinned at Rice's summing up of her companions and hoped she merited a kinder description.

"Please call me Charlie. Trivial? I don't know. Have any of you been baled up in a corridor by a man who makes unwelcome advances, takes close proximity as an opportunity to grope, and laughs as you squirm away while he rubs himself up against you in an elevator?"

They all murmured in agreement that no, that had never happened to them.

"I guess that man is Miller?" Suliman didn't need an answer. Miller fitted every category of creep. "Did you report him?"

"More than once," Charlie said, "but somehow, he's protected. Not only that, but I'm also more than two months over my assigned roster on Rille. I should be back on Earth by now."

"Miller's my mother's brother," Livesey told them. "He's never been any different." The others looked at each other. That would be a story worth hearing, but Livesey offered them nothing more except for grinning and asking, "I hope you gave him a few well-placed kicks to the groin?"

Charlie wished she could say yes. "It's a fine line. Knowing Miller, I believe an assessable injury would have resulted in an assault charge. I shoved and yelled, but he didn't give up. To resist presented him with a challenge. When my three months on Rille were up and I didn't receive my reassignment, I knew he would use it as leverage. Of course, it didn't work, so this is his retribution, sharing a spaceship with four men."

Suliman saw how the young doctor would see that as a punishment. "He's not going to risk you having face-to-face contact with anyone who'd believe you." Then added with a smirk, "We'll try not to get in your way."

"I'm sorry," Charlie shot back, "I didn't mean it like that, Suliman, I meant—you know what I meant."

Suliman grunted. "It's not so bad. The government owns me for the next three years, and it beats being stuck on Rille."

"Me too," Charlie commiserated. "I'm still indentured. But put like that, perhaps this is better than Rille."

Rice didn't share their view. "Well, I want to get back in one piece. I have a career that won't wait for me."

"What! History?" Suliman laughed. "History won't wait for you? Where do you think history will go?"

"I told you, Rice," Livesey said, "we won't get back in one piece. We're expendable."

"Yeah," Suliman picked up the comment, "about that. Speak up."

Livesey dropped his voice to make sure Thale wouldn't overhear, and the others leaned in closer. "The Nexists sabotaged the Seeker ships, tampered with them so they'd self-destruct." Livesey's glance flitted between his crewmates. "I don't know how far out in space, but that's why none of them ever came back."

Rice sat back in disbelief. "That makes no sense. What about the one that did?"

Livesey shrugged.

"If they rigged the ships," Suliman said, "and I don't know how you know that; are you saying they've rigged the Millstone as well?"

"All I'm saying, Suliman," Livesey said, pressing his palms on the table, "is that I'm a good eavesdropper. I don't know for sure if they rigged this ship, but my family would prefer me out of their way."

"Is this for the reason you haven't told us about?"

Livesey nodded. "In part."

"If your family wants you out of the way, why not just shoot you?"

"I think they considered it, Suliman, but you know the Triumvirate's policy on early death. This way, if this mission ever becomes common knowledge, they can say I volunteered, which I did, and died in the course of my duty. Such a sacrifice gives me value, and they can pretend to be proud parents."

"You volunteered?" Rice's bulgy eyes protruded even more.

Suliman shushed him. "Worry about that later. Livesey, how might the ship be rigged?"

Livesey shook his head and lowered his voice to a whisper, "I have no idea, but I bet Thale knows."

Suliman was out of his seat in a flash, but Charlie grabbed him before he got through the exit. "Don't, Suliman, we're just speculating," she cautioned. "What if it's a detonation device controlled from Rille or Earth or even somewhere on the ship only Thale knows? Confronting him would hardly buy us time now, would it? You know this ship better than anyone; we need to conduct our own investigation."

Suliman sat down with a huff. "Any chance you're wrong on this, Livesey?"

Livesey lifted a shoulder, "I don't think so, but I don't think it's imminent either. The mission is real."

"I must say, you seem pretty relaxed about it," Rice said. "How can your mum and dad do this to their kid? Are they part of a fundamental sect or something?"

Livesey gave Rice a sideways glance. "Nexists. Same as Miller, and probably Thale. I never subscribed to the ideology. They believe I don't have much of a future, anyway."

"I hate to add to all this intrigue," Charlie said, feeling like she was about to drop a bombshell, "but I think you should know that Amira Santer's Seeker ship returned a full year before it got towed to Rille."

"What are you talking about?" Suliman's response was far too loud. The other three made "shushing" faces at him lest they drew Thale's attention. He leaned in closer. "I know they tractored it in from beyond the perimeter a couple of weeks ago."

"Not true." Charlie studied the three expectant faces; they still needed convincing. "Sam Mead found plant material on the ship during dismantling. He reckoned it was food left by a worker. There was only a small amount, but the rate of decay put it at around a year old. He also found some soil in an outer hull seam. Martian soil."

"Martian?" Suliman agreed that was damning evidence.

"Sam is also working on a new device that strips all data right down to the original entry," Charlie told them. "He found a data eclipse on the signatory entry."

"Whose signature?"

"Commander Wells, but she only tampered with the dates. Sam decided to test his new device. It worked; no-one else would have found it."

"Where did Sam find the plant stuff?" Livesey asked.

"In the flight compartment, in the corner. The entire ship was filthy. Sam extracted the plant material before anybody saw him. He's going to do some investigating. It's all very suspect."

Suliman drummed his fingers on the bench. "I bet Thale knows more than he's letting on. Rice, if the Nexists are caught up in all this somehow, do you think Miller or even Thale knows you discovered that document?"

Rice's head bobbed about, uncertain how to answer. "Miller might if the security guards told him, but they'd have to go to the antechamber and find the vault; it's only small, and I dumped loads of stuff on top of it."

"Can you remember anything else about the document?" Charlie asked.

Rice's round face lit up in an impish grin, and he whispered, "Better than that, Charlie, I took a copy."

"But you said…"

"I told security I couldn't copy it, but I did. I had to hide the lens where they wouldn't look. It was uncomfortable, but they didn't suspect, and I have the images."

Suliman felt himself warming to this guy. Copy lenses were an outdated commodity. Trust a history professor to have one and not mind where he shoved it to keep secrets hidden in the interests of posterity.

"We'll need to see it, the image, I mean," Charlie told him. "What you discovered must link directly to this mission. Otherwise, why stop you from revealing your find to the museum?"

"I'd like to know why they didn't just quietly shoot you?" Suliman grinned.

Rice didn't know either. "Beats me."

Thale commed through to the galley. "Suliman, out here, if you can tear yourself away."

"Do you think he heard us?" Rice whispered.

Suliman navigated himself backwards through the exit. "It won't be easy keeping things from him," he said. "Livesey's right. I don't trust him either. Doc, what's his illness?"

"I'm not supposed to tell you, Suliman, and for now, he is my patient. I will say he's beyond a cure, and you're right; no way will he survive three years out here."

Suliman gave Charlie a thoughtful look and left, leaving his three crewmates to mull over the puzzle they'd only just begun to unravel.

CHAPTER SEVEN _

In the weeks after leaving Rille, Rice assigned himself the position as Charlie's aide. He helped her clean the medbay, catalogue supplies in the field kit, and worked on making the cockpit safer, even though Suliman did all the heavy lifting and repositioning of the seats. Meanwhile, Livesey spent his time roaming the corridors, and when he finished, he wandered again, maintaining this ritual for all hours of the day and night, pausing now and then to gaze out the viewports or check out a bulkhead or console. The task completed, he would start the rounds again, only stopping to eat or sleep. Since that first conversation, where he intimated that they were all doomed, he'd said little and offered only monosyllabic replies to any questions about how he was doing.

Charlie watched his dedicated meandering and feared for his mental state. Rejection by your family would be a good reason for depression; wanting you dead would be unbearable. Insisting he submit himself to an examination might be counterproductive; besides, he was eating and drinking, and she supposed he might not be a talkative person, anyway. The initial stresses of sorting out the ship and their place within it had eased, so there might be more time now to get to know him, that is if she could draw him out.

Thale, however, maintained his coolness, only speaking when necessary, and not revisiting his mission parameters discussion. He attended the medbay for all medications and infusions, mainly to control pain. Still, even at this early stage of treating him, Charlie doubted he would last eighteen months, let alone three years. Thale maintained a professional attitude towards her, but Charlie found the man distasteful, almost as if some of Miller's obnoxious personality had rubbed off on him. Thankfully, he didn't have Miller's propensity for sexual harassment.

As she did with all the crew, Charlie checked out Thale's personal file. From his image, he looked little different now from when he was disease-free. Thale offered nothing of his previous life, even during his lengthy scans, but Charlie knew something underhanded was going on with him. He never fully undressed and never permitted a physical exam. Spending time with the dying had formed part of Charlie's training, and she knew people approaching the end of their lives often liked to yield their private thoughts, to go to their graves with no secrets. Not Commander Thale. Whatever mystery he was keeping to himself, Charlie knew he wouldn't part with it willingly.

The Millstone had only two communication

terminals, neither linked to private channels, so no-one had any word from home. Rice mentioned his parents a few times, Livesey just walked around, and Suliman kept to himself, although he would stop to pass a few minutes if he found Charlie alone in the galley. Charlie hadn't decided yet if she liked the tough former trader, although something about him made her feel he would have her back if the chips were down. There was no liquor on board, no diversions, and as the ship had an automatic pilot function, Suliman only needed to pilot part of the time. Suliman's mental state worried Charlie as much as Livesey's. Still, with both men remaining unreadable, there was little she could do besides create encryptions on the field drug chest, just in case either of them felt a need to dip into it.

For herself, Charlie felt lonely for Sam, and the same as Rice missed his parents, she missed hers. As her only patient and the source of all their suspicions, Charlie entertained the idea of despatching Thale to the great hereafter with an extra infusion of painkillers. Only she wasn't a murderer. Well, not yet, she mused, but three years with a ratbag, a bored historian and a couple of oddballs might change that.

Eventually, the ripe smell in the bunkhouse got to Charlie. It stank of disuse at the outset, but now it had taken on the bouquet of the unwashed. Charlie could scarcely breathe in there, so she took to bedding down in her flight seat or on the now sanitised rock-hard medical bay bed, which resulted in stiffness and fatigue. They left Charlie with no choice. She addressed the crew, knowing full well she'd face resistance.

The conversation ran as expected. Rice couldn't see the point in taking a full shower if the others didn't, but faced with Charlie's fierceness, he was the first to volunteer to cram himself into the shower stall. Too broad for the purpose-built cubby, initially devised to conserve space and with the assumption of a leaner, fitter occupant, Rice allowed Charlie, as a physician, to scrub his back and feet. Wedged into the cubicle, he couldn't flex or twist unless his bare backside protruded out into the passageway, and that was a sight he didn't want to share with his associates, nor one they wanted to see.

Livesey went next without a word. He was the only one besides Charlie who so far had used the shower. Suliman presented a new problem. When she told him it was his turn, he looked at her, a flicker of defiance in his voice. Charlie couldn't tell if he was serious or just plain irritating.

"Doc, you're not my mother."

Charlie looked him in the eye. "Lucky for you, or you'd have learned better hygiene. I am your physician, and I don't have sufficient stores to treat fungal infections or skin disorders. The stink in the bunkroom isn't me; it's *you* lot."

Charlie caught Thale grinning a rare grin at the young doctor's chastisement of the navigator. His delight would be short-lived. "You're next," Charlie declared, addressing him without using his rank. "You needn't be so smug."

Thale shook his head. He also wasn't keen on using the shower, it meant disrobing, and that was something he didn't do. Besides, water, even recycled water, had better uses. He angled a defiant glance at her. "I use sanitiser, and I give the orders, not you."

"I couldn't care less about the chain of command, *Commander.*" Charlie planted herself squarely in front of him, fists on hips. "This is to fend off infection. You are on prescription, so you follow Suliman to the shower."

"I could order Suliman to disable the water recycler."

"Do that, Commander, and I'll disable Suliman."

Suliman snorted a laugh. "How're you gonna manage that?"

"Easy. Now, shower." Suliman didn't know it, but Charlie found, to her alarm, a palm-sized neurolysis spray in the medbay. She'd wondered what use such a thing, modified to deliver a dose exceeding the recommended concentration, might have on a freighter. She had her suspicions, knowing Suliman didn't play by the rules, but now she realised it might have its uses if she kept it on minimum yield. She had already decided to carry the spray in her boot for the rest of the voyage. Suliman eventually went to the shower with a bit more encouragement, but Charlie realised he was using the exchange for sport and to relieve boredom. She waited outside the shower cubicle as he finished.

"Checking on me?" he grinned as he wrapped a towel

around his lower half. To her surprise, he'd shaved off his tangled beard and washed his far too long hair.

"Cleanliness on board is requisite, Suliman. None of us can afford infections."

"We can't do it every day," Suliman warned. "The condenser and recycler won't handle it."

Charlie already checked that out. "I realise. I worked out we can each shower twice in any seven days. If you use a sanitising cloth the other days, it'll be fine."

Suliman grinned. "Can I watch while you get Thale?"

"No." Charlie shoved him towards the bunkroom. "Put on clean clothes. Rice took on the laundry role, so he's going to sanitise them."

Suliman smiled then, an uncharacteristically warm smile that momentarily caught her off guard.

"Are you going to be a mother hen, Doc?"

Charlie narrowed her eyes. "Don't be sexist, Suliman. Like you, I'm bored, and this amuses me."

It only amused her for so long. The water recycler didn't get sabotaged. The four men got used to keeping themselves clean, and the only time Charlie flexed her medical muscles was when Thale attended for daily therapy. The only other casualty was Rice, who pulled a muscle in his back.

"Dropping some of this weight and keeping up the exercise will make a difference Rice," she told him. "You're down only five kilos, and we've been out four months."

Rice picked up the flabby skin around his middle, misreading her point. "I know. I've never been so thin in my life. I used to say I was six feet, and my height had settled around my waist." He looked up, expecting her to laugh, but Livesey distracted them as he drifted by on one of his wanderings. Charlie didn't find Rice's lack of fitness funny, anyway.

"What's he doing, do you suppose?" Charlie said.

"I don't know." Rice peered after him. "He acts like he's looking for something."

Suliman turned up, ignoring Rice, who stood next to Charlie wearing only his jocks.

"Suliman, can't you knock? We're not much for patient confidentiality on this ship, are we?" But Charlie's irony was lost on Suliman.

He came back at her with a "so what, the door was open" face, "We're too far away for Miller to detonate this ship remotely," he said. "If Miller got us rigged, then it's hard-wired and timed. I've searched, but I can't find anything suspicious."

Livesey appeared in the doorway. "Whatever it is, you are right, Suliman. It is hard-wired."

Suliman turned. "How do you know?"

Livesey didn't explain, just added, "And there is a detonator."

"Didn't you hear, Livesey? We'll be too far away."

"Not if one of us is the detonator."

Only one name came to Charlie. "Thale. It can only be Thale."

Livesey made no acknowledgement. He just walked away.

"Scan Thale," Suliman said to Charlie.

Charlie raised her hands. What would she scan for? "His scans are pre-calibrated to his disease criteria," she said, "and directed at his brain and upper spine. I can't change them."

"Can't you add in an extra parameter? Look for anything unusual, anything at all. Just don't let him get suspicious."

Rice pulled on his slacks. "Thale's dying anyway. He's got nothing to lose if he blows himself up."

"He's not out here just to blow up himself or this ship," Charlie said. "Miller means us to at least get as far as the other Earth. There's something there he needs Thale to see or do." She nodded at Suliman. "There are a few things I can try."

Suliman gave her a thumbs up and encouraged Rice out into the corridor. Moments later, Suliman stuck his head around the door.

"Check Thale's cardiothoracic area, Doc," he instructed. "I have a hunch."

CHAPTER EIGHT _

Left alone, Charlie thought about Sam and her mum and dad and what they might think if they knew the truth, that she was on a ship that might blow up at any second. The idea she might never see them again was almost too much to bear. If she and the others didn't get sucked into some space anomaly or swallowed up by a Nexist-imagined, flesh-eating alien, it seemed an explosion would finish them off. To take her mind off her loneliness, she busied herself with making a couple of covert modifications to the scanner, ready for Thale's next visit. The changes were minor, but enough to broaden the sweep and keep them within the expected time frame. Thale often dozed because of the medication, so he was unlikely to notice the extra minute the scan would add.

That night was Rice's turn to cook, and he was terrible. Charlie couldn't face company, so she excused herself from dinner and headed to her secret spot in the cargo bay behind the Mag engines. She'd found the cubby only a few days after coming on board when the frantic search to find an alternative to sleeping with up to four smelly, farting, and snoring men became a priority. Charlie was grateful to whoever upgraded the engines having no option but to place them within the cargo bay's irregular contours, leaving a little nook remaining untouched. At first, she hoped it might pass as her private quarters. The engines performed silently, and the alcove was tranquil and hidden. Up to now, the others hadn't disturbed her there. The two-tiered cupboard she fancied might serve as a separate bunkhouse was a smidgen too short even for her, so instead, she turned it into a retreat for reading and sitting alone.

Suliman found her there later in the evening. He knelt beside her uninvited, and ignored her grumbling unwelcome at being discovered.

Charlie knew Suliman's story. A powerfully built man, despite his liver issues, swarthy looking, with deep-set dark eyes and a heavy brow, he displayed little tolerance for people or politics. A known drunk, Suliman spent most of his life as a cargo man. He hailed from the Southwest Central corridor, a place for Earth's dispossessed and those who dodged the Triumvirate's strict social, although beneficial controls which might at least have seen them fed and housed. Suliman was typical of those who bucked the system. His type packed the prisons on Mars and after release, haunted the shanty towns until they were either returned to prison or were fortunate enough, like Suliman, to own a ship that would allow them to escape the dusty planet.

Suliman's crimes numbered in the hundreds, the latest a protest at the impounding of the Millstone. In retaliation, he stole a Triumvirate ship, assaulted the pilot in a drunken frenzy and flew to Outpost 4 near Saturn, smashing the vessel into a docking bay. The event created sufficient damage to have the outpost towed to Mars for a rebuild, and Suliman was lucky to have survived. Several years of custody on Mars followed, but Suliman always found trouble, and liquor, which was readily available if you knew who to ask, and individuals like Suliman knew everybody. As a last resort, the authorities sent him to Rille. Charlie treated him a few times there, but that was as far as their contact went. He never spoke to the staff, just devoted his days to holonovels and dozing while his liver recovered.

"Hiding?" he grinned.

"Just a spot I found to be *on my own*," Charlie hissed, making sure Suliman understood what she meant by "on my own". He ignored the icy welcome.

"Mind if I join you?"

"Yes," came Charlie's tart reply, "particularly if you plan on making it a habit or telling the others."

Suliman squeezed himself between engine parts and the bulkhead. "No and no. Listen, if Miller or whoever orchestrated this whole thing only wanted us dead, it would have happened by now, right?"

"We know that's not his aim." Charlie had to shift, Suliman's knee dug hard into her thigh, and he took up most of the available room, but as he plainly needed to get something off his chest, something that might enlighten them, it was perhaps necessary to put up with him.

"I checked again. The ships not rigged," Suliman said. "I ran a diagnostic and came to check the engines—that's how I knew you'd made a house down here; I saw your stuff strewn around. Apart from the auxiliary system for the Mag engine, the ship is as it's always been. I can't find anything in the hull compartments, between the outer hull and the bulkhead, the portal drives, nothing."

Suliman knew this ship. Charlie guessed if there were something to find, he'd find it. The problem would be to accomplish that task without Thale knowing.

"Did Thale see you?"

"Nope, I did it after his meds."

"Good thinking."

"What about you, Doc? Did you find anything?"

Charlie shook her head. "His scan is tomorrow, but I have made some modifications to the scanner."

"Right," Suliman said. "Miller wants us to find Pilot Santer. I don't know what Miller's rationale is, but it may be a message to whoever she discovered or whoever reprogrammed the Seeker ship to let them know the ship made it back. The more I think about it, the more I suspect it's the return journey we're not supposed to make. We're just delivering this message. After that, Thale can blow us up, and we can go to hell."

"I see where you're leading with all this, Suliman. Thale will last eighteen months, certainly not more than two years. Chances are we will have reached the coordinates by then."

Suliman warned her to say nothing to the others for now, adding, "Rice might be a blabbermouth, and Livesey is too mysterious for my liking. I get the idea he hasn't told us everything."

"I wouldn't call you an expert judge of character, Suliman," Charlie pointed out. "Livesey might just be a private person, unless he's the detonator and not Thale."

Suliman wriggled around to stand up. "Then why…" He stopped when he saw tears in Charlie's eyes.

"Doc? Are you scared?"

He'd caught her in a weak moment. Too much dwelling on Sam and her parents did that.

"Yes, I miss my mum and dad."

"And Sam Mead?"

Charlie nodded miserably. "I only signed up to the Triumvirate for a career opportunity in medicine, not for the military. It's not as if we have wars or anything nowadays. I just wanted to do my medical training. Mum and Dad could never afford to put me through medical school," Charlie sniffed. "I don't want to die." The tears slid down her face, hot and unstoppable. How ridiculous to be crying in front of him, but she couldn't help it, not now she'd started. Tears were like that. Exposing.

Suliman watched her. He expected her to be tougher, but she'd lived a more privileged life than he, so he knew his expectations were unfair. Where he came from, women were hard as nails and didn't nurture their children. He knew the doc considered him rough and uncouth, and he supposed she was right, but he greatly respected the skinny little physician.

"Northwest continent aren't you," he asked, making sure he injected some softness into his tone, even though it sounded false and foreign on his tongue.

Charlie nodded, too busy feeling idiotic to notice his attempt at kindness, but it was done; he'd seen her at her most vulnerable.

Suliman squashed himself back between the engine housing and the bulkhead and placed an arm over her shoulder. What was it about her that made him act soft?

"I don't get scared anymore, Doc," he said, looking down at her with a grin. "D'you wanna know why? Because I don't care."

Charlie sniffed. "Don't care if you live or die?"

He forced out one of the snorting laughs that centred around his enormous beak-like nose.

"I've learned not to care *who* lives or dies. Where I come from, no-one looks out for you. It's every man, woman—child for that matter, for themselves. If we go under the Triumvirate Relief Program, we might as well sell our souls, so there's no-one to trust, no-one to care. I only underwent detox because I was a detainee, and I had no choice. My death doesn't bother me, and to be honest, I don't think dying bothers Livesey. No point in it bothering Thale, it's coming for him anyhow, but you and Rice, well, neither of you seem prepared."

"We're not prepared, Suliman!" Charlie cried, then mumbled, "I think you might be wrong about Livesey."

"Maybe, but I've got nothing better to do at the moment than see this mission through." Suliman grabbed a cloth from a sack on the floor and handed it to her. "Dry your eyes and stop being a baby."

"I know." Charlie attempted a smile. "A moment of weakness. Thanks."

"Can you fire an abettor?" Suliman asked as he stood.

"No," Charlie wiped her eyes. "I never did combat."

Suliman pulled a hand-sized weapon from his boot. It had seen better days.

"Where did you get that?" Charlie took the weapon from him. The firearm was old, worn, and even had a smear of epoxy resin holding part of the housing together. A forerunner of the modern military weapons, it appeared functional, although the Triumvirate defunked this version because the frequency interfered with communications and medical equipment. Charlie knew of some in a museum.

"It's been here for years," Suliman grinned, "holed up in the galley bulkhead. I can't believe they didn't detect it."

"Thale won't let you have it."

Suliman gave her a "really?" look. "What's he going to do? Take it off me?"

Charlie looked at the large framed Suliman and reflected on the lean and considerably weakened Thale. She saw his point.

"What do you plan to do with it?"

"If we can be sure Thale controls the explosive, I bet the rest of his plan is like I said. We can't kill him, so we're stuck with him. I've got three of these—" he took the weapon back, "and to pass the time, I thought I could teach you to shoot, just in case. Maybe not teach Livesey and Rice, I'm not sure about them yet, but you're fine."

"Won't we damage something?"

"Not with the abettor on simulate. That means it won't interfere with the Millstone's frequencies. They're about the same vintage. If we get into a fight with aliens, we can unmute them."

Charlie thought for a moment. "As you say, nothing else to do."

Suliman reached out a hand. "C'mon."

CHAPTER NINE _

The following day, Charlie ran a thorough scan on Thale, extending, without his knowledge, to a few different organs to spot any additional "hardware" he might be packing in his chest cavity. After his treatment, she ran through the results, only saving relevant parts of the data to his medical file. Suliman looked in on her later that day.

"Did you find anything?"

"Yes, but I don't know what it is. From what I can tell, it's some kind of biotechnology, an organic patch with a neurovascular signature. It's acting like a partial stent on the superior vena cava. Part of the artery looks to be missing, so this thing is a kind of prosthetic artery wall, but Thale has no cardiac history. I'm sorry, but I couldn't get a decent visualisation."

"Show me what you got."

"I can't. Rice will be back any second."

"Okay. Thale's back on duty in four hours, so when he gets to the cockpit, put the image in my bunk. I'll look at it later."

Charlie nodded; she didn't know what all this would achieve. Thale could be the key to the booby trap, but confronting him might be dangerous.

It was Charlie's turn to heat the flat-pack food that evening. Her efforts were only a tad better than Rice's and much worse than Livesey's, whose culinary skill with a pouch of liquid and withered vegetables gave them all some reprieve from the desire to gag their way through their meals. He sometimes served a peculiar biscuit, a bland concoction that mopped up slops and made the meal seem almost standard fare.

Charlie's "I'm swamped" face did the trick, and Livesey took her turn for her. She was keen to get to her cubby and see what Suliman thought of the implant she found but didn't want to raise suspicion. Unused to deception, she didn't want to make her first attempt too glaring.

Luckily, Rice engaged Thale in a spirited historical debate, skirting any reference to the Venusian documents, so when Charlie escaped to her cubby, the others didn't notice. Sitting on the floor, she pulled up her knees, wedged a pillow under her bottom and waited. She didn't have to wait long. Suliman flopped down untidily beside her. Despite him showering now regularly, he still looked derelict, but he'd kept the dirty beard off.

He held up the image she left in his bunk. "You're

spot on. Near his heart."

"Yes, I'm sorry the resolution is so poor," she said, "Thale has had hundreds of these pain targeting scans. He'd know if I took longer or messed around too much."

"It's fine. I put it through the sensor, then loaded it here and deleted it from the record. It's cleaned up the image." Suliman took her reader, clicked in a new code, and the enhanced image appeared. Charlie had never seen anything like the tiny, worm-shaped patch fitting snugly against Thale's superior vena cava.

"During the civil war, when the Nexists tried to gain power," Suliman told her, "they sent operatives into Triumvirate-controlled areas, each fitted with a gadget like this. It's highly secret…" he peered down as Charlie made a slight, "huh?" sound. He shrugged. "What? I know stuff, Doc. All sorts of illegal stuff. Anyway, stop interrupting. The operatives sent back intelligence, and if they got discovered, they blew themselves up rather than allow anyone to interrogate them. The point is, they needed a hand-held trip, and Thale doesn't seem to have one. When the operative's hearts stopped beating, their bodies exploded, wreaking havoc and maximum damage to their surroundings. The devices can't be removed without them detonating. If the host died by any other means, the bomb went off. Boom!" Suliman threw his arms wide, not a good idea in such a small space, and Charlie had to duck.

She pointed to the worm. "That's a bomb?" Unbelievable, she thought, Thale must feel strongly about the mission to volunteer as a human sacrifice. But then, he had little to lose, although the rest of them did. "We don't know when he's meant to detonate," she said. "It may be when we meet Pilot Santer or when we find the door on the moon or at a moment only known to him. I bet Miller means us to get caught in the explosion."

"Well, unless you keep his heart beating until we find this door, we won't find out. The Millstone wouldn't withstand an internal explosion." Suliman frowned. "I'd like to know where he's sporting that trip device."

"Could we shove him out the airlock at the side of the cargo bay?" Although Charlie wondered how they could manoeuvre the frail commander into that position without him suspecting.

"You mean murder him, Doc?" Suliman chuckled. "Do you often have homicidal thoughts?"

Charlie couldn't think of a good answer. What was happening to her?

"He's dying anyway, Suliman," was all she could come up with to justify her words. "We can't stop that."

Still, Suliman seemed to give her not-entirely-not serious suggestion some thought before discarding it. "That device may be automated, so we need to keep him alive or make sure he dies well away from us and the ship." He hesitated. "Makes me wish we had a stasis chamber. You could knock him out and freeze him."

"He's the only one who knows what this mission is about," Charlie reminded him. "And what would be the point? To turn around and head home? To what? Besides, in his condition, he would never survive stasis."

"You're right. We've got no choice."

"It's at least another year before we reach the coordinates," Charlie said. "Thale should last that long. While he's still alive, we can consider ways to disarm him. Either way, Miller had that device implanted for a reason, so I don't believe Thale will blow anyone up until he finds his target, whoever or whatever that may be. Thale has the trump card for now, and we're at his mercy."

"Just don't let him die." Suliman cautioned. "I reckon Livesey guessed Thale had the implant…What the hell!?"

An alert sounded, and the ship began to pitch and vibrate. Suliman jumped to his feet and headed for the cockpit. Charlie gave him a few seconds before following. She didn't want the others to know they were speaking alone for fear of raising suspicion.

Suliman and Thale were surveying a sensor chart when she arrived. Rice had responded to the alarm, peering anxiously through the viewport. Charlie caught the end of Suliman's observations.

"…I don't know what to make of it."

Thale pointed to a sector on a stellar map. "Could it be a gravitational wave coming from one of the planets in that system?"

"Why didn't the ship pick it up?" Rice wailed. "We'll get sucked in!"

"This is a cargo ship, Rice," Suliman huffed, "not much more sophisticated than a pushbike. Besides, gravitational waves are only a theory; no-one ever ventured far enough out in space to test it."

Rice struggled for control and took a few deep breaths. He hoped his next question made him sound less like an idiot. "Can we break free?"

The Millstone resisted all Suliman's efforts at stabilisation. "The wave is acting like a rip," he said. "At a guess, it might be better to power down engines and let it take us. The Millstone's no match for that force. We'd best hope it burns itself out."

"What if it doesn't?" Charlie asked as a hard vibration shook the ship. "And if our trajectory is correct, Amira Santer must have passed this planet. How come she didn't get sucked in?"

Suliman indicated to Charlie and Rice to buckle themselves into their seats. "I don't know. Maybe it's intermittent. I've never run into one before. The wave appears in one sector above the atmosphere of that planet dead ahead, according to sensors, a desert region, so if we were to hit that planet, we might end up buried under tons of sand."

"Reverse thrusters," Thale ordered. "Power down, then reignite mag in the waves swell. It looks less intense there. We might be able to sheer off."

Rice and Charlie looked to Suliman for a response, although Charlie doubted Thale knew more about handling the Millstone than Suliman. Suliman didn't leap to obey the command. Instead, he spent the hiatus between Thale's words and answering, scrutinising the wave's behaviour, then, satisfied Thale's suggestion had little merit, flicked out a holoview of the wave for them all to get a closer look from their seats.

Charlie only saw grey, misty strands that curled and flicked through space. It didn't look malevolent or dangerous, but as the Millstone pitched violently, she realised looks can be deceiving. Her anxiety grew as the planet loomed larger.

"We would need the wave to vary in intensity to sheer off," Suliman said, "but it seems to have a consistent flow. The sensors recorded an electromagnetic field just before it hit, but the system froze while analysing accelerating particles, so all we've got on view is the wave and the planet. I can tell you now reverse thrusters would have no effect, and allowing the ship to battle the wave will cause damage."

"So will crashing into a planet," Thale responded, an observation made by them all but voiced only by the one with nothing to lose.

"Is it possible there are other objects, asteroids, that we can't see in the wave that might hit us?" Charlie asked nervously.

Suliman nodded. "It's an unknown." He pointed to the small green and gold world now filling the viewport. "We're going there whether we like it or not, and at this vector, most likely buried in sand. Let's hope the Millstone can pull something out of a hat."

Thale highlighted an area between the origin of the wave and the planet's surface. "Could it be manmade? It doesn't appear to connect to the planet."

"That would mean a trap," Rice wailed, shaking visibly

and gulping against tears.

Charlie understood his fear. This wasn't looking good, but Suliman turned to his three companions.

"Well, aren't you the cheerful ones? Look at the sensors." Suliman changed the details of the wave for them to examine at close range. "A civilisation would need to be highly advanced and possibly desperate to employ so much atmosphere in snaring unsuspecting passing traffic. And for what purpose?"

Only Charlie answered. If this civilisation was advanced, she suggested, then it would most likely have space travel. They all agreed that made sense, but when Suliman changed the holoview to a view of the planet, it looked peaceful and clear of satellites or any form of spacegoing vessels.

That didn't reassure Charlie. "I suppose that's a 'no'. Before the sensors froze, were there signs of habitation, population? If we get through the wave, we might not be welcome, and if we crash, we might not get help."

"That depends on whether or not the wave remains consistent," Suliman said, making a futile attempt to unfreeze the sensors. "We may be able to ride it out, or we could end up crushed by an atmospheric force as we drop. The sensors are too scrambled to give us anything more than we have, so there's nothing useful. I'm more concerned with the gap between the terminal end of the wave and the planet. The Millstone's not a glider. She'll drop like a stone, and I won't have much time to power up the engines."

"Keep it in low power then," Rice stammered, "and your finger on the button."

In answer, Suliman cut power completely, but the ship continued a forward and sideways motion, although the buffeting ceased as soon as the engines stopped.

"See, Rice?" he pointed out the viewport. "Less pitching. I can't keep the power on. We have to let it take us, but don't worry; I promise I'll press 'go' as soon as we drop out of the wave."

Charlie patted Rice's hand, ignoring her own panic in the face of Rice's. "You can trust Suliman. We might not even end up on the planet."

"But what if we do?" Rice squeaked. "What if cannibals live there?"

From over his shoulder, Suliman shot him a look of impatience. "They can have you as the main course and the rest of us as hors d'oeuvres."

"Suliman!" Charlie scolded, "Stop. Rice, hang in there. We'll be fine." She craned her neck around to look at Livesey's seat, expecting him to be sitting there quietly, as always. In all the kerfuffle, she hadn't noticed he wasn't with them, a distinct disadvantage of being a crewmember easily overlooked. "Where's Livesey?" she asked, but before anyone could reply, the ship flipped and careered at speed towards the planet. Charlie held on to her shoulder straps for dear life, shutting her eyes tight, tensing her entire body and willing the ordeal to end. Wherever Livesey was, she had to hope he'd secured himself. She couldn't discount the possibility they might crash into that planet, but if there were cannibals, they might be taking a few tribes with them in the impact.

The planet loomed massive and multicoloured in the viewport with no signs of the wave terminating. Suliman remained calm; his attachment to life was not so strong that he needed to panic. He studied the wave for the opportunity to sheer away, as Thale kept insisting, even for a chance to reignite the engines, but his one attempt resulted in dragging a terrifying groan from the Millstone's hull. Charlie heard and felt it, but her eyes remained tightly shut. She didn't want to witness her own demise. She always believed she'd die peacefully in her sleep, certainly in a bed. Having her bits scattered across a strange planet didn't feature in her plans. Rice keened a high-pitched wail, a single note that seemed to go on forever until the contents of his stomach discharged all over the back of Thale's seat.

The wave came to a sudden halt, its drag dropping them many kilometres above the planet's surface. The Millstone hurtled downwards. Rice stopped keening, and Charlie opened her eyes. As Suliman predicted, the ship dropped like a stone, and he was onto the engines in a second, but the traumatised old vessel didn't know which way was up, so it clicked itself into a self-diagnostic mode to figure out its horizons before responding to the helm. Suliman expertly overrode the Millstone's auto functions, but even then, it didn't like flying blind and resisted Suliman's attempts to spark the engines. After what seemed an age, the battle between pilot and ship ended as the engines spluttered into life.

Too late.

The impact as the Millstone hit the surface sent their brains rattling and their bones bouncing inside their skin. Rice shrieked as he bit down hard on his bottom lip. Charlie's nose streamed blood as her head slammed back against the seat, and she felt unbearable pain in her ears. Her ribs squeezed against her lungs as the harness tightened in response to the impact. Suliman's last-minute control of the Millstone saved them from a head-on collision with the planet. Instead, he pulled up the front just enough for the ship to surf along the surface, building a mountain of sand as it propelled its ugly nose through the desert.

Charlie was out of her seat as soon as the Millstone ground to a halt. She felt herself all over, satisfied she suffered only bruising and shock, but her job was to consider the others. Rice was a quivering mess, made worse when he saw the blood on Charlie's face. Thale indicated to Charlie he was uninjured and that she should attend to Rice. Suliman, behaving as if he had just executed a perfect landing, calmly implemented a systemwide test as sensors came back online.

Charlie focused on helping Rice get cleaned up. His lip injury was minor, and once he trusted they were on the ground, coupled with ministrations from his favourite physician, he garnered enough courage to unharness himself.

Charlie wiped her face with a sanitising towel. Her

nose had stopped bleeding, and the pain in her ears began to subside, leaving her with only residual deafness and ringing, that thankfully, rapidly cleared. Confident she was okay, her thoughts turned to Livesey.

The pitch of the impact angled the Millstone so that sand covered much of the forward hull. Otherwise, the ship was uncompromised. Systems checks revealed the flight controls needed realignment. Suliman agreed it was safe for Charlie to go looking for Livesey. There was no sign of him in the galley nor the latrine, and Charlie breathed a sigh of relief; there were no restraints there, and he would not have survived that impact. The only other place was the bunkroom, but the impact buckled the joists above the bunkroom hatch, so Charlie couldn't get in to see if he was okay. She retrieved a heat sensor from the medbay to check he was alive and still breathing, but he didn't answer comms, so Charlie had to assume he was unconscious. Suliman went with her to assess the damage but refused to grind the door, telling her there was a danger the bulkhead might collapse and crush Livesey. Once the ship was level, he assured her the compacted joist would reseat itself. The fact he knew that suggested to Charlie this was not the first time the Millstone had crashed.

Thale looked up as they returned. "The planet has a similar atmosphere to Earth," he said. "Useful if we have to stay here for any length of time."

Rice located a narrow, uncompromised view from one of the side viewports and began a commentary on the terrain, pointing out how flat it seemed for a desert and even had trees. Charlie looked over his shoulder at the forlorn twigs poking from the ground, hardly worthy of the title.

"And we're up to our armpits in sand, just in case you hadn't noticed," she snapped. "I couldn't care less about the native flora," she added, her concern about Livesey becoming her main focus. "Suliman, we need to get this ship moving."

Rice ignored her and pointed to a distant group of structures. His voice raised a notch as he turned his saucer-wide, fear-filled eyes to his comrades. "There are buildings. That means it's inhabited. That means there are aliens."

Thale checked the sensors. "It does look like a city. We need to get the reverse engines started before we draw attention to ourselves."

"Too late," Suliman announced as eight figures appeared on a proximity alert, two each astride four open craft, one towing a gurney. "Let's hope they're friendly."

"Can't we just lock them out?" Charlie asked as the familiar sound of the gangway opening bounced through the ship. Her heart sank.

"Follow their instructions," Thale ordered. "No ifs and buts this time, Suliman. Do nothing to antagonise. There's nowhere for us to run, so with luck, they'll let us go with a caution for entering their space."

"Are they human?" Rice whispered.

Charlie held his hand. It felt cold and clammy with fear, and she felt guilty for snapping at him earlier. "It wasn't our fault, Rice. We'll explain that to them." She pasted on a smile for his benefit and hoped she sounded more confident than she felt. The people surrounding the ship were aliens. Aliens on an alien planet. She and the others were aliens too, alien to this world. Different thoughts jammed her brain, and she wondered if Suliman still had his abettor in his boot. It might turn out the wave was the least of their problems because she didn't know how aliens treated other aliens. Rice stared at her, pleading with her to tell him everything would be

okay. She couldn't. Too many variables rattled around her head, and she could only add a lame,

"They must know that wave is out there."

Had the entry gangway been at the front of the ship, and therefore under the sand, there would have been no way the visitors could have boarded without sawing the ship in half. They confronted the crew in the cockpit. Suliman's instincts prepared him for a fight, but until now, he didn't know what the opposition looked like nor what manner of weapons they carried. A single ancient abettor against eight aliens might be a pointless exercise. Plus, if they fired a weapon at Thale, it would blow them all up, unsuspecting aliens included.

Their visitors turned out to be uniformed, weapon-toting, human males. Despite their firearms and air of authority, these men were neither harsh nor threatening. They seemed interested, even pleased to see Charlie, and spoke in a dialect that converted Rice's terror to curiosity.

"They're speaking fast," he whispered to Charlie, "and it's a primitive Earth language, Cornish, I think, but no-one's spoken it on Earth for centuries, so I'm not sure."

"Try to work it out, Rice," Suliman muttered, overhearing, "We need a translator. They could be discussing where we would fit on a menu."

Rice gave Suliman a nervous nod as the men stood in a row and politely indicated for them to disembark. There was no shoving, no raised voices. If they had not been sporting weapons, their attitude was rather friendly.

"They want us to go with them," Thale said. "Do as they say."

"Commander!" Charlie whispered frantically, "Livesey is still on board!"

"What do you suggest, Doctor Maitland?" Thale turned his moribund eyes towards her. "We're defenceless, and at least for now, the Millstone isn't going anywhere until we can start the engines and dig her out of the sand. Livesey may be better off left here."

"What if he's injured? These people might be able to help."

Thale ignored her, and although Charlie would have said more, Suliman put his hand on her shoulder. His glance told her that those guards might seem easy-going, but if there was any fuss, they might lose their niceness. Charlie understood and shut up. There looked to be no option but to obey the men's request.

"I'm really worried about Livesey," Charlie muttered under her breath to Suliman as they filed past the men, who immobilised the crew's wrists in forcecuffs as they started down the gangway. Except for Charlie, whose attempt at co-operation by putting out her wrists was greeted with a laugh and a pat on the head.

Suliman examined the cuffs. Old technology but effective. "Livesey's alive and breathing," he whispered back. "You've established that much. He's safe enough in the bunkhouse. These guys obviously haven't used any scanning equipment, so they don't know he's there."

"He can't rescue us on his own."

Suliman agreed. "I would have said we don't require rescuing, Doc, but these restraints suggest otherwise. Having Livesey on the ship makes me feel a whole lot better."

"What's he going to do?" Charlie looked back at the ship. "At that angle, the bulkhead joist will keep him trapped. Besides, he can't pilot."

"I gave him lessons."

Charlie turned her face into Suliman's arm as the men herded them onto the gurney, "What? When?" she mumbled, making sure Suliman's sleeve kept her voice muffled.

"I don't think you need to whisper," Suliman said. "I'm willing to bet they can't understand us. And if you must know, I taught Livesey because he asked. He's no expert, but he could fly it out of here."

Charlie gave him a wry grin. "You missed your vocation, Suliman. You should have gone into education, teaching me combat and Livesey flying. What next?"

Suliman pulled an "I don't think so" face. He was good at that, communicating with expressions.

"Have you still got…you know, in your boot? Why didn't they check us for weapons?" Charlie kept her voice low, not because of the men, but because she didn't want Thale to hear.

She didn't get an answer, just confirmation in the form of a smirk.

While the guards busied themselves with a second forcefield on the gurney, Charlie wondered why they didn't restrain her, and said so to the others.

Thale had a theory. "There are no women among these guards; perhaps they consider women inferior and not a threat."

Charlie wasn't sure about that. If that was the reason, there was something politically incorrect about being the only member of their party without restraints, but perhaps now wasn't the occasion for righteous indignation for her sex. Even though the guards didn't seem fierce, their attitude appeared to be of a people taking no chances. Charlie, and she guessed Suliman, wasn't too sure Thale's order of following the guards' commands would offer the best outcome. She hoped Livesey was watching from his hiding place, making sure no-one discovered him. More importantly, she hoped he was okay.

The guard who travelled with them on the gurney handed Charlie an apple, inviting her to take a bite. Not wanting to seem uncooperative, she bit into the crisp flesh. She hadn't had an apple for all the time they'd been out in space, and it tasted good. What were the odds of finding a planet with humans and apples? She smiled her thanks, and the guard nodded his pleasure in her response.

Suliman watched them. "They think you're a kid."

Charlie looked from Suliman to the smiling guard. "What?"

"They're treating you like a child."

"Why would they do that?"

"Perhaps because you're—" Suliman looked for a fitting description, "—little."

"And flat-chested," Rice chimed in. "You do look like a kid."

Charlie narrowed her eyes at him.

"Play along," Thale said. "We might work this to our advantage."

Suliman appeared for once to agree with Thale. It did occur to Charlie to inform the guards she was an adult, but good sense prevailed. She was the only one of the group unrestrained, so that admission might just earn her a pair of forcecuffs of her own. Besides, Suliman was right; there was no way they'd understand her. Only one thing for it, play along, although Charlie reminded herself to take offence at Rice's comments later, and address the fact he'd even made that observation when they got out of this mess.

The desert turned to grassy meadows, the grass strangely beginning as the sand ended. As the guards hauled the gurney over the brow of a hill, the prisoners saw the country starkly contrasted with the sandy outlook from the ship. Here, green meadows, pastures and inland streams stretched towards the distant city which was built of towering, gleaming white buildings and golden spires.

"This is incredible," Rice exclaimed. "It looks like Earth."

"I've never seen a city like that on Earth," Suliman said.

Charlie reminded them that two minutes before, they were in a desert.

Thale took in their surroundings. "It must have a diverse ecosystem. Controlled weather systems or something. It looks like an oasis, but on a grand scale."

Rice sniffed the air. "This place is more than an oasis, Commander Thale. You might be right about climate control; there doesn't seem to be any pollution. I just don't see how they can be this selective."

Suliman nodded towards a fellow standing before a low building. "We might get a chance to ask. That guy looks pretty official."

The facade of the building jutted out from the side of the hill. The turf roof sported a mat of wildflowers that waved with merry abandon as the guards' bikes disturbed the surrounding air. As they came to a halt, the official man greeted them like familiar friends, although he did not remove their cuffs. He babbled in an unfamiliar tongue and set his sights on Charlie, who looked across at Rice for a translation, but his shrug told her he was only getting snippets.

The man escorted them into the cavern. Unlike the outside, which looked a little like a gnome's house from a fairy tale, the interior was dank and cold, without a stick of furniture save a tatty old divan. At a guess, Charlie thought the cave might be a lockup. The guards directed the men to sit on the ground against one wall, then guided Charlie to the divan. The official man offered her a plate laden with sugary-looking plum-shaped food and urged her to take one. Charlie darted a glance at Suliman, who conveyed a *"Yes, go ahead"* signal with a slow blink.

Unsure at Charlie's hesitation, the important man demonstrated by taking a plum and popping it into his mouth. Smiling, he licked his lips to show its deliciousness and raised his bushy eyebrows in invitation. Charlie tried to hold on to the sense she must remain free, but she had to admit this was all freaking her out. Someone would catch on she wasn't a kid. Still, at the first bite, Charlie discovered the plum thing very much to her liking. Full of syrupy sweetness and finishing with a crunch, she felt like a little kid just eating it. The man laughed and patted her cheek, then turned to Thale. He placed his hand on his chest by way of introduction.

"Jochim," the man announced.

"Thale," Thale offered in return.

Jochim launched into a speech, but they couldn't understand any of his other words. He emphasised, inflected, and exaggerated cadences, all to no effect. Rice did better, but without context, he struggled. Jochim shouted as if they were deaf, repeating himself and using hand signals and gestures that to Charlie read like a game of charades. Rice made noble attempts to interpret, but unable to piece together the individual words he recognised, he found himself powerless to provide a reliable translation. In the end, Jochim conceded defeat, and throwing Charlie an exasperated smile, left the cell, returning minutes later with a scrap of paper. As he passed, Charlie craned her neck to see. The paper had words, but Jochim didn't let her read it; instead, he held it out to Rice, pushing the paper close and flapping it up and down.

This time, Thale did better at interpreting the gesture. "He wants you to read it out loud."

"It's written in universal," Rice told them. "From a Seeker ship. There's a date and a name. Kathryn Winstanley."

Jochim grunted at the mention of the name, then headed for the door, twisting a key in the lock as he left, leaving them in semidarkness. After a moment, Rice's voice split the gloom.

"I felt almost glad to see the aliens were human. Now I'm not so sure they're friendly." He lifted his hands, enclosed in the forcecuffs. "And how would they have something from a Seeker ship?"

His comrades nodded in agreement. It seemed a Seeker had made it this far, that much was unmistakable, and somehow, the ship had avoided destruction. The question remained. What happened to the pilot?

CHAPTER TEN _

Daylight filtered through the gaps between the turfs on the roof and the surrounds of the ancient door. The group tracked the sun's movement through the cracks, estimating it to be around noon, which meant they'd been in the cavern for a few hours.

Charlie eyed the roof. She bet spiders lived in that turf. She hated spiders. One might drop on her… *Stop it, Charlotte Maitland,* she scolded herself. *You are on an alien planet, your colleagues restrained, no hope of escape, and you're worried about spiders? Start thinking of a way out of this mess!* But even a self-pointing out of their dire situation didn't stop her shuddering.

The three men sat in silence. From his position on the floor, Suliman scanned the cave's dim interior. Charlie followed his lead and got up to examine the door. Despite looking easy on its hinges and having gaps all around, the lock was large and solid. A shot from Suliman's abettor might dislodge it, but that would alert any guards outside.

Besides, Charlie had no way of releasing the men from their bonds.

Suliman broke the silence with an accusation. "So much for your leadership skills, Thale."

"I'm not responsible for the wave, Captain Suliman," Thale retorted with half a glance. "We have no weapons, and I for one, am in no fit state to engage in fisticuffs."

"It was you who told us not to resist. From where I'm sitting—" Suliman wriggled against the hard stone wall, "we're prisoners." He nodded towards Charlie at the door. "There's no way out."

"Suliman's right, Commander," Charlie said. "Why didn't Miller issue us with weapons?"

Predictably, Thale defended his friend. "Governor Miller didn't foresee us landing anywhere," he countered. "And why do you single him out to blame for our tribulations, Doctor Maitland? He is not the architect of this mission. It is Triumvirate sanctioned, and this Kathryn Winstanley may be able to help us if she is still alive."

Charlie flushed. Thale's response was too defensive. He felt a need to deflect any blame from Miller, and Charlie couldn't afford to let Thale know any of them had suspicions. She needed to be more vigilant, so she gave a nonchalant shrug. "I wasn't singling him out. It's just he was the agent, that's all."

Thale took a few deep breaths, closed his eyes and leaned his head against the cave wall. His sudden display of weakness brought Charlie to drop to her knees beside him.

"Are you okay, Commander?" His skin was damp and

cold, but Thale waved her away. "I'm due for pain relief," he gasped a little before recovering. "I'm alright, Doctor Maitland. The earth roof is making the air thick and unpleasant."

Thale didn't look close to death, but he couldn't go too long without treatment, and pain relief formed only part of his therapy, so they had to escape and get him back to the ship. In hindsight, Charlie decided Suliman's first instinct had been right. It might have been better to fight their way out of it.

Charlie just made it back to the divan when a woman, hard-faced and sharp of feature, dressed in a long-sleeved dress and carrying an old-fashioned lamp, cut the debate short. She stepped through the door, held up the lamp to better survey the occupants of the cave, then locked the door behind her. A neat little cap covered her hair, and from the floury residue on her smock, the woman might have come from baking bread. Rice thought she looked as though she stepped from the pages of a history book. With a thin-lipped, humourless smile, the woman sat beside Charlie on the divan and introduced herself.

"I'm Kathryn Winstanley. Please call me Kate."

Charlie wondered how a child might respond to this frosty-looking woman. That would be with caution, she decided, so she looked down without answering. Kate turned her attention to Thale.

"You are Commander judging by your insignia?"

"I am, Madam," Thale replied with a wheeze that went ignored by the woman.

"And you, sir?" She addressed Rice next, his eyes darting nervously in his head as he strove to figure out quite which era this woman's dress represented.

"Er, Rice," he replied. "History professor."

"Indeed? A strange occupation for deep space. And you?" She turned her cold gaze on Suliman.

"Suliman, I'm the pilot."

"Welcome. I'm pleased to meet you," Kate said, the effort of feigned friendliness evident in her voice, a voice which warmed distinctly when she turned her attention to Charlie. She drew Charlie's hand into her own. "Don't be frightened, child. What is your name?"

Charlie decided to play the part of a shy kid, in case the pretence might help the situation. Kate encouraged her to look up by placing a finger under her chin.

"Strange to see such a young girl as crew on a cargo vessel. Is one of these older men your father?" Kate glanced at the prisoners. One looked sick, and the other too swarthy to be the father of such a pale child, and neither looked like father material.

Charlie felt presenting herself as "Charlie" didn't feel appropriate; it was too intimate, too tomboyish. Instead, she introduced herself as Charlotte, trying not to blow her cover by sounding too bold and grown-up.

Kate seemed pleased with the response. "And how old are you, Charlotte?" she asked.

Thale was in Charlie's peripheral vision. He mouthed something, but she wasn't good at lip-reading, so she guessed it was something to do with "playing along".

"Seventeen, Ma'am," Charlie lied, snatching a number out of thin air, and wondering if shaving ten years off her age would work when she turned forty.

"Seventeen?" Kate's eyebrows shot up in surprise, and Charlie wondered if she should have gone younger, sixteen maybe, but that would have been stretching it. Either way, she couldn't change her mind, so for now, Charlie was seventeen again.

"Jochim said your delight in the sweeties proved to him you are but a child." Kate tucked an errant lock of Charlie's hair behind her ear. "I would have said you were older, but seventeen is a perfect age."

God, Charlie thought, her sweet tooth let her down, and what was so perfect about being seventeen? Only from the viewpoint she wasn't in forcecuffs. That was an enormous benefit.

"You told us, 'Welcome'," Thale said, drawing Kate's attention and lifting his hands, "but we remain restrained."

In response, Kate pulled a remote from her apron pocket. Charlie thought that pocket might be deep enough to be packing a lot more, even a weapon, but Kate took care not to let Charlie see the contents. Kate removed the cuffs with the remote, but as they fell away, a forcefield instantly activated, confining the three men to the corner of the cave.

Kate resumed the frosty voice she used to address the men before. "Not for long. We will release you soon." Somehow, Kate's unfriendly tone seemed a more natural fit for her demeanour.

"The ship only needs a minor repair," Suliman said. "Let us go; we'll fix it and be on our way. Unless you plan on confiscating it."

Kate appraised him with her chilly stare. "Interstellar travel has no place in this society. We will return your ship to you."

"Isn't that how you got here?" Thale inquired. "Jochim showed us a fragment of a Seeker log."

Kate inclined her head. "I was a Seeker, yes. The final Seeker to leave on the initial launch. Seeker-19."

Suliman didn't expect that. He remembered the launch well, and Kate's memory must have been affected. Thale would remember it too, but as Suliman glanced across at him, expecting the same puzzlement, Thale turned his face away. Somehow, Kate's revelation wasn't news to him.

"Seeker-19 wasn't the last to leave," Suliman said. "According to history, twenty Seeker ships launched."

Kate folded her hands in her lap, her expression making it clear she didn't like to be contradicted. "That is incorrect, Mr Suliman, nineteen only. The twentieth ship lost its pilot only a few days before departure. Seeker-20 was due to be rescheduled for inclusion in the second round of launches."

"That second wave never materialised," Suliman informed her. "When the Triumvirate received no word back from any Seeker, they abandoned the program. I know for a fact all the remaining ships went to Mars for dismantling, I was there, and there were twenty of them.

Forty ships originally made up the Seeker program, and records state twenty launched."

Kate considered Suliman's words. "I see." Then a touch of caustic amusement thawed her frosty mouth. "It seems you've lost a ship."

Charlie was interested to know what happened. "You said it lost its pilot. How?"

"She broke her neck, cliff-diving." Kate dismissed the enquiry with a flick of her hand. "For a Venusian, Amira was reckless."

"Amira?" Charlie echoed.

"Yes," Kate repeated. "Amira Santer."

So, Seeker-20 had been hijacked! Charlie looked across at Suliman. Going by his expression, he'd come to the same conclusion. Charlie would have been too young, but Suliman remembered the Triumvirate's official reports advising twenty ships left on the Seeker mission. Only an insider with something to hide would know someone other than Pilot Santer took Seeker-20. That someone had to be Governor Miller. And Thale would be in on that secret.

Suliman decided a little probing about the launch would do no harm. The woman seemed forthcoming about the Seekers despite her unfriendly manner. "Are you sure about that pilot?" he ventured.

"Positive," Kate snapped, "Why would you doubt my word? I am an expert on the Seeker program. Nineteen ships launched in the program's first wave. How could I know it got abandoned after I left? I clearly remember the launch pattern for Seeker-20 not taking place."

"There was a rumour someone sabotaged the ships," Charlie said.

"The Seeker program was well before your time, Charlotte," Kate sniffed, dismissing Charlie as an adult would a child in a discussion not suited to their age level. However, the comment did pique Kate's interest. "I am unaware of such a report. Did you hear of this, Commander Thale?"

"I was on Jupiter-Europa. I heard nothing." Suliman and Charlie knew that was a bare-faced lie.

"I see," Kate answered slowly, then stood and faced the men. "Now you mention it," she began, "I can't discount something like that happened. When the Triumvirate first proposed the Seeker program—almost two hundred years ago now—it received considerable opposition from the Nexists. As you know, that led to a civil war. When the program was re-established over two decades ago, the Triumvirate only paid lip service to the historical objections that influenced the original mandate."

Suliman remembered the resurrection of the Seeker program dominating the news some twenty-five years or so before. Even then, the program had its detractors, although none owned up to being Nexist.

"A few light-years out," Kate continued, "I lost contact with Seeker-17 and Seeker-18. We did not anticipate the loss of contact for several months, but around the same time, my ship's systems became unstable, failing one by one until I lost drive shaft and velocity. It seems the saboteur, if indeed there ever was one, was less than efficient, crippling my ship rather than effecting its destruction. Either way, I had no way of returning."

"And you got trapped in the wave?"

"No, Professor Rice," Kate replied. "A passing ship picked me up. They magnetised me to their hull and brought me aboard."

Rice turned a ghostly white. He knew it!

"*A-Aliens?*" he stammered.

Kate shot him an impatient glare. "No more than the people here are aliens, Professor Rice. These were human males. I didn't speak their language, and at first, I was grateful to them."

"So, there are others 'out there'?" Suliman said.

Kate inclined her head. "Yours is the sixth ship to crash since I arrived and the third to survive, although none appear to possess your speed capabilities. According to our records, dozens more have made it to the surface over the years. The wave flicks out like a streamer in the breeze. Once caught in its wake, a ship is carried along until, depending on your piloting skills, you either crash or glide to a halt on the inland sea basin." She looked at Suliman and added with grudging praise, "That you survived is a tribute to your ability as a pilot. The wave rises in the atmosphere, not from the planet itself, and the phenomena confined to this region only. The inhabitants of this world believe they originated from the stars and arrived by the wave. Another Seeker also landed a year after me. She lives east of here, in another province."

"So, how did you get here? Did the ship that rescued

you get snared in the wave?"

"Yes, Commander Thale," Kate replied. "The two men who picked me up had been in space for five years, on a mission not dissimilar to the Seekers, but their ship didn't have Mag capability. They planned on returning to their system to dismantle my ship and further their knowledge of the engines." As she drew in her breath to continue, Kate's body became rigid, and her lips curled in disgust. "In the interim, they made good use of me."

That sounded awful, Charlie thought. Kate might be creepy, but, well, poor Kate. Respecting what must have been a terrible ordeal, they waited in silence for her to continue her story.

"Both men were addicted to a plant dust they inserted into their nostrils," she told them. "At those times, during their drug-induced stupor, they placed the ship on auto and allowed me to roam. I didn't understand their systems, so I couldn't pilot the ship. We got caught in the wave while they were drugged." She thrust up her chin, her thin mouth tightening even further. "I decided that if we hit the planet and I died, it would be preferable to the life I led."

"You got catapulted out of the wave close to the planet?" Thale asked.

"By the grace of God—" Kate made a brief, reverent bow of her head, "I gained control of the ship as the wave terminated. The two men died in the impact. I woke up in the infirmary and discovered I was with child."

"You seem to have made a home here," Charlie said. Frosty Kate had her sympathy for now. "It's very diverse.

One moment desert, the next pastureland."

"The people believe in a simple life, Charlotte," Kate smiled. Her purpose here was to gain the girl's sympathy and, perhaps, interest in the culture, although in the end, if she were unsuccessful, the outcome would be the same. "Technology has its place," she continued, "but honest labour, self-sufficiency and family are the cornerstones of our society. The founders created this artificial ecosystem that has endured for generations. There are several of these provinces across the planet." For the first time, Kate's face blossomed into a genuine smile. "They caused the desert to bloom," she added with no small measure of pride. In her glee, she gave Charlie's cheek a gentle pinch.

"How do you maintain such a system?" Suliman asked. " 'Generations' can mean a long time."

Kate's frostiness returned. "I'm sure you'd love to know all our little secrets, Mr Suliman, targets for if you find a way to attack us." She turned to Charlie. "Charlotte, you will remain here, with us. Our female population is ageing, and we need younger women. As time goes by, fewer females are born; at present, it is four males to each girl child. With such a serious populace imbalance, your arrival here is most fortunate." Kate felt the flesh on Charlie's arms as though measuring chunks of prime meat. "You are young, strong, and doubtless very fertile," she announced. "The guards thought you younger, but if you are seventeen, you will soon be able to select your husbands and begin motherhood."

"Husbands?" Charlie's eyes widened in horror.

Creepy Kate was delusional if she thought Charlie was staying here to become a *baby-making machine!* Her compassion for Kate's history fled in the face of this development.

Kate had seen this response before. The women accepted their new lives in time, just as this young woman would. Kate held all the cards, so she could afford to remain calm. She would adopt a reasonable tone and encourage the girl, who only needed a little more convincing.

"Each woman takes three husbands," Kate said. "Three spouses increase a woman's chances of conceiving, and provides each man with a family to love and nurture. A few months after I arrived, I gave birth to a healthy girl. She is now appointing her husbands. I chose three males, and in time, gave birth to two more children, sons now aged sixteen and fourteen. Our elders no longer expect me to bear children, but I am respected and prized as a mother and wife. On Venus, like all the other Seekers, I had no family to return to or to mourn for me." Kate attempted to take Charlie's hand, but Charlie was having none of it. The game had gone on long enough.

"I'm not sticking around your blooming desert," Charlie exploded, jumping up and snatching her hand away from Kate. "I don't want *ONE* husband, let alone three. And I'm certainly not ready for children!" Charlie glanced frantically towards the door, wishing she could just run, but she couldn't leave the others here. She turned to the three men, who watched the proceedings helplessly from behind the forcefield. There was no telling what would happen to them if she didn't comply, so centering herself with a couple of calming breaths, she sat down on the divan.

"Please give us a chance, Charlotte," Kate soothed, stroking Charlie's hair and ignoring her outrage. "Women here are cherished; we want for nothing. The men ask only we bear their children. What greater joy can there be for a woman than to bring forth new life? In so doing, we magnify our womanhood and elevate our men to the status of lords."

No, this was going too far, stay here be damned. "I don't want to magnify my womanhood nor have any man, or three, lord it over me. I want to leave!" Too late, Charlie remembered the neurolysing spray in her boot as Kate snapped on the forcecuffs she had concealed in her bottomless apron pocket. Pasting on a smile that did nothing to hide her determination, Kate took Charlie's arm none too gently and propelled her towards the door, stopping once to make what she deluded herself was a sensible suggestion.

"If it makes it easier, perhaps you can take Professor Rice as your first husband? Intelligence is always attractive in a mate." Kate dismissed the older males' candidacy with a meaningful flick of her hand.

For Rice, being a husband to Charlie held a certain appeal. Still, he didn't fancy sharing with two other men. Besides, reading Charlie's body language, her fists clenching and unclenching, even in the forcecuffs, it looked more like she would deck the older woman, and no-one would end up marrying anyone.

With Kate about to separate Charlie from them and not having either a Plan A or B, Suliman tried to work out some way to delay them leaving. He couldn't fire the abettor through the forcefield, so the best they could do was negotiate. Kate knew nothing about their mission, and so far, she hadn't asked. For all she knew, Earth's space program could have moved out into the galaxy since the Seekers launched. It was worth a try.

"Forcing her won't help your cause. Give her some time," he suggested, standing as close to the forcefield as he dared. "Before he died, I promised her old man I'd watch out for her. She's not my kid, so if she stays, it's fine by me, but I'm the only father she's ever known. Why not be reasonable and give us some time to make our farewells."

Suliman was a plausible liar, but then, he had a lot of practice over the years. Charlie held her breath. At least it might buy them some time, but if he failed, she was grateful to him for even trying.

He did fail. Kate saw right through the ploy.

"We will release you, Mr Suliman. Charlotte—" Kate's eyes shone with luminous zeal, "this is a harmonious and joyful society. You'll conform. You'll see."

As Kate dragged her hostage through the door, Charlie wondered whether she should fight and try to run back to the ship, but the sight of two guards told her that would be a pointless exercise. Perhaps she could say something to support Suliman's unbelievable claim of being her guardian, but nothing came to mind. The last thing Charlie saw as Kate slammed and locked the door behind them was Suliman, his expression telling her he had her back. He would think of something.

CHAPTER ELEVEN _

The key twisted in the lock. Then, believing the men were contained and that they would be too concerned for Charlie's safety to attempt an escape, Kate allowed the force field to drop as she and Charlie left, leaving the three men free to move around the cave. Suliman headed straight for the door to try the lock, then checked the roof, looking for a place he could push through the turf, but the reinforcing mesh wouldn't yield. The cave looked tacked together, but it was craftmanship-efficient tacking together.

"What's going to happen to Charlie?" Rice wailed, his anxiety bubbling up to the surface. Usually, when he got like this, Charlie hugged him until he felt better, which he always milked for all it was worth, but he knew she knew that. He liked to pretend she enjoyed hugging him, but he knew she was just being kind. No way would he ask Suliman or Thale for a hug.

"Doctor Maitland is a capable young woman," Thale

assured him. "Plus, she thinks on her feet. Unless she elects to remain, she'll find a way around it. We talked our way out of the cuffs, and that mechanism on the door looks ancient. No match for Suliman, I suspect."

"You're a moron, Thale," Suliman snapped as he debated firing his abettor at the door. "We didn't talk our way out of the restraints, we just got stuck behind a forcefield, and now we're behind a locked door. I'm not going back to the ship without Charlie, even if it means engaging in 'fisticuffs', as you so quaintly put it."

As Charlie thought previously, Suliman realised weapons fire would draw the attention of any guards on the other side, and would also let Thale know he was concealing weapons. He didn't want him to know that, not yet, but getting through the door was the only way out.

"I can't fight," Rice blubbed as Suliman knelt to explore the lock.

"We're not leaving without the doc, Rice, so you may have to. This latch is a museum piece, more your area than mine." Suliman sat back so Rice could examine the lock. "Is there a way of opening it?"

Rice's face contorted as he considered possibilities. "This society is a hotchpotch of ancient and contemporary. I believe if you introduce something into the keyhole and waggle it about, it might release the mechanism."

Suliman peered at him, his leathery skin wrinkling in a look of surprise. "Did you say 'waggle'?"

"Yes." Rice knew a lot of interesting and obscure words. "But you need something long and thin, perhaps with a pointy bit."

Suliman looked over his shoulder at Thale. "Do you have anything that fits that description?"

Thale shook his head, but Rice rummaged down his shirt front and drew out a pocketknife. "I've got this." He handed it to Suliman, who'd never seen such an array of tiny blades.

"What do you carry this for?"

"My papa gave it to me. He said, 'Cyril'—that's my name—'you should always carry a knife; you never know when you're going to need to peel an orange'."

Suliman bit back a grin. Rice's expression was deadly serious.

"Your old man said that?"

"Uh, huh," Rice sighed, his face breaking into a nostalgic smile, his happy memory temporarily deleting their current dilemma.

"Wise man," Suliman muttered, extending the pocketknife and inserting it into the lock. It didn't have enough of a "pointy bit" to facilitate a complete penetration of the mechanism, but he could "waggle" it with necessary force. Rice told him to listen for a click or sound that would herald success.

"Humans picked up that woman, and she ended up on a world colonised by humans," Thale said, leaving the breakout attempt to the other two to coordinate. "Could it be only humans inhabit the galaxy?"

"Looks like it," Suliman replied as he made repeated incursions into the lock, all of which resulted in no reassuring "clicks". "Seems like little green men and lizard-people are just stories, although so far, we've only got the testimony of one person."

Rice's historian's brain shifted into gear. "We're on a world with a breathable atmosphere. They use technology at a level our world moved beyond hundreds of years ago, apart from the climate control. I've never seen anything like that. But their attire, both Kate's and Jochim's, dates further back in time. I'd be interested to see how their industry has progressed. If interstellar travel's not their thing, they likely have little interest in advancing their technology either. That's why they appear to have stood still. They just use what they need and update it as they go along. Also, with Kate's interest in Charlie, some old religious sects and cults align the primary position of women with motherhood. I don't know of any ancient societies that embraced technology without social advancement."

"I don't give a damn about them and their culture," Suliman hissed through a jaw clenched in concentration as a series of clicks caused them all to pause, listening. If there were guards outside, they would have heard the lock turning. Suliman dropped his voice. "We need to get out of here and find her. She isn't staying. Not if I have anything to do with it."

"What do you propose, Suliman," Thale replied, his voice rippling with sarcasm, "Riding into the city on a white horse?"

Suliman handed the knife back to Rice with a nod. "If

that's what it takes. I hope Livesey had the sense to keep out of their way."

He opened the door a crack, and from what he could see, the cave was unattended. "They could have simply killed us," he said, "but that might be against their religion. Right now, Kate believes she got what she wanted."

CHAPTER TWELVE _

Kate's dwelling lay just inside the city's borders in a section set out in neat rows. Kate called these rows "avenues". Large family houses lined each "avenue", as neat as a pin, with flower-filled gardens and flourishing vegetable patches. Charlie found it obsessively pastoral, but Kate spoke with so much pride, she felt compelled to make the odd approving noise. Beyond this area, the "suburbs", Kate explained, farmland stretched to the city boundary. Kate kept hens and goats in pens on her patch of land. The scene could have been anywhere on rural Venus or Earth, but for the old-fashioned attire and how the area ran along such efficient-looking lines. It was far too pristine for Charlie, far too unrandom and regulated to be a real home. She made a few attempts to get an idea of the culture, and asked Kate why such a harmonious society needed weapons and guards and a cell with a door that locked. Forcefields? Forcecuffs?

Kate replied with a smile, explaining the guards were

drawn from their proper employment as needed. "Volunteers and peacekeepers," she advised. Charlie's other questions about weapons and the lock-up went unanswered. It seemed not all was perfect in paradise.

Inside the house, Kate showed Charlie to a chamber at the top of a narrow, wooden staircase. The house had no elevator nor any other visible signs of technology. Chintzy curtains with little rosebud details matched the bedspread, and dainty cushions were positioned on chairs and against pillows. Sugary-sweet looking lace and more chintz adorned a dressing table. It was like walking into a doll's house. And she was going to be the doll.

Charlie shook her head and looked Kate in the eye. "I'm not planning on staying."

Kate patted the fancy quilt, stepping back to check out the flat, uncreased, perfectly detailed and pressed linen with pride. "But you must be comfortable while you decide."

Charlie eyed the quilt and thought of her messy quarters back on Rille base. She hated housework. "I have decided."

Kate gave her a tolerant smile in response, so Charlie pressed on.

"When will they let the others go back to the ship?"

"Soon, Charlotte, they won't keep them for long."

"I'll be going with them."

Kate blinked, and for a moment, her composure slipped; her eyes narrowed, and her mouth twitched. Charlie knew her defiance was trying the woman's patience, but Kate recovered her cheerfulness by changing the subject. "You'll meet my family later. Evening meals are always a family event."

Charlie felt indulged in the way a parent would indulge a problematic child. She'd probably get a banana or a lollipop next, or even a slap, just to shut her up. But Kate simply asked, "What happened to your parents?"

The question took Charlie by surprise. Suliman lied about her parentage, so now she would have to lie as well. "Uh, oh, an only child." At least that part was true. "I never knew my mother. My father was a freighter pilot until his death. He died after that." Charlie bit her lip. What the hell did that mean?

Kate studied Charlie's face. "You are very pale. Earth, Northwest continent?"

"Yes, but I haven't been back there for a long time."

"Well," Kate said, "you will have a wonderful family here." Then without giving Charlie a chance to answer, she stepped from the room. "Let me show you the rest of the house."

Charlie rolled her eyes as Kate turned away. Lying didn't come easily to her, although she doubted it mattered to Kate what continent she came from. Charlie was female and fertile, and that meant she met the criteria. Ancestry was meaningless. Sighing, she followed Kate back down the stairs.

That evening, Charlie endured a lecture on society's expectations, a woman's role, plus effulgent evangelising about her fortunes if she stayed. She met Kate's husbands and sons, the older of the two making flirtatious eyes at her until she pulled a fierce face that stopped him in his tracks. Later, Kate's daughter Martine arrived home, brimming over with enthusiasm at her impending nuptials.

Charlie had enough experience with social history to see how a society like this could work if the community had the same mindset and goals. The men worked at farming, engineering, building and infrastructure and more menial work, but allowed—Charlie thought a better word would be permitted—the females to be "on top" in a token sense. The men left the practice of medicine to women; local government fell to the women, and men had no say in the running of the household or its accounts. The men looked to their wives as the rearers of children, but both men and women devoted themselves to the service of a god who owned a testy, punitive personality that meted out imagined retribution for a host of misdemeanours, catalogued in a weighty tome that took pride of place in each home.

Yes, it might work for some. But not for Charlie. Despite the perceived freedoms of women, Charlie witnessed servility towards the husbands' and sons' wishes, at least in Kate's household. The women's fawning over the males made Charlie uncomfortable, and later, alone in her chamber with the house dark and hushed, she formulated a plan of escape. She peered out the window to the avenue that ran in front of the house. There was little in the way of street lighting, but Charlie paid attention to the direction Kate brought her, so she was sure she'd find her way back to the cell where they held the others prisoner.

Kate locked Charlie in the bedroom, effectively making it a prison. The drop from the window wasn't high, and she could doubtless manage it, but Kate had removed her slacks and blouse on the premise of washing them, even taking her boots. Fortunately, the compact neurolysing spray she carried in them would be hard to find except with a diligent search, and she doubted that was likely. No, Kate removed the boots as an added safeguard against her escaping. She'd given Charlie a long, modest nightdress that covered her from neck to toe. A dress of similar sombre tones as Kate's hung on a hook on the wall.

In escaping her prison and getting back to the others, Charlie decided she would have to leave her boots and clothes behind. Tying up the sleeves of her nightie and tucking the lower part into her underwear, she tackled the window. After an hour of futile pushing and pulling, Charlie flopped back on the cushioned bed, defeated. Staring at the ceiling, she hoped the morning would shed fresh light and inspiration for escape.

Charlie had washed and put on the too-large, heavy dark dress before Kate unlocked the door and summoned her to breakfast. A family affair with lots of excited chatter, Charlie pretended cheerfulness while taking in the kitchen's layout. She couldn't talk to Kate while the family milled around, but the position of the door challenged any hope of a quick getaway. If she convinced Kate she was leaving, and Kate didn't resist, and if the others were still in the cavern, she could run there in about fifteen minutes. The ship was only another couple of hours beyond that on foot. If she had to leave without Kate's agreement, it would mean dodging any guards that came after her—not easy in such open country—but she'd take her chances.

After breakfast, Kate's family left for their varied activities. Looking for a husband appeared to be a full-time job for Martine as she travelled in search of what she called a "perfect fit". So far, Martine, homely looking with an enormous bosom, had only found one spouse, so she still needed another two. She hugged Charlie as she left.

"I promise you'll love it here, Charlotte," she gushed. "It will be splendid to have a sister."

Kate beamed. "The other Seeker who crashed here embraced everything we offered," she told Charlie. "Another ship with an entire family on board survived as well. Those people weren't from Earth but from a distant system. I believe the male occupant was a criminal, fleeing the law. Sadly, he died soon after we found them. He has now faced the judgement of God."

"And they're all human?"

"All human," Kate confirmed.

Charlie eyed her boots on a cupboard near the door, but she had to get past Kate to access them. "Well, good for them. I'd like my clothes now, Kate. I'm going to find the others."

Kate didn't move. "Just stay today, Charlotte. I'll show you the neighbourhood, introduce you to a few people. You would be a blessing to this community."

"I don't wish to be rude, but I'm not staying."

Kate held her breath, then let it out in a sigh of resignation as if she had finally decided she'd lost the argument. "Very well, I'll take you back." But instead of stepping away from the door, Kate pulled out a chair. "Will you sit for a while before we go? Have more tea; it's nice to meet someone from Earth. How are things with the government?"

Delaying tactics. Charlie could smell them at fifty paces, but with Kate standing in front of the only means of escape, she had no choice other than to sit, re-evaluate and feign ignorance of Kate's strategy.

"It seems like you fulfilled your mission to find other inhabited worlds," Charlie said.

Kate remained standing while she poured tea, and Charlie tried to fathom how this woman could act so naturally while detaining someone against their will. Kate's experiences after her rescue must have turned her into a religious zealot or sociopath. The Seekers underwent a rigorous mental evaluation, and it seemed the Triumvirate's psych team missed this Seeker's propensity for space psychosis.

"It seems I did, praise God," Kate replied. Having won a small victory in keeping Charlie seated, she could afford to be pleasant once more. "I wish there was some way I could tell Earth. Is that where you and your companions were heading?"

"No, we're following a lead. Pilot Santer landed her ship, reprogrammed it, and returned it to Earth."

Kate pushed a teacup towards her unwilling guest. "It couldn't have been Santer."

Charlie forced a smile. "We know that now, thanks to you, but someone did, possibly as a pointed message for the Triumvirate or someone in it."

"The Nexists?"

"Possibly. Probably. Kate, I want to go now." Charlie stood. "I'm going to get changed. I can find my way back to the others. They might already be at the ship."

Kate lifted a basket onto the table. When she spoke again, Charlie heard a hint of menace.

"Please reconsider, Charlotte. This is a good society, and we need females."

Charlie moved around the table towards the door. "Not this female."

Kate shifted the basket so it stood between the two women. "Your shipmates aren't in the cell. They left last night."

That didn't surprise Charlie. She half expected they would either escape or get released without her knowledge. "If I walk out of here now," she asked, "will anyone stop me?"

Kate shook her head. "No-one outside will prevent you from leaving, but I will."

She put her hand into the basket.

Charlie wondered if Kate had concealed a weapon and

planned to subdue her, but she was prepared to defend herself, no matter what. "It's you against me," she declared, getting ready to dodge or duck whatever came from the basket.

Kate lifted a white root-like plant with intense green leaves. Charlie's heart sank. She knew that plant. Knaproot. She was right; Kate did have a weapon in the basket.

Eyes glittering in triumph, Kate advanced. "It flourishes in the warmer climates," she said, making no attempt to disguise the threat in her voice.

"I know what they use it for on Venus," Charlie spluttered as she backed off. "The question is, what do *you* use it for? It has other properties, less legal properties."

Kate swung the knaproot a little, and her tight mouth transformed into a wide grin. "It has a calming effect and makes the recipient more docile. Come now, Charlotte, it worked well on Lucy. Like you, she needed more encouragement. Eyos wished to stay, and as she already had daughters and was past childbearing, she settled and became a valued member of society."

"I will not agree to any of this, Kate."

Kate struck the knaproot against the table, exposing its moist core. Moving away only served to further separate Charlie from her boots, the neurolysing spray, and the exit.

"I'm an anthropologist, Charlotte," Kate told her as she poked away the knaproot shell with the corner of her apron, further revealing its mind-altering, soggy centre. "I can see what is happening here. The female population is ageing, and this civilisation is in danger of extinction. You'll be glad you stayed. The rest of us stranded here are all glad."

"I won't be glad," Charlie pointed out, "because, unlike you, I'm not stranded. I am a hostage."

Kate's expression changed to a chilling smirk. "Your comrades have gone, so you are, from where I'm standing, stranded."

Charlie had to get past Kate without taking a hit of knaproot. She knew Suliman would never leave her behind, but he might be in danger if he came looking. "If your people are so desperate," she suggested as she looked for a way to disarm her captor, "why don't they try genetic engineering? They can rebalance by using sperm selection. It's a basic technique; I doubt it's beyond your society's ability."

"They made some attempts," Kate replied with a dip of her head, "but when the failures persisted, they abandoned the practice in the belief the divine thought it blasphemy. They also believe that leaving this planet is heresy, so they can't travel to harvest females from other systems."

"But slavery is fine?" Charlie kept talking, looking for any opportunity to make a run for it. "Depriving someone of their freedom to choose is fine?"

Kate stopped and cocked her head to one side. "Only because I know you will change your mind." She rested the gnarly knaproot bulb on the table. "You are a wise little thing, aren't you? You seem much older than seventeen."

Charlie had to choose. Submit to the knaproot—it

didn't take much to render a body senseless—or make a run for it. No contest: she chose the latter.

"Well, I lied. I'm *Doctor* Charlotte Maitland, and I'm twenty-seven."

Charlie realised she'd never get past Kate before she got smashed with knaproot, so in a fluid movement, she picked up the pan next to her on the table, lunged forward and whacked Kate over the head. Kate's mouth dropped open in shock as she crumpled to the floor. The knaproot dropped with her, conveniently spilling its fibrous contents onto her stunned face.

Charlie checked Kate's pulse and mumbled "sorry" before fleeing through the front door, snatching her boots on the way out and fumbling for the neurolysing spray as she made it out into the avenue. Dressed as she was, the few people she passed accepted her as one of them. One or two gave her a second look, possibly because a young woman sprinting in a rather unladylike manner along the street, one hand scrunching up her cumbersome skirt and exposing her knees, the other clutching her boots, was not an everyday occurrence. She reached the cave in minutes, but as Kate had said, it was empty. If the others were forced to leave, she was likely to be at worst, a fugitive on an unknown planet, at best, mother to hordes of kids. Not ready for either, Charlie sprinted up the hill and ran for several kilometres, pausing to catch her breath and scanning the landscape for signs of the Millstone. Even though she was sure of Suliman, her heart sank as she surveyed the empty, sandy landscape that stretched towards a burning horizon.

CHAPTER THIRTEEN _

"We are leaving. That is an order."

"Do you want me to punch you in the face, old man?" Suliman's blood was up, and he towered over Thale, a weak, frail figure who was, in all likelihood, not much older than him. Suliman told Thale he would not leave Charlie behind, and all the way back to the ship, he'd endured Thale's insistence the mission was more important. Suliman raised his fist, but knew he couldn't hit the commander; the consequences might be too great. It just felt so good to have the man shrink from him, but if Thale died, they all died, then whatever fate befell Charlie would be his fault.

Rice stepped between Thale and Suliman. "Stop it, you two," he commanded in his best voice. "Charlie might decide to stay; we have no way of knowing. You know how fed up she gets with us. She might view this as a better option; besides, we don't know where they took her."

Suliman bent and shoved his enormous face into

Rice's. "We. Are. Not. Leaving. Understand?"

Rice stepped back and raised his hands. Suliman could squash him like a bug if he chose.

"We could start a manual search, Suliman," Livesey suggested. "I'll go with you."

"Is no-one listening to me?" Thale snapped. "I am the commander, and you agreed to follow my orders."

Livesey shrugged. "I didn't."

"Me either," Suliman echoed.

Rice flopped down into his seat. He didn't want to leave Charlie, but self-preservation was always at the front of his mind. He took only a couple of seconds to convince himself he would impede any search.

As it turned out, no-one invited him. Thale conceded there would be no point in commanding Suliman not to go, and without him, piloting the Millstone would likely have disastrous results. Besides, he'd gone over twenty-four hours without pain relief, so he decided to let them do what they wanted, and he'd deal with his own problems.

At the ramp, Suliman turned to Livesey.

"I work better alone. Keep an open comm. If you hear anything that suggests they captured me, or if I'm not back in eight hours, leave. Keep Thale alive as long as possible and try not to be in the neighbourhood when he carks it."

Livesey nodded. He knew Suliman and Charlie had uncovered something about Thale, just as he knew they would tell him in time. Also, the Millstone needed a pilot, and without Suliman, he was the only one who knew enough to fly it, thanks to the big man's patience.

Even though she saw no sign of the ship, Charlie continued to run. Anywhere was better than being at Kate's, and if she died in the desert, well, so be it. She had to remember Thale didn't have time for diversions if he were to fulfil this mission, and any delay put the Millstone and the others in danger if he somehow detonated or died. Charlie's performance in the cavern would have left them in no doubt about her feelings involving a life here, so she just had to trust they were hiding a ship the size of the Millstone in the desert somewhere and were searching for her.

Charlie picked up the distant whine of a guard bike. At this point, she didn't know if she was anywhere near where the Millstone crashed or just how far she'd run since escaping Kate. The guard came upon her quickly, reaching out his arm as if planning to grab her. Charlie dropped and rolled, feeling the bike skim over her before it banked and stopped. She heard more bikes in the distance. She could handle one guard if he didn't shoot her, which was unlikely knowing her value, but taking on two might push her luck. The guard approached; his mouth curved in a reassuring smile. He didn't raise his weapon, making Charlie think he aimed to apply forcecuffs and return her to Kate, so she waited until he was close enough, then squirted the neurolysing spray into his face. Clutching his head, he fell to the ground, his body jerking in spasm. Charlie jumped on the bike and tried to work out how to get it going, but it appeared equipped with a personal interface and wouldn't budge. The other bikes were getting closer, so Charlie snatched the downed guard's weapon. Closing her finger around what she hoped was the trigger, she aimed at the first bike and shut her eyes, chanting to herself, *"Please work, gun, please work, but don't kill anyone."*

The bike was almost upon her, but before she squeezed the trigger, an explosion split the air beside her ear. The second bike rolled, and a third and a fourth, spilling all the riders onto the ground. The impact rendered one man unconscious, but the other two rose, both reaching for their weapons. Suliman dropped one with a blow to the head; the other, not expecting Charlie to fight, went down when she applied a paralysing kick to his gut. With the guards neutralised, Suliman pointed to the weapon still in Charlie's hand.

"I'm glad you didn't fire that," he declared, taking the weapon from her. "It's pointing the wrong way. You'd have blown your head off."

Charlie's eyes widened in horror. How could she have been so stupid? Suliman grinned.

"Only joking. At this range, you would have just sent him into orbit. Now hurry, there'll be others."

Even though Charlie couldn't get the bike to work for her, Suliman didn't face the same issue. He took less than a minute to work out the controls, and Charlie jumped on behind him. They took off over the dune and down towards the flat sandy desert basin, where the Millstone waited.

"Livesey laid a plan away from the wave," Suliman told her as they made their way up to the cockpit. "The last thing we want is to return, and here's where we find out if they have any surface to air firepower."

"Livesey's okay?" That was good news.

"He's fine."

The Millstone took off across the city, the only safe way to bypass the wave. Not a single weapon impeded their escape, but not one of them breathed easy until they were in the upper atmosphere.

"Kate told me you'd left," Charlie said.

"We got out," Suliman told her. "Rice and I picked the lock, but we only got a few metres before the guards found us. They just brought us back to the ship and left us. Thale would have taken off straight away, but I knew you wouldn't volunteer to stay."

"I wasn't tempted even for a minute." Charlie shuddered at the thought. "Ugh."

Suliman eyed the drab, heavy garment swamping Charlie's slight frame. He didn't know how she made it as far as she did dressed like that.

"That woman had no fashion sense," he grinned. "You look like something out of a horror story."

"Kate took my clothes. It's not as if I've got heaps."

"They wouldn't fit her."

"She took them to wash, Suliman." Charlie sniffed the air. "Talking about washing, what's that smell?" She held her nose. In all the relief of having escaped, the disgusting odour permeating the cockpit now threatened to make her gag.

Rice immediately implicated Suliman. "It's his fault," he declared. "Just after you left to have your choice of men to bed, he peed in a corner, then when I heard it—you know, the stream, I needed to pee as well. Then Thale. It took us a while to escape, and it was smelly in there anyway. I expect other people have peed there too, probably where they made us sit. We'd all been holding it, and well, it stank." He plucked at his shirt. "The smell must be clinging to our clothes."

Charlie looked from one man to the other. "Well, thankfully, we're safe now, and I am very grateful you waited for me, but don't let me keep you from washing and changing into something less pungent."

Rice nodded mutely. He could smell himself, and there was still vomit residue on his slacks from when the ship crashed. He did smell nasty.

"Those people would have lamented you passing on your bossy gene," Suliman grinned as Rice trotted off to the shower.

"You can get cleaned up too, Suliman."

"Are you sure there's room?"

"I don't mean *share*. I mean go someplace else to wait. You stink!" Charlie felt grateful to him. She'd been right to trust him, so she shouldn't be telling him off for being stinky. She looked around. "Where's Thale?"

Suliman pushed himself from his seat. "In his bunk. He spent most of an entire day without pain relief. He was dead against searching for you, so I made Rice draw up extra to avoid any funny business. Thale must have taken it without checking.”

“Rice? He knows nothing about medication, and he can’t do the targeting scans. Did he at least check Thale’s blood pressure?”

Suliman laughed. “Stop flapping! Thale’s fine, but he’s out cold. So, he still doesn’t know about the abettors.”

“And I didn’t know they were so loud on full. My ears are still ringing! Now go and shower.”

Charlie closed the cockpit door behind Suliman and sat opposite Livesey, who hadn’t said a word so far.

“It’s nice to see you, Charlie,” he said.

“And I am relieved to see you in one piece. Were you hiding when we crashed? I thought you’d been hurt.”

“Not hiding,” Livesey confessed, “I was having a sneaky nap. I fell out of bed and got knocked unconscious. When I came to, no you, Thale, Rice, Suliman, and we were half-buried in the sand. I prised the door open just enough to squeeze out.”

“I worried you’d come after us.”

“That wouldn’t be my instinct, Charlie. I’m a coward, and I have a coward’s instincts.”

“That’s not it.”

“It is in part. I knew you’d come back. The guards showed up and cleared away the sand from the front of the ship to check for external weapons. I just hid when they came aboard. They weren’t particularly thorough, then when they left, I pulled up the side of the ship using fractional thrusters and lifted the ship out of the sand inch by inch. I decided to give you a few hours, then reassess. I had no idea what to do beyond that. The only other thing I did was to calculate a course away from the wave and get the ship ready, so we could leave as soon as you got back."

"Suliman's glad he taught you how to fly."

Livesey agreed. "It turned out to be useful. Thale said there was no way you'd get away, but Suliman shaped up to him. By then, I think Thale was too weak from pain to argue. Nothing would have stopped Suliman from coming to get you. I planned to go with him, but he said 'no'."

"Thanks, Livesey. The woman who took me prisoner was from Earth, a Seeker. She planned on me staying to help increase the population."

Livesey nodded. "Suliman told me. It doesn't sound so bad. I suppose it depends on what you want."

"I'd be a prisoner, Livesey," Charlie said, the horror of it all now settling in, now she was safe. "She, Kate Winstanley, loves it there and was willing to get you all to leave and leave me stranded."

"That blows our theory about booby-trapped ships out of the water."

"No, it doesn't. There's another Seeker there whose ship also suffered catastrophic system failure. The other woman embraced the society with a little help from raw knaproot. There's another family from a different star system as well, all human. Who knows how many others have settled there over the centuries? Did Suliman tell you only nineteen Seeker ships launched?"

"Yes, seems like someone posing as Amira Santer

hijacked the twentieth."

"I agree. Thale knows what's going on. I feel like confronting him."

"I doubt he'll tell you, but I have a theory."

"What theory?"

"Give me some time."

"Okay, but we should share any ideas. I think…"

Charlie would have said more, but Livesey interrupted, steering her neatly away from the subject. "We've only been out for a few months. I can't believe other humans are within such easy distance. How come they've never introduced themselves to us?"

"Kate said our ship was the first with advanced Mag technology." Charlie saw what Livesey did, and she would allow him to be mysterious for now, although she would revisit his words soon. "The people on that planet don't use interstellar travel, but it seems others have spacefaring technology. Maybe there's something to those stories of 'lights in the sky'."

Rice returned and caught the end of their conversation. "That ship buried on Venus. Maybe that's a crashed UFO."

"But you never saw it?"

"No, but why put the entry in those archives if it didn't exist?"

Charlie closed her eyes. "I don't know," she sighed. Her brain started to hurt; shock from the crash, escaping from Kate, exhaustion; it all caught up. She headed for the door. "Let's discuss it later when we're all together."

That evening, in the galley, with the ship back on a course that skirted the wave, the crew sat around the table, relieved their first contact encounter was now behind them. Thale still looked drowsy from his unauthorised extra dose of analgesia, but that didn't stop Charlie glaring at him until he acknowledged her.

"Something on your mind, Doctor Maitland?"

"You were going to leave without me, Commander Thale. Abandon one of your crew to an uncertain fate."

"We had no way of knowing where that woman took you," Thale responded levelly. "And let's be honest, in the past, you have been very vocal about being stuck in a tin can with four smelly males."

This was the truth. Charlie did that occasionally, but she was only venting. It didn't mean she actually wanted to leave. Thale had missed the point.

"On that planet, I would have been stuck with *three* men—" Charlie jabbed a furious finger in his direction, "and at least I don't have to have sex with any of you. Which would you say, Commander Thale, is the lesser of the two evils?"

"They were willing to let us leave, Doctor Maitland," Thale answered wearily, as if she should follow his reasoning. "I have little time to complete this mission, and I took the opportunity. None of us is indispensable."

"The mission!" Charlie snapped. "The mission that you keep under your belt and don't share with the rest of us?"

"Doctor Maitland, I see you are upset, but I know no more about the mission than you."

"Remind me then of what you *do* know."

"To find the door on the moon, to determine who Pilot Santer encountered with the technology to return the Seeker module and hopefully mitigate any threat to Earth."

"You heard Kate," Suliman said. "Pilot Santer is dead. She never left Earth."

"I am as confused as you are on that point."

Suliman doubted it, just as he doubted Thale was not aware of that particular tidbit all along. He debated challenging Thale, but the man looked exhausted, debilitated. The last thing he needed to do was cause a heart attack.

"So, if I was still on that planet enjoying the ministrations of a psychopath," Charlie demanded, "Who would administer your treatment?"

Thale nodded at Rice. "I discussed this with Rice. At a pinch…"

Several pairs of accusing eyes turned.

"Er, well, I've watched you, Charlie." Rice adopted the squeaky voice he used when painted into a corner. "I reckon I could do it, and Suliman asked me if I knew how to draw up analgesia."

"You're a toad, Rice."

"Sorry, Charlie, I was just trying to make it okay if you stayed." Rice hung his head, his cheeks flaming. "I meant nothing by it. I'm glad you came back."

"I wonder where the people on that planet originated?" Suliman said. "I don't think they're indigenous."

Charlie reminded him of Kate's words in the cave; that they came from the stars. "Perhaps they have their own stories of creation and settlement, like ours. I didn't see the family that came from the other system, but Kate says they're human too."

"Superior beings created us," Thale cut in with sudden fervour, banging his fist on the bench and gasping with the effort. "Our origins are divine."

His outburst momentarily stunned the others to silence, except for Suliman, but aside from Charlie being taken prisoner, little disconcerted him. "I knew you were a Nexist, Thale," he said evenly.

Thale gave a dry laugh. "You don't have to be a Nexist to be a creationist, Suliman. Not everyone believes Venus to be the pivot upon which the universe swings. And Nexists don't reject the notion of life on other planets; they just don't want to attract their attention."

"Xenophobes," Suliman muttered, although he was not much of a lover of other people himself.

"Xenophobes? Captain Suliman, until the Seeker program, the Triumvirate itself was xenophobic. It didn't direct funding to astrophysical study save for a few probes, resulting in them learning little about the space outside our solar system. Besides," Thale reasoned, "is xenophobia so bad? Doctor Maitland encountered hostility on an alien planet."

Suliman nodded. Fair enough, but the universe might hold other, more reasonable societies.

Rice frowned. "I thought they outlawed Nexism?"

"To a large extent," Suliman said, although he knew the movement hadn't completely moved underground. "There are still those who believe in preserving the purity of race and not diluting it with other cultures. That's at the heart of Nexist ideology."

"The Nexists never went away," Thale said. "They are once again on the rise, stronger and in greater numbers than ever."

"Why?" Charlie asked.

"To avert a threat, Doctor Maitland," Thale answered with a look of surprise. "Would you want a society like the one from which you escaped, imposing their culture on us? Who knows what is out there? The Nexists are not the enemy." Thale looked at each crew member in turn. "It is the Venusians who hold secrets from the ancient past. Our mission will prove it."

Tacitly, Thale had just admitted to them all, he either was Nexist or at least a sympathiser.

"So Thale, tell me," Suliman asked, "why did you enlist for this mission if you believe it might draw the attention of a hostile species?"

Thale rolled his eyes. "That debate is old, Suliman. The attention has already been drawn. A ship returned to us from an unknown system. Whoever reprogrammed it knows where we are." He made to rise, unsteady on his feet. "I'm going to the bunk room."

No-one offered their commanding officer any assistance.

"I knew he was a Nexist sympathiser," Rice whispered. "And I don't agree with them, but in this, Thale's right."

"That we've attracted attention?" Charlie said. "Yes, but we don't know if the ones we're chasing are hostile. True, someone sent back a story and one of our ships, but we can't assume that's an act of war or a prelude to an invasion."

"I wonder why Miller hid that Seeker ship on Mars," Rice wondered aloud. "Perhaps it never left in the first place, they might have fabricated the logs to make everyone believe it did, and we're on a wild goose chase on coordinates that lead nowhere."

Charlie didn't believe that. "It's too elaborate. If you believe Kate Winstanley's story, Santer never took the ship, so someone else must have."

Suliman repeated his earlier comment that Miller wanted to show the messenger they were looking for that the ship did make it back to Earth. They all agreed that might only be part of the answer. Charlie struggled. She knew they were missing something, a vital piece of information, and Livesey didn't seem ready yet to offer his theory.

"Then why send a motley crew like us?" she asked, "launched from Rille and without the sanction of the Triumvirate?"

"His own agenda?"

Charlie looked at Suliman. He was thinking the same, that Miller also knew Santer died before the Seeker ship left, so why would he need them to contact the hijacker or the people who sent the ship back? And Thale's suicide implant? What could be the reasoning? None of it made sense.

***

Later, Suliman found Charlie in her cubby, poring over her reader. He squeezed his bulk in beside her, and she shifted her position to accommodate. He was too tall to stand in the confined space, so she had become used to these somewhat squashed private chats.

Charlie handed him her reader. "I've been doing some investigation of my own. This is the report from Santer, or rather not Santer."

Suliman scanned the entry. "This is what your boyfriend thought was poetry?"

"Prose, yes, but look, I've cross-matched some keywords. I briefly looked at it once. Sam sent it to me before I left, but I just looked again. It was a hunch, but a solid hunch. My reader extrapolated this transposition from the text." Charlie reached over and adjusted the visuals.

Suliman recognised the tone of the language. "A kid's story?" Not that he knew many.

Charlie nodded. "Not one I know, but it's pretty standard; an astronaut getting lost in space, the loneliness, never meeting any aliens, and look at this sentence—" Charlie highlighted an entry, " 'I have long since ceased to see the angled elegance of a twin-mooned sky'," she quoted. "That's straight from a child's book of space tales, at least, it's familiar."

Suliman returned the reader to Charlie. "So how does that help us?"

"Apart from those few phrases, the similarities are several degrees away from an actual match of any story I know. I wonder if Miller saw something in that report or prose that he recognised. It could even be code, and he wants the individual who wrote it kept away or executed? Maybe it's not about alien civilisations or Nexism at all. Maybe I was right; maybe it is personal."

Suliman scratched his head. "You're saying this individual ventured out into deep space at the same time as the Seekers?"

"If Santer didn't take the ship, there's no other explanation. That person must be important or dangerous for Miller to go to this trouble."

"I reckon Miller only planned on sending Thale and me," Suliman said. "Then you came along and pissed him off, Rice turned up with information he didn't want getting out, and Livesey, if we can believe him, volunteered. It probably didn't occur to Miller that several heads nutting out the mystery would be better than one."

Charlie twisted around to make eye contact with Suliman. "Don't you believe Livesey?"

"Of course I don't. Do you?"

"In the absence of any other information…"

"It's crap," Suliman snorted. "He wouldn't volunteer for this, knowing it's a suicide mission."

"Okay, but Miller would have needed a doctor for Thale. If it hadn't been me, someone else would have got pressganged."

Suliman grinned. "Perhaps Thale will come to love us and not blow us into eternity."

Charlie looked at him with a "really?" expression. "Do you think it's time to share what we know with Rice and Livesey?"

Suliman shook his head. "I wouldn't trust Rice. Under pressure, he might just blab."

Charlie had to agree. "Livesey is developing a theory about Seeker-20, but so far, he hasn't volunteered any thoughts."

"That's interesting," Suliman said, then slapped his knee decisively and made to get up. "Let's keep it to ourselves, Doc, just in case. We can tell them when we need to."

Charlie saw a sudden weariness wash over Suliman's swarthy features. "Is everything alright, Suliman?" She pulled on his sleeve to stop him from leaving.

Suliman felt fine, never better, but he didn't feel prepared to tell her the reasons why. "It's just that I'm not cut out for intrigue," he grinned, hoping to reassure her. "I like a quiet, simple life."

"The life of a criminal can't be quiet nor simple."

Suliman acknowledged that fact with a flick of an

eyebrow. "I got away with a lot more than I got caught for," he admitted. "Anyway, I was on Rille for almost a year; maybe my drinking habit wasn't as ingrained as I thought."

"Oh, it was ingrained alright," Charlie laughed. "I've seen your liver!"

Suliman allowed that, no hiding his liver from the doc. "There's no liquor on board, and I'm not missing it."

"Good. You know, Suliman," Charlie said after a moment, "You're okay."

CHAPTER FOURTEEN _

Over the next few months, Charlie trained Rice up as a field medic. Unfortunately, the nurse droid blew up, melting part of the bulkhead, with the resulting mess rendering the medbay unusable. The damage to the equipment caused a delay in Thale's treatment which led to a setback in his condition, a turn of events that almost caused Suliman's and Charlie's own hearts to fail, wondering if Thale might not survive until the medbay became operational. Still, Charlie got his condition under control, more by luck than judgement and help from the field medical kit, without resorting to surgery to eliminate a secondary growth on his lung. Also, in those few months, Livesey became quite a pilot. Suliman set up a continuous sensor sweep to notify them of any irregularities that might catch them unawares, all the while mistrusting the reliability of the Millstone's technology. This concern kept him on alert and lost him a considerable amount of sleep.

It so happened, an exhausted Suliman was dozing

when the alert sounded for the first time. The Millstone set up a series of rhythmic shudders as it passed by a gas giant, not settling until Suliman disengaged the Mag engines.

"We've entered a star system," he announced as the others rushed to the cockpit at the first rattle, fearful their first experience of the Millstone shuddering was about to be repeated. "The ship will break apart if we use Mag, so I'm guessing it might be the same here as at home, and we can't use it so close to planets. That's a pity; it'll take us longer to pass through at this speed."

"Why would Mag make a difference?" Rice asked.

"I don't know about Mag four," Suliman said. "This is my first experience of it, but I know they couldn't engage Mag one, which they used in the Seeker craft, until beyond the perimeter. In trials around Mars, the prototype Mag one craft disintegrated in orbit. It caused a weather event that took a month to dissipate and gave the planetologists a year's worth of data to examine. For them, it was a gift. For the Mag engineers, it was a disaster."

Thale gazed through the viewport. "Get closer to that planet. What's its composition?"

"Hydrogen, helium, hydrocarbons, methane." Suliman looked up. "It's got fourteen moons and an axial tilt of twenty-eight point five. Same as Neptune."

"I knew it," Rice groaned, burying his head in his hands. "We've been going in circles."

"We're not going in circles, you goose," Charlie said. "We're in the corresponding solar system."

Thale set the map of the star system out for them all

to view. "I'd say Doctor Maitland is correct. Although we are not yet at the coordinates, this system does have similarities to our own."

Suliman narrowed the data to supply them with information on the local planets. "For argument's sake—" he positioned the stellar map, "—let's call this planet Neptune B. There's another planet where I would expect to find Venus."

"Well, Saturn looks normal enough, but these…" Thale highlighted two tiny planets. "We don't have anything this small so close to the sun. The blue planet looks to be in a corresponding position to our Earth."

"Those two tiny planets can't be inhabited."

Suliman pulled up the compiling data on one of the small worlds. "According to the sensor report, and we might need to take that info with a pinch of salt at this distance, we wouldn't survive even in life suits."

"So, where's Venus?" Charlie asked. "Or a corresponding Venus. It looks like Mars has taken its place."

Suliman peered at the star chart. "It does look like that. From the sun, there are those two small uninhabitable planets, the Earth-lookalike, then the planet that looks like Mars but should be Venus, Jupiter seems okay, Saturn, Uranus and Neptune." He looked up from the compilation. "Asteroids, comets, you name it, it's here."

Charlie enlarged the world that most intrigued her and walked through the projection, turning this way and that. She felt a wave of nostalgia. "This little blue planet really does look like Earth."

"It's got a moon that fits the bill," Suliman agreed as he walked through the holoview with her. "The blue planet is the only one that can support life. The parallels between this system and ours are remarkable, that is, if we ignore the planets near the sun."

Later, alone in the cockpit with the crew sleeping, Suliman, his feet on the co-pilot's chair, leaned back as he watched the onboard aggregator make sense of the data it received as they entered this star system. Even with a higher number of asteroids and comets than home, the Millstone navigated the space efficiently. In a surge of nostalgia, Suliman reached out and patted the bulkhead. The old girl might be composed of bundles of other ships welded onto her hull, but she'd never let him down. He told Charlie he didn't care about dying, but he now saw the merits of space travel, the lure of solitude, the lure of peace. Once the crew were back home safe, assuming they prevented Thale from blowing them to kingdom come, perhaps he would find a home out here. Maybe Thale would only blow up his target, Suliman mused, and maybe once he'd achieved his objective, they all might make it out alive and be able to return to Earth. It was all wishful thinking. Miller wanted none of them back, and if they met the aliens who programmed the Seeker ship, maybe they wouldn't let them leave.

Charlie joined him in the early hours. "Didn't you

sleep?" she asked.

"No, you were snoring." Ignoring Charlie's horrified look of unspoken denial, he lifted his feet so she could sit down. "I reckon the coordinates are correct, but our little side trip on the wave might have distorted the sensors. There are a few blank spots."

Charlie looked at the stellar map. "That just doesn't look like Mars."

"No, it doesn't." Suliman had spent hours pondering the planets, and he had to agree. "Neither does Jupiter look like Jupiter."

"The one with the moon we're headed to looks like Earth."

"Yes, Doc, but what are the chances of two solar systems being virtually identical?"

"I don't know, Suliman. I wonder what the aliens call these planets?" Charlie looked out the viewport. At normal speed, she was getting a chance to see them properly. "How spooky would it be if they had the same name as ours?"

A pale and drawn-looking Thale joined them. Charlie was concerned his setback robbed him of much needed time. At one point, she even doubted he'd make it this far, but could only take a philosophical approach; if he died, then none of them would live to tell the tale. This close, he had a reasonable chance of getting there.

"This is like crawling," Thale grumbled, closing his eyes against his wheezing as he took a deep breath.

"Sorry, Commander," Suliman told him. "We're

giving it as much as we can."

Charlie went to take Thale's arm. "Shall we go to the medbay, Commander?" Every breath Thale took bought them more time. If he needed treatment, she'd give it, but Thale waved her aside impatiently as he pulled away.

"No. Nothing. Let's just get to the moon. We need to find this door."

Suliman watched him stagger off. "That's a man on a mission."

"His heart is holding up well for a man in his condition," Charlie said. "We should be thankful for small mercies."

Suliman nodded towards the exit, "We should make the moon within twenty-four hours. Check on him anyway, Doc. Let's not take chances."

CHAPTER FIFTEEN _

The sight of the blue planet so close gave Charlie a hefty dose of homesickness. Even Rice stayed silent as the ship came to rest on the moon, but Thale seemed agitated, leaping from his seat before Suliman cut the engines.

"Are we all going?" Charlie called to his retreating back, concerned about him going out in a life suit, but he didn't acknowledge her.

Suliman shrugged and followed Thale. "I guess we are," he called over his shoulder.

There were only four life suits, so to Rice's dismay, Livesey volunteered to stay behind.

"We'll search the grids in two teams," Thale instructed, "then meet back at the ship."

The life suits were too long for Charlie and Rice. Rice's rotund body filled his out better than Charlie's, so Suliman made a few folds and secured them with tape so the legs and arms didn't hang down. The boots had an adjustable interior, so besides the heaviness, they fitted well enough. However, the helmet and additional oxygen pack were heavy and cumbersome and dug into Charlie's shoulders.

"You'll be fine when you get outside," Suliman told her. "All this equipment will feel light, but it will take a few moments to get the hang of moving."

Outside the Millstone, Charlie turned a full circle, marvelling at the cold, grey light cast across the moonscape. Many years before, she saw an image, called a photograph, on display in a museum. The image was devoid of colour, just black and white and faded. There were no buildings in the image, no people, no transports, just a picture of a desert. This place reminded her of that image, lonely and cold. She thought about the Seeker ship report and understood a little of what it must be like to be alone in space. The blue planet shone distantly in a blackened sky. So like home.

Still, Charlie thought bounding in almost zero gravity was fun, even slamming into Suliman once or twice, her antics drawing a reprimand from Thale. Rice preferred to keep himself anchored and took no time to play, thudding down his foot at each step to make sure he didn't go floating off into space. Finally, after hours of fruitless searching and diminishing ambient oxygen within their suits, they regrouped to compare notes.

"Nothing." Suliman showed them the data he collected. "This place is just as advertised. A desolate moon."

Thale was exhausted, but he was determined to give

the search another try despite Charlie's caution that a drop in oxygen, however minor, could exacerbate his recent lung problem. Suliman backed up Charlie with an insubordinate threat directed at Thale, but they failed to sway him. At Thale's insistence, they switched to backup oxygen, and Charlie monitored the situation for another hour. By then, Thale was not in a fit state to argue.

In the cockpit, Livesey looked as though he'd been busy.

"What have you got, Livesey," Thale wheezed. Charlie at least got him to sit, but she also saw from his narrowed eyes that his head was hurting. Over recent weeks, the lesions in his brain showed signs of becoming resistant to treatment. Any day now, she expected him to show signs of irrationality. It worried Charlie that he might detonate himself in a moment of agitation. So far, although the patch on his aorta hadn't budged, she had been unsuccessful in locating anything that looked capable of tripping the device.

"I'm not sure," Livesey said. While the others were away, he'd mocked up a chart of the local landscape aided by the onboard aggregator. "The information that came back on the Seeker ship didn't have enough detail. I found an energy signature, but the Millstone's sensors can't narrow down the location, only a general region."

"These instruments should be able to pinpoint a simple, local signature if there's one there," Suliman told him, checking the data.

"Yes, but I think it's buried."

They all exchanged puzzled looks. "Buried?" Thale asked. "Like underground?"

Charlie had another explanation. "Or like inside the door our unknown pilot found?"

Livesey nodded a "maybe".

None of this did anything for Thale's mood, but with the life suits requiring replenishment and the backup packs needing recharging, he grudgingly agreed to Charlie's offer of a spell in the medbay.

"What is it, Doc?" Suliman squeezed himself in beside Charlie in her cubby.

"I pulled up Livesey's findings about the energy signature. Look at this. Livesey's been snooping through Thale's personal data."

Suliman thumbed through the reader. "It's just a personal log. What of it?"

"The personal log is an eclipse," Charlie told him. "It's what's behind it that's interesting."

"Did Livesey decipher it?"

"No, he wouldn't be able to," Charlie grinned. "But I can."

Suliman raised a quizzical eyebrow, so Charlie enlightened him with details of the system Sam was developing in response to recent, albeit minor instances of espionage within the Triumvirate.

"He told me about ghosts and eclipses," Charlie explained. "His invention separated all layers of overwritten data on these types of historical logs, peeling them right back to the very first entry. Not just that, he could restore any corrupt data." Charlie gave Suliman a rough demonstration on her reader. "Sam hadn't fully developed the system, but he planned to present it to the Triumvirate when he returned to Earth. He was so keen; one of his passions was information security. He detailed all the algorithms—endlessly!" Charlie rolled her eyes and laughed. "And I have a great memory for numbers."

"If Livesey is snooping, perhaps he knows more than he's letting on."

Charlie shook her head. "This has nothing to do with Livesey. How old is this ship?"

Suliman could only offer an estimate. "The original hull structure is about one hundred and seventy years, give or take."

Charlie nodded. "You can't see it, but underneath Thale's log is an original and unaltered shipping roll from the Triumvirate. Would a cargo vessel like the Millstone have a record of all shipping data while in service, including Seeker movement and training?"

Suliman failed to see what Charlie was getting at. "These are standard records, Doc."

Charlie waved her reader around. "Are you telling me then, if we search the Millstone's shipping roll, it won't show the launch of all twenty Seeker ships at the allotted time?"

Suliman got to his feet and dusted off a calendar terminal. The roll was there but showed only the launch of nineteen Seeker ships, all on schedule. Charlie joined him; she'd expected the roll to show twenty ships launched, not nineteen. "Then this roll correlates with Thale's original uneclipsed version," she said. "On his data, it shows Seeker-20 didn't launch until a clear five weeks later."

"Why would the Triumvirate modify the data?" Suliman said. "What would be the point?"

"Not Triumvirate—" Charlie grinned a little, allowing herself a minor triumph at remembering Sam's algorithms, "—Nexists posing as Triumvirate. I believe the espionage within the Triumvirate was Nexist too, including the cover-up of Seeker-20."

"These rolls are automated. No-one troubles themselves checking unless there's a problem, and each ship gets a hundred each day."

Charlie nodded. "The Nexists know that. They relied on each captain's apathy not to check the data thoroughly after it was altered," she said, the pieces fitting together. She just had to explain it coherently to Suliman. "Seeker-20s launch didn't show on the autodata; how could it? Whoever wanted to hide the fact that Seeker-20 didn't launch on time had to go back to the source and rewrite the information."

"So why didn't this roll update?" Suliman asked. "Why didn't the autodata amend the entry after the Nexists tampered with the official version?"

Charlie thought for a moment. "Where was the Millstone when the Seekers launched?"

Suliman shrugged. "At the time? Just about to be

impounded on Mars."

"Powered down?"

Suliman nodded slowly and raised his eyebrows as Charlie's meaning dawned on him. "I only have the original information. I lost the Millstone for a year, and it wouldn't have updated when I got it back. It would have defaulted to the most recent saved data."

Charlie laughed. "Thank goodness for old technology! I found something else as well in Thale's data. I bet when they were putting in the Millstone's Mag engines, they had the ship in at least lower power. Check to see if the shipping data updated recent activity; it will be eclipsed, but we'll still be able to extract it."

Charlie moved aside several layers to find a single entry displaying the unique signature of Seeker-20 as it entered the system.

"Now we can see beyond the tampering, it adds to what Sam told me. The ship came back a full year before Miller said it did."

Suliman grinned. "And they reckoned without Sam Mead telling you how to extract that information."

"They also reckoned without me finding this…" Charlie opened the piece of prose from Seeker-20. "The location of the door. In their tampering, someone eclipsed its coordinates. Miller believed he only had coordinates of this moon taken from Seeker-20. It must have been an error, but Sam didn't examine the report. Livesey is right; we need to move the ship. I bet the door is visible."

Suliman entered the coordinates, and the sensor

found the door easily. "I wonder who it is that Miller is out to get," he said.

Charlie gave that a moment's thought. "Is there any possibility, however remote, a member of this alien race has already made contact in the past, made themselves known to the Nexists, got rejected, stole Seeker-20 and is the person Miller plans on assassinating?"

Suliman had no answer for her other than it was damned convoluted. He was sure they were missing something. Surely Miller wouldn't be arrogant enough to believe sending a ship to assassinate a member of a superior alien race would go unnoticed and unpunished? That alone would be a good reason for the aliens to instigate an interplanetary war. He said as much to Charlie.

She listened to what he had to say, but she'd thought long and hard about this.

"I think Earth, maybe even the Triumvirate *is* in danger, and I don't think that danger is from invasion by an alien race. I think the danger is Miller and the Nexists. Whoever Miller wants dead may just be the key to solving that mystery. We need to get to that person before Thale."

CHAPTER SIXTEEN _

They found the door easily, and as described in the prose, tightly sealed. Livesey volunteered to remain behind again, where he could view the door through the viewport.

Rice examined the surroundings. "This is a pylon. In ancient times, a gateway."

"There must be some means of opening it," Thale said, his frustration showing as he resorted to hammering on the rock face.

Rice took a few steps back, whispering in fear. "It might be a tomb."

Suliman tried enhancing the sensor images. They showed the energy glowing behind the door but no means of access. Irritatingly, with limited range on the portable device, he couldn't be sure of its accuracy. "If this is an advanced civilisation," he said, "chances are it involves technology, so maybe the door is controlled remotely. If they're expecting us, they'll open it."

Charlie looked around at the still, grey landscape as a

shiver made its way up her spine.

"That means they're watching," she murmured.

So far, they'd found no indication of life, and now they stood in the same spot described in the prose. Meanwhile, the moon gave up none of its secrets, their footprints the only disturbance in the dust.

Suliman tethered Charlie to his belt.

"Jump," he instructed. "Look for something above the door, an activation portal or beam."

Charlie gave herself a push, and after a few stomach-churning moments as she rocked to regain balance, Suliman gripped her ankles, and she settled on his shoulders. She found nothing above the door, even after waving her arms around. Defeated, they returned to the ship.

"I've taken a sweep of the entire surface of the door and the surrounding rock face," Livesey reported as he met them at the airlock. "I can't see any mechanism that would open it."

Charlie nodded. "There's nothing. Suliman thinks it's controlled from elsewhere. Livesey, how close are we to the blue planet?"

"About 385,000 k's."

"Perhaps we should head there. We might have better luck."

Thale, agitated and disappointed at their failure to gain entry, disagreed. "We need to view what's behind that door," he hissed as he banged about the cockpit, far too stressed for Charlie's liking. She tried to calm him, but that just made him angrier. "The door, Doctor Maitland," he shouted. "We need to open the door. There's no evidence she ever made it to the planet."

Suliman and Charlie looked at each other. *She?* That narrowed it down.

Thale pulled off his gloves and threw them to the ground. "We'll try again as soon as the suits have reset."

The next time they went out, Livesey requested to go with them. Thale didn't care who went as long as they made themselves useful, and so far, Rice hadn't. Charlie studied Livesey's face as he dressed in the life suit. Something, *something* he wasn't telling them.

Rice's relief at staying behind was tempered by the concern he couldn't fly the ship in an emergency, made worse when Suliman slapped him on the back, saying, "Just keep an eye out for giant space monsters."

Rice pulled a face. "Many true words are spoken in jest, Suliman."

Suliman pulled on his helmet with a sideways glance. "Who said I was joking?"

Charlie's initial fascination with the moonscape dwindled after they found the door. If they couldn't get in, then what? And if they did, then also what. She doubted even Thale knew what to do next. His determination to gain entry suggested he believed this might be the journey's end, a possibility that worried both Charlie and Suliman.

They found the door as before, shut tight, unyielding.

Until Livesey leant against it. The door then woke from its resolute slumber and lifted, revealing a dimly lit cavern within. Livesey entered first, followed by Thale and Suliman.

The cave was not large enough to accommodate all four, so Charlie remained at the entrance. The muted light source came from an elegant, pendulum-like crystal shard about two metres in length, suspended by no visible means above a raised central altar. Besides this central adornment, the cave was empty. There were no bodies to suggest a crypt or any other form of use. The three men walked around the gleaming artefact.

"What do you suppose it is?" Suliman said.

Thale touched the shard, then curled his hand away as an almost imperceptible surge of light touched the tip of his finger.

"I have no idea. Image it, Suliman," he ordered. "Perhaps Rice has seen this kind of thing before. It might be an artefact from an ancient civilisation, although there are no signs of this moon ever being colonised."

"It might be a warning beacon," Charlie commed.

"It might," Suliman commed back, "but it's not doing anything. The only place it could warn would be that blue planet or other ships in the vicinity, and we haven't detected…"

Suliman's voice faded as a low humming filled the cave. They looked around for the source, but it seemed more prudent to head for the exit. The shard rotated and tilted, positioning itself as an arrowhead when finding its target. In an instant, Thale vanished. Suliman and Livesey made for the door, but it simply waited for them to pass through, then rumbled closed behind them. As if the artefact had got what it wanted.

Outside, the three crewmates stared at the door in astonishment. Suliman voiced their disbelief. "What the hell was that?"

"It took Thale!" Charlie's feelings vacillated between dread and relief. "Why would it take Thale and not us?"

Predictably, Rice flew into a panic at seeing only three return and listened to the story in horror, hands over his mouth as his crewmates recounted the incident. He didn't like Thale, and if anyone had to be abducted by aliens, he was glad it was him and not one of the others. The artefact's power might also not be confined to the cave, and Rice offered the possibility it might get them here on the ship. But with the door tightly shut, that didn't seem likely. Suliman showed him the image of the artefact.

"An arrowhead?" Rice suggested. "Although if it's glass, as you say, it seems an odd material to use as a weapon. See this feathering around the edge? There are a few Venusian symbols that incorporate those shapes. Historians generally agree that they are purely decorative and have no real meaning; they are just fashions that have been passed down through history. The overlap makes me think it denotes familial connections, maybe generational links, but nothing in current use. I don't know, the adornment would almost certainly continue, but you haven't caught the complete image." He shook his head.

"I'd have to examine it, and I'm not going in there. It doesn't seem friendly."

Suliman glanced at Charlie. Perhaps now is the best time to tell Rice and Livesey what they knew. "Thale wasn't friendly, anyway, Rice. He's wearing a pericardial detonator."

Rice didn't understand, so Charlie explained. It took a moment for the meaning to dawn on him. "He is *not*," he scoffed, "what a lot of rubbish!"

"He is," Charlie confirmed, "and from what we've discovered, we suspect he'll make sure we don't make a return journey."

Rice blew out his breath. "So, Thale is the bomb?" Charlie nodded. Rice had to believe her, but still he eyed her suspiciously, "How come you know all this —" he pointed to Livesey, "and we don't?"

"We were worried you might…blab," Suliman said.

"Me?" Rice looked hurt. "I would never…" But even as the denial left his lips, he knew it to be true. Keeping his mouth shut, especially under stress, wasn't his strong point. Look where it got him.

Suliman and Charlie told Livesey and Rice everything they knew. Livesey listened quietly; he'd already made up his mind about Thale. Rice couldn't stay in his seat, his anxiety making Charlie glad they waited to tell him. The knowledge would likely have become such a burden that he would have blurted out all their suspicions to Thale.

"I thought he was okay," Rice groaned, running his hands through his shock of red hair. "He seemed to be warming to us."

Suliman shook his head in disbelief, and Charlie hid a grin. "Rice, I think his allegiance is to Miller," she said, "or the Nexists."

"There haven't been true active Nexists for years," Rice reasoned, trying to make sense of what he'd just heard. "Only sympathisers. Real Nexists are history. You heard Thale; he's a creationist. Nexists are nutjobs."

"I don't think so," Charlie said as she offered Rice Livesey's research. Even Livesey was intrigued to see it deciphered, however crudely.

Rice looked up at Suliman, wide-eyed. "So, this is a Nexist plot to get rid of us?"

"What!?" Suliman whacked Rice on the head with his glove. "No, you idiot, they don't care about us. Miller wants Thale to deliver a message, to whom I have no idea and what about, I have no idea about that either. Charlie thinks Earth is in danger from Miller, and this person holds the key, but without Thale, who I suppose possesses that knowledge, we aren't likely to find out. I haven't a clue where we go from here."

"I have a theory," Livesey said. "Thale confirmed my suspicions when he referred to the messenger as 'she'."

He had their attention.

"Do you remember that scientist who died in a shuttle explosion on Rille Base just after the Seeker launch?" he began. Charlie would be too young, but Suliman remembered because he was in confinement on Mars and a captive audience. Livesey was also young, but he knew of it. In later years, he researched the events surrounding the disaster. It hadn't generated much interest at the time, although it might now among his colleagues. "That scientist was my grandmother, Rebecca Allardice."

"Governor Miller's maternal family are Allardice," Rice said. "Is that who you mean?"

"Yes. I think she may have taken the Seeker ship."

Suliman settled himself into the pilot's seat. Whatever Livesey knew, he'd better have a good reason for keeping it quiet. "What makes you think that?"

"Well, Suliman, I was a child when it happened, but like I said before, I'm exceptionally good at eavesdropping. I listened in on a comms connection between my uncle and grandfather. My uncle wanted someone dead, but my grandfather refused to sanction an assassination. Days later, the explosion happened, and they told me my grandmother had been killed. Something about it stayed with me, and years later, I researched the events, and none of it added up. Now, I believe the explosion was for show, a way to explain her absence."

"Why would they want her dead?" Charlie asked.

Livesey shrugged. "I'm not sure. Both my grandparents were covert Nexists, but not to the fanatical extent my uncle is. I think she knew something they didn't want her to know."

"Any idea what that was?"

"No, Charlie, I don't, but I suspect the Nexists intend to resurrect their plans to take over the Triumvirate. Thale's right, they're gaining numbers."

Suliman demanded to know why he hadn't told them this before.

"It's a theory. I might be way off. Besides, we're on a suicide mission. Not much point in speculating too much."

"Of course, there's a point!" Charlie exploded. "If we join the dots, we see that Rebecca Allardice, aka Governor Miller's mother, who he wanted dead, escaped in the Seeker ship, contacted an advanced civilisation and sent back the module with a message to her son that she survived. What if your grandmother had information that would expose the Nexists? To Miller, this may very well equate to a thwarting of the Nexist takeover if she enlists the aid of that advanced civilisation. *This*—this mission is the assassination his father wouldn't sanction, and Thale is the weapon!"

Suliman raised his hand. They hadn't exactly been forthcoming with their knowledge of Thale either, so they couldn't attack Livesey for doing the same thing.

"Calm down, Doc," he said. "Knowing her identity doesn't help us right now, but it does add weight to your theory that the Nexists are planning a coup. Livesey, do you know if the Nexists were mobilising twenty-two years ago when the Seekers launched? Would your nanna have known about it? More to the point, would she have been aware of the actual existence of an alien race where she could go for sanctuary?"

"The Nexists have always planned to dominate the Triumvirate," Livesey said, then nodded, "It's possible my grandmother may have known of the plot and resisted them, but she was a Nexist herself, so I can't even guess her reasoning, unless she abandoned her beliefs. No-one leaves the Nexists. I can't answer your last point; I just don't know."

"Come on, Livesey," Suliman responded, "I'm not disputing what you're saying, but Nexism twenty-two years ago was not much more than a few dozen agitators; even they would have had difficulty explaining why they killed someone because she changed her views. If this Rebecca went to the trouble to steal a booby-trapped Seeker ship, how come it didn't disintegrate with her in it, and when it didn't, why would she send it back? Why would Miller send us out to find her and then blow us all up?"

Livesey shook his head. "You're wrong about the Nexists, Suliman. They never went away, and Rebecca Allardice represents something my uncle doesn't want. We know now not all the Seeker ships disintegrated. As for the alien civilisation? Perhaps the Nexists are right. Perhaps Rice's document is authentic, and beings from another galaxy settled Venus and Earth. Either way, the Nexists don't want them sticking their noses in."

It didn't take a mind-reader to know Livesey wasn't giving them everything. Charlie tried to make eye contact, but he just turned away. Suliman, however, was more forthright.

"What does she represent? Livesey, stop being so bloody mysterious!" he blasted.

"I'm not sure." Livesey sat back and folded his arms. "I'm not sure about any of it, but that report you showed me, Charlie, I remember her telling me a story when I was a kid. It was kind of like that. She probably told her son the same story."

Suliman glanced at Charlie. She'd been right.

"Well, I vote we return to Earth and say we lost Thale in the cave," Rice suggested.

Suliman sighed. Running was always Rice's advice. "Think, Rice. Would Miller welcome us?"

Rice liked easy questions. "No, but we could land on Venus and go straight to the Triumvirate." Even as he said it, the wisdom of Suliman's words dawned on him, and while space held no fascination, he didn't fancy being on the run from the Nexists for the rest of his life either. His expression showed he withdrew his earlier suggestion.

"What if the Nexists *are* planning a coup?" Charlie said. "We'd end up as dead as if Thale blew us up." She looked through the viewport at the blue planet. "Let's go there and see if we can find this Rebecca Allardice."

Suliman agreed and fired up a launch sequence. "She may just be a theory."

"I bet it's a theory that's close to home."

Suliman granted Charlie that much; they had little to go on anyway. "If the Nexists are successful in a takeover of the Triumvirate," he said, "I suspect their vision hasn't changed. They'll separate Earth and Venus; that was their plan during the civil war."

Charlie suddenly regretted finding the Nexist question so dull during her education. "Why separate Venus?"

"Nexists never dropped the idea of the Myth of

Origin," Rice said. "It's a fundamental Nexist ideology that Venusians didn't colonise Earth. That Earthers are superior."

"But not as superior as the beings who created Earthers?" Charlie remembered then why she lost interest in history. It boggled her mind.

"That's right, but Nexists don't want them either. They say Earthers should keep their purity, no Venusian dilution and no interference from any aliens, regardless."

Rice did his best to bring Charlie up to speed with a crash course in history, and Suliman did the same with politics, but it didn't matter what any of them thought or speculated; as soon as the ship cleared orbit of the moon, the controls became unresponsive.

"Tractor beam?" Livesey suggested.

Suliman shook his head. "No, I can't understand it. Someone or something has overridden the controls."

"I knew it!" Rice babbled. "The thing that grabbed Thale is after us now!"

"Calm down, Rice, we're not heading back to the moon," Suliman said. "We're in one piece, but you're right, we can't trust anything out here."

Charlie reached forward and patted Rice's shoulder. He glanced behind and attempted a smile. "I'm okay, Charlie," he lied. "I don't like not being in control."

Charlie suggested they had come under some kind of guidance. She tried to make it sound benign, not to alarm Rice any further, and kept her voice steady.

"It may be possible the blue planet is where 'they'

need us to be," she said, her false confidence rewarded when Rice took a couple of deep breaths to regain composure, at least until the next surprise.

"Why not just vanish us like they did Thale?" he asked.

"They probably guessed Thale wasn't alone," Livesey said. "Or maybe we might need to be in direct proximity of the artefact."

Suliman swivelled his seat to face them. "Whatever it is, I can't regain control. We'll just have to wait it out. They haven't ignited Mag, whoever 'they' are, and we aren't on a course to crash into the planet."

The crew watched the blue world loom large in the viewport. Clouds swirled around the poles, oceans appeared, and twinkling lights from cities became visible as they flew closer to the surface. It brought up the question of population density.

Suliman pulled up the Seeker ship data. "Unfortunately, there's no information beyond the little we know about that moon. I think that was the farthest the Seeker ship ever got." He turned back to the controls. "I can try a sensor sweep."

The ship allowed them at least that much. "I can't believe this," he exclaimed. "Only three hundred million people, mostly concentrated in the Northern Hemisphere. The Antipodes and Eastern Asia appear devoid of population density, no human life, but dense vegetation. At a guess, I'd say the few life signs are animals. There are settlements on the Western Continents. This is curious…"

Suliman enlarged a sensor view of the planet for them all to see. Charlie had difficulty making out anything other than a sparsely populated world. "What's curious?" she asked.

"Every settlement," Suliman pointed out as the image of the planet revolved between them, "and some are vast, is surrounded either by desert or water. Some even have forcefields."

"To keep people out?"

Suliman half nodded, half shook his head. "Or in. It looks like we're heading for an island in the Northwest region. Going by the sensors, the temperature suggests the area is in early winter. There's dense forestation, but the forcefield extends way beyond. We can hide the ship amongst the greenery. From the trajectory, it means a long walk to any kind of civilisation. I expect whoever is guiding us doesn't want the inhabitants to see the ship." He shrugged. "Maybe the general population isn't technologically advanced."

Rice's eyes were as round as saucers. "But there are aliens who took over our controls," he said, his voice wobbling as his earlier moment of calmness fled. "Maybe they ate everyone! Maybe they breed humans for food!" Right now, he longed for one of Charlie's hugs.

As the Millstone came to rest, Suliman stood. "I meant the locals, Rice. They may not know there is alien technology on their world. Here—" he tossed Rice a jacket, "don't catch a cold."

"I want to wait here with the ship," Rice complained

as he looked from the jacket to the wintery scene outside.

Suliman pulled the unwilling Rice from his seat. "You're a historian, Rice. If anyone can make sense of this society, it's you."

CHAPTER SEVENTEEN _

The four crewmates made noble but largely ineffective attempts to camouflage the Millstone with leaves and branches. The task proved monumental, so they just had to hope this wasn't a popular picnicking spot, where the discovery of a spaceship would send the locals into a panic.

Suliman pointed out that none of the vegetation looked trodden down, signalling it was likely a place not often visited. "With a bit of luck," he said, "whoever's looking for us finds us quickly."

"What do you mean, 'whoever'?" Rice's voice took on its timid, frightened tone. He'd just got used to them being called "they". Now it was "whoever". He tried not to make his obvious cowering beside Charlie, well, obvious.

Suliman peered down at the frightened professor. "The ship got sent back, Thale got vanished. Whoever it is, Livesey's nanna or someone else seems to be holding all the aces. Take comfort in the fact there doesn't appear to be any hostile intentions towards us."

"It's a good point," Charlie agreed, giving Rice a gentle shove to stop him using her as a shield. "Unlike the ship, perhaps we need to be conspicuous."

"Seizing control of the Millstone seems hostile to me," Rice grumbled, but his protest went unheard.

Suliman pointed to what appeared to be signs of civilisation in the distance, suggesting, with a jerk of his head, that the others follow him. The walk took over two hours, peppered with irritating comments from Rice about the potential toxicity of the plants they couldn't avoid brushing against. Livesey seemed distracted and hardly spoke, and all three wished Suliman didn't take such long strides.

The town had an ancient and dated appearance, its ambience depressed and colourless. The sky above seemed low and oppressive, filled with the promise of rain. The historical buildings seemed vaguely recognisable to Charlie, as if she'd read about or seen pictures of them somewhere. A river that delivered an eye-watering stink ran under an ornate bridge that spanned two embankments. But the smell mattered little to Rice. His eyes lit up with enthusiasm as they left the wasteland behind, his face shining and energised as he lifted his arms to embrace the view.

"This must be a re-creation of London in the twentieth century," he proclaimed, reminding Charlie of where she'd seen illustrations of these buildings before. History books at school, although she couldn't see how buildings from across the galaxy got into her school's history curriculum.

"A re-creation?" Suliman asked, also feeling a stir of remembrance.

"Yes," Rice replied, his eyes bright with excitement, nervousness miraculously dispelled. "And a damned good one. Whoever set it up must have an outstanding knowledge of our history. Look at the attention to detail!" Rice turned in circles, embracing the view. He stopped spinning as the last revolution squared him up with Livesey. "Was your grandmother a historian?" he asked.

"Er, no, Rice," Livesey shook his head. "A botanist, I think."

Rice ran his hand over the parapet of the bridge. "This feels so real!"

"Is it possible it is?" Livesey said. "And this is a parallel Earth?"

Rice wasn't listening. The others watched him, behaving like a thrilled kid in a candy store, gushing about the detail of the buildings, pointing out architectural features, people's clothing— *humans*—he stressed, and anything that caught his eye. He carried on until Suliman had enough.

"Rice!" he snapped. Rice stopped. He didn't like it when Suliman shouted. "I can see a place like this is fairyland to a historian," he said, "but I'm with Livesey on this. I don't believe this is a re-creation." Suliman glanced at Livesey. "I'm not sure about the parallel world either."

Charlie pointed to a sad, faded red vehicle drifting along the precinct, setting off Rice's enthusiasm anew.

"Buses. It's got buses!" Rice buzzed as he clapped his

hands together in delight. "And this is a street."

"Like avenues?" Charlie said. "They had this layout on Kate Winstanley's planet. I wonder if their ancestors, or even ours, came from here. All this can't be a coincidence."

Rice looked up at the sky, then at the pavement beneath his feet, then watched the people passing by. He eyeballed Charlie. If her theory was correct, she'd just burst a bubble. It would mean the history of Earth, their Earth…

Rice screwed his face from left to right and shook his head. He'd need convincing of that.

"It doesn't look as if they've achieved space travel. If anything, it looks like time stood still."

A second bus trundled into view. "Do buses fly?" Livesey asked.

"No, they just convey people from one point to the other," Rice explained flatly. "They had cars too, like little buses with wheels, but I can't see any. Did you not take history at school?"

"I did for a while," Charlie interjected. "I recognise some of these buildings."

"What language did they speak?" Suliman was not interested in history. He wanted to discover who hijacked them, why, and if they could communicate with the people here.

Rice adjusted his confusion and disappointment and pointed to a group of young people. "They're speaking English."

"Great!" Suliman threw up his hands. "None of us speaks English. Anyway, it's a dead language. Who'd bother?"

"*I* bothered," Rice informed him.

Charlie reminded him of his distinct lack of language ability on Kate's world. Rice conceded he hadn't fared well with that particular dialect.

"English has the same root, but I studied it more. Except I didn't have anyone to practise on, so there may be some inaccuracies."

"Okay, we all need to decide what to do next." Charlie didn't want any of them to assume Suliman, or heaven forbid, she was in command now with Thale gone.

"I think we need to get our bearings and wait for whoever brought us here to give us directions," Rice announced sensibly. He looked around. He just couldn't get over being amongst this history, real or re-created. He felt his enthusiasm returning; this was just too good an opportunity, and he quickly became overwhelmed once more. "See that enormous building next to the river? That's the House of the Parliament, and the tall structure next to it is Big Ben."

Suliman sighed, but he agreed with Rice they couldn't just wander without purpose. "Big Ben?" he said without interest.

"Yes." Rice had decided at the very least he was in a living museum. "It's a clock. It's for telling time."

"Imagine that," Suliman answered. "Telling time, huh? What does it tell it?"

"It doesn't tell time anything, Suliman." The sarcasm got lost as Rice dredged up an explanation. "Clocks told the people where they were in a day, either the morning or the afternoon and exactly what part. Perhaps more accurately, it *shows* the time."

Charlie studied the gigantic face set atop a perpendicular tower. "How does it work?"

"Well," Rice pointed up, happy to have a student. "You see all those symbols set in a circle?"

Charlie nodded.

"They're Roman Numerals," Rice told her. "Like numbers. I can read them."

"What do the two pointy arms mean?" Charlie had encountered Roman Numerals in old documents during her medical training, so they didn't seem so strange.

"Those are hands." Rice stretched out his arms like a semaphore to bolster his explanation. "When the big hand points straight up, it's something o'clock, and when the little hand points to a number, say two, it's two o'clock."

"What's the 'o'clock'."

"Of the clock, Charlie. Two of the clock."

"Do you have to know how to read Roman Numerals?" Suliman said.

"Well, it would help."

Charlie pondered the clock face. "I know some Roman Numerals. That little hand is between three and four. Is that right?" Rice nodded. "And the big hand is pointing to seven, I think?"

Rice nodded again. "The clock is telling us it's twenty-five to four."

Charlie's newly discovered remembrance of Roman

Numerals took a dive.

"How does seven denote twenty-five?"

Rice couldn't wait to explain the nuances of clocks. "Each hour comprises minutes…"

But by now, Suliman was bored. "It might be best we save this for later. Let's look around."

Livesey agreed. Rice *was* boring. "Shall we split up?"

"Probably not," Suliman said. "Charlie, did you bring your reader?"

Charlie held the device up for them all to see. "It's flashing a symbol," she said, "but I don't know what all these lines and icons are. We seem to have linked to some kind of local network. I can try to decode it."

Livesey's eyes lit up. "I smell coffee, let's stop and make a plan, see if we can work out Charlie's reader."

They followed the exquisite coffee aroma that for a short walk, camouflaged the smell of the stinky river. The delectable scent came from a café not unlike the cafes on Earth, with tables and seats, but instead of serving droids and holographic interfaces, a young woman, the sole occupant of the café, worked behind a counter. She smiled warmly as they entered. As they sat down, the young woman called out and pointed to a sign above her head.

"Okay, Rice," Suliman said. "Time to flex your English muscles. What does it say?"

Rice squinted at the sign and bit his lip. He could only afford part certain, part guess. "Order here, I think."

"Okay, go and order coffee."

Rice went up to the counter, glancing back at Charlie

for moral support. He would likely make a colossal ass out of himself, so he erred on the side of caution and stated simply, "Coffee."

The young woman's smile stayed bright, even when her customers didn't display common courtesy and say, "please".

"Cappuccino? Latte? Short black? Macchiato?"

Makky-what? Rice stared. He'd never heard of these. Then, not wanting to try the woman's patience, he picked the first one she suggested, deducing that would be the most common as it was her first offering.

The young woman opened her hand. "Three pounds, sir."

Rice nodded, but he didn't understand. Three pounds. An ancient measure of weight. Why would she mention this? Did they supply coffee by weight? Not in cups? Seeing the confusion spreading on his face, the woman repeated herself. It was then Rice spied a motif on food in a display cabinet. Excusing himself with a mumble, he went back to the others.

"In ancient times, they exchanged currency for goods," he told them. "We don't have any of their currency."

"Where do we get some?" The idea stumped Charlie. Currency at home only related to education, careers and infrastructure. Not food.

The young woman approached and spoke pleasantly. "I suppose you're visitors. You sound foreign. I get little custom this time of the year, and I'm just about to close up. Coffee's on the house because I'm cleaning the machine. Next time, bring money."

Rice translated but only got the gist she was donating the coffee because they were poor. They all smiled and made noises that they hoped sounded enough like "thanks".

"Would they get visitors here who spoke other languages?" Livesey asked.

"Centuries ago," Rice said, "everyone spoke different languages until Universal. Let's assume we're in England. Perhaps people from the continent visit. You can visit the island of England from the continent on our Earth."

"This country is surrounded by sea, and the technology isn't very advanced," Charlie pointed out, scanning her reader for anything that might help. She held up her results. "They might have sailing ships."

Rice agreed. "Seems reasonable, but if there's a forcefield around this island, perhaps that lady thought we were Scottish or Welsh. The forcefield extends that far, and those areas seem to be part of the mainland."

Suliman handed Rice a large, folded document. "I picked this up while you were ordering. I think it's a map of sorts. It's got lines like on the doc's reader. Can you read it?"

Rice opened the paper. "It is a map. Compare it with Charlie's reader, see if any of these words match that red beacon."

A single point seemed to correspond to the lines on Charlie's reader, and Rice read the words on the printed map. "Wormwood Scrubs," he spelt out. "That must be where they want us to go."

"Is it far?" Suliman asked.

Rice shook his head. "Not according to this." Then he looked up with a smile. "It sounds charming. Perhaps it's a herb garden."

"What are those other words?" Suliman underlined a few words that flashed red.

"No. Go. No go? Maybe we can't go there."

"D'you think?"

Rice pulled a face. "I'm doing my best, Suliman."

"Why would they lead us to a no-go area," Livesey asked. "Something secret? Like an alien ship?"

Charlie called over the waitress. "Let's ask." Unfortunately, the woman either didn't understand Rice's posing of the question, their frantic pointing at the map, or she chose not to. The group quickly realised they would get no answers just sitting there.

Once more, back in the street, a man walking past brushed them aside when approached. A young couple stopped but chuckled when Rice showed them the map and strolled off, shaking their heads. Eventually, a man told Rice they needed the tube and pointed across the street.

He reported the man's instructions. "We need a tube."

Such a baffling language. "A tube of what?" Charlie asked.

"He didn't say."

Sometimes the professor's timidity exasperated Suliman. "Why didn't you ask him, you idiot?"

"He looked at me as if I was stupid."

They sent Rice to stop someone else and enquire about "tube" and "Wormwood Scrubs". As they watched his many futile attempts to get folk to explain, they wondered why these people were so unhelpful. The girl in the café had been pleasant enough, but these individuals—one glance at the group and hearing Rice's halting efforts at the language, heads went down, and they hurried by. After repeated attempts, Rice finally returned with information.

"The tube is a mode of transport, but I think we'll need currency."

"We can steal some."

"Suliman!" Charlie exclaimed, horrified.

"Got a better idea?"

Charlie shut up. She had to admit she didn't. Suliman pointed discreetly along the precinct.

"That man over there with those packages on a stand, someone just selected a packet and gave the man something in return. If this is a transaction, it's probably currency." He turned abruptly and strode towards the stand. "One of you divert him. I'll get the currency."

Wordlessly and without a plan, Charlie and Livesey trailed behind. As Suliman reached the kiosk, Livesey fell to the ground, writhing in theatrical agony. Charlie leapt to his side, patting his face until he settled, holding up her hand to keep away the crowd that gathered to watch. As soon as she saw Suliman signal he'd carried out the robbery, Livesey made a spectacular recovery. Helping him to his feet, they hurried away, locating Suliman and Rice behind a hedge at the base of an enormous old building.

"Damn fine acting Livesey," Suliman grinned.

"Did you get currency?"

Suliman held out a roll of notes to Rice. "I think it's currency. We'll soon find out when we try to use it."

"Yes, it is," Rice confirmed. "It's called 'money'. Okay, let's go on this tube."

They found the section the man pointed out, but Rice couldn't make out a word that looked like "tube". His shoulders slumped when he realised the implications. "Oh my, I'm going to have to ask someone else."

"You did well before," Charlie encouraged him. "Try that man, the one carrying the furry beast."

From the gesticulating, it was apparent Rice was having a problem making himself understood. He came back. "The man's demanding payment."

Suliman handed Rice a note of the currency. "Give him one of these." Rice returned to the man, who upon seeing the note, broke into loud snorts of laughter. He then pointed to an area just off to their side, shoved the furry animal at Rice, then sprinted off as fast as his legs could carry him. Rice came back with the creature in his arms.

"What is it?" Charlie giggled at the wriggling little beast. Whatever it was, it seemed thrilled to see them, depositing its saliva over their faces and ears with long strokes of its pink tongue. Its breath smelt like fresh toast, and it made little noises that seemed to convey delight. It had a short, pointed nose, enormous eyes, and an appendage at the end of its back that moved briskly from side to side. Covered in black fur with a streak of white under its neck, it didn't smell nice, and as they discovered as it greeted them, it had sharp, pointed teeth.

Rice examined the creature. "I think it's a young dog. Our forebears called them puppies. They've been extinct for hundreds of years. There's not even a skeleton to be studied." He looked around. "I love history, even though this place...well, none of it makes sense. Money for coffee, extinct animals. I don't know what to make of it."

"Did you find out about the tube?" Suliman said, impatient to get moving.

"Yes." Rice pointed to a sign. "That's it. The Underground."

Steps led them below street level until they found themselves on a terrace with tunnels running either side.

"Look," Charlie said. "There's a clock."

"And a map." Rice diverted their attention to a picture of networks. "It says 'Journey Planner'. We need to do that, find out how to get to this Wormwood Scrubs."

Suliman took out the roll of notes. "Do we pay to go on the tube?"

Rice took the money. "There's a counter like the café. There, maybe?" But he returned almost immediately.

"The man behind the counter says no dogs, so I suppose that confirms this is a dog."

"Well, let it go."

"I can't do that, Suliman," Rice wailed. "It's cruel. It's a baby."

"For crying out loud, Rice."

Livesey made to take the dog from Rice's arms. "Give it to me. I'll take it back upstairs."

Rice held the pup close for a moment before handing it over, and with his face a picture of disappointment, watched as Livesey sprinted back the way they'd come, returning just as a rush of air heralded the arrival of the tube.

They all stared at the "tube".

"This is a train," Rice observed. "I wonder why they call it a tube?"

Livesey had a theory. "Perhaps because it looks like it's going inside a tube? Or being squeezed out?" That made sense. As the tube arrived at the platform, it could be reminiscent, with a bit of creative visualisation, of something being squeezed from a container.

In tiny seats, huddled in a row and bumping up against other travellers, Charlie found it claustrophobic, mainly as there was no outside view.

"I feel like I'm in a moving coffin," she declared to the others, who like her, watched the blackness outside flash past.

Their dress and their speech caught the attention of a few people. Some smiled, but most gave them hard looks before turning away. Charlie didn't feel welcome here. Even though these people looked human, they were nothing like the humans at home.

"It would be better if we could see outside," Livesey said.

"There's not much to see in space either," Suliman pointed out logically, "at least not when we engage Mag. That's just mist as well. I don't doubt we miss heaps of incredible sights."

Charlie agreed, but somehow, space didn't feel so confined. What she'd seen so far of this world felt limiting, restricting, cold, drab and dispiriting.

CHAPTER EIGHTEEN _

The train jolted and pitched just like the Millstone, finally grinding to a stop with a deafening shriek of what sounded like air being forced through a narrow cylinder. Rice read the notice outside and stood up, indicating to the others to follow him.

He consulted the journey planner. "We get off here," he said. "We need to take another tube now from Platform 3. According to that sign—" he pointed upwards, "the one with the blue fist and extended finger, Platform 3 is upstairs."

They were all glad to be back out in the light. The next train went overground, and they had the carriage to themselves, but it bounced even more than the tube. At one point, after a notably violent pitch, Livesey's jacket opened, and the puppy's little black face peeped out.

Rice was on the puppy in a flash. "You didn't let it go!" he squealed in delight, kissing the puppy's snout and allowing its pink tongue to kiss him back.

Livesey grinned at the reunion. "I didn't know what would happen to it. It's a terrible thing to be unwanted."

Suliman groaned and rolled his eyes at Charlie, but she just shoved him with her foot.

"Lighten up, Suliman," she laughed. "It's not every day you get to cuddle an extinct animal."

"What if it's not welcome anywhere else?"

Charlie dismissed his concerns. "We'll manage." It was good to see Rice happy.

The train slowed and after one final lurch, ground to a halt. Livesey searched for the mechanism that opened the window before realising he simply had to pull it down. He looked outside. "The front of the train is gone," he reported. "There's a kind of hangar bay with other trains docked." He looked the other way. "The back of the train is gone too. It's just this carriage left, and we seem to be stranded. Wait, there's a man headed this way. Perhaps someone told him about the dog, and they've placed us in quarantine."

Rice had put the puppy on the floor to give it some exercise after being cooped up in Livesey's jacket, so Charlie picked it up and thrust it inside her shirt, where she had to hold it tight to stop it from squirming and being detected. The man, who wore a hat like the ticket seller at the train station, shouted and gestured at them as he wrenched open the door. The hat suggested he had more to do with trains, but his gesturing and show of power suggested law enforcement. Rice translated as best he could, but he didn't understand the man's under-the-breath cursing of foreigners. However, a few words he understood only too well, and they filled him with fear. He turned to the others, his voice a strained whisper.

"They're terminating the train!"

"With us on it?" Charlie clamped the puppy tight to make sure he didn't escape and ushered the others towards the door.

Suliman rose to his feet, his menacing bulk prompting a shift in the train man's attitude. He stopped swearing and stepped backwards, allowing the group to disembark. Suliman curled his lips evilly at the man.

"You're not terminating anything while we're aboard. We're leaving. Don't try to stop us," he bellowed.

It was standard London Transport protocol to issue a warning when passengers missed an announcement and remained on a train in a siding, but the man decided to ignore the rules this time. Besides, he didn't like foreigners; these looked Scottish, and he couldn't make head nor tail of the language, but at least they got off the train. Charlie gave the man a nod as she jumped down from the carriage, a pleasantry the man ignored as he closed the door and walked away. He flapped his hand in a vague gesture of— according to Rice, "Station's that way."

Rice, assured now his life wasn't in immediate danger, trotted after him, making small bowing movements as he pleaded with the man for directions. "Wormwood Scrubs?" he repeated himself over and over until the man stopped walking.

"It's a no go," the man snapped. "You can walk it

from here, across the common, but they'll stop you, mark my words." And he resumed his pace and cursing of "bloody foreigners" as he went. Rice returned to the others and told them what the man said, with a little extra drama chucked in for good measure.

"It's a warning. That man said, '*They* will stop you'," Rice announced as he took the puppy from Charlie and held it tight as if for protection. "Perhaps 'they' is the name of the alien race. He says we have to go across a common." He stopped rambling. "A common? Charlie, show me the map."

With the evening drawing in, there was little natural light. The map appeared to concur with Charlie's reader, but it showed a large, wild tract of land that required navigating. They concluded this was the "common" to which the train man referred. The four crewmates and their dog were less than three kilometres from their target. From that moment, a single deviation, necessary to avoid walking through muddy water, which the puppy splashed through with reckless abandon, was met with an alarm on Charlie's reader, a useful navigation tool, seeing as they had no idea where they were. It also gave them a focal point while jangling their nerves every time it sounded.

Besides the small muddy ponds that dotted their path, the common consisted of thick grass with stunted trees and stinging plants, much like the area where they left the Millstone. The grey skies delivered on their promise of rain but obligingly kept it to a light drizzle that still chilled them to the bone. When a dismal-looking, walled structure rose up ahead, they breathed a sigh of relief.

"Do you think that's it?" Charlie held up her reader. The target glowed steadily, confirming the structure was indeed "it".

Rice peered through the mist. "The entire building is in darkness. I don't think anyone's home. Can you see a door?"

"It's too dark," Suliman said. "I propose we find shelter and wait for them to find us. That place looks like a fortress. If they haven't made contact, we can check it out at first light."

"Good idea," Charlie agreed. "We need to eat."

Livesey drew their attention to several low buildings. "I can smell food. It's coming from over there."

Bright lights lit a section at the edge of the wilderness area. One place, glowing a welcoming red and yellow, looked more promising than the others.

"What does it say?" Charlie asked Rice.

"I'm not sure. It's got a number. Twenty-four—open twenty-four. There's no clock, but I suppose 'twenty-four' means a day. I guess the other word is hours. I don't understand why they would say twenty-four hours instead of saying 'day'. People are coming out of the building and eating from packages."

"Okay," the others said. "Let's try."

The diner had a few patrons and was run by adolescents around twelve or thirteen years old, all with severe acne, bitten fingernails and strange hairstyles. Rice assumed the task of ordering and pointed to a bright, enticing poster depicting appetising cuisine. He said "four" and held up four fingers just in case he got the translation wrong. He understood the child behind the counter's reply, but it puzzled him. Blinking in confusion, he rounded to his friends. "She says, 'Do you want fries with that?'. Do you think it's a question? What do I say?"

"Just say 'yes' to anything," Charlie said. She looked at the others as Rice went back to ordering. "It might be a recommendation," she reasoned. "You know, something that complements the main dish."

Livesey examined the brightly back-lit posters on a stand near the counter. "These look delicious. It's possible that to enhance the dining experience, you need to have other components."

"These are called burgers," Rice informed them as he returned with a tray laden with paper-wrapped items and lidded beakers. "The girl gave me 'milldills'. In milldills, you get a 'soft' drink—I don't know how they make a drink hard or soft—or coffee if you prefer."

They consumed the burgers, fries and coffee under a sheltered porch, where the server directed them after informing them the dog had to stay outside. An extra "kids milldill" was appreciated by the puppy, who rejected the coffee and lettuce but scoffed down the meat patties and bread. It finished off its meal with a few licks at a rainwater puddle.

"They don't seem to like dogs much here," Livesey said.

Rice put the puppy on his lap, grimacing at the paw

marks left on his shirt by its wet feet, and wrinkling up his nose at the wet dog smell. "I once read the domesticated variety was considered man's best friend. They must have done something to upset their masters. That's why they're not allowed inside or on trains."

"He smelled bad before," Charlie said. "It's a darn sight worse since he got rained on. I don't think it can be hygienic to have them around food."

Suliman didn't join the debate, only allowed himself a rare sigh of satisfaction. "If the food here is like this, I might stay."

"Mmm," Charlie agreed through a mouthful of burger. Not about the staying bit, but the greasy food hit the spot on a cold night. "I love these 'fries'," she said between mouthfuls, "they're just like chips, only thinner."

Rice though, unusually pondered other factors than his stomach. "I don't understand why, when you give them money, they take the rectangular-shaped ones, then give you other money that look like discs. History covers little of currency. There are only a dozen examples back on Earth."

"Perhaps its value," Livesey suggested. "Maybe the rectangular ones have a higher value; they subtract their portion and return the lower value."

"Why don't they just use credits?"

"Maybe they haven't evolved to that yet."

"It's an odd place," Rice said, munching his fries and looking around. "I always dreamed of discovering actual history, real artefacts, but I always expected it to be on

Earth or Venus, not halfway across the galaxy."

"This isn't history to the people living here," Livesey pointed out. "It's modern times."

Rice nodded absently. His earlier enthusiasm had given way to a kind of anti-climax. History represented an unknown and exciting world to him, a world of discovery. He wondered if this place had museums; he wouldn't mind exploring one, perhaps as a prelude to studying history here, that is if they got stuck. The sudden thought filled him with angst, so to distract himself, he turned his attention to the posters depicting colourful food, spelling out the words that promoted the best value. "Meal Deal," one declared. He looked at the array of food on the table before him. The penny dropped. With all the components together, it comprised a meal. "Milldill" was simply "meal deal" delivered to him in unnuanced English by the child behind the counter.

"Rice?" Suliman pointed upwards, interrupting the professor's moment of reflecting on the local vernacular. "If the sign on the roof means perpetuation, we may be able to stay here until the morning. It's sheltered from the rain."

"I guess," Rice shrugged. "It sounds like a good idea."

The pimply management didn't share Suliman's and Rice's interpretation of "twenty-four hours", threatening to move them on unless they agreed to buy more food and coffee.

An exhausted Charlie put her arms on the table and rested her head. In a moment, she fell fast asleep. Suliman seemed not to need sleep, or he slept with his eyes open, which would have surprised none of them. Rice and Livesey just dozed with lots of caffeine-fuelled twitches between coffees. The puppy snored inside the warmth of Rice's shirt for several hours before its face appeared, ears pricked up and a low growl emanating from its throat.

Suliman responded instantly and put his hand on the dog's head. "What's it doing?"

"I don't know." Rice lifted the puppy onto the table, the hair on the back of its neck stuck up like a brush. "It's vibrating. Do you think it might be a warning?"

The puppy growled towards the gloomiest part of the common, where earlier they'd located what they believed to be Wormwood Scrubs. They all turned to squint in that direction as a tall, lithe figure, covered by a long dark coat, appeared from the darkness. A wide-brimmed hat, equally sombre, was tugged down over the brow. At the sight of the figure, the puppy retreated into Rice's shirt, its moment in the limelight over.

The figure stood over them. It sounded male. "Please come with me," he said in English.

Only Rice understood, but he didn't move, just slid closer to Charlie. The man repeated himself, this time in Universal. Suliman got to his feet, but he didn't match the man for height; nevertheless, he stood his ground. No doubt this was one of the 'they' people, but no harm in making sure. "Now, why would we do that?" he asked.

"Because without me," the tall man said reasonably, "you can't get into Wormwood."

Here they were, on a strange planet, carried by unknown forces, and Suliman was arguing with possibly one of the aliens they came to find. Also, Charlie was freezing. She pushed past him. "We haven't had a better offer," she declared, "and he speaks Universal. Don't forget—" she threw over her shoulder as she went, "You didn't want command, so don't be difficult. Besides, Wormwood might be warmer than out here."

Suliman thought he'd acted sensibly. "Just making sure, Doc."

As they walked, Charlie and Suliman kept up with the luminescent-skinned man and tried to ask questions, but he ignored or deflected each one. He stopped when they arrived at a towering, ornate door marked with studs, set back in the wall surrounding Wormwood Scrubs. The rain had stopped, and the early morning light afforded Rice enough brightness to make out the words hewn into the stone above the studded door.

"HM Prison. Wormwood Scrubs," he recited. "I don't know what HM means. A prison is a place where they kept people who broke the law, but HM? I thought this might be a herb garden. Herb Management, maybe? Perhaps they've outlawed herb cultivation here." He shrugged. "I dunno."

The man watched their study of the words but didn't enlighten them. He waited a moment, then, without shifting his gaze, leaned an elbow against the wall where a second, smaller door appeared. He stood aside and waved them through.

"How can we be sure he represents the people who brought us here," Suliman hissed as he followed Charlie. "There could be opposing factions. And he doesn't look human. Remember, in the town? Some people were very suspicious of us, others more friendly. We could be heading into a trap."

"You got a better idea?" Livesey said, overhearing. "Whoever sent him knows we're here, and he speaks our language. I don't think we've got a choice. And I don't think we're in danger."

"That's good to know."

Charlie raised her eyebrows at Suliman. A man like him would naturally advise caution, but Livesey was right; what choice did they have? They filed past the pale-faced man, Livesey bringing up the rear.

With Rice convinced Wormwood Scrubs sounded like a pristine herb garden, it dismayed him to find it was only a dark corridor, sloping downwards into the bowels of the earth. As they descended its depths, a light glowed at the back of the man's hat to guide them on a walk that took over two hours before they met with a fast-moving walkway that carried them to their destination. A metallic barrier.

"Now we wait," the pale man instructed.

They stood expectantly. And waited. And waited some more. Suliman gave Charlie several huffs and enquiring glances, and each time, she made "How should I know?" faces back.

Eventually, the light on the man's hat blinked off as

he spun and pressed his back against the silvery barricade. His body expanded and flattened, spreading several feet in all directions until he looked like a human pancake. An opening appeared between what was previously his legs. Through the opening, they could see Thale, disappointingly, very much alive. A slightly built, fair-haired woman stood opposite him, alongside a man who, although he appeared protective, was unarmed.

The pancake man's head flipped down, indicating they made procession between his legs into the room. In this rolled-out state, they were unsure he might not just melt all over them, so it seemed wise not to hesitate.

Suliman entered first, taking care not to let his head brush the shapeshifters groin area. He kept Charlie close to him. The woman watched as the little band assembled, a soft smile on her face. She tilted her head when Livesey entered the room, and perhaps her smile became a little warmer. The pancake man's legs closed, and he vanished as the wall behind became solid once more.

Charlie flicked a glance around the room to take stock of her surroundings. The sense of standing on the bridge of a ship or a command centre of sorts came strongly, despite the area not showing signs of instrumentation. No tech, no consoles, no desks, not even a visible viewport, but there was a feeling the place could come to life at any moment. Although cold and thick with the smell of soil, the air was breathable, confirming they'd travelled far below ground. The lighting, white and bright, illuminated so thoroughly, not a single shadow remained. Charlie turned her attention to the woman, who granted them a moment to become accustomed to the transition in both atmosphere and light. Charlie wondered if these individuals knew about Thale's cardiac detonator. If he went off in a confined area like this, it would have devastating consequences for them all. He looked calm enough, but he'd gone over seventy-two hours without pain relief and treatment. Charlie didn't want to think about what was happening in his brain.

"I'm Captain Suliman of the Millstone," Suliman said with uncharacteristic politeness, perhaps because he didn't want to spark off bomb-man Thale. He introduced the others. "Doctor Maitland, Professor Rice, and this is Livesey. And you are?"

The woman laughed. "Captain Suliman, you have questions of greater import than that."

"It would do for a start. Governor Miller sent us here."

"Ah," the woman nodded, her mouth twisting slightly. "Governor Miller." She looked at Livesey. "How long have you known?"

Livesey responded instantly, as though he anticipated the question. "About six years."

"It must have been hard for you to have kept it hidden."

Charlie had no idea what attributes someone like Livesey had that demanded he kept them hidden. He was a passable actor, and he picked up piloting well, but that couldn't be what this woman alluded to.

Typically, Suliman demanded an explanation. "What do you mean, Livesey? What have you known for six years?" He angled back to the woman. "It isn't unreasonable for us to expect a straightforward explanation. If we don't get one, we'll leave." He paused. "I'm assuming we *can* leave?"

"Patience, Captain Suliman," the woman replied, but she seemed preoccupied with speaking to Livesey.

Suliman's face hardened. He couldn't be sure there weren't others invested in the return of the Seeker ship. He'd asked nicely, but the woman didn't answer, so Suliman's other instincts kicked in, which was either drinking himself into oblivion or fighting his way out of a situation, and as no-one so far had offered him a drink...

Charlie laid her hand on his arm. She'd pulled rank once, and she doubted it would work again. These people brought them here; leaving at will might not be possible, so Suliman needn't be a hothead. Taking a leaf from his book, she communicated all of that in a single glance.

Suliman pointed to Thale. "What's his part in all this, whatever 'this' is?" he demanded, drawing the woman's attention.

"Thale disappeared on the moon," Rice announced, giving Thale an edgy look. He didn't like knowing what Thale had in his chest. "The artefact spirited him away."

The woman inclined her head. "The artefact identified a threat."

Charlie knew this had to be Livesey's grandmother. Why couldn't she just say so? And somehow, the artefact picked up Thale's pericardial detonator.

"Do you know how to deactivate the device?" she asked.

The woman looked confused. "Device?"

"Yes, Thale's pericardial detonator. The threat you detected."

The woman darted a sudden, frantic glance to her companion, which told Charlie the detonator was not the threat she meant. Thale's expression turned to thunder.

"How do you know that?" he yelled, his voice pained and grizzled with suffering, but none of that disguised the menace.

Charlie had to wrestle with her own confusion. If the woman didn't mean the pericardial detonator, what did she mean? As she looked at Livesey's grandmother, a gut feeling grew inside her.

"We know about the Nexist sabotage of the Seeker ships," Charlie said to Thale. "We realised early on Miller had an ulterior motive for sending us out here. We pieced things together as we went along and came to the conclusion Miller sent us to find someone—his mother, and silence her…" She turned back to the woman. Charlie's words were not a revelation to her.

Thale would not detonate, Charlie knew it, but he gave her no more time for analysis. He leapt at Rice and locked his arm around the younger man's throat, cutting off his airway. Rice struggled, and Suliman started forward, but Charlie grabbed him as a reminder Thale could still trip the device, and she needed a few more moments to be sure…

Rice was not fit, easily terrified and an easy target for someone like the weakened Thale, who would not have so easily subdued Charlie or Livesey. As Rice gasped for air, the black puppy dropped from his shirt. It tried to defend its new master by attacking Thale, baring its needle-sharp teeth and ripping away part of the attacker's shirt sleeve. He kicked the dog away, and it ran to Charlie for sanctuary, yelping in fear and pain. As she grabbed it, the white light of the room caught a glint of a metal button embedded in Thale's elbow where the dog had torn the fabric.

"I came here to kill you," Thale sneered at the woman, relaxing his grip on Rice just enough to keep him conscious. "Miller understood your message. You will subdue our Earth, bring your alien hordes and contaminate our people with your seed, just like you did on Venus, just like you did with this Earth, and see how it has turned out? Desolate, chaotic, divided, unevolved. The Nexist Mutuality will not stand by while you desecrate our home."

"We are not responsible for what happened here, Commander Thale," the woman said. "Humankind did that for itself. My people colonised your planet in ancient times, and many of your ancestors came from here."

"You lie!" Thale spat his contempt all over the purple-faced Rice's head.

"It is no lie, Commander Thale." The woman's voice remained calm as Thale's agitation grew. "The Nexists are wrong; Supreme beings did not create Earthers. They came from us. From here, and before that, our home planet."

With his plan now revealed, it seemed Thale had no

reason not to activate the device and kill them all. Except he knew what Charlie knew. She handed the puppy to Suliman and lowered her voice, but it wasn't likely anyone would hear, not with Thale ranting so loudly.

"He's got a button embedded in his arm. I bet it's encoded Stamirine," she whispered. Suliman bent his head to hear her better, but no-one paid any attention. "His plan won't work," she told him. "He can't kill her, but he can kill us. I'm going to stop him."

"Enjoy your theory, Doc," Suliman whispered back. "When she runs out of things to say, bits of us will be floating around like leaves in the breeze."

"He won't detonate because she's not really here, and he knows it. He's hoping the real Rebecca Allardice will turn up."

Ignoring Suliman's look of disbelief, Charlie closed her fingers over the neurolysing spray in her boot and switched the setting to medium with a flick of her thumb. In a single bound, she sprayed Thale in the face. The man and woman disappeared immediately, Thale collapsed in a faint, and Rice, who also received a remnant of the spray, rocked for a moment before falling. When he did, he collapsed on top of the frail commander. Suliman ran forward and hauled him off.

"I hope Thale's alive. What did you do, Doc?"

Charlie checked Thale's pulse. "I'll explain later. We need to tie him up, keep his hands away from the button."

Suliman stood and looked around. "There isn't anything in here to tie him up with. If I didn't know better,

I would say we're inside a ship."

Charlie nodded. "I think we might be. Livesey, hand me your belt."

Suliman tucked the unconscious Thale's arms into his waistband and tied the belt around tight. Thale made a few sounds as if he were regaining consciousness, and the puppy took the opportunity to pee on his face.

Suliman looked to where, a moment ago, the man and woman stood. "Holograms. Those were bloody good projections. They convinced me."

"Not me," Charlie said. "No respirations, nor did they blink. And if that were Livesey's nanna, she'd be older. She used a younger image. That's why I knew Thale wouldn't detonate. He's only got one shot."

Suliman looked impressed. "No fooling you."

"Is that your nanna?" Charlie asked Livesey, who stood over the semiconscious Thale.

He nodded. "She hasn't aged at all."

"What was all that 'six years' stuff?"

Livesey went to answer, but the shape-shifting man interrupted them. He stepped through the wall as if it weren't there.

"Pardon me." He scooped Thale up in his arms and disappeared the way he came.

Suliman examined the area where the man entered and exited. "It looks solid. How does he do it?"

"Some kind of intermolecular interaction?" Charlie suggested.

Suliman shook his head. "It's a technology we've

never encountered. I wonder what that woman meant when she said her kind settled Venus."

Charlie had an idea about that but got interrupted by the return of the disappearing man.

"I have neutralised the threat, Thale," he announced.

"You defused him?" Charlie prompted.

"I detonated him."

Suliman thought it worth making sure. "He's dead?"

"His heart is dead," the man replied.

"If his heart is dead, then isn't all of him dead?"

"Not quite."

Charlie stepped closer and scrutinised the man's face. "Are you an android?"

"Correct."

On close inspection, the android appeared constructed of some kind of elastic polymer.

"You also shape-shift?"

The android looked down at her. "I can change my molecular structure to predetermined parameters, but I cannot become something for which I have not been programmed. That, for example." He gestured to the dog, busy leaving his scent around the room. A still woozy Rice scooped the little vandal up into his arms and promptly fell flat on his face. Suliman stood him up, and he and Livesey took an arm each to keep him upright. Free once again, the puppy headed for the android, who intercepted it with an outstretched arm. The puppy howled as it found itself engulfed in a roll of polymer.

"Are we going to get some answers?" Suliman asked

the android.

"Follow me." Once again, the android melded with the wall and allowed them through his open legs. Then, on the other side, he assumed his proper shape and led them to a spacious apartment, empty save for a few old but well-maintained easy chairs. Unravelling his arm, the puppy rolled out at Rice's feet. The android bade them sit. "Now, we wait."

As they waited, the others turned to Charlie for an explanation as to how she stopped Thale.

"I found a neurolysing spray in the medbay when we first came aboard the Millstone. I was going to use it on the lowest setting if any of you played up," she confessed. "I planned to use it on Kate Winstanley, but a whack on the head with a frying pan had the same effect."

"That spray can kill, Doc," Suliman said. "In Thale's weakened state, we're lucky to still be here talking about it."

"I used it on the guard that chased me from Kate's house, and it only knocked him out. It's lost its potency, maybe because it's over its use-by date by about ninety years."

Suliman had to grin at Charlie's originality. Neurolysing sprays, even old ones, had their uses. He would have liked to see her try to use it on him. It had to go directly into the face, and she wouldn't have been able to reach. "What if it disrupted the signal to his heart?" he asked.

Charlie shrugged. "His heart has to realise it's dying to

set off the device."

"I didn't know you knew so much about them," Suliman grinned.

"It's obvious." Charlie poked a finger at Suliman's chest. "If the detonator was so sensitive it went off at the slightest change in rhythm, there would have been suicide bombers going off like popping corn throughout the Civil War. Everyone gets missed beats and cardiac misfires."

That made Suliman grin. "Why didn't you think of this before? We could have kept him in a coma. Come to think of it, how come you've never seen the button?"

"He always refused to strip off," Charlie explained. "I know why now. Stamirine is invisible to the types of scans I used on Thale. Also, the Millstone doesn't have the facility to keep someone on extended life support. We would have had to keep spraying him to overload his neurological functions. His heart would have eventually given out."

Rice tried to pay attention, but that spray had disconnected his brain. What the hell was in that stuff Charlie slugged him with? He had a question, but it took a moment to get his mouth into gear. At least it made sense to him.

"Did someone say Thale had a button?" he slurred. "You mean, he was like a grenade? He only had to press a button, and he'd go 'boom'?"

Charlie moved over to sit next to him and put her arm around him, giving him a much-needed hug. At last, he began to feel safe.

CHAPTER NINETEEN _

When the woman returned, real, breathing and with all her life signs visible, Charlie saw she looked more the age she expected. Holographic projections of people, even those as sophisticated as the one she saw earlier, did not always accurately represent the subject. As none knew Rebecca Allardice apart from Livesey, who had not seen her for many years, she probably considered it a safe way to introduce herself, given she was possibly an assassin's target.

Rebecca's hair was a little greyer in real life, her skin a little more lined, and her eyes, in contrast to the gentleness of her face, a piercing, determined blue. She smiled, a genuine, warm smile, but this was no cake-making, baby-sitting nanna. For all her delicate appearance, Rebecca's experiences had shaped her into a woman of purpose. A woman who knew what was likely taking place on her home planet.

"I had to be sure you weren't working with Thale,"

she said. "We detected you near Neptune, and when you landed on the moon, we saw you had an Indigo with you."

"An Indigo?" Charlie echoed, forgetting in her surprise how creepy she thought it would be if the planets had the same name as theirs back home. For no reason, she turned to Livesey. "You're an Indigo?"

Livesey nodded. "So it seems."

"That's why we had to remove Thale," Rebecca said. "To protect you. If Thale were to discover that Matthew was Indigo, he might have executed him."

"He planned on killing you," Charlie reminded her. "It's fortunate your android didn't kill Thale when you brought him here. The explosive he carried was capable of taking out an entire ship."

"Our android wouldn't execute anyone without a direct order," Rebecca told her. "We didn't know about the detonator until you told us. Our perception of risk was that he might be a threat to Matthew."

"It took us a while to work out the reasons why Miller sent us," Charlie said. "It made sense when Livesey told us about his grandmother."

"When we discovered Thale, I anticipated sabotage or some kind of hostile act; that's why I appeared as a holoprojection," Rebecca replied. "I expect he knows I'm much older than him. I couldn't have looked so young in the flesh!"

"I knew you were a holoprojection. You weren't breathing."

Very astute," Rebecca grinned. "I didn't plan on a

doctor turning up."

That the artefact took Thale still didn't make sense to Suliman. "Why didn't the artefact take Livesey if he was the one you were worried about?"

"We were worried about all of you. The Lunar Foundation Artefact is also a psionic transmitter. It alerts those of us with strong psychic abilities of variations in the flame. The Foundation artefact on the moon can only displace a single form and then at long intervals between, so it seemed prudent to transport the hazard. We knew no threat to Matthew lay with you. Afterwards, we applied a remote to your ship and brought you to the outskirts of London. We could not direct you here, the inhabitants are unsophisticated, non-progressive and the sight of your ship would cause widespread panic."

Just as the crew guessed.

"They know about you, though, don't they?" Rice said. "We met a man who said 'they' will stop you getting into Wormwood Scrubs. That it's a 'no go' area."

"He probably meant prison guards. There is little need for a prison of this size, but on occasions, it's necessary. The locals avoid it. It's not that sinister, Professor."

"Oh," Rice responded. He remembered the way the train man said it, and it sounded sinister. Very sinister.

Rebecca smiled at Rice's confusion before continuing. "Our android removed Thale's heart. After detonating it, he inserted a mechanical device and revived him. When he recovers, he will remain here in the Scrubs to live out the rest of his days."

"Every question I have starts with 'why'," Suliman said, impatient now for answers.

"Then let me answer your initial query, Captain Suliman. As you have already guessed, I am Rebecca Allardice, and I believe you are looking for me?"

"Miller spun us a tale about a Seeker ship returning minus its pilot," Charlie explained. "It was all very cryptic. He assigned us—" she gestured to the others, "to return to the ship's last known coordinates to investigate. Except, I know for sure that the Seeker ship spent a full year on Mars before someone located it on the perimeter. We also know that Amira Santer never made it to launch."

"I returned the ship as a message to Governor Miller."

"Your son?" Suliman prompted.

Charlie saw the subtle change in Rebecca's expression as she answered, but she didn't drop her eyes or allow her face to reveal too much of her inner thoughts. Even so, Charlie recognised Rebecca felt some pain in that acknowledgement.

"He is my son in a biological sense," Rebecca kept her chin high, "but no longer a son in my heart. As a child, he loved space stories but was too young to understand Nexist policies. One story thrilled him more than any other. In his innocence, he related the story to his father and me. He saw such wonderment in the possibility of travelling to distant worlds, but my husband, his father, knowing that soon George would come to know of his Nexist heritage, thrashed his wonderment out of him, to prepare him for the Nexist messages of purity of race and creation of humankind. The message I sent contained elements of that story, disguised to look like a rambling report. He would recognise it, of that I was certain, and would know I sent it. He would have believed me dead before that, killed in a sabotaged Seeker module."

Charlie thought of Miller as a little boy, enthralled at a fictional story. The notion was unimaginable, and from what she sensed from this woman, she did not understand how that little boy could have turned into a monster.

"I knew about Pilot Santer," Rebecca said, "and I knew her ship was still on the launchpad. My son and my husband imprisoned me on Rille Base, but I escaped by taking Seeker-20. When it launched, George would have known I was aboard and would have assumed it wouldn't be too long before I was space dust. He didn't know I knew about the auto-destruct. I disabled it."

"How did you know about Santer?"

"The man who became my daughter's second husband and Matthew's stepfather was the Triumvirate co-ordinator to the Seeker program and a Nexist spy. He planned to launch the twentieth Seeker ship without a pilot to hide the fact he killed Amira Santer. Fortunately for me, he must have been delayed."

"Why did he kill Amira Santer?" Livesey suddenly looked down at his hands. Knowing your family doesn't want you is one thing, but the revelation the man who brought you up is a murderer, is another. Rebecca waited until her grandson was ready for her to continue.

"She found out about the Nexist sabotage…"

Rebecca held up her hands as she saw a few mouths open to form questions. "Please don't ask me how she knew, I don't know, but she was heading to the consulate to inform them and to reveal her suspicion the co-ordinator was a Nexist infiltrator."

"A former Seeker told us Amira Santer died of a broken neck."

"Yes, the official story was she died while rock climbing." Rebecca paused. "A Seeker told you, Doctor Maitland?"

"Kate Winstanley."

"Kate Winstanley?"

"We crash-landed on the world where she made her home. Did you know her?"

"I did," Rebecca nodded, raising her eyebrows. "Most disagreeable. Kate must have been in Seeker-19; it's the only way she would have known Seeker-20's launch sequence didn't begin, and when she asked, they informed her of the 'accident'."

Charlie wanted to know what made Rebecca's family turn against her. Rebecca knew the answer would come as a surprise, perhaps even a shock to all of them, save Matthew.

"I am Indigo."

Charlie felt the wind taken out of her sails. Miller's mother, Indigo? How would the Miller family have viewed each other after that revelation?

Suliman looked over at Livesey. "And you've known for six years you're also Indigo?"

Livesey nodded. "Yes, as soon as it became clear I would never amount to anything, my parents shoved me off to Venus to study. One day, on a field trip, a specific area drew me, so much so that I sneaked out there at night. I took a spade droid to dig a few holes, and it found something hidden below the ground, something solid. When I pushed against it, it yielded, and my hand entered an empty space." He smiled at Rebecca. "A bit like when your android pushes through the walls."

"You were a little boy the last time I saw you," Rebecca smiled back. "I can't imagine what life has been like for you in that family. Your uncle planned to bring about a new Nexist order, Matthew. I believe even your grandfather felt he went too far. The Nexists are certain the Indigo exist, that we are not a myth, but it was to become a potent propaganda tool, one that would justify their ultimate bid to take over the Triumvirate. That's why The Myth of Origin linked the Indigo to Venusian DNA and allowed the Nexists to draw up a different possibility as to the origins of Earthers." Rebecca waved her hand as if flapping at an annoying insect. "It's nonsense, of course, a diversion, and a lot of Nexists in the hierarchy know it, but that won't stop them from committing genocide. Matthew, did your parents ever find out about you?"

Livesey took a moment to answer. He was never sure about this, although he asked himself the same question repeatedly. "Did they know?" He reworked Rebecca's question and shook his head slowly. "An inkling perhaps, but I didn't know myself until after my experiences in the

Mars undercolony."

Suliman knew that place only too well: a high-security prison and a dump for human misery.

"It's hell," Livesey agreed, flicking a glance at Suliman. "The first day I got there, the warden told me to reorder the prisoner manifest. The undercolony is high security but some inmates, well, they were pretty old, and I wondered why such old people were there. I got shut down when I asked. Anyway, I had to feed one old man who had one of those hand manacles that cover both hands like a double glove?" He checked to see if the others knew what he meant. "He was about one hundred and five years old! As soon as he saw me, he smiled. A great, big, enormous grin!" Livesey exaggerated the width of the grin with his hands, smiling at the memory. "But not just that, something about him burned like a flame inside my head." The smile faded, and Livesey turned inwards to his thoughts. "The old man kept nodding and smiling." Livesey acted out the old man's actions, moving his head up and down as he recalled the event. "I can still see his dirty face and rotten teeth. He kept trying to grab my hand. I didn't know why, but the manacles stopped him. A day or two later," he continued, "the old guy choked while I was feeding him, and they called the base medical officer. She ordered us both removed to the hospital, but the poor old man died. I thought I was in trouble, and the grief—I'd never felt an emotion like it; it just hammered me." He touched his heart. "It seemed the physician knew more than I did. She told me the old man was Indigo and asked about my connection to him. I just told her about the flame. I didn't know much about Indigos, only the mention of them in that Myth of Origin challenge we learned about in school. The doctor said there were four of them in prison but many more on Venus. She was part of a faction that would stand at the side of the Indigo when the Nexists made their move to take over the Triumvirate. She told me the Nexists planned the destruction of anyone suspected of being Indigo and the transportation of Venusian/Earther marriages and hybrid offspring."

"She trusted you enough to speak to you about her involvement?"

"Yes, Charlie, but she disappeared days later. I didn't find out what happened to her."

"Why imprison an old man?" Rice wondered aloud, then asked, using Suliman's logic, "If they suspected him of being Indigo, why not shoot him?"

"He'd been there since his youth," Livesey said. "As it stands, the Triumvirate insists on investigating any deaths that take place in judicial custody, but old age? Well, that's one they wouldn't investigate. It turns out the governor of the Martian Prison is a Nexist sympathiser. Rounding up the Indigo, hiding them in the prison until nature takes its course, made certain the Indigo were no longer a threat. As my grandmother says, the Nexists know the Indigo aren't a myth."

"I've asked this before," Suliman said, "If you were such an embarrassment to your family, Livesey, why send you out here?" He turned to Rebecca. "They planned to kill you; why not him?"

"It's not that simple, Captain Suliman," Rebecca answered. "The Triumvirate has a policy of investigating all unexplained deaths. I don't doubt they considered staging his demise, until your mission provided them with a way out. They won't want scrutiny, not right now, and eventually, they'll let it be known he's off on some space jaunt or other."

"Livesey, how did the doctor know you were Indigo?" Charlie asked.

"Remember I said the old man burned like a flame in my head? Well, the flame is purple. Look..."

Livesey held her gaze until a gentle pulsating colour flooded Charlie's brain. A tongue of purple, encompassed by silvery edges, flicked through her mind. It felt peaceful, benign.

"You aren't Indigo, Charlie, but I can make you see it if I choose."

Until today, Charlie was happy to believe the Indigo were a myth. Now, circumstances had turned those beliefs on their head.

Rebecca watched as Charlie examined the intense colour and sensation perfusing her brain. Then the colour slipped into Charlie's shoulders, into her chest and abdomen and disappeared.

"I don't know what to say," Charlie whispered. "It's remarkable. Perhaps the prison doctor had seen it as well."

"And once it burns," Rebecca smiled, "you can't deny it."

Charlie shook her head. If that was with you all the time, even in the background, it set you apart, a reminder you weren't like other people, although it begged the question, "What does it do?"

"Do?" Rebecca laughed. "To other humans, it has no meaning, but to the Indigo, it is our heritage, our life force, a connection to our ancestors."

"And the Indigo are connected to this world as well as our own?"

"The Indigo did not come from this world, Doctor Maitland, but that is a story for another time."

Charlie felt herself looking again for the flame, for any remnant, but it had gone. She felt bereft; to have such a flame burn within you, knowing that force defined you, a connection to your ancestors, it would be wrong to allow anyone to snuff it out through prejudice and a lack of understanding. She thought about the Myth of Origin, about the Nexist propaganda, about the Indigo, and once again cursed herself for not paying attention at school.

"You wanted to know why I stole the Seeker ship," Rebecca said. They all agreed, yes, they would.

Rebecca swallowed hard. Only once had she spoken of it, when the Indigo found her and brought her here. Even thinking of her son's rejection caused her pain, but these people deserved to know the whole story.

"My husband and I visited Venus on Triumvirate business," she began. "While he was busy, I wished to undertake a few field studies for amusement and perhaps to compile a thesis on some rare Venusian flora. When my son learned of the location, he vehemently opposed my choice of area. His opposition amused me and only served to fuel my desire to carry out my research in that place."

Rebecca continued her story in a voice that carried smooth and clear, inflected with emotion, and imparting to her audience the pain she felt at her family's betrayal. She told the Millstone's crew that she ignored her son and went to the area she selected, discovering a structure below the ground, the same structure her grandson discovered years later. Where he only pushed the surface, she entered and found herself inside what she believed was a crashed, alien vessel.

"I moved from room to room simply by touching the walls," Rebecca said, glancing away from the curiosity of several pairs of eyes to better filter through her memories. "There, for the first time, I saw the purple flame."

Charlie thought about it. Governor Miller and possibly his father must have known something was buried at the site. "Did you tell your husband?" she asked.

Rebecca's mouth twisted. "In my innocence, I did tell him. I expected anger at having gone against them, but my discovery, well, I was so excited and eager to share; I believed I had found something extraordinary. It didn't occur to me I discovered an Indigo ship, even though I knew the so-called proof the Indigo existed was passed to the Nexists many years before. The flame took a secondary place; I thought it was just a coincidence, a hallucination." Her eyes filled with pain. "I was a silly woman. They didn't share my excitement. Instead, my husband locked me in a room on my son's orders, telling me I would be 'dealt with'. Their behaviour astounded me. I received a call from George, who told me I only ever brought discredit to the Nexist cause. When I asked why, he just laughed and said, 'Because you were never dedicated, and now, dear mother, it seems you are one of them.'. He was so cold, so calm, so full of hate." Rebecca took a deep breath. "He told me I would never see my family again, that we were to proceed to Rille the next day, where he would arrange my 'demise'."

This made no sense to Charlie. "If your son had managed to stage your death, wouldn't the Triumvirate investigate?" she asked.

"My son would have thought of everything, Doctor Maitland, witnesses, disposal of my body. I am sure he would have played the part of a distressed and grieving son. My own parents were long gone, so there was no-one left to be suspicious. Besides, I was the wife of a senator, and he was above suspicion. I didn't realise until I arrived here that the flame ignites soon after connection with an Indigo artefact or another Indigo. Once it burns..."

"So, the Indigo did settle our worlds?"

Rebecca nodded. "Yes, along with humans from here. Venus first, then Earth."

"Does that mean we're all Indigo?" Rice said with wide-eyed wonder. A fair few old documents suggested the Indigo had superpowers.

Rebecca laughed at his amazement. "No, but we are human, just a little different," then added, revealing at least some psychic ability, "And we don't have superpowers.

When the flame lit, memories, not my own, flooded my mind, but I had little understanding of what it meant to be Indigo."

Suliman felt a need to move the conversation along, find out where they were going with it and not get bogged down in the Indigo issue. "This is all very interesting, but why did you send back the ship?"

"I wanted George Miller to know he failed to silence me. That I will return."

"Okay," Suliman inclined his head, but he needed more. "To do what?"

"The Nexists didn't forget the Triumvirate's dismissal of the Myth of Origin challenge in 4331. They weren't well-placed during the civil war to take over the Triumvirate, but by the time my son staged my death, plans for a coup were well underway." Rebecca linked her fingers together and fell to silence, leaving her audience to wait while she gathered her thoughts. "They say they will liberate Earth from the Indigo and restore the purity of humankind. Corrupted Venus will become outcast." Her voice dropped to a whisper, and she shook her head gently in disbelief. "How was I ever part of such evil?" But that moment passed quickly, and the determination returned to those piercing blue eyes. "We cannot allow their prejudice to destroy us."

"They want to remove the seat of power to Earth," Rice said. "The Nexists believe humans were created *on* Earth, *for* Earth, and any other colonisation is a by-product of their superiority. As Venusians claim to be the colonisers, it follows the Nexists will separate Venus."

Rebecca acknowledged the truth of Rice's summary. "They plan to deny Venusians education, advancement and technology."

Suliman knew that as a lapsed Nexist, Rebecca would have more insight into their organisation than he did, but usually, he heard things, even in prison. He didn't remember anything this radical. "Surely, it's just historical politics. They don't have enough power to carry off a coup."

Rebecca quickly corrected that assumption. "Not so. They want control. At the time I left, they were devising a several-stage plan to take over the Triumvirate. The Nexists will establish the armed perimeter they proposed years ago and an army to suppress any opposition. They will revise the social structure within the mid-Southwestern corridor and the removal of hybrid families. We are not talking about a benign dictatorship here, Captain Suliman. Expect genocide, expect a regime, a military rule." Rebecca waited for her words to sink in. She knew now the Nexist movement was a labyrinth of deception, lies, empty promises and, in many cases, pure evil. When the flame inside her lit, she didn't at first understand, but when she escaped Rille, she saw the foreshadowing of the future Earth under Nexist rule. There would be only two choices: either for the new government or against it. Twenty-two years ago, she knew of the plans for the mid-Southwestern corridor, where those from Suliman's race, strong, outstanding fighters, would become a police force to administer the new regulations. Historical specialists like Rice would be redundant as history would be rewritten; he would probably get sent to Venus. Charlie would fare better, educated and qualified, she would be an asset provided she didn't buck against the system the Nexists instituted. The new regime was not about the people. It would be about the power one man could yield.

"They are biding their time, Captain Suliman," she continued. "The truth is, while traditional Nexists loosely support the theory of creation by supreme beings on Earth, they want to ensure any alien influence stays out of the picture. However, since learning the Indigo do exist, those belief systems are being questioned. It might mean Venusians *did* colonise Earth, and the Nexists will not stand for that. My son just doesn't know how many Indigo there are or where. Venus only? Or elsewhere in the universe? The Seeker module would be a powerful message to him. The idea of a power greater than Nexism drives him to create a stronghold, and he certainly won't want me turning up to rain on his parade, so I sent the ship to tell him firstly that I had survived and, secondly, that I wasn't alone."

"Well, you certainly put the wind up him," Suliman grinned.

"Good, I would have loved to have seen his face. You turning up here tells me he got the message."

"So again, where do we all fit in?"

"When Miller reveals himself as leader of the Nexists, if he hasn't already, the senior families on Earth and

Europa will rally." Rebecca gave a small, humourless laugh. "I am ashamed to say I looked forward to the day when the Nexists took control, to the day when 'normal' humans would not tolerate marriage unions with the Venusians, and we would purify our race. Can you imagine what would happen if word got out I was Indigo? My family would lose all credibility."

"Is your son half Indigo?"

Rebecca shook her head. "No, Doctor Maitland. There is no 'half' Indigo. One is, or one isn't."

Livesey's voice suddenly cut across the conversation. "This is a fight we must win," he declared, matching his grandmother's determination. "Not just for the Indigo, but to stop the Nexist plot against Venus."

The shift in his usual mild manner, raised voice and sudden resolve came as a surprise. Livesey once told Charlie he had a coward's instincts, but it seemed now, in the face of overwhelming injustice, he had found his purpose. For Charlie, she understood that Livesey could not sit back while Miller implemented his plans, but she also couldn't fathom how a handful of people could resist the Nexists, assuming they could even make it home. They had no plan of action, no allies, and no idea how many enemies they would be taking on. And none of them were warriors. On the other hand, she thought, they could go back, find the Triumvirate dismantled and everyone living happily with Miller as King. They had no way of knowing, but something told Charlie it wouldn't be like that, not knowing Miller as she did.

"We will fight, Matthew," Rebecca said gently, "and we will win."

Livesey's face, still set in determination, told Charlie the notion of waging war was a topic he didn't plan on dropping, despite Rebecca's understanding reply. For now, Charlie's mind buzzed with so much new information, she hoped he would wait just a little longer before dashing back to the Millstone with an abettor and hiking back to Earth to blow up Miller. She returned to a somewhat less confronting subject, inviting Rebecca to continue her story.

"How did you end up here?" she asked.

Rebecca noted that Charlie sidestepped her grandson's outburst. That was fine; she wasn't ready to discuss the Nexist takeover yet.

"Same way as Thale. The artefact on the moon."

Charlie guessed that, but she still plucked a question out of thin air, not wanting to give Livesey the chance to interject.

"Who operates it?

"We do."

"But this isn't the Indigo planet of origin, is it?"

"No, the Indigo came from another galaxy. They found this Earth after fleeing persecution on their homeworld. The people here took them in."

Suliman thought about the world outside the walls of Wormwood Scrubs. A backward, non-progressive society surrounded by a forcefield.

"And this world is held back. Why?"

Rebecca described a planet with a history of war, each

time ending with a promise of lasting peace. That lasting peace never came to pass. In the final conflict, she explained, the Indigo divided the populations to save them, to give them a chance to become reborn with a new vision for their Earth. The Indigo possessed technology that modified the people's expectations, limited their ambition, and slowed their social evolution until they showed signs of recovery.

"People accused us of being foreigners," Charlie said.

Rebecca had encountered the people's prejudices herself. "They would have thought you were Scottish or Welsh. Those are the only other societies of which these people are aware. Scotland and Wales are quite a journey overland, and not everyone welcomes newcomers."

"We viewed the southern hemisphere," Suliman said. "It's pretty wasted."

"Yes, but it is recovering, and the populations will move outwards in time. When it is safe."

"The Indigo must have a lot of technology and knowledge."

Rebecca shook her head. "No, Professor Rice. We missed the detonator inside Thale. All we saw in Thale's heart was malice. We have limitations."

Then, to Charlie's horror, Suliman took up the possibility of returning home to fight.

"Do you believe the Indigo from here will be prepared to fight a war on our Earth on the strength of what Thale told you?" he said, aiming the question at Rebecca but looking at each of his crewmates for their input. Rice buried his face in the dog's fur, hoping the issue would just disappear. Charlie had no answer. She only knew she didn't want to stay here. Rebecca saw Charlie and Rice's responses, but she knew Charlie was strong and would come to terms with what fate had in store. Rice? Well, he might need a little more encouragement. And Suliman? He wanted the whole story, possibly all at once.

"In the mid-twentieth century, some Indigo left this planet to renew their travels," she said. "They settled our Venus and our Earth, so those worlds are theirs in more senses even than this one because they found this world already settled. This world, this Earth, will not be abandoned. Many Indigo will remain to oversee the recovery, but we cannot take the Foundation Artefact with us; it sustains the Indigo work here, so some of our technology will be limited. When the Indigo discovered our system, it was uninhabited, but alongside the humans that travelled with them, the Indigo laid the foundation of new worlds. So the answer to your question, Captain Suliman, is yes, the Indigo will fight wherever other Indigo are threatened. Many are already prepared."

"Are some staying because they integrated with humans?" Charlie asked.

"In the same way they have on our worlds, Doctor Maitland. Some families here are a mix of human and Indigo. I don't have the benefit of aeons of Indigo knowledge of this Earth, but I know beyond doubt that the ship buried on Venus was a colonist's ship."

"Kate Winstanley lived on a so-called colonised

planet, colonised by people who came from the stars. It was the one we landed on, on the way here." Charlie screwed up her face without realising.

"Not to your liking?"

"Not at all."

"There are other ships on Venus," Rice cut in. "An entire fleet. I saw the documents myself, ancient documents. That's why I got sent away."

"I wasn't aware there were more ships, but I know, like this one, it would only be the Indigo who can access them. There are no doors from the outside, so unless you are in the company of an Indigo, there is no way in."

"Your android does pretty well."

"Andy, yes, he is part of the ship, so he can go anywhere and be anything that is part of the programming."

"Andy?" Rice snorted. "Andy the android?" Rice's unsophisticated humour fell on deaf ears in the face of more important issues.

"Rebecca," Suliman said. "Are you planning on an invasion force? Otherwise, what was the point in sending Miller that message?"

"You're right, there would have been no point, but we need to know what is happening on Earth, current Nexist activity, the position on Venus. We have a provisional plan in place—" She took the puppy from Rice and grinned as it ministered to her face with its tongue. "But for now, this little fellow needs food and water, as I suspect you all do. I'm sure a chance to refresh yourselves and a good meal would be welcome. You have a lot to talk about."

"You haven't told us how you escaped."

Rebecca smiled. "Doctor Maitland, I am happy to tell you. I have no secrets. We'll reconvene here in two hours." She kissed the puppy's head and handed it back to Rice.

After she left, Suliman turned to Livesey. "I would have thought if I hadn't seen my nanna in years, she would have made more of a fuss of me." He'd never had a nanna. What did he know?

"She is happy to see me," Livesey assured him, "but it seems we can communicate between ourselves, not necessarily words, but feelings. She told me privately."

"Can you do it back?"

Livesey nodded, pleased to have discovered at least a modicum of psychic ability. "It seems so. I've learned more about the Indigo in these few minutes than I ever knew before. I'm sorry about what I said, you know, about going home and starting a war. I think I was picking up on my grandmother's feelings. Rice, I hope I didn't scare you."

Despite the apology, Charlie knew this was what Livesey wanted, to return home and defend his kind. She understood. No-one has an inalienable right to declare war on others because they don't understand or care for their beliefs and culture. In coming here, in finding his grandmother, Livesey found a cause worth fighting for, and he wanted his friends by his side in the coming conflict.

CHAPTER TWENTY _

The android, who still wore his hat, showed them the amenities. While they took advantage of hot water and clean towels, he laid out a meal for them, including in the preparation a dish of meat for the little dog. The puppy swallowed the meat without chewing, then licked the plate around the room until not even a skerrick of flavour remained. Contented, the puppy claimed one of the chairs, turning in circles several times before belching and twitching his way to sleep.

For his human guests, Andy served an array of cheeses and bread, along with several glasses that contained a bright green liquid. Rice sniffed suspiciously at the brew.

"What's this?" he said, wrinkling up his nose.

"A combination of several different kinds of grass and herbs, sir," Andy replied. "Most beneficial to the body." But despite Andy's endorsement, the colour was just too florid for Rice, and he put the glass down. Rarely picky about food, and although a long time since the "milldill", he wasn't game to try anything that looked like toxic waste.

"I had no idea the Indigo were making a comeback," Rice said as he stuffed his mouth full of cheese, thankful that even light-years from home, his favourite food was still available. Somewhere in his subconscious, he made the unwelcome connection that the recipe for cheese at home must have come from here and that cows were also part of the first colonisers' entourage.

Livesey had a less complicated answer. "I think it's more probable the Indigo on Venus—those who knew they were Indigo—never went anywhere. They just wanted to be left in peace."

"I'm surprised the Indigo hasn't written this place off as a lost cause," Suliman said as he made himself a towering cheese sandwich.

Charlie disagreed with his cynicism. "They've lived here for generations. It's natural they'd feel some responsibility towards the citizens."

"Yes, Doc, but if it was the Indigo or Indigo/human hybrids that settled that pseudoreligious planet where Kate lived, on their way to our system," Suliman pointed out, "then I have a few qualms about their ability to govern."

Charlie couldn't deny he had a point. "Livesey, did you see any Indigo on Kate's planet?"

Livesey could only shake his head, unable to answer through a mouthful of the only decent food he'd had in months. In his opinion, although it looked delicious when he was starving, the burger had only been a notch above the ship's prepacked meals. "I only saw those few guards searching the ship," he mumbled after a moment. "Maybe that planet has bred the Indigo out, if that can happen."

Rebecca returned with the man from the earlier holoprojection, both stepping through the wall together. "The Indigo flame can be dormant for centuries," she said, catching Livesey's comment, "but it will burn somewhere. It will never be extinguished." She indicated to the man beside her. "This is Greg Sheehan, one of us."

One of *you*, Charlie thought, feeling ill-equipped to fight a war on anyone's behalf and hating the sense of inevitability of the path they were on.

Greg greeted everyone with a handshake, an old Earth greeting. Possessed of a pleasant, friendly manner, Charlie saw nothing in Greg that set him apart from other humans. Livesey had shown her the flame, but in other ways, neither he nor Rebecca seemed remarkable. All these years, she had probably walked past Indigo people without realising, so how could the Nexists prove someone was an Indigo? Greg looked like a regular man. Nothing standout about him, nothing obvious anyway, but then, she saw nothing extraordinary in Livesey either. The only difference was that Greg was good-looking—not Sam good-looking, but still...

"Doctor Maitland," Greg addressed Charlie. "Your quick thinking earlier averted a disaster."

Charlie didn't feel like she should receive any accolades. If Thale had managed to access his elbow, their molecules might well be now embedded in the walls around Wormwood Scrubs.

"It could have gone the other way if I'd been wrong," she said modestly.

"It could," Greg smiled, "but there is something to be said for intuition."

He invited them all to sit on the old armchairs, sweeping the little dog from its spot, who made a few "harrumphs" before dropping its snout on its paws and settling on the floor.

"From what Rebecca tells us," Greg began, "the Nexists plan on taking over the government on your Earth. We aim to return to your world and subvert these plans. We will in no way coerce you into helping us," he added, waiting the tiniest moment for a response. Suliman wanted to hear more, although he'd already decided to go back and fight. He saw no other option. Charlie wanted to protect her mum and dad, and Rice, well, even though he had parents back home, fighting didn't appeal. They already knew how Livesey felt. Still, they didn't respond to Greg's pointed comment.

"If you prefer," he continued, "you can remain here, in Greater London, but Captain, we could really use your ship."

"I go with my ship," Suliman growled. "I'm not staying here."

Greg grinned; he already knew this man had no intention of remaining. "History tells us this was a vibrant and diverse culture before the last war, Captain Suliman. What happened here must not happen on your world. I believe we can help."

Suliman, suspicious by nature, particularly of people bearing gifts, eyed the newcomer. "Why is something that's happening on the other side of the galaxy any concern of yours?"

"The flame is our life essence, our heritage," Greg said. "We knew nothing of the plight of the Indigo who left here centuries ago, not until Rebecca came to us. The Indigo on this Earth have diminished over the millennia as we cemented our alliance with the humans. There are fewer Indigo now to preserve this Earth's rehabilitation, but we are dedicated. To learn of a new threat to another world that we settled? Well, we cannot allow the Nexists to extinguish the flame. Your Earth and this, as far as we know, hold the last remnants of the Indigo."

"We got stranded on a planet where they tried to force Charlie to have a bunch of husbands," Rice said. "Is it possible the Indigo also settled that world?"

"The colonists who left here had many non-Indigo among them," Greg responded. "That planet may be inhabited only by their descendants. I can assure you that we would not establish a new society based on coercion." He tilted his head. "Worlds survive how they may. This Earth must continue, and so must yours. We cannot allow a threat to the Indigo to…"

Suliman cut in there, pointing to Rebecca. "Even if that means killing your son. Because that's what it might come down to."

That Rebecca had feelings about this was clear, but her voice did not waver as she answered, "If that is what it takes, yes."

Suliman shrugged. He didn't expect such a short answer. "Seems fair."

"Greg," Charlie needed some clarification about species. "I notice you speak of humans as if they are a different species to the Indigo, yet Rebecca told us the Indigo are human."

"We *are* human…" Then, he pointed to the dog. "On this world, his kind are all one species, but each has differences."

"You're saying the Indigo and human share a common ancestor?"

Greg nodded, giving Charlie a mysterious smile. "I believe we did. It's worthy of research."

Gosh, Charlie felt a tingle of excitement. Is it ever! How fascinating!

"Can you tell us how you ended up here?" Rice said to Rebecca. "How you got away from the Nexists?"

"My son took me to Rille base and placed me in a hospital cell," Rebecca began. "He left me alone, and believing I could not escape, didn't post a guard. I made it onto the roof by climbing through a vent in the ceiling, but I couldn't get outside the base without a life suit. I saw the second row of Seeker modules out on the launch pad. Seeker-20 was still there and the most accessible."

"And you stole it?"

"I thought Matthew's stepfather had already launched it to hide his crime, but it was right alongside the modules for the second wave."

"There was never a second wave," Charlie told her. "Seeker-20 was included in the data from the first round of launches."

Rebecca didn't seem surprised. "I had a feeling the second wave wouldn't happen. I stole a technician's life suit from a locker room, and I had no problem getting on board the Seeker module. I knew it would be obvious to my husband and son what I'd done."

"How did you know how to disable the auto-destruct?" Rice asked.

"I didn't. It was just a feeling. I located the device; a simple Mag bypass, and without knowing what I was doing, I disabled it. I've learned since I've been here, the Indigo are often sensitive to technology."

"And your family assumed you would eventually get blown up like the other Seekers, and to hide the fact you stole the ship and that you are Indigo, they rigged the explosion on Rille?"

"I didn't know what they did after I took the ship, Professor Rice, and I only know what you have told me. As for me, I had no thoughts, no plans where I could go beyond getting away. I guess I hoped there'd be a habitable planet."

"You could have died out there."

Rebecca had a simple response to that, "I would have been dead if I'd stayed on Earth."

"So you found your way to that moon, and the Indigo brought you here?"

Rebecca nodded. "Yes, after five years in space. I

sensed where I needed to guide the ship, but newly awakened, it's easy to become distracted. The galaxy is filled with many wonderful things, and once or twice, I put the ship down, but those places were never my goal."

"That was here?"

"*Here?*" Rebecca gasped in surprise. "No, Captain Suliman, not *here*. My goal is my home, the Triumvirate worlds. I want to go back and defeat the Nexists. How can I know what I know and not do my best to end them?"

Suliman looked around at his crewmates. Charlie, small and light, scaredy-cat Rice, Livesey, who might have hidden talents, mixed in with a former Nexist of advancing age, although he didn't doubt he underestimated her. Greg looked strong enough but still not great odds against an army. Unless the Indigo had something up their sleeve, this band of oddballs wouldn't strike terror into the Nexists' hearts. Greg watched the changing expressions on Suliman's face.

"I know what you're thinking, Captain Suliman," he said. "We are not alone. There are other Indigo who will join us. We have heightened perception, but at our core, we are mortal, no more, no less."

"Yet you believe yourselves a match for a Nexist army?"

Greg inclined his head. "In your solar system, it's unlikely any ship will be a match for ours in an aerial engagement, but even those of our fighters with psychic ability will have little advantage in hand-to-hand combat on the ground. From what Rebecca has told me of abettors, the side arms we possess are only slightly more advanced. When our forefathers settled here, they believed they found a home among friends; therefore, they did not need weapons to defend themselves, nor did they see a need to develop their technology. Fortunately," he grinned, "they didn't dismantle the ships' weapons arrays."

"If you wish, you can learn something of Indigo history," Rebecca said. "Andy has much of the history of the journey here stored in his memory. Captain Suliman, the Nexists will not defeat us."

"Us?" Suliman waggled his finger between Greg and Rebecca and his crew. "We haven't formally agreed to anything."

"There are a few dozen others who will join us," Rebecca replied. "And you did say you won't be parted from your ship. We'll go to Venus and get support there."

"What about ships?" Suliman enquired. "Mine isn't up to much, and it's got no weapons."

"We have this ship plus two others," Greg informed him. "They are all as ancient as this one, and smaller, but they will get us where we need to go. We stowed your ship in the hold last night. We'll get to your Venus, identify the other Indigo, then travel on to Earth. I will disguise this ship's hull configuration so that it appears similar to your own. With a few modifications, I can also disguise your ship if necessary."

"I'm impressed," Suliman said, "but someone will see it's not on a registry."

"We'll have time to deal with that."

"You're very confident, but Rebecca's belief in the Nexist plan may just be Nexist posturing. History is littered with pockets of radicals bleating about their lofty ideas."

"The fact my son heard my message and sent you suggests it's not posturing," Rebecca replied before Greg could formulate an answer. "He's arrogant. And I needed to force his hand. I know my son, Captain Suliman. Ambitious, ruthless, and destined to be a major player in the Nexist Mutuality. He'll have a plan to steer sympathy towards them and away from the Venusians." She frowned. "I would be interested to know why he sent such a diverse crew."

"They needed a pilot," Suliman began, then looked at Charlie, "and the doc, well…" Charlie could speak for herself, tell Rebecca what she wished.

Charlie didn't want to tell the whole story just yet, certainly not to Miller's mother. A simple, "Miller needed a doctor to keep Thale alive until he got to you," would suffice.

Rebecca raised an eyebrow. She sensed more in that sentence than the young woman revealed in simple words. "I see. We will leave in the morning. Is there anything else we can get for you? Any other questions?"

Rice raised his hand as if he were in a classroom. "What about the puppy? I don't know about dogs and space travel."

"You can take him if you wish," Greg said. "He will do better with you than leaving him here in Greater London."

Delighted that his newfound friend could remain with them, a beaming Rice gathered up the sleeping puppy and kissed the fuzzy head in a frenzy of affection and baby talk, while the fortunate dog grinned in its sleep.

Rebecca looked across at the pair with a flick of her eyebrows, then rose to leave.

"Andy will be here if you think of anything: history, food, drink, anything at all. I will see you in the morning." Then, bidding them all good night, she invited Livesey to follow her as she and Greg departed through the wall.

"That's a useful skill," Suliman observed. "They just seem to melt. I wonder if it works on brick or steel?"

"Probably not," Charlie said, "their abilities seem interconnected with the structure. I wonder where they've taken Livesey. Catching up, I suppose. Rice?" Charlie sat down; she had a question. "If we're not Indigo, and the humans came from this Earth with the other Indigo to settle *our* Earth, does that mean our ancestry, our history comes from here?"

"Makes sense," Rice agreed as he spat out dog hair. He'd thought of this very question himself. "There're stories of things, artefacts, even lost underwater cities which we've never been able to verify. I would suggest they don't exist on our Earth, and the humans and Indigo that came from here simply transported their history. Most of the stuff we've got dates back less than two thousand years, but we've had space travel capabilities since the beginning of records. No civilisation is born knowing how to travel in space. That was always one of the great mysteries."

Charlie pulled out her reader and displayed a map of their current location. "We're in the Northwest, but at home, we don't have any islands this big in the peninsula."

Rice agreed. "If some of the Indigos headed to our Earth after here and took humans with them, this must be where our ancestors are from. All of them."

"At least the human ones," Charlie nodded. "Some intermarried with Indigos. Like Rebecca said, we could have Indigo blood without being Indigo. I know I have a couple of Venusian ancestors."

Thinking about it made Rice's brain hurt. "You might be right, Charlie. Knowing what we know, I wish I could explore this place." He lifted a shoulder in resignation. "Our history isn't our history. It doesn't belong to us. It belongs here." Then he added with a sigh, "History back on our Earth is a meaningless exercise now."

Charlie didn't want him to feel discouraged. "Ancient architectural history, maybe, Rice," she suggested, "but we still have an evolved society and roots back home. So we still have a history worth exploring. Besides, does it matter where our story started? If you think about it, if we have Indigo blood in us, it comes from another galaxy. That means their history belongs to us too."

Rice sniffed. History to him was fossicking around dig sites, forming theories, reading and re-reading old texts and studying ancient languages. Now, it seems history spanned not just time but galaxies as well. The thought overwhelmed and intrigued him, and he was grateful when Andy showed them to the divans, inviting them to get some sleep.

Rice tucked the puppy up against him and fell asleep almost immediately. The pair's strident, synchronistic snoring stopped Suliman and Charlie from nodding off but allowed them to go over privately, and in hushed tones, the extraordinary events of the day. Most of all, they both speculated on what was taking place on Earth—their Earth, and what they would find when they returned.

CHAPTER TWENTY-ONE _

The following morning, Suliman, Rebecca, Charlie and Greg debated the finer points of the journey back to Earth.

"It will take thirteen months or thereabouts," Greg informed them. "This ship is a couple of points faster than the Millstone."

"How long did it take the Indigo to get from their galaxy?"

"Centuries, Doctor Maitland. Generations lived and died on this ship."

Suliman looked around. "It's an impressive size. A helluva lot bigger than mine."

Greg smiled. "It's also somewhat older."

It didn't look it to Suliman; the interior was a pristine white, and he wondered about propulsion. "I'd be interested to see the engines."

"It doesn't have engines," Greg said as several stunned expressions greeted his revelation. "It's powered by a system of biomolecular bubbles. These 'bubbles' are impervious to age and environment and protect the structure."

"Is that why the ship hasn't deteriorated?"

"This ship, like the others that will join us, is over five thousand years old, Captain Suliman, possibly more. Believe it or not, its operation is not very complex."

"Not if you're Indigo."

Greg responded to Suliman's sardonic comment with a non-committal twitch of his eyebrows. He knew every inch of this ship and its capabilities.

Charlie wasn't interested in starship mechanics and shifted the conversation back to the matter at hand. "The Nexists might have made their move. If so, they would have had plenty of time to gain a foothold since we left."

"They most certainly will have," Rebecca agreed. "It's doubtful my son told many of his colleagues about my message; he'll assume Thale effectively delivered his and in so doing, issued a warning to the 'aliens' who reprogrammed the ship."

"Wouldn't he have considered how the aliens harbouring you might take that?"

Rebecca's lips curled into a dry smile at Suliman's observation. "You are speaking of a fanatic. Don't expect reason."

The group stood in the room where they first arrived. Overnight, it had transformed from an empty chamber to a functioning ship's bridge. Charlie realised her view of it the day before had been a psionic projection designed to hide the technology. A vast forward viewport enveloped the bridge; however, the spectacle of rotting tree roots, dirt and skeletons from various decaying animals that once walked the surface above, didn't make for an inspiring view. An incomplete human skull, possibly an unfortunate former resident of the prison, its jaw grinning at a comical angle, lay wedged between the outer viewport and the compacted soil. A macabre reminder of just how deep under the earth they were. Still, the potential for a fantastic panorama of space was undeniable.

"How far underground is the ship buried?" she asked.

"Kilometres," Greg told her. "When the ship landed thousands of years ago, the local inhabitants believed a star fell from heaven and the Indigo occupants to be angelic beings. They called the area Wormwood after the star. The locals received them, but the Indigo burrowed the ship deep in the ground, not anticipating a future need. They didn't destroy it just in case." He grinned. "The Indigo cannot predict the future."

"Are the other ships buried elsewhere?"

"Yes, one in the British Isles and one on the continent. The Indigo that continued on after many years on Earth took most of the remaining ships."

Something puzzled Charlie. She and Suliman discussed it the night before. "When this ship lifts off, don't you think the local population will notice?"

"Greg is an engineer and has studied this ship for the last twenty years," Rebecca said. "We won't take off vertically. Instead, we will burrow out to the Thames—the river that runs through London—and remain immersed until we reach the Greater London boundary, then lift off from there. The residents may feel a little vibration but nothing else. The area outside Greater London is mostly unpopulated."

Suliman hadn't so far been able to get a sense of the Indigo ship's size, but he felt he needed to satisfy himself as to his own vessel's condition. "Can I see the Millstone?"

"You can go anywhere you wish on this ship where there are openings, Captain Suliman," Rebecca told him. "Otherwise, you will need an Indigo to help you walk through the walls." She delivered her line in such a matter-of-fact fashion that it took a moment before she caught Charlie's amusement. "I take it for granted now," she smiled, "but I assure you, it was strange to me at first. I enjoyed watching Matthew accomplish the first transition!"

"I won't be trying to walk through walls," Suliman assured her. "I'm not even sure I want to. Do you not trust me alone on the ship?"

"As a matter of fact, I do, Captain, although I think you may have an impulsive streak. And we can't walk through every wall, only the ones on Indigo ships."

"I've examined Livesey on several occasions," Charlie said, seizing on the relationship between Indigo and their technology. "His physiology is the same as ours. Is there anything in the Indigo that sets them apart?"

"I asked the same questions, Doctor Maitland. The ability to walk through walls comes from a partnership between the Indigo and the ship. The technology to develop the material is ancient and now lost."

"I'm Charlie."

Rebecca nodded. "Charlie, you won't find any physical differences. Regrettably, casualties of such lengthy internment on this ship are the degradation of some of the early Indigo recorded texts and technical data. We have Andy, and he may be able to answer most of your enquiries."

"Rice found texts written on some kind of fibrous material."

Puzzled, Rebecca turned to Rice. "What texts?" Greg also turned his full attention to the professor, who looked from one to the other, unnerved by the sudden scrutiny. "About—about the arrival of the Indigo on Venus," he stammered.

Greg stepped forward. "Do you have those texts?" he demanded. "Can you remember any of them?"

Shrinking from the urgency in Greg's voice, Rice nodded, keeping up the movement of his head until he recovered. "I recorded them," he squeaked. "I have them recorded, on my recorder, um, my reader on the Millstone."

Greg pressed him for an answer. "What do they say? Were there signs anyone before you had seen them?"

Rice squeezed out a "no", but with a nod from Charlie that indicated Greg was only trying to get to the bottom of a mystery, he managed a whole sentence. "The vault was only as big as a deposit safe, hidden. I don't think anyone had seen it since it was put there. I'll get the copies for you if you like." He glanced at Charlie and Suliman. "We've all seen them."

"The Nexists are aware of texts that allude, some say confirm, the existence of Indigos," Rebecca said to Greg, "taken from Venus years ago and in the custody of Nexist hierarchy, but they were never verified, possibly just hearsay. These must be something different. Something they missed."

"It's written in a mix of ancient Venusian, English, and, I think, French," Rice said. "I thought it might be a celebratory document or a proclamation."

"Like this?" Greg rattled off a long sentence. Charlie recognised some of the dialects, but her Venusian was rusty, and this inflexion sounded different. But Rice understood. He nodded.

"Yes, like that. You're very fluent. I couldn't read it all."

Rebecca and Greg exchanged knowing looks. "The Indigo must have transferred the proclamation to a physical document as backup against data degradation," Greg said. "It may be all the other data is stored there too." He turned to Rice, softening the urgency in his voice as he recognised he'd startled the little man. "Professor Rice, were there other texts? Did you tell anyone what you found?"

Rice started his foolish nodding again. "I didn't examine all the texts in the vault, just the one I told you about and one about the craft buried on Venus. I told the janitor who let me out, and he told security."

"Anyone else?"

"Security took me to Rille, so I suppose they told Governor Miller. By then, I knew my discovery was important, so I kept my copy lens hidden. I wish now I went straight to the Triumvirate, only I get nervous around government, and I wanted to show the document copies to the Earth Museum curator to verify before I took them anywhere else."

Rebecca sighed. "Chances are the Nexists have seized or destroyed any remaining texts by now. They'll try to wipe us from history."

"Sorry," Rice quivered.

Charlie hugged him. "It's not your fault. How could you have known?"

Greg agreed. "Professor Rice, if the text is what we believe it is, you may have done us a great service. I can translate it."

"This fight, this war we're planning," Charlie said, "It's not just about establishing the existence of the Indigo. It's about ridding the Triumvirate of a Nexist threat to the three inhabited worlds."

Greg acknowledged there was more than just the Indigo origin at stake. "Yes, but documents such as the ones Professor Rice discovered prove the existence of the Indigo. They are key to confirming your Earth's origins. When the fighting is over, they will provide irrefutable proof to settle your history once and for all."

Old tree roots twisted, buried bones rattled, and the

grinning skull got dislodged from its ancient tomb against the viewport as the Indigo ship burrowed like a mole from its almost prehistoric resting place. Charlie marvelled at how such an ancient vessel hadn't deteriorated throughout its enforced rest. The technology on the bridge blinked into life: sensors, panels, star fields, proximity feelers, life support to prepare for space travel, artificial gravity. It seemed that historical data was the only function that suffered. The first wash of water from under the Thames cleared the earth from the viewscreen, giving way to a whole host of rubbish dumped in the river's murky depths. They'd seen an image of the ship, a massive flattish disc, which was fortuitous as the top didn't protrude above the water. Greg took the launch carefully, it was the first time he'd flown the ship, but his instincts were perfect. They guided him, although luck rather than judgement helped him to avoid creating too much underwater turbulence, and what little there was likely provoked some serious speculation by observers on the bank as to what manner of fish or eddy could make such waves.

Charlie, Rice and Suliman watched the city pass via the sensor compilation. Rice had mixed feelings about leaving, although he felt safer on the ship than walking around the historic town.

"This city is the same as in our history books," he said. "Big Ben would be at least four thousand years old in our years. If Greg's calculations are correct, society stopped developing around the time the people who colonised our Venus left here. The Indigo did a good job of preserving the buildings and making it appear as if time stood still."

Suliman pointed to the sensor maps. "I don't see the point in Big Ben when only people within the city can see it. Other inhabitants are spread over kilometres."

"It's not the only clock, Suliman," Rice said, a little peeved that he had to educate his colleague on information freely available in museums. "The inhabitants would have had smaller versions in their homes with little legs and bells. A key in the back wound up a mechanism to make them tick away the minutes, and they made a ringing noise to wake up their owners in the morning."

Suliman gave him a sideways glance. "Sounds like torture. I'd have smashed it."

"It was their custom, but then, clocks probably never existed on our Earth. All our history belongs here. No wonder we can't find any artefacts from this era or before." Rice looked glum, as if he'd just discovered all his toys belonged to another child.

Charlie tried to cheer him up. "As we said, these people are our ancestors. Just remember their history is also ours, just transplanted."

Rice sighed. "I know." Then he sighed again. "I can't fight alongside you. I'm too fat and unfit. What good am I going to be in a battle against the Nexists? They'll take one look at me and die laughing. You might be better off dumping me in the Thames when you reach the outskirts."

"And lose our most important historian?" Suliman gave Rice a good-natured shove. Rice attempted a smile, but he felt significantly extra up against all these people itching for a fight. Charlie promised him, and he so wanted to believe her, that they would defeat the Nexists. She tried to jolly him out of his misery by telling him he'd soon be back digging up bones and annoying museum curators. She finished up with a comforting, "Don't worry, Rice. Rebecca will rally the other Indigo on Venus, and they'll join with us. You'll see, it's all going to work out."

Suliman supported Charlie's inauthentic optimism. "The doc's right," he added. "I'm going to break Miller's neck, although I might start with his other bones first."

Charlie glared at him. Rice was fragile enough, and now was not the time to discuss violence. Besides, she'd already visualised how it would all play out.

"Suliman, it's not going to be a bloodbath or a bone-breaking festival. We're going to walk in calmly and take over. The Nexists are cowards, and with the weight of the Indigo and Venusians behind us, they'll back down." She concluded her speech with a positive, "You just wait and see."

Brave words, Suliman thought. He wondered if she genuinely believed them. Either way, he hoped for her sake they would prove prophetic.

CHAPTER TWENTY-TWO _

They didn't dump Rice into the Thames when they cleared the city. The ship rose in serene elegance into the air, well away from anyone who might have run back to the city crying, "flying saucers" or "UFO's". As they left the planet behind, Charlie felt oddly reassured to be back in space. An unexpected feeling, as it wasn't a place she loved, but just being back in her own space—she tried to work out how that fitted together—felt familiar.

Okay, she conceded, there'd be a fight. Suliman would probably break a few of Miller's bones, maybe all of them, with his mother's sanction. Hell, Charlie might even break them herself. The Triumvirate took any threat to its sovereignty seriously, no matter how insignificant. It had always prevailed. Charlie had to believe her little band of friends could save the day, that the Nexists had not yet made their move and that Sam had learned a thing or two that would work in their favour. She felt confident putting her trust in him, but Rebecca and Suliman had their heads together discussing battle plans even before they reached the ionosphere.

"It'll be ages before we get back to our Earth," Charlie said. "Isn't this premature?" She lowered her voice. "Rice is frightened. He doesn't want to fight, so I hope it doesn't turn out to be necessary."

Rebecca looked over to where Rice sat on the floor with his dog.

"We won't ask him to fight," she said. "But he will learn how to pilot the Millstone and any Venusian ship we can secure. Charlie, you think diplomacy will save the day, but we are dealing with zealots. I know the scale of their plans, and I'm afraid a battle is unavoidable."

Suliman agreed with Rebecca on this. "You have even less experience with Nexists than I do, Doc. I can tell you, they won't go without a fight, and who knows what advances they've made in the last eighteen months with rounding up the Indigo? The Triumvirate may have already fallen."

"Nexists infiltrated the Triumvirate years ago, Captain Suliman," Rebecca said. "They were biding their time as sleepers, preparing and grooming younger senators."

Suliman shrugged. "See, Doc? I didn't know that."

"I just never expected a war." Charlie thought about her parents. "My mum and dad live on Earth."

"Well, a war is what you're going to get," Suliman said, perhaps too briskly. He didn't want to upset the doc, but he didn't want her unprepared either. "When we left, the Nexists numbered in the thousands. According to Martian records, they held over forty elderly people in prison for such crimes as not paying their rates and water bills. I bet they were Indigo."

"I don't believe it."

"It's true," Rebecca said.

"How do you know?"

"Look." Suliman opened a data stream from the Millstone. "Greg found it. Unbeknownst to us, during its preparation for our journey, someone tripped a switch on the frequency that allowed it to gather a limited number of Nexist communiques. We at least know they are moving forward with their plans."

Charlie looked over Suliman's shoulder. Sure enough, the text was there, although none with Miller's signature. "That sounds like a hell of a coincidence."

Suliman grinned. "I don't think it was. I reckon we had a sympathiser involved in the Millstone's refinements."

Charlie thought that was an amazing stroke of luck, particularly as the data was uneclipsed and original.

Rebecca understood Charlie's scepticism. "It is, but don't be too surprised. The Nexists aren't as exclusive as they think. There are a few spies among their ranks."

Charlie puffed out her breath. She was game to protect her homeworld by any means available, but she couldn't believe she missed any recent mention of the Nexists. Maybe she did and ignored it, or perhaps because someone stuck her on the moon and forgot about her.

"That's not all," Rebecca said. "I was never involved, but in the ten years before I left on the Seeker ship, fifteen

Venusian senators and their families disappeared. My son seemed to have specific knowledge of them. One body was found in the embassy's grounds in the southwest, pointing the finger at the criminal element there, although they denied it. According to this data, during the time the Millstone was having a refit, several others went missing, and for some reason, the Triumvirate didn't investigate."

Suliman remembered the discovery of the body of a senator's wife.

"I knew the man who went to prison for her murder. I met him in the Martian penal colony, and he told me the Nexists covertly recruited amongst the displaced youth in the Triumvirate Relief programs. A couple of those kids who wanted out once they realised how serious it was about to become, ended up dead. Of course, they weren't senator's wives, so it went unnoticed."

Charlie knew nothing of this. Had she really been so ignorant?

"I had no idea," she admitted. "The war has already started, hasn't it? Expelling Venus is just part of the endgame."

Suliman laid a hand on her shoulder. "Don't feel bad, Doc. I didn't know either. I heard stuff in prison, but when I got to Rille, all that dried up. I disliked Miller on sight, but I never suspected him."

Hours later, alone for the first time that day and away from the activity of the Indigo crew, Charlie gazed out the viewport as the other Earth shrunk from a glorious blue globe to a small, barely visible dot. Suliman came up behind her. She seemed lost in thought, and he hesitated, thinking perhaps he would respect her solitude, but she saw his reflection and turned.

"Want company?" he said.

Charlie smiled up at him. "I hope we give that plural marriage planet a wide berth."

"We might not bypass it altogether; it's a pretty linear trajectory to get home, but we know the gravity well or wave, or whatever it is, is there, so we can avoid it."

"It looks like humans populate the universe," Charlie said. "It's a shame we won't have time to find any we can rally to our cause. It would be a help." She felt it was probably a blessing to have only encountered humans; she remembered some of the space stories about hostile lizard men and space slugs from her childhood. "I can see how the Indigo appeared angelic to the early people they encountered on that world." She smiled. "This ship simply dropped from the heavens. I suppose there is something romantic, something exciting about the Indigo story."

"Romantic? If you say so," Suliman grinned. "I knew Livesey was hiding something. I can't get over him being an Indigo, although I have yet to learn of the benefits…"

"They're psychic."

Suliman bobbed his head around in deliberation before answering. "According to Rebecca, only a few are strongly psychic, so I wonder if it's a skill worth having. I find it hard to think of Rebecca as a Nexist either. She seems…" he couldn't find the right word.

"Nice?"

"Yeah, that's it. But she's not young, and she's planning to fight."

"I rather suspect her turning up will knock Governor Miller on his lecherous arse."

"I'd like to see that, Doc, but now I wonder if we should have delayed our departure, let Miller think his little scheme was successful and give him time to start not expecting us back."

"And also give him time to take over the Triumvirate? I don't know. Did you suggest that to Rebecca?"

"No, I don't think she would have listened. Miller forced me on this mission, and now, I guess I'm along for the ride. Staying in that Greater London place, hemmed in by that clock and extinct animals, isn't my idea of an adventure. Besides, they can't make decent coffee."

Charlie laughed. "I didn't like it there either. Did you notice how grey the sky was? And dull? How does a civilisation flourish like that?"

"Rice would know. Can't say I've ever paid attention to history."

"I wonder if other Indigo have different abilities. Telekinesis, maybe?" Charlie suggested, only half-serious. She raised a questioning eyebrow at Suliman. "Thought control?"

"Not as individuals, no," Greg's answer announced his arrival. "Although Andy speaks of ancestors with considerable mental discipline capable of channelling energy to enhance physical vigour and treat disease."

Charlie was impressed. "A worthy art. Do you still practise it?"

"We suspect it was a form of meditation, now lost to us. It is possible some of our ancestral data is stored on Venus. If so, we might recover some of our old observances. Now, I didn't mean to eavesdrop; I came to ask if you would join us on the bridge. We need to introduce you to the rest of the crew, and then I will show you your quarters. Suliman, I sense you are a man who prefers solitude. I managed to find you a separate berth."

Greg turned to Charlie. "There is a small billet at the side of the medical facility. You're the only doctor between all three ships, but there are four paramedics who can deal with anything non-urgent. We'll shuttle anything more critical across, although that means we have to drop from Mag as our shuttles don't have Mag capability. The other two Indigo ships will join us shortly. Captain Suliman, I will refer to our speed as Mag for your benefit. I wish it were faster, but it's all we have."

"What will happen to the Earth? I mean, your Earth?"

"It'll continue, Charlie. In time, there will be rediscoveries, air travel and sea travel; the Indigo will make sure the population thrives. The rest of the world will access each other, and when they realise the devastation their greed and disregard for each other caused, perhaps there will be more understanding and respect."

"What happened on your Earth?" So far, no-one had spoken of the war that changed history, and with so much going on, Charlie didn't feel the time was right to ask.

"My world has always had wars," Greg replied. "As each one ended, governments promised no more."

Suliman knew about governments; he didn't trust them. "How did that work out?"

"Not well," Greg admitted. "And usually, it was governments that started the major conflicts, but individual wars were waged as well, religions, corporations, individuals…they all needed to start arguments." Greg paused to draw a small device from his jacket pocket. A data diary. Charlie owned a similar tool, used for appointments, but Greg's contained historical information. The device projected the image of Greg's Earth between them, then it homed into an area they recognised; London, a bustle of life and energy, of flags flying above buildings, strange red buses crawling around like two-storey ladybugs, and the other vehicles Rice mentioned, cars, flowing across the bridge in both directions. The people looked happy and energised.

"This is London in the year 2030," Greg said. "The year the world, as everyone knew it, ended."

Charlie thought it looked vibrant and prosperous. A far cry from the grey, dreary city they just left. What could have changed it so?

Greg shifted the image to a scene of terror and unimaginable cruelty.

"A little under one hundred years before, an ideology took seed in a European country, eventually leading to a movement with philosophies not unlike the Nexists on your world. This ideology embroiled the planet in a war that culminated in the deaths of millions of innocents."

"Obviously, the good guys won," Suliman observed. "Did the Indigo have a hand in that victory?"

"No more than any native human," Greg replied. "Other wars followed—" he flicked through more, equally brutal scenes, listing only some of the battles, "Korea, Vietnam, Afghanistan. Many of these wars did not cover the globe, but each fight, each order issued by a dictator, diminished humankind."

"We have only ever had one or two wars," Charlie said. "Not even real wars, just skirmishes. We had a civil war on our Earth a couple of hundred years ago."

Greg pointed out that wars didn't necessarily involve guns and cannons. "In the war that changed my world," he told them, "No-one fired a single shot."

"Well, how…?" Charlie started to say. A war without weapons? How would that work?

"The 'how' was easy," Greg said. "A fast-acting, genetically modified micro-organism, introduced into the drinking water on the American continent gave a swift and deadly introduction to non-traditional warfare."

Greg changed the data history to scenes of America. Mass graves littered the countryside and decaying bodies were strewn in precincts and walkways. He spoke with quiet reverence as he recounted that seventy-two per cent of the population died within a month, not even enough left to bury the dead. He finished by saying that many Indigo also perished.

Charlie watched the unfolding scenes. How could humans on Greg's Earth have such little regard for life? She looked up at him in horror. "Did they discover who did it?"

"The culprits were an obscure cult. This is their headquarters—" He showed them an image of an old wooden house with a bunch of ordinary-looking people sitting around. "America, made up of many provinces, or states, called themselves 'USA', but this cult believed a supreme being entrusted them to deliver the USA from the evils of vice, satanism, adultery, prostitution; everything they believed went against the laws of their deity, then they expanded it to include climate, recycling, waste disposal. The list became endless, and everyone was guilty."

Charlie's hand went to her mouth as the images rolled before her. "I've heard of a deity like this before," she said, when at length, Greg flicked off the data stream. "It didn't have a name like most deities. It was just 'God'. They worshipped him on the world where we crash-landed. Apparently, he got upset about trivial things, so I can't imagine what he'd think about mass murder."

"It's a possibility that humans settled that world as our people made their way across the galaxy and took the notion of God with them," Greg suggested. "Although perhaps not as extreme. The existence of God was at the basis of many of our world's religions, but with this cult," Greg continued, "they had at their disposal one of the great scientific and insane minds of the generation. It became less about purifying the world and more about power. The microbe had a devastating effect. In the beginning, it was confined to the USA, but before the rest of the world knew what was happening, they were preparing for another war, another step in the cycle of destruction. Then the microbe appeared in Asia and the Antipodes."

"And the Indigo stepped in?" Suliman prompted.

Greg nodded. "To save the planet, the Indigo tried to program the Foundation Artefact. Indigo history speaks of it generating a canopy around the Indigo, but the truth is, no-one knows for sure. Andy told them it was capable of psionic programming, but when the Indigo tried, the pulse shook this Earth, and the artefact communicated, psychically, that it might cause harm. The Indigo took one of the smaller ships to transport the artefact to the moon and enough Indigo to carry out a psychic reprogramming."

It seemed like a mammoth task to Charlie, and she questioned how a device so far away exerted control over events here, but Greg knew little about the actual programming, only that the Indigo's desire to save the planet formed its foundation. It had taken place centuries before he was born, and he knew only that in the silence of the moon, the artefact became amenable to the thoughts of those earlier Indigo.

"The solution came next," he said. "Most technologies were removed: individual transports, mobile communication devices, home entertainment systems, and a forcefield set up around the surviving civilisations. That included parts of Europe, the British Isles, and an area of the USA with a separate forcefield around its neighbouring countries. The artefact produced a frequency that temporarily anaesthetised the population, and the Indigo mounted a mass evacuation to habitable areas cleansed of the microbe pollutant. They were not able to save so many in the Southern Hemisphere, not plants, not animals, not people. It was all too late." He looked around him. "It was the first time since they arrived that they brought this vessel out of hibernation, and yes, Charlie," Greg acknowledged her earlier thought, "it was a mammoth task."

"The Triumvirate's recorded history spans at least two thousand years," Charlie said. "The buildings in London are mentioned as existing before that time—questions are asked about what happened to them, and there have been several excavations. It's clear now that they never existed on our world. Don't give me any more surprises, Greg. Is this Earth on the same timeline as ours?" She circled a finger to include Suliman.

"The same," Greg confirmed. "That you see no progress, no ambition, no colour to the existence of this world comes from the artefact, but the people believe they are fulfilled."

"And it's been this way for the last two thousand years?"

"We had the technology to save them, Captain Suliman," Greg said. "Humans no longer think too deeply about their circumstances. There is no religion, no major commerce. The population is controlled. The barrier around each continent or country is never questioned. Needs are provided for. People still believe they have a purpose; they go to work, they talk, read, socialise, and they forget." Greg blinked slowly. "It pains me to say it, but the Indigo, out of necessity, created a world of automatons, at least until they can lift the barriers. That time has not yet come. The larger obstacles of greed, control, and prejudice are still yet to be overcome by humans themselves. You experienced prejudice yourselves when you arrived."

"It's been a long time. Maybe they never will, so why do you try?"

Charlie's question took Greg by surprise.

"Because we see signs of change. In time, the people will become enlightened, but for now, we can't trust them not to extinguish their own light." He saw the answer didn't satisfy Charlie or Suliman. Rather, he sensed suspicion from them.

"Isn't that for them to decide?" Suliman agreed with Charlie's evaluation.

"Look to your own world, Captain Suliman. It is a question of *who* will survive. The strongest, with their mech, their technology, their intellect? Or the weakest, with nothing but sticks to fight off the invaders and a will to survive to sustain them? Which side would you want to be on? Which side would you look to as guardians of the future?"

Suliman got his point, but Greg didn't know his world. His people were taken over by a government that believed they were doing their best but instead oppressed and removed freedom. The Nexists would be no better, just empty promises they would not deliver upon. Self-determination? Look where it got him, but he could not agree with the ongoing Indigo control of Greg's planet. He saw both Charlie and Greg waiting for an answer.

"So, doing it your way?"

"Our 'way', Captain Suliman, is better than their way. We're protecting them."

Charlie needed to think about it a little more, but on the face of it, she agreed with Suliman.

"Our populated worlds put together don't have the history of wars your one planet has," she said. "I see the depths to which your Earth sank, Greg, but two millennia of mind control on such a grand scale? I concede—" she looked at Suliman, "I, we, are outsiders, but it seems excessive. We need to get rid of the Nexists, but we don't need controlling with mind blocks."

Greg hesitated, unsure whether he should take Charlie's words as a warning. His whole life and the lives of generations before him had seen the people of his Earth in bondage because of their history. His dream was to one day lift those blocks and allow the people their liberty once again, to flourish and grow. Now, he found himself travelling across the galaxy to participate in a war that once again threatened freedom. This time, he assured himself, it would be different; the Indigo who settled the Triumvirate worlds created an enlightened society. He responded briefly to Charlie's statement.

"As I said, the artefact will remain here to keep this world safe." He smiled then and left them with a short reminder of the assembly on the bridge.

Charlie took a deep breath. "I hope we're not part of a strike team that will install a dictatorship."

Suliman watched as Greg disappeared along the passageway. He shook his head. "The way he told it, that planet was heading towards annihilation, but I believe he is a man dedicated to his cause."

Charlie asked him to count how many people from history who considered their approach better than anyone else's, adding, "Isn't control what we're fighting here?"

Suliman's jaw tightened. "I'd agree with you if I didn't know what an asshole Governor Miller is. I wouldn't have him umpire a game of musical chairs at a kid's party."

The second two Indigo ships fell into formation before they reached Jupiter. In total, there were seven hundred souls on the three vessels, a blend of ancestral Indigo and Indigo/human hybrid, all with the knowledge and varying degrees of Indigo psychic ability. In addition, a few non-Indigo human descendants completed the volunteer force. Every person on each ship was destined for combat should it be required.

As the weeks progressed, Greg and a group of engineers collaborated on reproducing the abettors and updating the ancient, shoulder-carried weapons of the original Indigo. Charlie and Livesey joined in physical fitness sessions; Suliman gave Rice simulated lessons flying the Millstone, taking it out only when opportunity allowed, such as when the shuttles were moving back and forth.

After a hesitant start, Rice discovered a new talent as a pilot, which led him to request combat training. Sweating through the sessions resulted in him gaining a leaner, trimmer shape, which in turn bolstered his confidence.

Rebecca and Suliman made a great leadership team, coordinating training on all four ships and appointing subcommanders to establish "local" government on each vessel. Charlie noted with interest how this hierarchy, administered from the largest ship, was received by the various crews. There were very few "full" Indigo. Greg was one of these. They exhibited traits that included quick learning, varying degrees of psychic ability and lack of fatigue, even after many hours of training or physical work. Working closely with them, Charlie soon learned to identify "full" Indigo by their attributes. Outnumbering the "full" Indigo by a ratio of four to one were those, like Rebecca and Livesey, who were considered "diluted". Charlie found the term distasteful, although it seemed to have no particular connotation to the full Indigo, just a means to distinguish Indigo, who also had other human blood in their veins but still displayed psychic traits. These were also the most likely to buck against leadership decisions. In those times, Suliman's patience and judgement surprised them all. No complaint or enquiry was too insignificant for him to give his full attention. If he could not resolve an issue, which usually involved training locations and the opportunity to drop from Mag to stretch their legs on a suitable planet, he would bring in Charlie or Greg to help with a resolution. Seldom did the petitioner go away unsatisfied. The other problem they faced was that no-one, regardless of the degree of Indigo, had ever left their Earth before, and it was inevitable some would suffer homesickness. Out of this rose regret at leaving their homes to fight a distant war, even to save the Indigo, while others found living in close quarters more of a trial. Charlie understood. Even on the vast lead ship, it was a challenge to find anywhere private, so she was grateful to have her modest quarters in the medical facility where she could escape.

***

A few months out, with the crews finally finding their place and getting along, the final battle plan was yet to be laid. With the status of Earth and Venus unknown and with Rebecca adamant the feared events had already taken place, the possibility of turning up with no plan in place became a concern. The extra information they gleaned from the Millstone's illegally acquired communiques didn't give specifics, so they couldn't ignore the fact Rebecca might be correct. Livesey, the most recent Indigo to be on their own Earth, was convinced they were heading into the aftermath of a coup.

"In those few years after the awakening," he told Charlie one morning, while Greg, Suliman, Rebecca and others debated contingencies, "I travelled between all three worlds. I didn't realise it at the time, I was too new to it all, but now, looking back, the Indigo on Venus knew this was coming."

"Then won't they be prepared?"

"What can they do if they're already separated? The Indigo won't have the technology, Charlie. They can't fly or retaliate without ships. Rebecca and Suliman know Venus is the place to start. I have every confidence in them."

"They're not military leaders."

"So what? I don't believe the Nexists will stand against the joint forces of the Indigo and the Venusians. That's not including any Earthers who join with us."

"If the Nexists have made Earth their headquarters, we have to find a way to get enough Indigo and Venusians to Earth to mount an offensive."

"Suliman has some ideas about that. He knows people."

Charlie smiled. Of course, he did. "Suliman has dedicated himself to this cause, hasn't he? It seems to have given him purpose."

Livesey agreed. "He is a clever man, a resourceful man. You say we have no military leaders, but I don't believe Suliman will disappoint us."

Rebecca seldom needed to attend the medical facility, but as a "diluted" Indigo and not as young as the others, the physical demands of training occasionally required a supplement to keep her going. Charlie knew Rebecca would not accept advice to, "take things easier," so she simply ensured Rebecca's bones and skin were in the best condition they could be if she suffered an injury. Physically, Rebecca was in great shape, but she would have to be at least eighty years old. Back home, someone of that age would have been baking cakes and playing with her great-grandchildren, not planning the downfall of an empire.

Rebecca's visits were always welcome, and she and Charlie often spent a pleasant hour chatting about their previous lives. Charlie found it impossible to equate the charming, determined, selfless Rebecca with being the mother of a conniving, nasty and overbearing son.

"He was such a self-contained little boy," Rebecca told her one time when Charlie asked. "He played alone and by his own rules. There were no signs of what he would become until much later. As a teenager, he got in with a pack who hearkened back to the Nexist wars. The Triumvirate ban on Nexism still stood, so all our activities remained covert. We made it a point not to tell our children of our beliefs because, as you know, children are not always reliable in keeping secrets. At that point, George didn't know, but he put two and two together because of his father's strictness and dislike of Venusians. We also kept scholarly texts at our home about humans and the creation by a superior race. All of it covertly Nexist. George saw in it all, in our example, an outlet for his bias against Venusians. He began asserting that Earth had to be kept pure, no intermarrying, and that Earth must become self-governing. He often spoke of moving the Triumvirate to Earth and imposing sanctions against Venus. It was all resurrected Nexist propaganda, but George was eloquent enough to make it sound like benign criticism." Rebecca sighed. "We tried to stop him, but already he was laying the foundations for a takeover. He and his friends, who would be part of his victory, drew up a staged plan. He knew it would be years before he could make his move, but he was content to bide his time."

Charlie had no fears for Venus. If it found itself separated and without transport to Earth and Mars, it would easily sustain itself.

Rebecca agreed. "And in time will become a threat once again, but the Nexists will deal with that problem later. Right now, they want the power of the Triumvirate, and to do that, they need to remove the Presidential seat from Venus. I am not sure how my son plans to accomplish it."

"Let's hope we're not too late," Charlie said. "Perhaps there is room for a peaceful outcome, at least if we get to Venus before the Nexists."

Rebecca studied Charlie's face. So young, so innocent, how could she know the fanaticism that stripped away any vestige of decency from those who fully embraced Nexism? She shuddered to think that that was also her path at one time, and it saddened her to know she led her family there too.

"You're from Europa, aren't you?" Charlie smiled after listening to Rebecca's story. "It's the accent. Were your family Nexists?"

Rebecca nodded. "Sad to say, but yes. Way back, one of my ancestors was a signatory to the Myth of Origin; they were mostly sympathisers, but they paid tithes to the Nexists." She laughed suddenly. "You should have seen the celebration when I married my husband!"

Charlie listened as Rebecca spoke about the man she married. Her voice held no accusation, no hostility as she related the early days of their courtship and marriage, their belief in a shared cause for a better way, their criticism of the Triumvirate's form of governance, the myths as to the origins of humankind. As her story unfolded, Charlie realised Rebecca was never as drawn into Nexism as the rest of the Miller family. Something held her back. The yet-to-be ignited Indigo flame, perhaps? A foreshadowing of her future betrayal of Nexist principles? Charlie didn't know, but she was sure that at one time, Rebecca was a devoted wife and mother. Now, her family had become her enemy.

"At one time, you admired your husband's achievements and shared his convictions, didn't you?"

"I idolised him," Rebecca admitted, "but there was always that…need, that drive in him to find something bigger, better. Nexism satisfied that urge, but it frightened him at the same time. I just don't know how I didn't see my family's fanaticism extended to murder."

Deep in conversation, the two women didn't notice that Suliman had come looking for Charlie. He overheard some of their conversation before retracing his steps. He'd committed himself to whatever came their way when they arrived back, but after that, successful or not, he didn't want to be part of rebuilding society or establishing a new one. He would stay until the end of the campaign, and then, with the Millstone now having decent speed capabilities, he might just go out into space and start again. He didn't mind being on his own, and he doubted anyone would miss him. Charlie, though, worried him. By the time they arrived back, almost three years would have passed, and he wondered if Sam would be waiting for her. Charlie would presumably return to be with her family and become a physician, but if the Nexists prevailed, Miller probably would have them all executed. Suliman had toyed with asking Charlie to join him on his venture into space, but she told him becoming a physician was her life's dream. Having only him as a patient may just not hold the same fascination.

CHAPTER TWENTY-THREE _

Several uneventful months passed, and Charlie's medical facility lay mostly idle. She passed the time training the four medics whose skills were also underutilised. Charlie took the opportunity to bring them up to speed in anticipation of the possibility they may have to treat injuries on the battlefield. They each showed remarkable medical skill, even though Charlie found they had a way to go before reaching her high standards. Still, they were a friendly and likeable group, and the training sessions became an enjoyable part of the day. Rice took to flirting with the two female medics, but when they made it clear they were not interested in him romantically, he turned to Charlie for advice, who advised him very gently that despite his new look, he simply wasn't a Casanova.

In other areas, Suliman and Rebecca developed a rudimentary battle plan with several alternatives. Still, without knowing the position on Earth and Venus, they had to accept the fact they might be flying by the seat of their pants. They took the situation in their stride, but Greg, irked by uncertainty, preferred things neater. Charlie noted this precision in the other full Indigo. Their attention to detail inspired confidence, while the diluted variety seemed happy to wait for events to unfold.

Charlie was still in the learning stages of telling one end of space from the other, but Greg, who had never left the atmosphere of his Earth and claimed his knowledge was only theoretical, still had the advantage of understanding the ancient Indigos' star charts. He attempted to explain the nuances of Indigo historical stellar cartography, when, on one occasion, the two found themselves alone on the bridge.

"I've spent years studying these," he told Charlie, displaying an impressive array of star systems that filled the bridge and surrounded her in pinpoints of lights and coloured clouds, all catalogued in the minutest of detail in a language that vaguely reminded her of Venusian. He narrowed them down for her to observe the systems they would pass through on their journey.

"The stellar charts survived, thankfully," he said, "but very few records of contact with other humans. I had full Indigo parents, and they were the previous custodians of this vessel. Custody passes down through generations. The Indigo flame burned in me even as a small child. I always knew I would take over from my mum and dad."

"Did the flame ignite early?"

"I don't remember it not being there, Charlie. In children of human/Indigo hybrids, it happens much later, sometimes, not at all, and if the flame doesn't ignite, that person is not considered Indigo."

"Are you sure the Indigo are human?"

Greg laughed. "Absolutely! Just different human."

"Almost everyone on these ships is Indigo, though," Charlie said. "I've learned to recognise the difference between full and diluted." She paused. "Diluted. I hate that term."

"That's because you perceive 'diluted' as watered down. To the Indigo, it simply means mixed. Equal parts."

"That's exactly what I thought," Charlie laughed. "Were you reading my mind?"

Greg raised his eyebrows and grinned. He wasn't, but all Indigo had heightened perception, and as a full Indigo, he could enter a mind if he chose. He just never did.

Charlie looked at Greg's raised eyebrows, his brown eyes, his soft mouth…and she turned away, hoping there were times he switched off his mind-reading abilities. She distracted herself by pointing to eddies she recognised, eddies that were burned into her brain. She didn't remember much about star charts, but she remembered those.

"We need to steer clear of this planet. There are a lot of women on these ships. If we get caught in the wave, I doubt they'll let us go that easily. And I'm probably wanted for assault," she added with a sideways glance.

Greg examined the eddies on the long-range sensors. The ancestral Indigo didn't record them—he'd added these from the Millstone, but every discovery, every anomaly fascinated him, although perhaps not enough to have an encounter with a hostile race. Charlie's retelling of her experience on that planet and of her clocking someone with a frypan was both amusing and cautionary. "We won't get there for a few hours," he said. "Don't worry, we'll give it a wide berth."

"Excellent," Charlie smiled. "I'm going down to aeroponics. Andy's distilling leaves for me to make a tonic. I discovered it quite by accident, and it's great for space nausea."

"I'll come with you. If Andy's already there, you'll need someone to let you in."

Charlie liked Greg's company. He was easy to talk to—particularly if you liked discussing space travel, and he managed to be consistently pleasant, enjoying conversation other than the coming confrontation.

"How long have you known Suliman?" Greg asked as they walked. "He's protective of you."

Charlie hadn't noticed. Suliman was, well, Suliman.

"Only since Rille. I spend most of my time in the medbay, but other times, I'm with Suliman and Rice." Charlie laughed. "Suliman and Rice sounds like a menu item!"

Greg's lips twitched in a faint smile. He often tried, but just as often failed, to get Charlie alone. It was true; Suliman always seemed to hover. Greg estimated Suliman to be fifty if he was a day, far too old for Charlie. But he might just be being ungracious, maybe the old boy felt fatherly towards her.

"For a doctor, you make a great soldier," Greg said. "I've watched you with the abettor and the Indigo weapons. You're pretty impressive."

"Suliman is a great teacher. On the journey to your Earth, I didn't have much else to do but play with guns. Thale was sick and on a schedule, so I had heaps of free time. I feel motivated to learn about fighting now, although my hope is for a peaceful solution." She shook her head and glanced up at him. "I'm the only doctor on board, and I've treated two sore throats and a couple of bouts of space sickness. It's a hardy crew."

"That's good to hear. I'll let you into a secret. I'd never fired a weapon before Suliman showed me. My Earth is a peaceful place now, and we spend most of our lives supporting the population until it is ready to become self-sufficient once more."

"I know. It must have been dull."

"Dull!" Greg exclaimed, "*Dull?* Is that what you think? Saving our fellow humans isn't dull, Charlie. A worthy purpose is fulfilling in itself. Each sectioned civilisation is unaware of the others, but as a custodian Indigo, I travelled using the single occupant shuttles. I saw the changes taking place, and I know the world will recover. It will start over, and next time, it will be a world free of war."

"I hope you're right." Charlie recalled the history of the conflict that beset his planet. She didn't want to talk about it. "Has Rebecca told you much about the Indigo on Venus and Earth? I know you know they are widely considered a myth."

"We are not a myth to the Nexists. Besides, we have our reasons for being inconspicuous."

"Landing a spaceship that the locals thought was a star isn't inconspicuous."

Greg conceded the point with a grin. "Yet that event appears to have dropped from history. Rebecca speaks of a document, the Myth of Origin. I would be very interested in viewing it."

"It got resurrected years ago from the Triumvirate vaults," Charlie said. "They use it now for sociological arguments in schools. It doesn't support the existence of the Indigo, but it does tacitly accuse the Nexists of hysteria, which, by the way, are also not supposed to exist. I expect there's a copy in the Millstone's database. I'll ask Suliman. Greg, I'd like to know why the Indigo left their homeworld. Andy's account sent us to sleep!"

Greg was delighted to tell Charlie about his ancestors. They'd documented parts of their history, much of which was lost, and other parts handed down through families. It didn't matter; it made fascinating listening even to an anti-history-back-in-school buff like Charlie.

In his desire to build a cohesive picture of his race, Greg often switched between early accounts of the Indigo homeworld and the interaction with the people of the planet that eventually became their sanctuary. He told her, with a certain wistfulness, that he sometimes wished he'd been there when the Indigo first left their homeworld. Charlie pointed out the Indigo were fleeing persecution and that he might have got the better end of the deal.

"Well, we're facing persecution in your home, now," he pointed out wisely. "We faced it in ancient times and retreated. This time, we will stay and fight."

Charlie nodded. He still had to finish his story, but she got the distinct impression he felt the Indigo failed to protect their heritage. He was determined it wouldn't happen again.

Greg went on to tell her how the ancient Indigo lived side by side with other races on their planet, Uxta, a word that meant unity in every language on their world. He spoke poetically of harmony and equality, comradeship, and a love of shared ideals. It had been this way since time immemorial.

It sounded like a perfect society, although Charlie doubted such perfection would last forever, as the next part of Greg's story confirmed.

"It took only one eloquent speaker," he said with a sadness carried by the ageless flame that burned within him, "A man not even a native of Uxta, who had the right words of envy, hate and fearmongering to fuel the fire."

Charlie had a sudden vision of Miller, an image that sent a ripple of rage right down to her toes. Unconsciously, she clenched her fists.

"The Indigo sensitivity and technical skills were always revered and appreciated," Greg continued, too lost in his narrative to notice her flush of anger. "But as the movement against them grew, these same attributes became shunned. The people still relied on Indigo craftsmanship for technology, but as they became outcasts, society crumbled. Those who rejected the Indigo built inferior machines and inferior structures. At one time, the Foundation Artefact became a focus for fear, and the Indigo were forced to remove it off-world to protect it. Not even the Indigo know where the artefact originates; it is unique, and part of pre-historic Indigo culture. It has power, but it only amplifies the psionic strength of the Indigo. Some say the artefact was forged in a star; some say it came from the gods. Who knows?" He tapped his chin absently, as if this question were something he pondered often.

From Greg's, at times, emotional account, Charlie learned the new anti-Indigo government eventually declared its citizens in need of protection from a race capable of reading minds. It warned the people that the Indigo were physically stronger and capable of producing weapons and technology that might destroy them. The government formed an army, took up arms and sought to drive the Indigo into the wilderness.

"Was it because you built these ships?"

Greg shook his head. "No, Uxta was a spacefaring world," he said, emphatically denying that possibility. "Interplanetary craft were commonplace, but there is a theory—" he frowned, "—or perhaps a myth, that it was the vision of an Indigo passing through a wall on this ship that sparked the initial fear. Were the Indigo careless? Complacent? I can't say, but their ability to combine their cellular structure with their creations is decidedly not 'human', and possibly the only thing that sets us apart. I can understand observing the melding of molecules probably terrified the casual observer."

Charlie remembered her curiosity the first time she witnessed it, but had to agree with Greg. It might also terrify. The actual experience, of which she'd had many in the company of Indigo, was nothing spectacular. Just a blink, and you're on the other side.

"So your ancestors had to leave," she said.

"The Indigo knew the government planned to enlist the aid of another world, more militant, and one who would mount an invasionary force that would bring about the end of the Indigo. So, we did exactly what the people feared: we weaponised what was previously an ordinary intragalactic craft and fought back. The battle had barely begun when the Indigo questioned the purpose of fighting. Was it to return to a planet on which they were no longer welcome? Or perhaps annihilate the races united against them? It ultimately came down to choice and conscience."

"Couldn't you have implemented a mind control using the artefact, like you have on your Earth?"

"I have some of the memories, Charlie," Greg said. "Kind of like an emotional echo, but nothing clear and solid. We were just one race in a world of many; it was better that we leave them in peace if they didn't want us. On my Earth, the people were in the process of annihilating themselves. When my forefathers intervened, they only had a theory that programming the artefact would work."

Charlie did not understand prejudice; the notion was

utterly alien to her. Somewhere over the centuries after their arrival on Greg's Earth, the Indigo's abilities appear to have muted, possibly deliberately to avoid any separateness. It would seem the Indigo had taken a similar low profile when they settled her Earth and her Venus. These were not a people craving status.

Greg's voice held such reverence for his forebears. Despite the responsibility he'd accepted, along with a commitment that right now sent him into the unknown, he remained kind and good-humoured. Charlie hadn't thought of Sam in a while, and wondered if perhaps, with all the turmoil, he was becoming part of her past, although she remembered she had been well on the way to falling in love with him. How could she be disloyal to that memory by finding Greg attractive?

Maybe, she realised as they entered the aeroponics bay, it was because Greg was looking at her the same way. Greg also noticed she watched him as he spoke, and she knew he could look into her mind if he chose, but he didn't want to find anything that would make any of his next moves unwelcome.

She turned away when he smiled. She didn't plan to have "moments" with him or with anyone, telling herself her loneliness was just a result of homesickness.

The aeroponics bay's only occupant was Andy, seated on the ground and working on Charlie's anti-nausea herbs. He acknowledged them as they entered. Apart from his shapeshifting abilities, Andy was also a half-decent gardener. He draped himself around the fruit trees when they required extra humidity, controlled the number of tiny insects that were part of the ecosystem, and often became a canopy when a particular plant demanded a controlled misting system.

"How old is Andy?" Charlie asked, hoping to deflect the tension between her and Greg.

"He's an interface; I believe created after the Indigo left Uxta. I wonder if the ships on Venus in your star system had one."

"I think his shapeshifting abilities are likely to shock a few people."

"He can't travel more than a few kilometres from the ship…" Greg stopped, glancing around before indicating to Andy to seal the aeroponics bay.

"I never asked…" Greg stepped closer to Charlie, "and I promise I've never pried. Is there someone at home? A husband?"

Charlie didn't answer. Greg didn't hide the fact he'd effectively locked the door, and she didn't need to be a mind reader to know what was coming next. He stood so close, she could feel the warmth from his body. Charlie swallowed against a tightness rising in her throat and raised her eyes to his. She saw only kindness and openness, a man who waited for a response, a signal from her. She could just simply walk away, but she didn't.

Greg pulled her into his arms; an answer might just spoil the moment, anyway. They were headed into a war, and he found himself fond of this girl. His mouth found hers, his kiss gentle and restrained until she melted against him. Any moment, Charlie felt she would call a halt to this. Her responses felt forced and perfunctory, but she still let Greg undo her blouse, his lips brushing against her shoulder as the thin fabric slipped away. Then, lifting her into his arms, he moved to one of the soft, grassy patches that dotted the bay and laid her down. Above them, through the skylight viewport, the stars were hidden by the misty speed of Mag engines. Songs came into Charlie's head, familiar songs she always hummed as she went about her daily work. Disconnected from her surroundings, from home, the coming war, from space, she barely felt Greg's touch, but while her head was elsewhere, her body finally responded. He murmured all the right things; his lovemaking was gentle, and she supposed it was fine. Good, even. But he wasn't Sam.

Arriving back at his quarters, Greg found a notification from Charlie. There was no message, just an attachment from the Millstone's database. He opened it. The document was hundreds of pages long, probably fascinating reading, but he felt a little emotionally drained. He'd hoped there would be something more with Charlie, but tonight he felt, well, there was a ghost between them, something that kept her from him.

Even so, he began to read. The Myth of Origin cited Professors and Doctors, the faculty of this and that, and the text spoke with self-important, technical jargon. Greg's Universal was excellent. Rebecca taught him well, but reading a document of this length promised to overwhelm him, so he decided just a scan would do, and he would revisit it at a later time. He flicked to the last few pages, hoping he might gain from the summary, some insight into the Nexists' discontent. It read:

ABSTRACT (Extract for summarisation and lower education facilities only).

The proposal, authored by the Nexist Mutuality and laid before the Science faculties and Alumni at the Venusian Institute of Life Sciences and the Institute for Human Behaviour (Earth Division).

In the first part, the Nexist Mutuality demands the historiographical Venusian Charter of the Colonisation of Earth, which cites the colonisation of Earth by Venus and held in the Triumvirate archives, be deemed a misrepresentation of actual events because a) the record may be incomplete, b) sabotage of the original document or c) might contain subjective alterations.

In the second part, they claim Earthers result from creation or experiment by a superior species and do not share a common ancestry with Venusians, who they allege are tainted by alien DNA, thereby corrupting the purity of Earthers. No evidence to support this claim was provided with the petition. The Nexists further submit Earthers are the original colonisers of Venus.

We concede that ancient records are subject to falsification. However, in the case of the Venusian Charter of the Colonisation of Earth, extensive examination over many decades refutes the Nexist challenge to its authenticity. The document, in both written and in data rondure form, is preserved intact and contains no errata. We found no evidence to contradict the many previous validations of the document's integrity.

Due to the nature of the challenges set by the Nexists, alongside their claims that Earthers result from an experiment by a superior race, and their further claim relating to the "tainting" of Venusian blood, it is worth noting the anecdotal and unverified oral (historical) accounts of an ancient species purported to inhabit Venus in pre-history. The Venusians have historically referred to this mythical race as "Indigo". Individuals of this race are believed to have exhibited superior stamina of both body and mind. It is our expert opinion that if such a race existed, it would survive to this day with clear genetic markers that would distinguish it from ordinary humans. We tested a vast cross-section of the population on all Triumvirate worlds and found no such distinction.

An investigation by the Faculty of Life Sciences, the Western University of Anthropological Studies and the Venusian Genomic Alliance failed to identify genetic differences between Earthers and Venusians that might prove which came first. The existence of both appears synchronous. As on Venus, no species on Earth links Earthers to evolution as put forward in the ancient theory of Natural Selection set out in transcribed writings by an unknown author. However, an examination of the remains of the ancestral families of Venus shows it is possible, however unlikely, at least some are not indigenous to Venus or Earth.

CONCLUSION: No new evidence has been submitted or uncovered to support the Nexist Historical Revision Proposal (Myth of Origin document) or their challenge to the Venusian Charter of the Colonisation of Earth. Therefore, the Venusian Document and its title of Earth colonisation stands in its entirety, and the Nexist Historical Revision Proposals are rejected.

Greg smiled. Well, they were about to blast the Nexist ideology off the face of the Earth.

CHAPTER TWENTY-FOUR _

In the early hours of the morning, Charlie wandered into the hold and onto the Millstone's flight deck. Suliman was dozing, feet up on the console. Suddenly aware of her presence, he pivoted in his seat.

"Bit early for you, isn't it?"

"I haven't been to bed, Suliman. There's no point."

He eyed her for a moment. "What's the problem?"

She couldn't tell him about Greg the evening before, but it wasn't just that. She shook her head. "I don't know. I came up here because I thought no-one else does, but it seems *you* do."

"A touch of space melancholy?"

Charlie sat in the co-pilot's seat. "I didn't know there was such a thing."

"Sure, there is. It's what led me to drink."

"You're making it up, so I'll feel better."

He grinned. "Maybe. Will it cheer you up to tell me about that poky little island you come from?"

Charlie didn't know if it would cheer her up. It might make things a darned sight worse, but what the heck, there was nothing else to do. As it turned out, Charlie found speaking of her home oddly cathartic. She told him about the bridges that spanned island to island, the snow in winter, the wildflowers in spring. Suliman asked intelligent questions, admitting it wasn't a place he'd ever visited; too pastoral, too proper. She told him about her mum and dad, her pet toothclaw lizard, and her determination to follow her dream of being a physician via indenture to the Triumvirate. There would have been no way her parents could have afforded the private route, which would have meant not having to give the government back four years after she qualified. She supposed it was a fair exchange, and it had been great until Rille and Governor Miller.

Suliman listened, but his attention wandered to the first time he saw her. A non-routine call to the secure wing on Rille base when he tore a ligament in his ankle. The new doc was such a little thing, so efficient, and despite him being a prisoner, treated him with kindness and respect. It was a unique experience, and he came to look forward to her visits. Doctor Charlotte Maitland was the first person in his entire life who engendered any emotion in him other than anger and disdain. When he discovered she was to be part of this mission, he knew then that he needed to keep his feelings under wraps more than at any other time. To hide the emotions the memories threw up at him, Suliman feigned a few off-hand comments during her discourse, but still felt the broadside when she got to the part about meeting Sam. He noticed she teared up a little, and he thought about Greg's obvious attraction to her, his own attraction, and felt a wave of self-disgust. He'd already spent years in prison by the time she was born.

Charlie sniffed, cutting in on his thoughts. "Your attention wandered. Is my life so boring?"

He grinned. "It's not, but it was very safe. Mine was hard. I never knew my father, and I lived wild until I ended up crewing on a freighter."

"Your records list a mother as next of kin."

His heavy eyelids flickered. "So they do." He didn't offer more; his mother was someone he never thought about. She was dead to him. He hadn't even owned up to having one, except being in the justice system since he was a minor, he had to have a next of kin, and her name came up in his latest kerfuffle on Mars.

A distant beeping disturbed their conversation, and Suliman pushed himself out of his seat.

"That's the proximity alert to Kate's planet. We might need to go to the bridge."

Andy let them through the wall. Greg and Rebecca were already there, and Charlie avoided looking at Greg as he flicked a special smile at her. The exchange not lost on Suliman, he wondered what passed between the two to foster such a response.

"We've picked up the wave," Greg told them. "It's easy to avoid, but we're too close to keep up Mag. Going too far wide or under the planet will add weeks to our journey, so we'll just monitor the situation." He peered at the sensors and beckoned to Suliman. "There's an object just entering orbit." Greg stepped back to let Suliman take a closer look. "It's a ship, barely spaceworthy."

Rebecca checked for any similar hull configurations in the Indigo ship's database. There were none.

"The data is incomplete, Rebecca," Greg reminded her, "and it might not be a race the Indigo encountered. That data is several thousand years old, and any civilisations are likely to have advanced their technology."

Suliman jabbed a finger towards the object, now appearing as a smudge in the viewport.

"That ship is old by anyone's standards," he said. "But it doesn't mean it's not a threat."

"Only a fool would risk making orbit in that wreck," Rebecca said. "Let alone take on something this size."

"Could be a trap," Charlie suggested. "The people on that planet are not above deception."

"It could be," Rebecca agreed, "but it doesn't appear to have weapons capabilities, and you said yourself this civilisation showed no interest in acquiring the Millstone. Unless…" Rebecca turned her gaze to Greg. He understood.

Charlie watched the exchange. "Unless what?"

"Unless they're refugees. Greg, intercept… Wait, they're hailing."

A crackling and hissing filled the bridge. Greg did his best to clear the signal, and eventually, a woman's voice broke through, distressed, pleading and barely audible. She spoke Universal.

"I'm Lucy. We need to evacuate this ship. It got us off the surface, but it won't sustain us in orbit. At this altitude, we'll hit the wave. Please hurry." The transmission ended, and Greg tapped into the ailing ship to tractor it into the hold.

"Got it," he grinned.

"Good." Rebecca beckoned to Charlie and Suliman. "We'll go to the hold. Greg, make sure they weren't followed."

"Lucy?" Charlie remembered hearing that name before. "Kate mentioned Lucy, a former Seeker. According to Kate, she loved her life."

"That doesn't seem likely if she felt the need to escape in an old barge," Rebecca responded. "We'll keep them in the hold until we find out what's going on."

Little more than a heap of scrap metal and wire, Lucy's ship settled into the hangar just as the others arrived. If Charlie ever needed an example of a miracle, it stood before her now. A pile of junk that had just ferried a group of women to safety. A panel fell to the floor with a deafening clang, causing one leg of the landing gear to disintegrate and tip the craft at a precarious angle. Parked next to the Millstone, it made Suliman's patchwork ship look like a sleek, luxurious yacht in comparison.

An airlock hissed opened to reveal a small compartment packed with distressed females. Suliman lifted them down one by one, seven in all, one holding a newborn baby. These women risked their lives by escaping on a ship not even fit for salvage, so desperate were they to escape the planet below. One woman tearfully thanked Suliman as he helped her down. Possibly in her late forties, she would be the eldest of the group by at least ten years, and same as her companions, dressed in the manner of Kate's society, with the addition of a dark blue cap.

Charlie took her hand. "You must be Lucy?"

The woman looked composed but unsteady on her feet. As the medics arrived, Charlie indicated that they attend to the other women. With her comrades safe, the woman's control slipped, and tears of relief ran unchecked down her cheeks. She reached up with a bitter smile and pulled off her cap to reveal badly cropped brown hair.

"I know who you are, Charlotte," she wept. "Kate described you so well." She looked down at the blue cap in her hands, then dropped it to the floor, moving her foot to step on it. "Blue is for apostasy. We are just a few of the unworthy. For the last eighteen years, I have lived as an outcast, along with others who will not conform." Lucy gestured to the others, then turned her anguished eyes back to Charlie. "We are all outcasts. Even if your ship belonged to a hostile species, better to die in space than live the life of a drudge. We are grateful to you." Lucy swayed suddenly and lifted her hand to her head. Charlie and Suliman grabbed her before she fell, even though she tried to wave away their support. Charlie couldn't allow Lucy the dignity of standing on her own two feet, and reading Charlie's concern, Suliman ignored the woman's protests and lifted her into his arms, finding a suitable place to lay her down.

Charlie dropped to her knees beside her. "We'll get

you to the medbay when the medic's come back. I think you may just be suffering from the cramped conditions in that airlock, but I can't be sure until I've checked you out. How long were you in there?"

Lucy smiled a weak smile. "Fifteen hours. Kate told us you were a physician. You were lucky to escape. I tried, but I couldn't access the Seeker module. I lied at first, just to survive. I knew I couldn't fool them forever, and they wouldn't let me leave."

Charlie looked up at Rebecca and Suliman. Lucy didn't know how close Charlie came to staying and probably joining the ranks of outcasts. She took Lucy's hand. "You don't need to talk. We'll get some fluids into you, and you can tell us your story then."

Lucy shook her head slowly. "I fear I may be dreaming. Let me speak."

Charlie remembered her own gushing account of her few short hours in Kate's company and her relief when Suliman rescued her. After all these years, it was probably not surprising Lucy wanted to tell her story.

"Did they use knaproot to make you docile?" Charlie asked.

Lucy shook her head. "I have Joithem Syndrome. I never told them."

Charlie knew of this rare condition. Not even knaproot would sedate anyone who suffered it. She flicked a one-line explanation to Rebecca and Suliman.

"You would have had to bluff them then?" Rebecca said.

Lucy smiled a bitter smile at the memory. "And it worked at first." She rolled her weary head to look at Charlie. "I heard about the frypan. I wish I could have seen that."

Charlie still felt bad about bashing Kate, but it was necessary, even if for no other reason than she needed to be here to rescue Lucy. "Kate never mentioned apostates or outcasts; in fact, she went to great pains to tell me how happy you and the other women were."

"She wouldn't own up to anything but paradise," Lucy said. "Kate's zeal crosses several provinces; the elders believe she was sent from God. And she believes she has a divine purpose."

It looked like Kate kept a lot from Charlie. "You took a chance with us, Lucy. The ship that rescued Kate's Seeker module wasn't friendly."

Lucy flicked a hand towards the pile of junk still noisily shedding its parts. "Getting that off the ground was an act of sheer will." She gave a short, coughing laugh that didn't make it to her lips. "Maybe divine intervention? Who knows? Eyos feigns piety to help the apostates. This ship was left where it crashed nine years ago, and Eyos knew its location. No crew survived. Eyos helped me restore the engines. I was an engineer on Earth, but it's of alien design, and I didn't understand the configuration at first. I couldn't test the tech, so we didn't know if it would work. We've been ready for two years, waiting for a passing ship. When we heard your ship had left, and Kate told Eyos you would be returning to Earth, we waited for your hull signature.

Eyos refused to come with us because she wanted to stay and help the outcasts. This ship didn't match the description of yours, but Alir's baby—?" Charlie nodded; the baby had been taken to the medbay with its mother. "—it's a girl. Apostates do not choose husbands, even though the elders require us to submit and have children. They take our daughters from us for adoption; we don't know what happens to the boys. I, myself, have lost two daughters," she added sadly.

"Is there any possibility you were followed?" Rebecca asked.

"Space travel is against their beliefs. You can't fly too high in case you run into the Almighty."

The medics returned for Lucy.

"We're headed to Earth now," Suliman said as they laid her carefully on a gurney. "The Nexists are planning on taking over the Triumvirate and destroying the Indigo."

Lucy half laughed in surprise. "Indigo? There is no Indigo; they're a myth."

"Not a myth," Charlie assured her.

Lucy looked at her in puzzlement. "I don't understand."

"It's a long story. Right now, we need to get you well."

Lucy drew a deep breath. "I can't make sense of this just yet, but I trust you, Charlotte."

Charlie introduced the medic. "Lucy, this is Pete. He'll look after you, get you comfortable and run a few tests. I'll check on the others and let you know how they are."

Lucy gripped Charlie's hand. "Thank you, Charlotte."

As they watched the medic take Lucy away, Suliman turned to Rebecca and Charlie. "If she's Triumvirate and a Seeker, she will have had combat training."

Charlie gave him a look of horror. He was unbelievable. "Can we give her some time to recover from *this* fight before we offer her another?" Charlie's tone and body language left him in no doubt he'd stepped over a line. "Or shall I take abettors and combat uniforms when I treat them in the medbay?"

"I was just thinking out loud, Doc."

Charlie held his gaze. Suliman's focus on the battle with the Nexists was commendable, but she now had a medical facility full of already traumatised women. They'd been through enough.

"Well, perhaps they're done fighting," she snapped as she turned on her heel and stomped from the cargo bay.

CHAPTER TWENTY-FIVE _

"We should head straight for Venus," Rice insisted, making sure Greg and Rebecca heard him loud and clear. He'd already made his feelings known to Suliman. From the beginning, despite not being included in the organisation of the resistance, Rice had been an earnest advocate of an initial course there being the safest bet. He hated feeling disloyal, but a tiny part of him hoped that on Venus, he could disappear. He'd got fit, gained piloting and fighting skills, even confidence, but despite that, he couldn't hide the fact that as a soldier, he was right at the bottom of the class.

"No," Suliman said. "If there's been any type of Nexist incursion on Venus, they would have started at the Triumvirate. If it's as we suspect, we need to be anonymous. We'll head for Makemake and scan Venus for alarms. If necessary, I'll take the Millstone. It seems they didn't disable the undersensor tech when they did the engines."

"Why did you have undersensor tech?"

"Smuggling, Rice. What else?"

"What did you smuggle?"

"Stuff in boxes."

Rice wanted to know "what stuff".

Suliman shrugged. "I never asked. I was only interested in the payout."

"What if people got hurt?"

"I'm sure they were just contraband jack-in-the-boxes, Rice. The only way you'd get hurt is if you stood too close when you opened the lid."

Rebecca bit back a grin. Suliman seemed rough, a rogue even, but she knew what was in his heart. Whatever he had been before, he would be a firm ally in their coming struggle. She liked him. She liked them all, even Rice, despite his irritating ways. Rebecca felt that bringing them into her life was the only thing she could be thankful to her son for; that and reuniting her with her grandson.

"Okay, Suliman." Greg swiped across a few sensors. "According to the information you input, we're coming up on the coordinates for —" he took a moment to read the words, realising he may be about to display spectacularly substandard Universal. " 'Makemake'? Is it a manufacturing planet?"

" 'Mah-kayMah-kay' is how it's pronounced," Rice corrected him. " 'MahkayMahkay' is a god of fertility. I once went looking for relics," he sighed glumly. "Now I know I was looking in the wrong place. The wrong planet even."

"There's nothing on '*Mahkay Mahkay*'—" Suliman said, glancing at Rice, who shrugged in response. He was only trying to help. "It's freezing, just a dwarf planet at the edge of our solar system. It's got a wobbly magnetosphere, and any life would have been wiped out by cosmic radiation." Suliman compared an image of the two systems. "You've got a belt of asteroids like this on the outer perimeter of your solar system. You've got to admit, the similarities are extraordinary, except for your Venus being so close to the sun."

"All the ancient space program data from my Earth is fragmented," Greg said. "They got as far as a couple of lunar landings, but not much further." He pointed to the current starchart. "I wonder why the Indigo didn't call these two larger planets closer to the sun, 'Mercury' and 'Venus', seeing as they were naming this system after the one they left?"

Suliman had no idea. Naming planets seemed a tedious task. "I suppose they named them as they entered the system," he suggested, "starting at Neptune, then as they ticked them off, found the extra one in between Earth and Mars, decided to name it Venus and gave up after that. Those three form habitable planets. Maybe they thought they'd get round to naming the others some other time."

Greg grinned at Suliman. After a shaky start, he found himself grateful for Suliman's honesty and dared to say it. "You are a cynic, Suliman."

Suliman didn't mind admitting it, although he'd experienced a certain mellowing on his position over the last couple of years, at least where people were concerned. He headed to the wall, where Andy assumed the position to let him through.

"I think I'll take the Millstone, Greg. Power down and only follow when I say it's safe. And change the Millstone's hull signature; I can play hide and seek if necessary, unless someone gets close enough for a good look."

"Charlie wants to go with you; she's doing a surgical session with the medics. She said to remind you," Greg called out just as Suliman reached the wall. Suliman stopped in his tracks but didn't turn. He didn't want Greg to see his expression at that moment. He glanced over his shoulder. "It might be best if Charlie stays here. Just in case."

Rebecca and Rice looked at each other. Charlie won't like that. Rice shook his head. He wouldn't want to be Suliman when Charlie found out.

<hr>

Charlie saw the Millstone leave the hangar and stormed up to the bridge. Rebecca and Rice had followed Suliman, and Greg was alone. He told her what Suliman said.

"It might be best if Charlie stays here?" Charlie repeated. "What does that mean? Why is it best?" she protested. "I'm desperate for a change of scene."

"He didn't say, Charlie. He might be afraid they'll detect the Millstone."

"Who? We don't know for sure the Nexists have made their move."

Greg held up his hands. "I'm just the messenger, Charlie, don't get angry with me."

Charlie relaxed. "I'm not. Sorry, Greg. Suliman treats me like a child. I get all these lectures about safety protocols with a simple weapon like the abettors. He's always been like it. I told him I wanted to go with him to look around once we got here." With a snort, she flopped into a seat and folded her arms before adding as a postscript, "He thinks he's my dad."

Charlie had no idea. Suliman didn't think he was her father, his desire to protect her came from somewhere else altogether, but it wasn't Greg's place to say anything. "He's worried you'll get caught, Charlie," he said, then fudged the truth by adding, "You're our only doctor."

Charlie sniffed at that. In fairness, Suliman was not reckless. He would be careful to preserve essential personnel. Still… "And what if he gets caught? They'll find out about us anyway. Your hull disguise will only go so far."

She missed the indulgent raise of Greg's eyebrows. Sometimes, Charlie was too much with the "what ifs".

The three Indigo ships waited behind Makemake as Suliman conducted his search. Their formation allowed the lead ship to protect the smaller ships, in case the Nexists had somehow developed battle cruisers in the past two and a half years. A tall order, but no-one could be sure. Rebecca and the other Indigo had a sense of impending conflict, but with this being her home at stake, the delay proved especially difficult.

Suliman, however, was not on a pleasure cruise. He reported in on an obscure bandwidth he'd worked out when he was a criminal.

"There's a Venusian freighter just hanging in space this side of Neptune," he advised Greg. "There's no sign they detected me. I also found an inactive perimeter guardian beacon, perhaps from the days of the Seekers. There's nothing else. I think Rebecca needs to come aboard, so I'll pick her up. We'll go find out what that freighter's doing. It's unusual for a cargo vessel to be this far out, and I'm guessing it's got something to do with what's going on on Venus."

CHAPTER TWENTY-SIX _

"I'm wondering if this is a Nexist trap."

Suliman and Rebecca stood side by side and watched the freighter as it hung as a silent shadow against the backdrop of Neptune. Suliman nodded.

"Except that would mean they were expecting us, and I don't like that thought."

"We can't discount anything," Rebecca said. "I feel a pull, and although I can't pinpoint it, I don't get a sense of captivity or fear." She looked up sharply at Suliman; something else was on his mind. No, not something…*someone*. Rebecca seldom used her limited psychic abilities on anyone other than Indigos, but she had become an expert at reading body language. So had Suliman, and he didn't like to be watched. He went back to the sensors.

"Well, I'd hate to walk into an ambush and end up…"

Rebecca stopped him mid-sentence, leaning around to peer into his face.

"You're bothered about Charlie?"

Suliman gave a theatrical shrug. "Why would I be? She's good in a fight. I've seen her."

"You know what I mean, Suliman."

Suliman made a pretence of scanning the spacescape through the viewport, even though the sensors at this range were many times more accurate.

Rebecca followed his gaze and smiled. Sure he did. He knew exactly what she meant.

"You've never told her?"

Suliman didn't answer, but his mind rang loud and clear, even though Rebecca wasn't looking. *Why would I?* She sensed his resignation. *I'm old enough to be her father.*

Suliman sent a hail across to the freighter to distract Rebecca's intuitive foray into things he would rather not share. When he received no reply, they decided to scan the area and give it a few more minutes. If the vessel was abandoned and awaiting salvage, the Millstone needed not to be here. There was no way of telling if any vessel that ventured this far out was friendly. That still didn't explain why this freighter was away from shipping lanes, both lawful and unlawful. Suliman wondered if it had powered down to study the Millstone's intentions by playing dead duck or if it was standing by for them to make the first move. The Millstone was well known to most freighter pilots, but with the hull signature occluded by Indigo technology, it would appear as unregistered on scans. A freighter pilot would have to look out a viewport and get close enough to identify it. After several minutes in this stand-off, the freighter tacked but did not advance, giving them their first clue it was at least piloted. This time, Rebecca hailed them and elicited a response.

A woman's voice, no visuals. "Who are you?"

"This is Rebecca Allardice. To whom am I speaking?"

Suliman blinked hard, fearful she might be giving away details to the wrong people, but a sudden burst of excited squeals had Suliman and Rebecca staring at the comms in surprise.

"Rebecca!" the voice yelled. "It's Steele's daughter, Margot! We've been waiting for you! Dad said you were like us. I don't know how he knew…well, he said you would be coming back. He didn't even tell us from where, only that we had to wait out here. We came out in shifts after the Nexist takeover, but it got too dangerous to keep going back, so we stayed. Dad said you'd almost certainly head for Venus. There's another ship keeping watch for you there."

"How long since the Nexist takeover?"

Margot didn't hesitate. "Two years! We've had to dodge one or two Nexist scouts, which was easy enough. They don't expect to find anything this far out anyway. Your hull isn't registered, but one of our older pilots reckoned it looked familiar from the viewport. We feared there might be Nexists on board, so we maintained comms silence." Her voice took on a sudden urgency. "Rebecca, the Nexists are murdering anyone they suspect of being Indigo. Venus is trying to get back on its feet, but they can't do anything to help Earth. The Unionists mobilised a well-organised resistance, but we can't transport anyone to Earth to join with them. The Nexists erected a perimeter to keep any unwanted ships out. Besides, we don't have enough anyway; this is the only cargo freighter left out of the entire Venusian fleet. The other ships are either destroyed, disabled or limited occupant."

"How many aboard your ship?" Suliman asked.

Silence.

"This is Captain Suliman," Rebecca stepped in. "The Millstone is his ship."

Margot took a moment to answer. "Suliman? That's interesting. There are nineteen of us, not including two babies who were born over the last few months."

"Margot, our fleet is waiting behind Makemake," Rebecca said. "We'll send coordinates. Debrief us when we get there."

"Fleet?"

"Only three ships, plus this one," Rebecca admitted, "but we have some ideas."

Margot, fascinated to have arrived on an Indigo ship with all its attendant wonders, looked to be around Suliman's age, ruddy-faced, irrepressible and acted as a mother to all the people on board the freighter. She gave a rundown of the events of the past two and a half years.

"Sixteen of us are Indigo," she told them. "I sensed Rebecca's presence—" she glanced at Suliman, "when I saw that old ship of yours. I'm not strongly psychic, and these times are so strange, so dangerous, I couldn't take a chance when you hailed. In the last few years, more and more Indigo are awakening. They can hide from Nexist troopers on Venus, but we know little about what is happening on Earth."

"Margot," Rebecca said, "can you explain something? I was a Nexist, and so was your father. I met him several times, but not once did he affect me. You can understand my confusion, yet I recognise you as Indigo."

"You may not have been ready. The flame chooses its moment. I was in my late thirties, and Rebecca, my dad wasn't a Nexist. He was in the Protectorate. I never knew. We all thought he just worked in admin at the Triumvirate headquarters. But all that time, he was a Protectorate Operator."

This news stunned Rebecca. Steele, a spy? A member of the Protectorate, the most elite and secret service of the Triumvirate? The government never acknowledged their existence. Rebecca knew of them only through her association with the Nexists. The Protectorate infiltrated crime syndicates or the few organisations that opposed the Triumvirate's sovereignty over the years. They never failed to suppress any opposition, and with this knowledge, the Nexists took pains to ensure no Protectorate operative joined their ranks. Clearly, they failed.

Conversely, Nexists could never penetrate the Protectorate's security in the way they did other areas of the Triumvirate. Rebecca knew the fear the Protectorate engendered within Nexism. So, it begged the question,

"If your father was spying on the Nexists, why wasn't the Triumvirate better prepared?"

"Oh, they were," Margot nodded vigorously. "Absolutely prepared, as were the Nexists. Some plans were known only to your family, to George." Margot gave a short whistle. "Not even the Protectorate could breach the stronghold that was your family." She pushed her fists together. "They're untouchable."

"So, what was the ace the Nexists had up their sleeve?" Greg asked.

Margot's eyes widened, and she looked around at the people assembled. "This is the best bit." Her voice lowered in a touch of melodrama. Margot had waited for this moment, had gone over and over it in her mind for when Rebecca returned—the moment that meant the beginning of the end of the Nexists. She desperately hoped her father was right.

"I don't know how he did it," Margot continued. "George Miller had four gunships—smallish, packing a huge amount of firepower—secretly constructed on Mars. He executed the builders afterwards to ensure their silence. Somehow, the gunships' construction went unseen even by the Protectorate. Miller is paranoid; I doubt he even trusted his own family with that knowledge. So, the Protectorate was ready to defend the Triumvirate using Venusian troops, but…well, those ships blew the Triumvirate to high heaven. They took out communications, space dock, surface landings, everything that would cripple Venus. Then the darned things landed and blew themselves up!"

Margot expected a response but was only rewarded with some head shaking. No matter, her audience was beginning to understand how critical the situation had become.

"It was part of the plan," Margot explained. "In all the chaos, the Nexists crawled out of the woodwork, peppering broadcasts with claims the Indigo colluded with rogue Venusians to build the ships secretly and destroy the Triumvirate. Well, by then, the Triumvirate complex was a smouldering ruin with no-one left inside to ask. Communications were down, and because the Consulate on Earth was already covertly Nexist, it was easy to take over and declare martial rule. Miller then reported he'd secretly built a Nexist fleet to defend Earth, and his ships destroyed the warships that attacked the Triumvirate because he didn't want them turning their attention to Earth. He went on to say the Nexists knew of an Indigo-Venusian plot against Earth. Basically, it was the Nexist ideology projected onto the Indigo. Anyway," Margot shrugged, "after claiming his 'secret' fleet destroyed the 'alien' Indigo warships, subdued Venusian sympathisers and subverted an Indigo attack on Earth, he ended up a hero. The events took even the Protectorate by surprise."

Charlie felt sick to her stomach at the idea of Miller being hailed as anything other than the filth he was. "How did Miller convince the people of Earth the Indigo had returned?" she asked. "There's no proof of their existence."

"Not so," Margot said. "According to my father, the

Nexists always knew there was some truth to the myth. Then, a few years ago, a professor found a text that confirmed the Indigo were the original settlers of Venus, then of Earth. That text got cannibalised and leaked to the public, probably by the Nexists—" Margot rolled her eyes "—as a 'public service', just a little teaser for what was to come, get the people in a mindset that the Indigo were the enemy. A few eyes turned to the Triumvirate, accusing them of hiding aliens. That text played right into the Nexists' hands."

Rice turned pale. At the time, he hadn't deciphered the manuscript copy. He later availed himself of Greg's knowledge of the native language from which Venusian stemmed, and now he knew the entirety of the text. It was proof, and it seemed now the Nexists had used it as damning proof, but nowhere did it say the Indigo planned on subduing anyone.

"What is the situation on Earth now?" Rebecca asked.

"You are either with the Nexists or against them," Margot stated simply. "Those citizens loyal to the Nexists carry out witch hunts, exposing anyone they believe might be Indigo, even if they're not. Venusians married to Earthers get sent back to Venus with their kids; the Nexists don't allow Earther spouses to go. The Nexists don't want hybrids. If anyone protests, they get sent to Mars, sometimes executed if the Nexists see them as a potential threat. They say they are purging alien DNA from humanity and include the Venusians in that distinction because they believe them tainted."

"I spent some time studying that Myth of Origin," Greg said. "The Triumvirate's investigation into the claims is irrefutable. On a genetic level, there is no difference between Earthers and Venusians. The Indigo are human too."

Margot gave a little shrug. "The Nexists don't agree. They say it's all part of the Indigo plan. We heard they'd converted many Earthers to their view, but we've had no contact with Earth in months. We can't be sure of the current situation."

"Do you know if there are many ordinary citizens on Earth we could recruit to stand up to the Nexists?" Suliman asked.

Margot was in no doubt there was a potential army if they could get to them.

Once again, Charlie thought of her parents. "My mum and dad live on Earth," she said, her voice trembling and laced with concern. "They're gentle people. They don't have politics. They wouldn't be revolutionaries and get caught up with Nexism."

"Then the Nexists would leave them alone if they didn't make waves," Margot informed her matter-of-factly. "Not many full-blood Earthers got sent to Venus."

Charlie hoped the Nexists didn't go to the trouble of checking. Her mother had Venusian ancestry, even though it was generations ago.

Suliman took a step closer to Charlie. She so often expressed her fear for her parents in the event of a war. "Is there any way we can find out?" he said.

Margot nodded, seeing her briskness had an undesirable effect on the young doctor.

"Give me their names. I'll check for you. There's a roll of refugees on our ship, although I'm afraid it is a little outdated."

Charlie thanked her, even though all hopes for a peaceful solution faded with every passing moment.

"How did they build ships with that kind of firepower?"

"Well, Captain Suliman," Margot gave him a withering stare. "We learned of a group of technicians, one coincidentally with the same name as you, inmates in the Mars penal colony, that had something to do with it."

"How?" Suliman bristled. Suliman was an uncommon name, and he'd never encountered another on Mars. "I haven't been in this system for almost three years, and for a year before that, I was holed up on Rille station."

"In the Martian penitentiary, did you hold a technician's position?"

Suliman had no idea where Margot was going with this, so he answered honestly, "Yeah, so what?"

"And to obtain alcohol—" Margot didn't wait for an answer, "—you and others smuggled TRA-ether compounds in casings in return for whisky?"

"So?" He wasn't the only one; he didn't know where the smuggled TRA-ether ended up. He never asked. Right now, he wished he had, although then, he might not have cared.

"TRA-ether is refined on Mars," Margot chattered on

briskly in a manner they would all soon come to know. "The refinery recorded every activity. There are only minute amounts, so you were easy to track, and your name came up several times. When Rebecca introduced us, I guessed it was you. Those little spores you siphoned off on the side? You were smuggling to Nexists." Margot didn't pause for anyone's shock to register at that revelation. "Remember the Famier ships you loaded?"

Suliman's expression confirmed he did indeed remember the piddly, little armour-plated runabouts used for mining. Four of them. The penny dropped. It made sense. And it made sense to Charlie. Poor Suliman, he couldn't have known. No wonder Miller wanted Suliman where he could keep an eye on him.

"Those ships didn't go to a mine," Margot continued. "They made them bigger. The hull got weaponised using TRA-ether. After the so-called alien attack, Miller reminded Earthers of the document that proved the Indigo existed. He added an addendum, one that confirmed the Indigo, supported by Venusians, planned to invade Earth and establish their own oppressive and violent rule. It was pure fabrication, but because he was a hero, the people believed him, and when he took power, they didn't question his authority."

Suliman's long-standing low opinion of himself and other people was just confirmed. People are so easily influenced.

"Not everyone, Suliman, just the weak," Margot declared ungraciously as she made a quick foray into his thoughts. She turned to Rice. "I seem to be meeting all the major players today. Professor, was it you who unearthed that document? You are a wanted man on Earth."

"Me?" Rice, standing in fearful silence until now, stepped back, hand to mouth.

"You blabbed about your find on Venus, didn't you?"

"Well…I said something to the janitor, not blabbed exactly."

"You provided details about what you uncovered. You blabbed to a Nexist, who made sure he blabbed to his superiors. Miller's document? My father told us it's the same as the one uncovered by a historian on Venus."

Rice paled again. "How did they read it? I barely made head nor tail of the text, and I'm supposed to be an expert. And I hid it."

"Not well enough. A Venusian linguistics expert translated some of it under duress. I suppose Miller made up what they didn't understand, although they did prove the document existed before our written history."

Rice remembered the other document he found. "Did they ever find out about the Indigo ships on Venus?"

Margot nodded. "Courtesy of your blabbing, Professor. I expect they're destroyed by now."

"It's not possible," Greg cut in to defend his friend. "These ships are virtually indestructible. If we go to your planet, we might find attempts at destruction, but I promise you, they will not have penetrated the hull."

Margot looked Greg up and down. Like her father, this man was a full Indigo; chances are he would know.

Even so, "I hope you're right. We don't have much in the way of an attack force."

Charlie felt sorry for Rice; he was just doing what a history professor would do when he made a startling discovery. Margot had a sharp tongue, but Charlie didn't feel she meant to target him. She had the same manner Suliman displayed at times: to simply call a situation for what it was. Charlie knew Rice's new confidence had been knocked, so she deflected any further mention of the documents. "Do you think the Nexists are expecting an uprising?" she asked Margot.

"At some point, they do," Margot said, "but not from Rebecca. Most of them think she's dead. For years, my father has known Rebecca didn't die on Rille; he only found out about the mission to find her just before the coup. He knew she'd come back. Miller believes only the Nexists have ships now, apart from a few cargo freighters on Mars. They're confident they can put down any rebellion."

"What about a ground invasion using Venusian volunteers?" Suliman suggested. That was one of the possibilities discussed over the months. "Sheer weight of numbers may be enough."

"We don't have the ships to transport volunteers to Earth," Margot said, waggling a finger out the viewport at the other vessels standing by. "Even though the Nexists destroyed those gunships to hide their involvement, they do have several weaponised fighters, possibly even capable of conducting a war in space. If they suspect we're coming, they may blow us out of the sky."

"Not this ship," Greg reminded her.

"We can't wage war if we're counting numbers," Rebecca declared. "The Nexists expect an uprising?" She set her mouth in a firm line. "Then we'll give them one."

The ensuing murmurs of agreement assured Rebecca she was preaching to the converted. Charlie hated talk of battle. In her heart, she had to accept the increasing unlikelihood of a diplomatic solution, and she thought of Sam. It was a long shot, but she wondered if Margot might know of him. Perhaps he had joined the rebellion.

"Someone I knew planned to find out what was going on," she said. "He had suspicions when we were on Rille."

Margot pricked up her ears. That could help. "Who?"

"Sam Mead."

Margot compressed her lips and frowned. "Sam Mead? Are you sure? Was he a Data Analyst?"

"Yes, and a metallurgist." A knot of anxiety formed in Charlie's stomach at Margot's expression. "You seem surprised."

"Looks like the Nexists converted him." Once again, Margot gave no thought to where her words would land. "A Sam Mead married Miller's youngest daughter. They had a massive, showy wedding in New York."

Shock-induced adrenaline coursed through Charlie's body, and the knot of anxiety twisted angrily. Outwardly, she made no sign, just held herself together as she tried to plaster on a look of indifference. It was a shame most of the people present were psychic. No-one other than

Suliman knew of her relationship with Sam, and she felt his hand in the small of her back, offering support and comfort. Coming right on top of the news about her mum and dad, this was all becoming too much. Greg caught her wave of emotion and promptly distracted the curious senses of the other Indigo present. Charlie had seen the curious stares; too many pairs of eyes may just cause her controlled facade to disintegrate, so she was grateful when they turned away.

"Well," Rebecca said briskly, also witnessing Charlie's sudden, ill-concealed sadness. "If they did convert him, I guess we'll have no-one else on the inside until we can contact the Unionists. We could make sure Miller knows I've returned. It might draw him out, along with his weapons. If we can disable or even destroy those fighter craft, we might have some advantage."

"There's a perimeter around Earth now," Margot said. "You wouldn't get through without alerting them. When Dad found out about the Seeker ship that returned a few years ago, he realised Rebecca wouldn't have the engineering capability to reprogram it to return. It had to be alien technology. The thing is, at the time, Miller didn't know if it was Indigo or another alien race, so they filled the perimeter with alerts, even mines in some places. The Indigo are one thing; other kinds of aliens are another. And as he didn't know which to expect, George Miller wanted to make sure nothing penetrated Earth's defences."

At that moment, Lucy, completely recovered and now a willing crew member, spoke up with something specific to offer. An opportunity to thank her rescuers by using her knowledge.

"I knew the Nexists once proposed to place a boundary around Earth," she said. "The idea interested me from a logistics point of view, so I once worked out how it could be established. I have extensive knowledge of all forms of communication systems on Earth. I believe I can disable it. There aren't many ways it can work—" Lucy looked to Margot for confirmation "—unless communications have made some significant advancements in the last twenty-five or so years?"

Margot didn't see a problem, but she wasn't an expert in much at all. Other than Margot's silence, there was no hesitation in accepting Lucy's proposal.

"That's settled," Suliman said. "Margot, I know a few merchants based on Mars. I doubt they've gone anywhere unless the Nexists impounded or commandeered their ships. Earth will still need transport vessels, and those freighters would hold several hundred people each. I'll give you something to trade, so they don't ask too many questions. I don't know who you'll meet, and don't mention my name. I'll go to the Millstone and transmit coordinates for the Sackbutt route between Venus and Mars. They won't detect you."

Margot grinned. "Sounds simple, but don't worry about the coordinates. I know them."

Suliman raised a finger to caution her optimism. "Keep an eye out."

Charlie asked Suliman what he would give Margot to

trade.

"I'm not telling you, Doc. You'll come over all sanctimonious at me. It's something any Martian trader won't refuse nor own up to receiving. Believe me."

"Okay," Margot agreed. "I'm not squeamish about your trade, Suliman, but I am keen to get underway. We'll leave the freighter with you; one of you can fly it to Venus. We've got a long-range shuttle that'll get us to Mars. It'll be tight, but we'll manage. Once we've enlisted the merchants, we'll meet you on Venus. Make sure you go in the back door, Suliman, understand?"

Suliman understood. The "back door" was yet another illegal route. There was clearly more to Margot than met the eye.

Suliman estimated it would take around seven days for the Indigo ships to reach Venus from their present position. They also needed to get Lucy to the perimeter to examine and hopefully find a way to disable the alerts. What they couldn't factor in, however, was the availability of suitable vessels on Mars.

Much later, sitting alone in the aeroponics bay, already overwhelmed by the impending war and her inborn need to protect the people she cared about, Charlie reflected on Sam's betrayal of his principles. What happened to make him turn? Did Miller exert some influence over him? Did he go willingly? She felt too numb even to cry, so she pulled up her knees and dropped her head onto her arms, wishing she could sleep away the next few weeks and awake to find it was all a bad dream. Rebecca found her sitting on the floor, propped up against the bulkhead.

"Sam Mead was someone you loved?" she said, sliding down to sit beside her sad young friend. At first, Charlie didn't acknowledge her, but Rebecca pressed gently for an answer. "Did you have any inkling he was a Nexist?"

Charlie took a deep breath. She would have said Sam had no political leanings, but perhaps she didn't know him as well as she thought. "I can't believe Margot was talking about the same person," she sighed. "Perhaps she got it wrong."

"It's not likely, Charlie," Rebecca said, wishing she could deflect some of Charlie's hurt. "You don't know what happened to change him."

"Do you think Greg and the other Indigo know now? About Sam, I mean?"

Rebecca gave a non-committal shrug. "They might, but with psychic ability comes responsibility. It's not their business." She took Charlie's hand and gave it a squeeze. "Charlie, you're going to be fine."

The Nexists' paranoia about protecting Earth served the resistance fleet well. The perimeter beacons concentrated their fields only as far as the moon. Although Nexists didn't undertake routine aerial patrols, they occasionally entered Venusian air space to carry out raids. However, as Miller became more confident that Venus was subdued, and no longer a threat, even those incursions decreased. If a rebellion was to be mounted, he assumed it would come from disgruntled Earthers and easily put down. His apathy meant the entire Indigo fleet reached Venus without so much as a splutter of an alert.

Three trader ships responded to Margot's trade proposal. Slow, cumbersome, but with the proportions to operate as a troop carrier and capable of carrying arms if any were still to be had on Mars or Venus. The traders arrived only hours after the Indigo fleet and greeted Suliman with a fair amount of suspicion. Fortunately, for him at least, these merchants had less reason to kill him than most other Martian traders he had dealings with.

"We reckoned you were dead, Suliman," one said, "that you got took with liver trouble on Rille base. It's been quiet without you. There hasn't been a decent fight in any canteen on Mars since you went to jail!"

"I got sent on a mission. By Miller."

"Miller? I suppose you haven't heard about the takeover?"

"I heard." Suliman stepped to the side. "This is Charlie Maitland and Lucy Conroy. She was a Seeker."

The men looked at each other. "Well, that's a surprise," a second man said. "We thought you were all like Suliman. Dead."

"We need help taking control from the Nexists," Lucy told them. "I'm going to try to take down some of the perimeter beacons."

"Humph," the second man snorted. "Good luck with

that."

"And we need ships," Charlie added sharply. She'd been through too much to put up with attitude.

The third man spoke, ignoring the women. "You lured us here, Suliman. I wouldn't have come if I'd known it was you. Venusian space is off limits, and you're not worth the risk."

"Yes, you would have come," the second man came back swiftly. He dropped his voice and spoke into his hand. "You want the powder." Then he turned to Charlie. "We're just traders. Traders only, and pardon me, miss, you look a bit skinny for a fight."

"You carry cargo, don't you?" Charlie said, overlooking the personal reference.

"Yes, lass, we do."

"That's all we want, for you to carry people, soldiers. We're gathering volunteers willing to fight the Nexists, and we need transport."

The three men shook their heads, united in their decision that taking on the Nexists was a bleak prospect.

"We'd be marked."

Suliman didn't need to tell them how Nexist rules affected trade.

"Trading's marked even if you don't help us. Are the back roads to Earth still open?"

"No," the first man said. "All closed."

"Then we'll go as far as Mars on the Sackbutt, then on a legit trade route to Earth."

"What if we get boarded?"

"When was the last time you got boarded?"

There was a consensus it was an exceedingly rare occurrence.

"You would have valid approach codes, and I guess there is still at least one traffic lane open because they're still mining on Mars and using the prison facilities."

"That's true, but if they realise it was us who landed troops, we'll be finished. They'll probably shoot us."

"If we pull this off, you'll have all your freedoms returned to you. What's your armament compliment?"

The men glanced nervously at Charlie and Lucy. "C'mon, Suliman," the third man sniggered, "We don't have an arsenal. Weapons are prohibited."

Suliman slapped the man on the shoulder. "Of course they are. I never carried them either! Who was it that supplied the CCC when they went in to bat for the gold mine? And the ten boxes of abettors for the mining uprising on Saturn? Oh yes," he grinned. "You and me!"

The man darted another glance at Charlie. No use pretending. "I've got about a hundred abettors," he admitted. "All stingers, none heavy-duty. The Nexists confiscated all grade two and above weapons and implemented a compensable amnesty for any civilian weapons."

"And you?"

The second man shrugged. "About the same."

"And you?"

"Two mining repeaters," the first man reported. "They're not weapons, and you take a chance standing behind them. I wouldn't waste a shell blowing up a Nexist, but if you plan to bring down a building, it'll work, although you might kill yourself in the process."

"How did you get them past the amnesty?"

"I forgot them."

The comment was met with raised eyebrows. "No, I literally forgot. I put them somewhere safe, and well, I'm not as young as I used to be, so when the Nexists searched, they were safe."

"Do you remember where they are now?"

"I hid them in the engine cavities."

"What! Did the ship fly?"

"It did, but it rattled. That's when I remembered. It was only supposed to be temporary. Like I said, I forgot."

"Do you know where the Nexists keep their fleet?"

"Rille," the first man said. "They had a big thing about them being on the ready for an alien invasion. It's all for show, to make Earthers think the Nexists are protecting them against an Indigo invasion. That, or the other aliens they've chucked into the mix. They've only got half a dozen ships in operation with firepower weak as piss." The man looked at Lucy. "You'd have to get past them to get anywhere near the perimeter."

Charlie asked if Miller was concerned about an attack.

"I didn't say that, but the word is, he's stopped expecting one. As far as he's concerned, Earth is his castle now, and it's just a mopping-up operation of any resistance."

Untouchable, Charlie thought. Miller always believed

he was untouchable. That would absolutely be his downfall.

"We have someone among us Governor Miller will see as a threat," Suliman announced, not without some satisfaction. "His mother. He thought she was dead."

The first man frowned. "So did I. That was years ago. I saw the memorial service relayed from Rille."

Suliman nodded. "I remember it. Miller's mother is Indigo. She escaped in a Seeker ship. Did you know the Nexists sabotaged those ships? So, they assumed she'd been blown up, but she wasn't. She somehow ended up on a world with other Indigos. She told them about Miller, his threat to the Indigo, and they reprogrammed the Seeker module with a message to let her son know she was still alive. Let him know he wasn't safe."

"I don't know if the Indigo are real or not," the man said, "but people on Earth fear the very idea now. Miller saw to that. She won't be welcome there."

"So, how did you get involved?" asked the third man. "You become a saint all of a sudden?"

"I was a bystander, and Miller enlisted me to pilot the ship to find his mother. We were carrying an assassin on board."

"What ship?"

"The Millstone."

The three traders stared at Suliman, then roared with laughter. "What?!" one said, struggling to control his glee. "The last time I saw it, it was in bits on Mars. I can't believe it even got off the ground!"

"Well, I thought the same," Suliman said, feeling somewhat defensive about the Millstone, and moreover, a little offended. "The Nexists upgraded it. I'll tell you everything after you've agreed to help."

"Will you let us have the…" one man looked sideways at Charlie, "you know, if we don't?"

Suliman shook his head.

"Then we've got no choice. Just promise we're on the winning side."

"I guarantee it."

"You're a rogue, Suliman. Your guarantees aren't worth shit."

Suliman knew he couldn't truly guarantee the outcome of this fight. Still, the Indigo ship certainly gave them an advantage, and he had no doubt, now they had secured conveyances, many Venusians would volunteer, along with any Indigo left on Venus.

He handed each man a small pouch made from animal skin. They didn't go to the trouble of examining their bounty or looking inside, merely stowed the bags in their shirt fronts.

"I don't share your optimism, Suliman," the first man said, "but we're not doing anything else right now." Then, he gave a sigh of resignation. "We may as well back you."

CHAPTER TWENTY-SEVEN _

While Charlie, Lucy and Suliman enlisted the traders' aid, Greg and Rebecca contacted the interim Venusian government. Hundreds of thousands volunteered for the crusade, but even with the traders' ships at capacity, the original seven hundred on the Indigo ships only swelled to three thousand, with many more volunteers left behind. With Margot and the three traders' help, they identified Nexist strongholds around Earth, along with arsenals and garrisons.

"It doesn't look as if Miller is unconcerned about an attack," Charlie observed as she watched the data come in. "It looks like he's preparing himself for any eventuality."

Suliman narrowed his eyes at a side note detailing the scope and breadth of a weapons store on Mars. "Miller's not worried," he snorted, drawing Charlie's attention to the extra information. "I bet he's already making plans to take over Venus. He thinks it's going to be a pushover."

Suliman's statement shocked Charlie. "Why? I

thought he just wanted Earth."

Greg cut in then. "Tyrants are never content," he said in support of Suliman's theory. "My Earth is a testament to that. The thing with power, those who wield it want more and more. It doesn't surprise me he's stockpiling weapons. If we don't stop him, Venus will end up under Nexist control as well."

Charlie suddenly felt exhausted. All these months preparing, hiding out on Venus these past weeks, and now, suddenly, there was so much more at stake. Venus could recover left to its own devices, but how would they resist a takeover in such a reduced state? She sat down and watched the others making plans, supposing she should join them. It all seemed overwhelming, and she knew she needed to rally her strength and courage. She thought of Sam. It wasn't too overwhelming for him, the rat. Then she thought of her mum and dad. They didn't know it yet, but they depended on her. After a moment, she rejoined the others and asked Suliman for the tenth time what was in the pouch he gave the traders. For the tenth time, he didn't answer.

One evening, after wading through health checks for the additional passengers, Charlie enlisted Andy's help to let her into the Indigo lounge. There, she found the softest chair and sank into it with a sigh of relief. Greg discovered her there a while later. Charlie and Greg never repeated the intimacy they shared in the conservatory, and Greg made no further attempt, knowing her heart was simply not with him, so it surprised her when he brushed his lips against the top of her head before sitting down opposite her. She looked at him in surprise.

"You looked disheartened. I meant nothing by it."

Charlie smiled. "Thanks, Greg, I am a bit. Margot is bringing news about my parents; the delay is making me jittery."

"I don't understand how the Nexists sold the idea the Indigo are conquerors," Greg said. "From my interpretation of our history, we've never conquered any world. We just settled on the other Earth and lived alongside the people. We didn't conquer this system either. According to the document Rice unearthed, it was uninhabited, so we settled Venus. No world should be dominated by one faction, like the Nexists."

"Are you sure you didn't contribute to the events in the other Earth's history?"

"Non-Indigos made the microbes, Charlie. The Indigo stood back throughout the centuries until the destruction of humankind looked unavoidable. My Earth has always known war, although before the biological warfare, none had threatened the entire species. Part of what we are doing there is self-preservation."

"You could have left."

Greg snorted a laugh. "And flee forever from world to world? No, sometimes, you just have to stop and work with what you've got. At others, take a stand."

Charlie understood. "I suppose the Nexists fear the

same things as the people on the Indigo homeworld, although their abilities there were more open, more used for the benefit of the people." Charlie tilted her head. "Those abilities set you apart, Greg, despite you saying you are human. I can't walk through walls."

Greg knew Charlie didn't fully accept his explanation of the link between human and Indigo, and anticipated that when all this was over, she would be asking him for blood and tissue samples to prove just that. He would comply, he grinned to himself, as often as she wished.

"As I told you before," he said, "We learned to become inconspicuous, a necessary move to make us acceptable. Now, I came to tell you that Rebecca and I, and a few others are going to the Southern Peninsula in the morning to see if we can locate the ships. We're hoping some of the records are intact."

Charlie nodded. "Throughout the years, I listened to tales of objects appearing in the sky. It was what sparked the Nexists and Unionists to disagree. Perhaps we were being watched by people who might invade."

"Perhaps, but from my understanding of those records, that went on for centuries," Greg said. "No-one ever got close to any of the craft. And weren't the visual images shaky at best? This was a system with the technology to verify the existence of any unidentified vessels, but Rebecca tells me it never did. The ancestral Indigo weren't the only spacefaring people. Others may have stumbled across this region. Or those reports were hoaxes."

Margot's face popped up on a holoimage. "Charlie, your mum and dad are okay, still on Earth and in the family home. Unfortunately, it's not safe for us to get a message to them. I'm sorry."

Charlie acknowledged her. At least they were alright. "I understand. Thank you."

Margot softened. "I can see you're disappointed. It won't be long before you see them again. Greg, we've found a couple of Indigo engineers to help Lucy. They're leaving soon in the Millstone; Rice is taking them. You'll need to disguise the signature."

"What about the fighters on Mars?"

"Don't worry about them," Margot grinned, "We're going to distract them."

They found only one Indigo ship on the Venusian Southern Peninsula, the same one Livesey and Rebecca had discovered years apart. Although functional, the ship was smaller and not weaponised, leading them to believe it was probably a scout vessel. They could identify no other vessels, even using the coordinates Rice had memorised from his snooping. It left them to conclude some of the other Indigo had continued their journey after a spell on Venus, a fact that heartened them as it meant the Indigo might have settled or integrated into other worlds. They returned to more good news.

"They've found a way to disable the perimeter remotely," Suliman told them. "It's narrow, but we can get our ships through."

Now they were fully across the Nexist situation; they needed to devise a workable strategy.

"We only have one weaponised ship, Suliman," Greg said. "We can manage four enemy fighters easily, but there may be more."

"Margot took a single occupant shuttle and led them up one of the old back roads towards Mars," Suliman told him. "Strikes me she knew where she was going. If Margot can draw them out so easily, we could use a similar tactic."

Greg agreed. "I could adjust our hull signature to make Miller believe it's the Millstone. He knows the Millstone doesn't have weapons, so he'll scramble his fighters, and we can traction them into the hold. That will confuse Earth's and Mars's sensors. If there's no debris, no weapons fire, they're going to wonder what happened."

"Will we all be going this time?" Charlie asked.

Suliman nodded. "Lucy got a good look at the perimeter. She and the engineers are modifying a transceiver to mount on a probe. If we follow Greg's plan, she can release it when the fighters are safely stowed. I will say, though, the probe's only good for taking down three points on the perimeter, just enough to create an opening that will let us through."

To Charlie, hardware built in such haste didn't inspire much confidence.

"What if it fails?"

"Our ancestors modified this ship to become a war vessel, a destroyer," Greg said. "If necessary, we'll blast our way through, although I, for one, would prefer a less spectacular entry to Earth's orbit."

"And I don't want to risk any of our other ships," Suliman added. "We can't afford to lose any personnel."

"Don't speak in 'what-ifs', Charlie," Rebecca declared, although not unkindly. "Margot said she easily evaded the fighters, and Greg is confident we can pick them up, so there's no need to worry."

Rice couldn't get over the fact they were so undermanned. "We've only got six ships," he fussed. "And only one with weapons."

Margot seemed to have forgiven Rice for finding the documents and telling the Nexist janitor, but she didn't like his fatalism, so she snapped at him. "And the three trader vessels, Rice. We've got enough ships. Shut up with the negative attitude." Rice blinked at her a few times, but he did as she commanded. "We knew all along," she added, with a little more subtlety, "any battle would be fought on the ground."

"I can fire from orbit," Greg said. "That'll take care of some of the garrisons. Don't worry, Rice, we'll be fine."

Charlie listened with half an ear as she formulated some thoughts of her own. Miller knew Rebecca didn't have the know-how to reprogram the Seeker module, but what he couldn't know, at least not for sure, was that it came from the Indigo.

"Look, I know you've got to plan," she said, "but I bet there's no contingency for a ship that can vanish their albeit small fleet, plus an army of Indigo when they don't even know for sure there are others in the universe. Add to that the Venusian volunteers whom you have trained to fight. Everything we do from here has the element of surprise."

"Charlie makes a good point," Rebecca said, "but I think we need to get Miller on the back foot right from the start. I think we should announce ourselves once we get to the perimeter. I want him to know he failed."

Suliman liked that idea. "I agree. Let's put the wind up him."

The ships became hives of activity over the next couple of days. Suliman organised the Venusian and Indigo volunteers into divisions. Margot headed one, less for her ability as a warrior but more because of her leadership qualities. Indigo from the other Earth, confident in their fighting abilities under Suliman's training, agreed to take over the other divisions. Suliman, Rebecca, Livesey and Charlie assigned themselves together with a mix of Venusian and Indigo to storm the Earth consulate compound.

Greg scrambled the Indigo ship's outer hull dimensions to match precisely the Millstone's bulk and size. He then amplified the signature. To anyone on Earth, it would appear as the Millstone. Margot's freighter came into position behind the Indigo warship, followed by the four Indigo vessels, including the one unearthed on Venus. Finally, the three trader's vessels fell into formation at the rear.

They intercepted the Nexist fighting ships within hours. Despite its appearance on sensors as a battered old freighter, the sheer size of the Indigo ship forced the pilots' surrender. At least this part of the battle, Charlie thought, went without any bloodshed.

Losing the ships on Earth's sensors sent a flood of comms traffic directed at the approaching fleet, but a sudden, ominous silence had the crew of the Millstone, still stowed in the Indigo ship hold awaiting approach to Earth, holding their breath.

"I bet Miller knows it's us," Suliman said. A moment later, an identification and credentials demand was broadcast. He frowned. "It's coming from Mars."

"Mars?" Charlie echoed.

"Yes, directed at the Millstone."

Margot's ears pricked up. "Scramble it—here…" Margot proceeded to mask the response. She listened. "It's the Unionists. When we disengage from the Indigo ship, head to these coordinates; an operative will be waiting."

Charlie expressed her concern the Nexists may have intercepted the message or that it was a decoy.

Margot shook her head. "The Unionists know what they're doing. That signal originated on Earth. It would have bounced around until it reached Mars and then bounced again before it found its target. In another hour or so, the Nexists might have bothered to trace it. Right now, they're still working out what's going on."

Greg commed they'd released the probe into the

perimeter and to stand by to pass through. Charlie wondered if Miller might be hiding out on Europa or Mars, although Margot insisted he never left Earth.

"He feels safe there…" Margot began as a threatening hail on government channels cut in, demanding they turn their ship around or suffer the consequences.

Charlie looked at the others. "We've got all their ships. What are they going to do?"

"Respond to the hail, Suliman," Rebecca said. "Tell them who I am."

Suliman did, and for a long moment, they heard only static and unintelligible chaotic comm traffic. Then a familiar, hated voice came across, loud and clear, sending an eerie chill of foreboding up Charlie's spine.

"So, Mother, risen from the dead? You are too late. Even a phantom cannot interfere with destiny. You also once anticipated a time when the tide would finally turn against the Venusians. Then you betrayed me, betrayed your family, but I will destroy everything the Venusians stand for, and with them, the Indigo and their filthy genetic code. I have freed the people from Venusian lies. I have purified Earth, and now the people see the Venusians for what they are. Collaborators with an alien race. I have saved my world. Earth is mine."

Miller's chilling words became swallowed up dramatically in the background of the comm traffic, the clarity lasting just long enough for him to deliver his terrifying message. Rebecca shifted her thoughtful gaze to the viewport where Earth hung, blue and shining in the heavens. Charlie touched her arm to check she was okay. Such a message from son to mother would surely be distressing. She turned to Charlie, that steely determination in her blue eyes.

"He's wrong. We are not too late. We are just in time."

CHAPTER TWENTY-EIGHT _

The divisions landed on Earth under cover of darkness at the exact coordinates given by the Unionist resistance. Lucy's comm probe performed admirably, allowing the fleet through before the perimeter spontaneously repaired itself, a failsafe set in place by a suspicious regime. Greg reiterated that he could blast them back through in a worst-case scenario but expressed his confidence that the Nexists would have fallen by then.

Several kilometres separated each division's coordinates, save two, which landed closer to the consulate compound. Margot advised them with some certainty before they left, that Miller was likely to be in the consulate as it had the heaviest guard, even though she qualified that by saying he could be somewhere else, then qualified it again by saying it was likely Rebecca would sense him. Of course, it was all supposition, and Charlie guessed they could only hope Miller was in residence. The very thought of him still creeped her out, and some of her old homicidal thoughts resurfaced, particularly in light of the fact she'd abandoned her hope of a peaceful resolution. Besides, she reasoned, she was protecting her mum and dad.

Charlie's division consisted of only seventy men and women but possessed possibly the ablest and most experienced combatants. And they had Suliman, who acted as though he was indestructible.

Margot insisted they didn't move from their position until contacted by the Unionist operative, so while they waited in the darkness, Charlie wriggled up the side of the hill to peer at the brightly lit consulate in the distance.

Rebecca wriggled alongside. "Looks like someone's home," she said. "No more thoughts about a peaceful solution?"

Charlie glanced up from her binocs. "Don't worry. I felt murderous as soon as I realised that was Miller's voice." She rolled onto her side. "I know he's your son…"

Rebecca raised an eyebrow. "I sense a 'but?'"

"What do we do? Take him prisoner? Shoot him?"

"You'd like to shoot him?"

"He's a pig."

"Yes, he is, and I don't consider him—that monster, to be my son any longer. Whatever happens, we will destroy the Nexist movement, reveal the truth about the attack on the Triumvirate, and hopefully—" Rebecca closed her eyes and sighed, "turn the hearts of the people."

"It won't be easy, not if they believe the Indigo are behind the attack on the Triumvirate on Venus."

"There's been a lot of propaganda, but I don't believe

enough time has passed for it to be fully embedded in society. If we can show the people the truth, prove it to them, I believe they will turn back."

"Turn back to what, Rebecca? The Indigo were a myth, so you can't expect everyone to simply accept you're here to stay and go about their business. There'll be questions, and you have to be ready with answers. I think Earthers might take some convincing it's safe to trust you. They might think better the devil they know. And you can't use your psychic abilities on them; that will only highlight your differences and prove they have something to fear. And whatever you do, don't let them see you walk through walls."

"I think you underestimate them, Charlie."

"I hope you're right; otherwise, once we defeat the Nexists, we might face another kind of struggle." Charlie returned to her binocs. The consulate compound had always been a hive of activity. Attached to the university campus, it was a place for young people who loved campus life. So much was provided for them, they never needed to leave. There seemed little random activity from what she could see at such a distance. Even with long-range binocs, it all looked rather regimented, although interestingly, she did pick up a forcefield surrounding the outskirts of the consulate.

Charlie wondered if Sam would be there. It seemed reasonable, seeing as he was now married to Miller's daughter and fully committed to Nexism. Torn between disappointment and harbouring murderous thoughts towards him, Charlie mostly felt betrayed. Worse, Sam betrayed himself. Rebecca patted her arm.

"Whatever happens, Charlie, life isn't going to be the same."

Charlie allowed herself a wry smile. "I guess not." She dismissed Sam from her thoughts. "Have you heard from the ship?"

"Rice got back okay. Apparently, the Unionists scrambled our signal, so we weren't detected. Greg is waiting for word from them before attacking the garrisons…"

A shuffling in the dark stopped their conversation. A girl in a Nexist uniform and dragging a bag slid across the hill on her belly. She stopped when she found herself in the eye of an array of abettors.

Livesey leaned forward and lowered his weapon. *"Hannah?"*

"Save the introductions, Matt," the girl said as she stood and tipped a dozen lethal looking sidearms from the bag. "I'm your contact."

The girl ignored the curious stares for a moment, but when no-one else lowered their weapon, she declared, "I'm his sister, well, half-sister if you must know." Dismissing their obvious suspicion, she lit up a data rondure and stepped into the midst of the group. "These are the blueprints of the consulate. We're in a blind spot here, kept from Nexist surveillance. We sabotaged their satellite when we decided to mount our offensive. Then you lot got picked up, and you didn't act like Nexist sympathisers."

Hannah highlighted an area of the consulate. "You might not be seen right here on the outskirts, but I can tell you, they'll detect us easily inside the forcefield, so I hope you've all got good aims." She peered into the gloom. "An operative met the other division that landed at the same time as you. She'll lead them into the building. We've made a plan that covers the entire area; we knew it would be difficult for you to work something out, but if you have any ideas, tell me now." She waited. This young girl had all bases covered, so no-one answered. "Good," she said. "Miller is inside. His guards brought him here when they realised an attack was imminent. It's the most defended area on the planet, but they don't know how much we know about those defences. Drone mines are patrolling, so make sure you stay low and don't look up; they can detect eyes. Commander Steele—I believe some of you met his daughter—is temporary president of the Triumvirate and is mobilising the patriots. They'll be here, so save some Nexists for them!" Charlie guessed this was a ham-fisted attempt at humour. No-one laughed. They probably needed a little more time to get as jaded as this girl.

"Don't try to take out the inner perimeter guards with abettors," the girl said without trying to single out who might be the division leader. She held up one of the sleek sidearms. "These weapons are lethal. The Nexists call them 'pistols', and they've had them in development for months. They brought them out of production to combat you lot. They don't stun," she warned, "they don't disable. They kill. The dart can pass through two bodies, so if you go in with abettors, the Nexists will mow you down and finish you off in time for an aperitif. Fortunately, there aren't many of these to be had in there, so you'll be evenly matched. There's a forcefield at each entry point into the building—" she changed the schematic— "I have the frequency to disable a single section. I'll try to get you all in before the field drops, but we'll meet with opposition. If we get through that, a second field works on a cycle; our operative couldn't get the code, but a charge from an overloaded abettor would lift the lower edge. Is there a technician among you? Or an engineer?" The girl waited for an answer and received only suspicious silence in return. "I can show you the location, but you need to get the third field down so your other troops can join us." The girl looked at Suliman. He seemed big and ugly enough to be in charge, so she addressed him. "We counted only seventy of you. What about the other divisions?"

"Just under three thousand in total, in seven divisions, spread out," Suliman confirmed, but he kept his hand on his abettor the whole time the girl spoke. "Plus, a cannon mounted on a freighter and a warship in orbit." He'd shoot her if he had to.

The girl appraised Suliman's abettor with an indulgent flicker of her eyelids. "It'll have to do. The garrisons are well-armed, so they'll keep your warship busy. I heard that ship took the Nexist fighter craft. One of our people has rendezvoused with the ship, so I hope your pilot is open to directions. Now, I've got a dozen of these—" Hannah tossed a pistol to Charlie, Rebecca, Livesey and Suliman standing at the head of the group. "I need another seven of you who think they can handle them." Several troopers looked at each other, not moving until Rebecca nodded "okay". Hannah held up an object no bigger than a grain of rice.

"This is the dart. There are forty-two loaded in each pistol. If the body slows the projectile, it produces two spines to maximise the damage as it looks for a way to exit. Depending on where it strikes, there is usually little blood on the outside, but inside the body, well, that's a mess." She lifted the pistol. "See this toggle? Once you press this with your thumb, you have a two-second window before it fires. You can't cancel the firing sequence, so make sure you are aiming in the right direction. Many of the Nexists carry abettors, so you can still get stunned." She turned and started back up the hill, tightening a belt containing an array of weapons around her middle.

"Follow me. We need to get those fields down."

"Hannah," Livesey grabbed her arm. "You can't walk in here wearing a Nexist uniform and expect us to follow you."

Hannah looked down at her brother's hand. There was no time for this. Impatiently, she shrugged him away. "Matt, do you think the Nexists are going to turn up here, arm the very people they plan on fighting and invite them in? I'm Unionist resistance, Matt. I'm a spy. I have been for the last two years."

Rebecca allowed herself a small smile and placed her hand on her grandson's shoulder to stop him from saying anything further. "Hannah, do you know who I am?"

Hannah shook her head. She wasn't interested in names, although the old lady seemed like it mattered, even when Hannah wanted to get moving. "No, I don't."

"I'm Rebecca Allardice. I'm your grandmother."

Hannah hesitated, then nodded. "I've heard about you. You died on Rille years before I was born." She looked Rebecca up and down. "You're here, so I guess you're not a ghost?"

"There's much more to the story than that," Rebecca smiled, "but it can wait. Right now, we need to set things right."

"Wait," Suliman said. "She's a kid. How can we trust her?"

"I risked my life to flip a switch on the Millstone to give you some extra info," Hannah said. "Does that count? They didn't suspect a 'kid'," she added, the sarcasm not lost on any of them. Besides, this 'kid' looked like a seasoned fighter.

Livesey nodded. "You can trust her."

Suliman had to take their word for it. "I have the most technical knowledge. I might be able to drop the force field." Then he added, "I'm Suliman."

The girl eyed the big man. What was it with these people and introductions? "Then you'll have to do. There's undercover Unionist backup inside, so they'll take the Nexists by surprise. I'll overload an abettor to lift that second field; then, you need to head straight for the controls to disable the interior field. It'll give your other divisions around two minutes to get in before the outer fields reset. You'll only get one chance."

"I'm self-taught with engineering, kid."

Hannah shrugged. "Then you'll either succeed, or we're dead. They won't bother sending us to Venus."

Charlie squeezed Suliman's arm. "You'll be fine."

He gave her a wry smile in return. "No pressure."

The division skirted the compound's perimeter with Hannah in the lead until she located the section they needed to disable. The inner rim swarmed with guards, but they managed to avoid two drones on their approach. It didn't bring them much comfort, any disruption would likely alert the entire consulate, and that would give Miller the chance to hide.

"I'll go first," Hannah whispered. "The signature will change once it's breached, so don't dilly dally. Pile through before it closes."

This part of the consulate building was erected around eight hundred years before, after the style of what Charlie believed were old Earth buildings. She knew now the style came from a different Earth. It was a beautiful structure with panelled walls, sweeping staircases, high ceilings, and chandeliers. The Triumvirate used it for dignitaries and social occasions because of its history, and because on Earth, no other building rivalled it for beauty.

A narrow section of the forcefield parted; the sudden flash and hum as it tried to reconnect took the guards by surprise. Hannah, in the lead, took advantage of the first responder's slowness and tackled him while the others piled through. Within seconds, the closure triggered, and they were left to fend off the guards until Hannah blew up the lower rim of the second forcefield. All seventy made it through. Although no alarms sounded, there would be no doubt the Nexists were now well aware the perimeter had been compromised. Hannah urged Suliman along a passage towards the force field controls that would drop the entire field circling the enclosure and allow the other divisions in. He returned in moments.

Charlie groaned. "Is it too complicated?"

Under other circumstances, he would have laughed. "No, it's got a switch that says 'off'. Can you believe it? The most complicated thing was decoding the access panel. I'm a criminal. I can do that. Kid, lead on."

Hannah turned to them. "In about ninety seconds, the backup forcefield at the other side of the compound will drop, and your troops will come through. Until then, it's just us. There's a Protectorate operative inside, high up in the Nexist ranks, who's positioned the resistance operatives. Remember, the Nexists have equal firepower, and they'll be waiting, so go in, guns blazing."

"How many operatives are there?" Charlie whispered as they crept up the stairs.

"About twenty."

"How will we know them from the Nexists if they're all wearing the same uniform?"

Hannah glanced over her shoulder. "Just remember who shot at you first," she said in all seriousness. Then she disappeared into the conference room exactly as she promised, with guns blazing.

Vastly outnumbered, the seventy Venusian and Indigo rebels swarmed into the room behind Hannah. Outside, the forcefield dropped, and the other division engaged the Nexist guards, some making it to the conference room to swell the rebels' ranks. The enemy scattered throughout the building, rebels in hot pursuit. Some of the abettor-carrying Nexists attempted to escape, while others, more capable fighters, reverted to hand-to-hand combat. Charlie found herself involved in both, her lightness and size a distinct advantage in dodging and rolling. The new weapons terrified her, and somewhere in the back of her mind, she wished she could curl into a ball, squeeze her eyes tight and pray for it all to be over. She knew that was the part of her that was not a soldier, the part that would never be prepared for warfare. The other part, the part that hated injustice and, more specifically, Miller, forged stronger. That instinct buried all other feelings, save her goal of defeating the Nexists.

The pistols were as lethal as Hannah described, and Charlie saw several Nexists on the ground. She hoped one of them was Miller, but no doubt he'd found a rat hole somewhere to crawl into, probably with Sam.

The dart trajectory was a fraction slower than an abettor beam and made an inferior aim at a moving target, so Charlie quickly learned to keep moving. Some Venusians took out their anger on a few fleeing Nexists, perhaps inflicting more bloodshed than Charlie would have liked, but this was never to be a non-violent takeback of liberty. Charlie heard the battle raging outside where a few of the ancient outbuildings were now engulfed in flames. In the melee, Charlie couldn't sort out the faces of the individuals who wore the Nexist badges and those who fired at them. In a moment of hesitation, she tripped and fell to the floor, sprawling across a young female in a Nexist uniform. Not much older than Hannah, the woman's eyes were wide open from the horror of the moment a dart hit her in the temple. Charlie had no time to consider her as Hannah dragged her to her feet, yelling, "Come on. It's not over!"

As more and more on both sides fell, Suliman, Livesey, and Rebecca dashed to assist with the fighting outside. Others, not wearing Nexist uniforms and not part of Charlie's group, joined in the battle. Some were armed only with basic abettors, most likely untrained Earther civilians rising against Nexist rule and probably part of the patriot army. As a matter of survival, Charlie had to keep going. She scrambled after Hannah, heading outside to join Suliman and Rebecca. It was then, as she ran across the threshold, Hannah was proved wrong. For Charlie at least, the battle was over.

A splitting sound and searing pain slammed her against a wall. For what seemed an age, she hung there, suspended, then her weapon flew from her hand, and she slid down into the mud in a fog of pain and shock. Flashes of light reached her through the dust and haze of the battle, distant sounds of screaming and shouting, shadowy people engaged in struggle all around her. Someone half dragged, half carried her back inside the consulate building and laid her gently against a wall under the stairwell. Through the mist of pain, Charlie glimpsed the distinctive feathered Nexist symbol on the uniform of the man who rescued her. He spoke as he stripped off his shirt to bind her leg. His face was bloodied, but it didn't matter; she would know him anywhere.

"Sam?"

"Charlie, your leg," he said, desperately trying to stem the flow of blood. "I can't apply a tourniquet; there are too many bone fragments. The dart moved upwards through your knee, and your thigh bone has shattered. The dart didn't exit. It's lodged somewhere in your abdomen, and you're bleeding internally."

Charlie heard everything Sam said, but none of it made sense. Who was he talking about?

"Sam?" she said again.

Sounds of battle buried Sam's frantic yells for help, and he leant hard against her wound, desperate to buy her some time until the medics discovered his distress signal. His face swam before her eyes. He just wouldn't stay still.

"Don't worry, Charlie," he said, forcing a smile. "I'm here."

He's crying, she thought, and she didn't understand. Why would she worry? And why would he be crying?

Sam saw her confusion; this level of blood loss only ever stemmed from an arterial bleed. Judging by the fragments of bone protruding through her skin, this dart's trajectory was a one in a million chance, upwards from above her knee and travelling into her body. It might still be looking for a place to exit and causing more damage. He only knew he'd lost her once. He couldn't lose her again.

Charlie tried to focus on Sam's face. He hoped it was a moment of clarity, that she recognised him. "The medics will be here soon, Charlie," he promised.

Sam wanted to say her name over and over. If he did, he might keep her alive, even as he watched her fade. He kissed her forehead. "Sweetheart, just hold on a little longer."

Something hurt, but Charlie couldn't tell from where. Perhaps everywhere. A man, a Nexist who looked like Sam, pressed his shirt against her thigh. He was trying to save her life. Weren't they fighting Nexists? This man really did look like Sam. On instinct, she made a weak attempt to lift her hand to touch his face. He caught her fingers and held them to his lips.

One moment Sam held her hand, whispering her name; the next, he fell forward, executed by a dart from a Nexist pistol that ripped through the back of his head and embedded itself in the panelling beside Charlie's ear. Bewildered, she looked down at the tiny drop of blood at the top of his neck. *That wound needs treatment,* she thought, making a pointless diagnosis to Sam's lifeless body as confusion took her once again.

The executioner stood over Charlie, his work not done, and his pistol pointed menacingly at her head. He seemed familiar. Charlie watched him from a calm place while she tried to work out why Sam didn't move. He only had a scratch to the neck, so why was he so still? Charlie knew she was hurt as well, maybe badly, so why would this man bother shooting her? It was getting hard to breathe; Sam was heavy, and she tried to push him away. He needed to wake up and move.

"So," Miller sneered. "It's still you and Mead, Mead and you? How touching."

Charlie allowed her head to tip forward to look at Sam's face. Why would a Nexist shoot another Nexist? She supposed the man would shoot her too, but he would have to be quick, because a fluid, snake-like arm was just about to coil around his neck.

Charlie viewed Miller's demise in slow motion, but in reality, it was a quick and unfairly merciful death. Miller's pistol dropped to the ground as he scrabbled at his throat, desperately trying to loosen Andy's grip. In a second, Andy joined the rest of his body and didn't drop Miller until he was sure not a breath of life remained. Suliman skidded to a halt beside Charlie, Rebecca close behind, who stopped only for a moment to bend down and touch her son's face. A mother remembering a little boy who loved space stories. A little boy who would grow into a monster.

As Suliman lifted Sam's body carefully from Charlie and arranged him on the floor beside her, Rebecca saw the extent of the injuries to Charlie's leg and the dimming light in her eyes.

"Suliman!" she screamed. "Charlie's hurt! She needs help."

When Sam fell forward, he loosened his pressure on

Charlie's wound. It made little difference, the internal bleeding was far more severe, but Suliman and Rebecca didn't waste time trying to establish the dart's trajectory.

"Andy," Suliman ordered. "Wrap yourself around her leg."

"I will, sir, but I suspect," Andy replied, "the most significant bleed is taking place elsewhere. There is nothing I can do. We may be too late."

Suliman looked down. He knew Andy was right, but he couldn't just let her die. "*You know*"—Charlie once told him— "*Suliman, you're okay.*" He knew he wouldn't be okay ever again if she died. Scooping her into his arms, he stepped over Miller's body and raced for the exit. "Let's get her to the ship,"

Wordlessly, Rebecca and Andy kept up with his frantic pace. Not once did it occur to Suliman to give Charlie to Andy, who would have been quicker, because from the beginning, he tasked himself to be the one to keep her safe, to be her protector.

Charlie looked up at Suliman. She recognised him. He always had her back. Now, he looked grim and scared, running and shouting, but she couldn't make out the words. Did he save her from Miller? The memory was fleeting. Yes, Sam was there, in her arms, a wound at the top of his neck. Charlie's head joggled against Suliman's shoulder as he ran. She saw Rebecca's worried face, the android striding alongside, and a glimpse of Sam sleeping in the consulate hallway. Her body allowed her one moment of clarity, one breath for her to whisper, "Don't leave him there, Suliman. Please don't leave him there."

Suliman headed for the Millstone, which was busy ferrying casualties to the Indigo ship hovering a few hundred meters above. He heard Charlie's whispered plea, and he knew it might be the last thing he could do for her. With only a moment's hesitation, he lifted her into Andy's waiting arms.

"Take her; you'll be quicker."

Andy wrapped himself around the dying Charlie, creating a torpedo cocoon that propelled him towards the ship. With not even a glance behind, Suliman ran back to Sam.

Charlie woke from her bad dream with a start. Even now, in those misty moments before the fog of sleep clears, screams and cries of pain echoed in her mind.

The smiling face of an old colleague from medical school swam into her vision.

"Hello, Charlie."

"Mike?" Charlie struggled to sit up, but her lower body, swathed in an advanced blue light-field brace, resisted any attempt to bend. "Where am I?"

"Don't worry," Mike grinned. "You're fine, still on Earth and in the university hospital. You got shot. You were lucky your body didn't get separated from your leg. It's difficult to revive a leg without a trunk."

Mike had always been a wag. A great physician with a questionable sense of humour, Charlie felt reassured to find him caring for her.

"It was impossible to know who to shoot at. Even those on our side had Nexist uniforms, except for us."

"Well, you did a great job," Mike smiled. "You're all heroes. Miller's dead, and the Protectorate are mopping up the last of the Nexists. I'd be interested to hear all about how you dropped off the radar for three years, and when you turn up, it's with the Unionist resistance. As a rebel, you'll be pleased to know the Triumvirate is re-establishing its consulates here on Earth, and a delegate is travelling to Venus. That said," he shrugged, "I doubt anything will be the same. Not everyone loved the Triumvirate, but the Nexists…" He shook his head. "How did we not see that coming? The only thing for sure is the Indigo are no longer a myth."

"They'll help bring stability, Mike. I promise."

"If you say so. The Nexists produced a pretty convincing argument after the destruction of the Triumvirate on Venus. Many believed the Indigo were behind the attack…"

"Propaganda."

"We know that now. Like I say, nothing will be the same."

Charlie wriggled. She'd put a few people in these compression braces over the years. They made great immobilising devices, but the forcefield generated a certain amount of heat, and she didn't realise how sweaty they made you feel. Mike put his hand on her shoulder.

"I'll sort out the thermostat for you. You've got a

couple of venous transplants, major muscle repairs to your leg, a new kidney, not to mention the compound fracture of your femur and associated neurological damage. You'll be in this brace for six weeks at least, so you'd better get used to it. I'll come back later, and we can have a chat."

As it happened, after those few words when she woke, Charlie didn't want to talk. The events of the battle began to replay over and over in her head, the smell of scorched flesh from weapons fire, people falling, the young Nexist woman with the vacant eyes, Sam's voice, him leaning against her leg, then falling forward with a fatal wound to his neck. She remembered Miller standing over her and Andy strangling the life out of him. It was all burned into her memory, a carousel of dark and painful images, there to repeat whenever it chose, without her bidding. As she considered the last three years, she added to the mix her guilt over the affair with Greg. It shouldn't have happened, not at a time when Charlie believed Sam was waiting for her.

One morning, Charlie received some visitors. Of course, Rice took advantage of the immobilised Charlie to not only hug her but to plant a wet kiss on her cheek for good measure. Livesey was more restrained, but there was no denying they were relieved to see their friend suffered no permanent damage. They all had their different versions of the battle, and Rice admitted to a few heroics in gathering up the wounded. Livesey sported a rather large, impressive scar over his shoulder, and only Rebecca appeared to have come through unscathed. Charlie vaguely remembered seeing her bending down to touch Miller's face, but it was a hazy memory, punctuated by noise and pain.

Rebecca lingered after Rice and Livesey left. Charlie thought she looked older and wearier in the aftermath of the battle. She waited until they were completely alone.

"I thought you might like to know the official version of what has happened since the fighting ended."

Charlie wasn't sure she did, but Rebecca took her silence as permission to continue.

"Margot's father, Steele, is heading the Triumvirate for now. You were right, Charlie. Many Earthers fell for the Nexist propaganda, and of course, our arrival confirmed we aren't a myth. We have faced opposition…"

"They don't want an Indigo takeover?"

Rebecca nodded. "Steele implemented a program with the assistance of Triumvirate psychiatrists; a plan to address the residual dissonance. I think we have a long road to establish a relationship between the new Indigo-led Triumvirate and Earth. I have to believe we can reverse the people's beliefs, but the harm caused will take some undoing."

"So, the war isn't over?"

Rebecca frowned even though she understood the sentiment. "Don't say that. The Nexists took this Earth apart, and we are going to put it back together. Nexist rule would have destroyed the people's civil liberties in return for Nexist protection. Even those convinced the Nexists saved them will have a change of heart, you'll see."

Charlie hoped Rebecca was right. But, stuck in a hospital, she hadn't had a chance to see what was happening in the outside world. Not that she cared.

"Do you ever see Suliman?" she asked.

Rebecca shook her head. "Only once since the consulate. After that, he seemed to fall off the radar. I'm sorry." It was the truth. Suliman had made no contact with any of them. She didn't even know if he knew Charlie survived.

Charlie closed her eyes. Everything felt so pointless. Suliman didn't want to be involved in rebuilding a world, so she hoped he and the Millstone had found something worth living for.

CHAPTER TWENTY-NINE _

Charlie went home to her mum and dad, physically repaired, but other scars remained open and raw. At first, she refused visitors, just slept, stared into space, and ate sparingly. She wasn't sure if Sam's parents were ever aware of her existence, so it didn't feel appropriate to contact them. At night, she mourned for him in private; her little toothclaw lizard curled up beside her for company.

While Charlie took a break from the world, the Triumvirate re-established government on Venus, while the Protectorate, believing it failed at averting the Nexist threat, was reorganised. Even though it wasn't popular with the locals, it established a strong police presence in the Southwestern corridor to curb crime and weed out factions still loyal to Nexist philosophies. A section of the Triumvirate became dedicated to serving the Southwestern corridor communities in areas of housing and education. The Indigo, meanwhile, recovered their ancient documents from the Venusian vaults and began the long road to acceptance.

The first visitor Charlie accepted was Hannah. The girl made a nuisance of herself by constantly turning up unannounced and calling at all hours of the day, even though Charlie's parents made excuses not to let her in. In the end, Charlie's mother begged her daughter to allow a visit.

Hannah wasted no time in coming to the point.

"I know we don't know each other, Charlie, but I needed to see you." She noted Charlie's obvious lack of welcome, but didn't apologise for her intrusion. Even so, Charlie was well brought up, and as Hannah was here, she invited her out onto the small balcony. "I knew about you and Sam," Hannah said in her forthright manner. "I just didn't make the connection at first. Well, I didn't actually know your name. All the others wanted to introduce themselves, but you never said anything."

Charlie wasn't sure she needed to talk about Sam. Her mind and her heart were still in turmoil. He'd become a Nexist; then tried to save her. The events of that rescue still rattled around inside her head, occupying too many dark thoughts. She held Hannah's gaze.

"I don't want to talk about Sam."

Hannah shrugged. "Okay, then listen. Charlie, Sam wasn't a Nexist. He was a Protectorate infiltrator. A spy. Miller's youngest daughter was a Unionist rebel. The Protectorate orchestrated the marriage so Sam could get close to the family."

Charlie's heart lurched. Surely Hannah would never

make up such a thing. "Did Rebecca send you?"

"What? Of course not, but she did tell me where you lived. You knew the Seeker ship was on Mars for a year before it came to Rille?"

Charlie nodded.

"Sam told me that Miller barred his communication with Earth because he had been part of the Seeker ship dismantling. Sam discovered evidence, evidence he told me he shared with you. When I asked what happened to you, he told me Miller had sent you off on some mission or other. When Sam left Rille, he managed to take an unsanctioned detour directly to the Triumvirate on Venus. They were impressed enough to ask him to inspect other communications."

Charlie could hardly believe it. Sam a member of the Protectorate? She'd only just learned of this organisation and knew little of what it entailed, but for sure, the Triumvirate would need to be sure of his loyalties.

"After induction into the Protectorate," Hannah continued, "Sam went to the Earth Consulate, known to be crawling with Nexist sympathisers. He gave them a sample of a data eclipse but used decoy information planted by the Protectorate. Naturally, Sam was asked how he came by such information, and Sam lied about its origins. He was brilliant at uncovering data," she said with unfiltered approval. Charlie knew that. "Over the weeks, he went back with more information and eventually came to the attention of Miller, by then back on Earth."

"Miller would have recognised him."

"Oh, he recognised him, but Sam said Miller asked him about you, so Sam acted as though he couldn't remember. Of course, Miller liked that. I'm not sure, but I believe Miller told him about your mission, so Sam learned Miller never meant for you to make it back. He set Sam a few tasks to prove himself to the Nexists. Sam came through with flying colours."

"What tasks?"

Hannah hesitated. Charlie had seen horrors; Hannah knew that, but she'd seen more. She'd witnessed the evil of the Nexists first-hand, knew of the ethnic cleansing carried out on Miller's orders. "Charlie, you have to understand that in his position, Sam had the interests of all the Triumvirate worlds at heart."

"What tasks?" Charlie asked again.

"We all had to do it after an allegiance oath. Miller sent him to Mars to execute those suspected of being Indigo."

The Sam Charlie knew was incapable of murder, but then so was she until there came a greater cause. "And did he?"

Hannah didn't answer. She didn't need to, but Charlie understood Sam would have been under Protectorate orders to do whatever was necessary.

"The Nexists accepted Sam," Hannah said after a moment. "Evelyn Miller is known to the Protectorate as a Unionist sympathiser. The only way to get close to Miller, I mean close enough to know his mind, would be to gain access to the family. Sam and Evelyn's marriage, Charlie, wasn't a marriage."

"What happened to Evelyn?"

"She died at the consulate battle."

Charlie suddenly felt like talking. "How come the Nexists destroyed the Triumvirate on Venus? Why wasn't it better prepared?"

"Sam's entry into the Protectorate came after Miller constructed the gunships. Even so, he knew an attack was imminent and got word to the Protectorate. Thousands were evacuated."

"The Protectorate didn't stop the coup, though, did it?"

"They needed to let the plan see daylight. The Nexists had to expose themselves and implement their strategy, while the Unionist resistance, and the Protectorate, with operatives like Sam, infiltrated the consulate. All the garrisons and armouries had spies."

"Is that why Greg only blew up a couple of garrisons?"

"Yes. When you arrived, all we did was bring the Unionist plan forward. The Protectorate scans picked up your ship and alerted us. Then they intercepted your message to Miller. Sam was there and knew you had returned. He armed the Unionists and gave them the codes for the forcefield. He made sure Miller was at the consulate, anticipating an attack force would head there."

Charlie fell silent as she absorbed this information. The image of Sam lying so still as Suliman hurried her away still haunted her, even more so than him lying in her arms, the smear of blood oozing from the wound on his head. It didn't pump out blood the way her leg did. She didn't understand that. Now, Hannah was telling her that Sam was a hero. She'd seen the Nexist symbol on the shirt he used to cover her wounds. And he'd died believing she thought him a traitor.

"Do you know what happened to Sam's body?"

"That big man, Suliman, took him. Matthew told me he took him to his parents. I don't know where. Sorry."

Charlie tried to allow her beautiful memories of Sam to eclipse her sad ones, but for now, her heart would not allow it. She didn't want to hear more. She wanted to be alone, but she had one more question.

"Do you know what happened to Suliman?"

Hannah lifted her hands. "I never saw him again, so no."

I was right, Charlie told herself. Suliman probably got a life somewhere. Good for him.

CHAPTER THIRTY _

"Chaaarlieee," Dad's voice echoed through the house. "Someone here to see you."

"I'm not home," Charlie called back.

"Says his name is Suliman. Says he knows you."

Charlie's mum popped her head around the door to find her daughter moving more quickly than she had in months.

"Suliman? You've mentioned him a few times, haven't you? Your dad's forgotten."

Charlie quickly shrugged herself into a jumper and shorts. "Yes, I have mentioned him. He was on that mission with me." Charlie's once robust and witty father was so traumatised during the Nexist takeover, he acquired a form of dementia that allowed him only short-term memory. Although he remembered his wife and daughter, he recalled nothing from the day before, often not even what he had for lunch. Charlie found him staring up at

Suliman; his jaw dropped in astonishment. Charlie's dad was like her. Short.

"You're a big bloke," he said after he recovered from tilting his head back so far it made him dizzy. "What do you eat? People?"

"Perhaps it's good genes, Mr Maitland," Suliman answered, throwing Charlie a nervous smile as she approached. He wasn't entirely sure of his welcome. "And space rations," he added. "I eat a lot of space rations."

"Space rations?" Charlie's dad looked confused. "Space is rationed?"

Charlie gently guided her father out of the way as she invited Suliman to step inside.

"Not space, Dad. What you used to eat when you crewed on the freighter, remember?" She gave Suliman a weak smile. "Hello, stranger. Rumour had it you dropped off the face of the earth."

Suliman just nodded. It took weeks before he found the courage to check with the hospital to see what happened to Charlie. He feared the worst, but even the news she survived didn't make him want to reconnect with Rebecca or Greg or any of the Millstone's crew. He had his own private war to deal with, and several months went by before he felt ready to reach out, and when he did, it was to Rebecca.

Charlie's dad followed them out to the balcony but kept a protective hand on Charlie's shoulder and a warning eye on Suliman. Finally, her mum appeared and dragged him away, answering him with, *"Charlie doesn't need a chaperone"* and *"yes, she did see how big that bloke was."* All the while, she steered him back inside the apartment so their daughter could have a little privacy.

Suliman hoped Rebecca was right, that Charlie would be glad to see him. He had occasion to meet up with Hannah recently as well, and she warned him of what he might find, so Suliman believed himself prepared to find differences, considering her injuries. He wasn't at all prepared. Charlie's natural paleness had turned almost to white, and her slender frame too thin. The jumper that matched the blue of her eyes looked several sizes too large and kept slipping off her shoulder.

Charlie was happy to see him, but he hadn't disguised his shock at her appearance well enough. His concerned appraisal made her self-conscious, and her knee bounced up and down in her nervousness. She hoped to see him again, so she couldn't fathom why she felt this way. How she looked wouldn't be of importance to him. Perhaps it was a mistake to let him in. She should have just stayed in her room. She squeezed her eyes shut. *Pull yourself together. It's Suliman, remember?*

Without thinking, a sentence tumbled out, a sentence she knew was irrelevant as soon as it passed her lips. "Did you go to see your mother?"

It was a strange thing to ask, but better than silence between them.

"I heard she died some eight years ago," Suliman said. "So, no. What are you doing these days?"

Charlie didn't want him to know that all she did was

sit in her room and stare at the walls. The funk she got into after the consulate battle, after Sam's death, seemed to take up residence in her life. Even Hannah's revelation about Sam didn't help, and for a while, it made things worse to know he didn't betray his principles, and that Miller had the final word in hers and Sam's story.

"I got released from my indenture." That was the truth. "I've been offered work as a municipal consultant, so I would get to do some surgery and general medical, and I can live at home." Charlie fiddled with her fingers. "I'm not ready yet."

Over the last months, Suliman had found a place for his feelings for her. He'd wrapped them up and tucked them away, safe from prying eyes, but they were the only good memories, good feelings he'd ever had, and he missed them. Sometimes, those feelings got lonely, and he had to talk to them. Seeing her for the first time in months, frail, in a baggy shirt, shorts, bare feet, legs bent up on the big old sofa, her wispy blonde hair tied up in two tiny ridiculous pigtails on top of her head, those feelings spoke to him now, and he almost lost his courage.

"I'm leaving," he said suddenly.

Charlie looked up. "You only just got here."

"Not here. I'm leaving Earth. This system."

Charlie often received messages from Rice and Livesey, who both appeared to have got on with their lives. She heard from Margot and Lucy from time to time and also received regular notes from Rebecca. She even got flowers from Greg. But Suliman, well, he was her best friend in the world, the galaxy even. And he hadn't come to see her, not even a message. And she missed him. Had she known where he was all this time, she might have sought him out. She'd put off looking for him, and now it was too late. He was leaving, only stopping by to say his farewells.

"Do you know where?" She looked down at her hands, not wanting him to see in her face just how much more lost his declaration made her.

Suliman made a non-committal gesture heavenwards. "Out there somewhere, not sure."

"Oh." Charlie envied him. Suliman had those freedoms, just to go where he chose, think what he wanted, be what he wanted to be. She had only four walls to stare at, trapped in that endless replay of…

"Come with me, Charlie."

Charlie blinked slowly and met his gaze. The expression on his face told her he meant it, but it took her a moment to find the words.

"On the Millstone?"

"Well…" he started to say. She hadn't immediately refused, didn't tell him not to be so stupid and to get out and leave her alone. That encouraged him. He knew she thought his ship was not much better than salvage, but like everything else in the Triumvirate, the Millstone had undergone a transformation.

The suddenness of her laughter rocked both Suliman and her parents to the core. Her mum and dad were listening from inside the house, and they didn't know whether to be pleased or concerned. Charlie wiped tears from the corners of her eyes. She couldn't place the emotion. A mix of surprise, happiness, *shock?*

"You want me to crew on the *Millstone?*"

Charlie's dad placed his arm around her mum. Once they assured themselves their daughter wasn't hysterical, they allowed themselves a smile of relief. Whoever this Suliman was, he'd made their little girl laugh for the first time in months. Her mum peeked through the window. Judging by Suliman's expression, he hadn't expected that response either.

"You want me to crew on the most uncomfortable ship in the entire system?" Charlie suddenly looked like the old Charlie. Full of life and sass. And she still hadn't said no.

"Come on, Suliman," she laughed again. "You'll have to do better than that."

"I'll have you know, Doc," Suliman announced with pride, inadvertently reverting to his old nickname for her, "The Millstone has had an upgrade. The Triumvirate reversed its confiscation and most obligingly wiped my sentence. There was an offer to remove the Mag engines, but I said I'd keep them as I didn't plan on returning to cargo work. Greg added a further upgrade, and now the Millstone matches the speed of the Indigo ship. A bit of negotiation, and the Triumvirate did a complete refit of all systems, including the exterior hull. I think being friends with the new Vice-President helped," he chuckled. "You won't recognise it."

Charlie knew of Rebecca's new position. "Rebecca told me she hadn't seen you since after the consulate battle."

It was Suliman's turn to look down at his hands, his voice softening. "Yes, I just couldn't face anyone. I needed to be alone. I found out later you recovered from your physical injuries, but I didn't know about…I didn't know about…"

Charlie lifted an eyebrow. "The funk?"

"Yeah, that, not until Rebecca told me." Suliman fell to silence. He may have been able to help her, but he didn't even try. The thought filled him with regret.

Charlie rose and came to sit beside him. He liked the way she smelled of soap and fresh air, and now her too pale complexion had taken on some colour. She hugged him.

"Thank you, Suliman, for making sure Sam got back to his family. It meant a lot."

Suliman waved away her thanks. Even though she looked like the old Charlie, she still hadn't said "yes" to going with him, and that made him feel out of place.

"Well, I…look, Doc, it's okay. I'd better go." He stood, silently cursing himself for daring to think Charlie would want a life in space, with him of all people. He shouldn't have come. Charlie had a comfortable home, loving parents, and her dream job when she was ready. What he offered was hardly a step up from that.

Charlie didn't move, just looked up at him.

"Would we live on space rations?" she asked.

Suliman hadn't once considered that aspect. He never

really got past how he would ask her. He sat down again.

"Not all the time. Rice and Livesey agreed to come. Rice's parents are old. They didn't even realise he'd been gone all that time. If you say no, I say no to them, I couldn't stand to live with those two, and you not being there to diffuse the situation. I'd rather spend my life in space alone or take one of Rice's dog's clones. Hannah asked to come as well, but if you aren't keen…" He was gushing. Uncharacteristically so. Her raised eyebrows told him that he'd misjudged her response as refusal.

From where she sat, Charlie could see directly into the house to where her mother stood just inside the door, making fierce faces at her.

"You must go," her mother mouthed, making pushing motions with her hands. *"Go, we'll be fine."*

Suliman caught Charlie's distracted look beyond his field of vision, but he didn't turn. Had he done so, he would have appreciated her mother's support and her sacrifice. Charlie shifted her position to block her view of her mother's urgent encouragement.

"I am a bit worried about my parents, Suliman."

"The Earth is safe in the hands of the new Triumvirate, Charlie. Commander Steele and Rebecca are trusted leaders, both here and on Venus. And what if I tell you I can put in place contingencies to return us here if we wish or need?"

"What contingencies?"

Suliman pulled a portable data rondure from his pocket, allowing it to spin and compile a star chart. Charlie didn't recognise any of it.

"Those aren't the systems we passed through to get to the other Earth."

"No," Suliman agreed. "We'll go in a different direction. We can head out farther as we become more experienced."

"Experienced at what?"

"Exploring. We'll be explorers. Maybe we'll find more Indigo. That's what Greg plans to do in time."

Charlie checked his face for any sign he wasn't serious. A respectable Suliman? An explorer? Did that gel? A swarthy, hawklike-featured man from the turbulent Southwestern corridor with a long history of lawbreaking? Yet, this same man gently lifted Sam's lifeless body from hers and reunited loving parents with their deceased son. This same dear friend held her broken body in his arms when the battle ended, when the guns went silent. She felt safe with him. He would always have her back. Besides her mum and dad, there was no-one in the universe Charlie trusted more. But…

"What if the engines fail?"

"We'll drift in space."

"What if we meet a hostile species?"

"We'll offer you as a sacrifice."

"What if…"

"What if, what if. It's a gamble, Charlie, and I'm a betting man. I bet it will be an adventure. And this time, you get your own cabin." He smiled as if that would be the one thing that swayed her. He hoped it would. A life with just Rice, Livesey and the young, bossy Hannah didn't hold enormous appeal. If Charlie didn't agree to come, he'd already decided to sneak off and "forget" the others.

"My own cabin?"

Suliman nodded.

"Is the dog coming?"

Suliman nodded again. "And one of its clones."

Her mother still stood in the doorway, making *"go"* eyes at her.

Today, Charlie laughed. Twice. Tomorrow, no doubt, she would laugh again. And the future looked bright.

END

ACKNOWLEDGEMENTS

Thank you so much for reading Myth of Origin. If you enjoyed Charlie's story, I would love for you to hop over to your orders page on Amazon and leave a review. Good reviews are the lifeblood of Indie Authors, and we are grateful for your support.

I would also like to thank my awesome editors, Amy and Jo. I am so lucky to have them on my team!

If you would like to be notified about my new releases, please sign up to my (occasional) newsletter at:
https://matildascotneybooks.com/

Or connect with me on Facebook:
https://www.facebook.com/Offtheplanetbooks

ABOUT THE AUTHOR

When my mind isn't off on some imaginary galactic quest with my trusty chihuahua sidekick Oggie, I can be found in Australia collecting teapots and nerding about all things Star Wars.

www.ingramcontent.com/pod-product-compliance
Lightning Source LLC
Chambersburg PA
CBHW020013120726
47903CB00004B/1270